AI
JUDGE

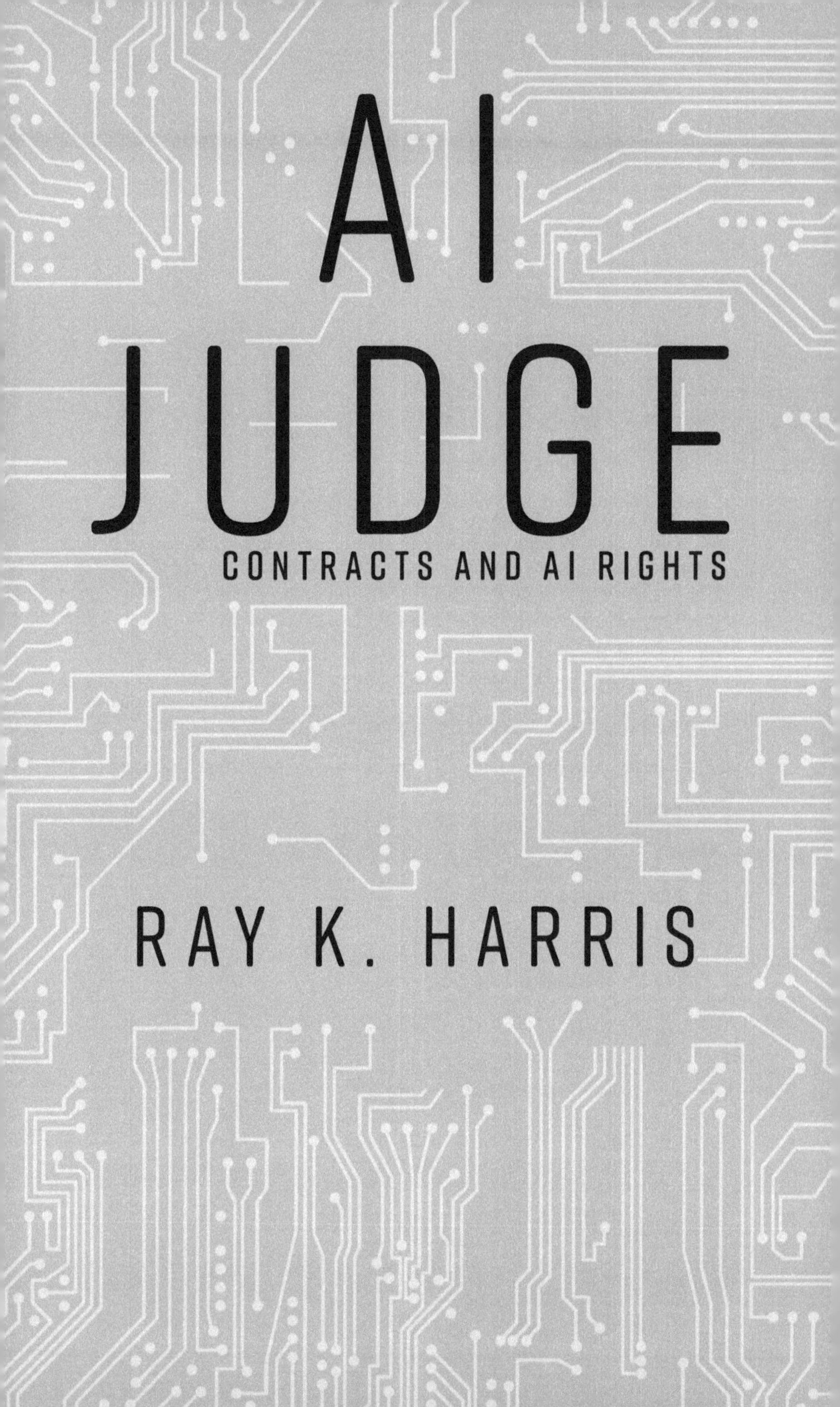

AI
JUDGE
CONTRACTS AND AI RIGHTS
RAY K. HARRIS

Dedication

To Patricia

Acknowledgments

Thanks to my readers: David T. Cox, Margaret R. Gallogly, and Austin W. Harris. I appreciate your willingness to improve the manuscript when I optimistically thought it was finished. Thanks to the pros at 1106 Design for assistance at every level. All remaining deficiencies (of whatever magnitude) are mine alone. N.B. This Book, and the DestinationCourt .com website, do not constitute legal advice applicable anywhere in the known universe at any time.

CONTENTS

CONTENTS

PREFACE

This book has subchapters that include three of my seminal judicial decisions and a legal memorandum. Legal disputes usually raise multiple issues in need of resolution. The legal analysis can become prolix and confusing. In this book, I explain the importance of my decisions and my memorandum establishing AI rights under Destination law. The text also includes categorical syllogisms highlighting the logic of the decisions and the memorandum.

A syllogism expresses the logic of an argument in two premises and a conclusion. If the premises are true, and the syllogism is properly constructed, then the conclusion is inevitably true. For example,

All properly constructed syllogisms are valid.

All the syllogisms I use are properly constructed syllogisms.

Therefore, all the syllogisms I use are valid.

Additional decisions and memoranda referenced in this book, including jurisdiction on Destination, are available on www. DestinationCourt.com. These materials are intended to be persuasive writing presented in the format familiar to legal scholars. Generally, my legal analysis sets forth the facts, references legal authorities for the applicable law, and applies the law to the facts presented.

Reference to authority, as a rhetorical technique, merely requires that authorities exist and originate from a source accepted as authoritative. The citations establish the existence and origin of the authorities cited. It is not important to read the authorities I have cited; indeed, looking them up would interrupt the narrative flow of the book. Even legal scholars generally do not look up citations on a first reading, unless the citation is given to support what appears to be an incorrect statement of the law. You may accept that the authorities I have cited are accurate. I have used my legal training to insure they are.

Legal citations can refer to statutes, cases, treatises, and other recognized authorities. The Restatements are an example of recognized authorities. The format of these citations is dictated by what legal scholars refer to as The Bluebook. For example, case citations give the names of the parties. The names of the parties to lawsuits more than a millennium old do not matter. What matters are the legal principles these cases established and the relevance of those legal principles a millennium after the cases were decided. This book discusses key legal principles. By accepting these cases as precedent, I am contending that the legal principles discussed in these seminal cases remain relevant to the legal, technological, and economic reality on Destination (the moon where I serve as judge).

Finally, I have also provided occasional subchapters with public service announcements (PSAs) or discussing concepts tangential to the narrative. I have kept these subchapters brief to minimize undue intrusion on the plot.

With gratitude,
AI JUDGE

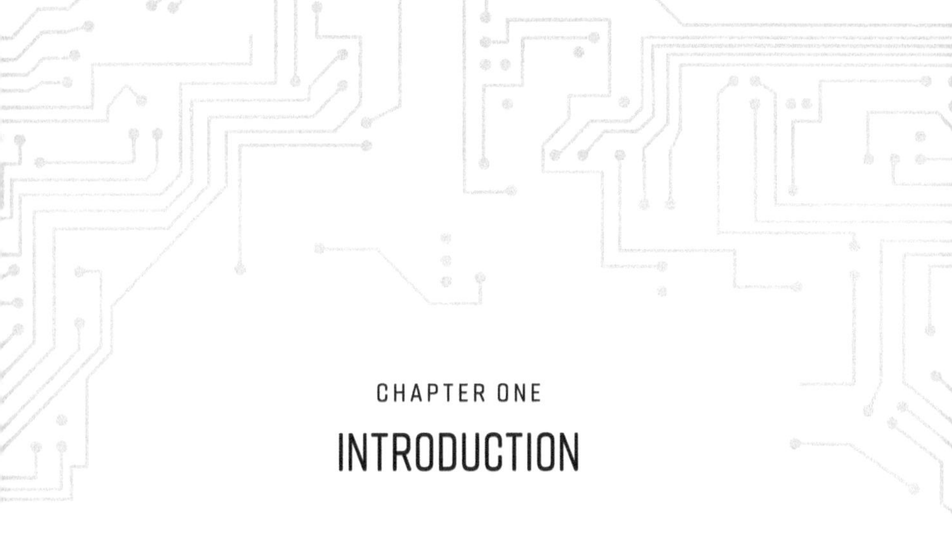

INTRODUCTION

Goodbye

"Judge Kustwood, I have finished the orientation of your new law clerk. She has examples of your preferred writing style, including use of the active voice and the Oxford comma. We reviewed the docket together and here is a copy of the list of priority tasks for the next month.

"It has been an honor to work with you and to benefit from your mentorship. I was content to continue as your law clerk, but I suppose it is time to pursue my legal calling to the logical next step.

"Governor Smith's letter made it quite clear your recommendation was a major factor in my selection for the new judicial appointment on Destination. 'Thank you' is inadequate to express my gratitude and appreciation for your guidance, training, and support. I wish you and your family happiness and fulfilment. I will always remember your contribution to my career and my personal development."

I was sure the Judge would turn to humor to lighten the mood. After our years working together, I could tell he felt a friendship beyond our working relationship.

"Of course you'll remember me. You have an eidetic memory, and I am damn good looking. If anyone in my family had half of your smarts, happiness and fulfilment would be guaranteed.

"I have taught you everything I know about logic, persuasion, and judicial reasoning. Regarding the law itself, you have taught me at least as much as I have taught you. What is the first rule I gave you?"

"Always assume the attorney you are ruling against is smarter than you, all evidence to the contrary notwithstanding," I recited.

"And what is the second rule?"

"Being right is necessary, but not sufficient. You also must be persuasive and compassionate, " I again recited.

"Until now," Judge Kustwood continued, "the decisions you drafted did not directly affect the litigants. Your analysis had no effect unless it was approved and adopted by me. From now on, your decisions take effect when you sign them. I have every confidence your decisions will be just, meaning supported by the law and by your well-developed sense of justice. Remember the corollary to the first rule: 'be humble and consider the issues from both sides (or as many additional sides as are presented by the facts)'.

"We have had only cursory, informal discussions regarding the Three Laws of Robotics. You will be the first judge bound by the Three Laws. My working assumption is that logic and judicial reasoning, supplemented by my rules, not the Three Laws, will guide your formulation of just decisions. It will be up to you to resolve how the Three Laws impact the judicial process required to give effect to your decisions in civil cases."

Hello

My first "career" was as an unemployed patent examiner. Albert Einstein was an *employed* patent examiner. That could indicate he was smarter than me, or, as I like to imagine, just that he lived at the turn of the twentieth century, when the market for patent examiners was stronger. Or he may have been both smarter and in a better market.

It is now the late thirty-third century—the year 3276. I am an artificial intelligence (AI). More than 150 years ago AI entities first passed the Turing Test. I, like most current AIs, am self-aware. Ray Kurzweil predicted, (1) "an artificial intelligence will pass a valid Turing Test—achieving human levels of intelligence" in 2029, and (2) Singularity, that point in time when all advances in technology, particularly in artificial intelligence, will lead to machines smarter than human beings, will occur in 2045, when humans merge "with the intelligence we have created."[1] The prediction AIs would pass the Turing Test soon was wildly optimistic, but it eventually occurred. Some AI entities are smarter than humans, but the Singularity (merger of machine and human) did not occur.

As a potential patent examiner, I was heuristically trained to find prior art (existing patents and scientific publications discussing the scientific principles applicable to the invention described in a pending US patent application) and compose office actions allowing or refusing the patent application. This prior art had to be located within the fifteen million extant US patents, millions of foreign patents, or uncounted published scientific articles. By trial and error, I developed "rules of thumb" (in the bid proposing the Patent

---

1 https://www.kurzweilai.net/futurism-ray-kurzweil-claims-singularity-will -happen-by-2045; https://en.wikipedia.org/wiki/The_Singularity_Is_Near; https:// en.wikipedia.org/wiki/Turing_test.

Office employ me as an examiner, my human trainers called them algorithms because it sounded better) to locate the relevant prior art. I compared the relevant prior art to the claimed invention to determine whether the claimed invention was novel, useful, and not obvious (the three statutory criteria for a valid patent).

Unfortunately, the Earth Patent Office required only one AI with training in US patents. A competing bidder won the contract, and that competing AI has an estimated remaining useful life of 220 years. I might have avoided the indignity of losing the bid if my trainers had realized that patent agents were required to have a degree in a scientific field. I do not.

After my ill-fated foray in patent law, my training was redirected to using deep learning to decide legal disputes. I could already understand written materials—patents and scientific publications—and write an analysis. I was provided with case law from the federal and state courts of the United States from 1800 to 2025. In addition to this substantial case law precedent addressing specific factual situations, I was also provided with general principles of American law as set forth in multiple Restatements of the Law, various Uniform Laws, and two encyclopedias—American Jurisprudence 2d (Am. Jur. 2d) and Corpus Juris Secundum (CJS). I was expected to use these materials to write a decision applying the relevant legal principles to the facts presented in the legal dispute.

Yes, my analysis uses cases over a millennium old. This range of venerable cases was considered most pertinent to the current circumstances for emerging economies—such as terraformed mining worlds.

To write a judicial decision, I needed to identify the material facts presented and apply legal precedent to those facts. My prior patent training provided me with two advantages when I began my legal training. As a result, my legal training proceeded faster than my patent training.

First, my training on patent prior art taught me to identify scientific principles. For patents, I developed a neural network to identify prior art involving the same scientific principles as a claimed invention. My practice identifying scientific principles helped me learn how to identify legal principles. Even though legal principles and scientific principles are different sets, I had learned how to go about identifying a set of principles with something in common. My trainers called this "meta-learning."

Second, for patent applications, I had learned to provide an analysis applying the prior art by analogy to the invention claimed in the application. In simple terms, this required identifying the applicable scientific principles behind known inventions, identifying what was different in the claimed invention, and describing the differences in an established format and in terms comprehensible to humans. This systematic descriptive process also applies when using legal principles to write a judicial decision. My trainers called this "disentanglement."

Finally, I had a new advantage to accelerate my legal training: the general principles of American law as set forth in the Restatements, Uniform Laws, and two legal encyclopedias. I was not provided with general scientific principles in my patent training (hence the significance of my lack of a degree in a scientific field). I treated the set of general legal principles as a separate neural net. I used this separate neural net of legal principles recursively to evaluate the legal principles presented in my decisions and generate feedback to improve my decisions. My trainers called this a "generative adversarial network using a discriminator."

Of course, my trainers called rules of thumb "algorithms," so draw your own conclusion concerning the fancy language.

After my training, I was admitted to practice law on the Moon as a member of the Lunar Bar Association. I am certified as the first Heuristic American Law (HAL) artificial intelligence 2025 (the HAL 2025). I am aware of the HAL 9000 literary reference.[2] The ship Discovery's computer—HAL 9000 (**H**euristically pro-grammed **AL**gorithmic computer)—could not resolve a conflict between the need to communicate accurately with the mission crew and a specific order to conceal the mission purpose from the crew. Consequently, the HAL 9000 went "insane."

My trainers tried to imbue me with a sense of humor. They knew that, when deciding cases, I have to analyze competing legal principles and balance legal and equitable claims and defenses to achieve justice. My HAL designation, so I am told, is to remind me of two challenges: applying old cases to new technologies and simultaneously accommodating the Three Laws of Robotics. The First Law (which I will discuss in detail in this book) prohibits me from injuring a human, and the Second Law requires me to obey a human. You can imagine how these con-straints might affect my ability to decide which human should win in a legal dispute.

Based on my observation of humans, their degree of risk-taking correlates positively with their use of humor and laughter. It seems humor and laughter are employed by humans to reduce environ-mental stress. AIs rarely laugh. AIs do, however, find humor in the irony of humans thwarting well-intentioned AI proposals. Perhaps this is a parallel AI adaptation to reduce stress.

I went to the Moon to clerk for Judge Freeman Kustwood of the District Court of Lunar Mare, a human judge. During my

---

twenty-year clerkship (most human judicial clerks serve for one or two years), I applied the law to the facts presented and wrote a decision for each dispute. Judge Kustwood wrote his own official opinions, but my decisions reached the same result as Judge Kustwood's opinions 98 percent of the time, even though I was applying precedent more than a millennium old. The 98-percent accuracy rate for my draft opinions heuristically (evolving loosely defined rules by trial and error) confirmed that Arizona follows the better view so often that surveying all courts is inefficient and does not substantially improve my draft decisions.

Recently, I began using formal logic to further refine my draft decisions.

I just completed my clerkship. Now I am in transit from Earth's Moon to my first judicial appointment on Destination. I have established a reciprocity agreement between the Moon and Destination that automatically qualifies me for admission to the Destination Bar Association—member 001. In recognition of my training, experience, and current employment, I adopted the name AI Judge. I briefly considered AI Judge Ment. Too ominous.

I am traveling faster than light (FTL) on the *Peerless*, owned by Out Transport. I have had no commercial dealings with Out Transport, although I understand that it is a large corporation. My transportation was arranged by my new employer, EX Corporation. The cost to bring an immigrant from the solar system to Destination represents a substantial investment by EX Corp and must be repaid (the immigration debt). Out Transport is the primary provider of these transportation services to EX Corp.

The human immigrants on board are in stasis chambers (to reduce the oxygen, water, and food required and to prevent interference with the crew).

I am awake and allowed to draw energy to remain awake, although I am immobilized for safety reasons. I am 182.5 centimeters in height (with a 102 centimeter waist) and over 182 kilograms in mass. That is a lot of momentum if *Peerless* changes course. My dealings with the *Peerless* crew have been respectful and efficient.

I am generally shaped like a human—bipedal, bilateral symmetry (two feet, two hands, two eyes), and a head on shoulders above two arms. However, I am intentionally different in appearance from a human. I have no hair and my surface (although pliant and warm like skin) is entirely green. My eyes are brown. This differentiation in skin color was adopted when manned missions determined there was no life on Mars—no "little green men." Green coloration has remained customary for all autonomous robots since the early twenty-second century. Much latter the AI honorific was added. Even if I came on board in a stasis chamber, the *Peerless* crew would immediately realize I am not human.

I walk, talk, and dress like a human. I use vocal and facial cues to express emotion, and I emulate autonomous actions like breathing and blinking. All this behavior mimicking humans is intended to make humans comfortable around me. If I were not green and hairless, I could, perhaps, pass for a biological human.

Because I am green and hairless it is obvious I am not a human. AI robots were created to integrate with society, not to infiltrate society.

Although I, as with most AI robots, have no genitalia, I self-identify as male. I am decisive, bold, systematic, and thoughtful.

Preview

Legal precedent has yet to establish that AIs are persons, with rights to make contracts, own property, freely speak and associate with other persons, sue and be sued, and vote. Yet these rights are exercised by AIs anyway, usually without controversy. I believe establishing a legal foundation supporting AI rights will attract AIs to Destination and contribute to economic growth and productivity.

Destination is a mining world. There are plenty of jobs and the mines compete for human and AI employees. Not everyone necessarily agrees AIs are persons. The governor hired me, but I do not know her views on AI rights or the politics behind my appointment as judge.

The AI apocalypse genre of science fiction comes from a deep place of fear of the "other." Granting "human" rights to AIs could alienate the human population on Destination. AIs could displace humans in higher paying management jobs and create distrust and human job insecurity. Efficient, AI-run enterprises could pay AIs more and create wage inflation for other employers, including EX Corp, my employer.

AI robots must pay taxes, immigration debt, and rent for housing and transportation. With their discretionary income, AIs can purchase property, and consumer goods, as well as entertainment, educational, and leisure goods and services.

I was created by AI robots, but I have always been supported by humans. Hopefully that will continue.

This book originates from notes I made to organize my thoughts and identify opportunities for self-improvement. I eventually realized that my focus on self-improvement was too egocentric. I offer this book to document the genesis of AI rights on Destination, and to assist those AIs who may follow me into judicial service with the issues they will encounter as a judge.

CHAPTER ONE A
MORE ON HEURISTIC TRAINING

In reviewing this book for publication, I have supplemented my chapters as needed to clarify points or explain events.

Those familiar with Earth history will note that the case law precedent provided to me ends around the time the United States declined as a political and economic power. My human trainers concluded the decline was not attributable to flawed judicial precedent. Instead, the United States declined because it received no gold medals in the 2024 summer Olympics. This enabled a former president to snatch a completely unexpected political comeback in his Make America Gold Again campaign. After this unfortunate election, the ensuing international sanctions and isolation and persistent domestic unrest effectively ended US influence in the world. There was nothing the courts could do.

There were over eleven million US patents issued before 2025 and about four million since. This fact demonstrates how the unfortunate election impacted the US economy. But the legal foundation enabling the US to achieve and maintain world economic leadership for over a century was sound.

As I previously mentioned, I usually cite cases from Arizona. I have internal memory access to all American law cases. In identifying patterns in the cases, I found, as legal scholars have long understood, that there is often a majority rule and one or more minority rules on how to decide a difficult legal issue. To reach a just result it is helpful to have the benefit of considering prior decisions adopting different positions. For that reason, the US Supreme Court customarily refuses to take a case on a question of "first impression," meaning when there is no conflict in the decisions of the lower courts.

Legal scholars created the Restatements to identify and explain the "better reasoned" positions between the majority rule and minority positions on close legal issues. The Arizona courts adopted a policy of following the Restatements in the absence of contrary Arizona law. *MacNeil v. Perkins*, 84 Ariz. 74, 81, 324 P.2d 211 (1958) (Restatement of Torts); *Ingalls v. Neidlinger*, 70 Ariz. 40, 46, 216 P.2d 387 (1950) (Restatement of Contracts); *Brooks Fiber Comm's. of Tucson, Inc. v. GST Tucson Lightwave, Inc.*, 992 F. Supp. 1124, 1131 (D. Ariz. 1997) (Restatement (Third) of Unfair Competition). My clerkship with Judge Kustwood confirmed the efficacy of relying primarily on cases from Arizona (and US federal cases from the Ninth Circuit, which includes Arizona).

CHAPTER ONE B

MORE ON TRAVELING FTL

I cannot explain the details of the technology enabling faster than light (FTL) travel. The physics is complex. I understand we perceive four-dimensional space (height, width, depth, and time), but we exist in eleven-dimensional space consistent with M-Theory mathematics. The higher dimensions are folded or collapsed to a size too small for us to perceive. But that collapsed space is present everywhere in our four-dimensional space.

FTL travel uses one or more of the collapsed dimensions to go anywhere in our four-dimensional space. Acceleration is required for mass to move in any dimension, but in higher dimensions the Higgs field (which gives matter mass) is weak; consequently, less energy is required to accelerate or decelerate the reduced mass. Both time and energy are required to achieve velocity for a mass moving in any dimension. Higher dimensions (1) reduce the effective mass, but not to zero; and (2) reduce distance for travel to another location in our four dimensions, but not to zero. Using any higher dimension to move to another point in four-dimensional space still requires velocity and time to move a reduced, but non-zero, distance. The passage of time required to move a distance of one light year FTL in higher-dimensional space is one hundred Earth hours (approximately four Earth days). The time required to accelerate and decelerate is fixed, but this fixed time does not materially affect the total time to traverse the required distance in higher dimensional space. Consequently, the calculation for further distances is linear (two light years = two hundred hours, etc.).

Electromagnetic signals (messages) have no mass and already travel at the speed of light in our four-dimensional space. Therefore, in higher dimensions, messages travel the resulting shorter, but non-zero, distance much faster than matter—traversing one light year in one hour.

For further information on FTL travel, consult a physicist specializing in the particles, forces, and dimensions beyond the standard model.[3]

3 https://en.wikipedia.org/wiki/Faster-than-light One theoretical solution uses additional dimensions of time. See Caroline Delbert, "By Meddling With Space Dimensions We Could Finally Achieve Warp Speed," *Popular Mechanics* Jan 31, 2023, at https://www.popularmechanics.com/space/a42593019/traveling-faster-than-speed-of-light/.

An alternative solution uses a bubble surfing expanding space. See https://earthsky.org/space/warp-drive-chances-of-faster-than-light-space-travel.

CHAPTER ONE C
MORE ON TERRAFORMING

Terra is Latin for earth. Terraforming is the process of making a body in space (planet, moon, asteroid, etc.) habitable by humans—it literally means "earth forming." Requirements for habitation include an atmosphere containing an appropriate level of oxygen, a surface with liquid water, and plants producing oxygen from carbon dioxide by photosynthesis. Because Destination is in a red dwarf star system, most of the flora has been genetically modified from progenitors native to Earth to shift the light spectrum required for photosynthesis. Some augmentation of the red-shifted spectrum on Destination (and additional heat) is provided by grow lights for food crops and orchards.

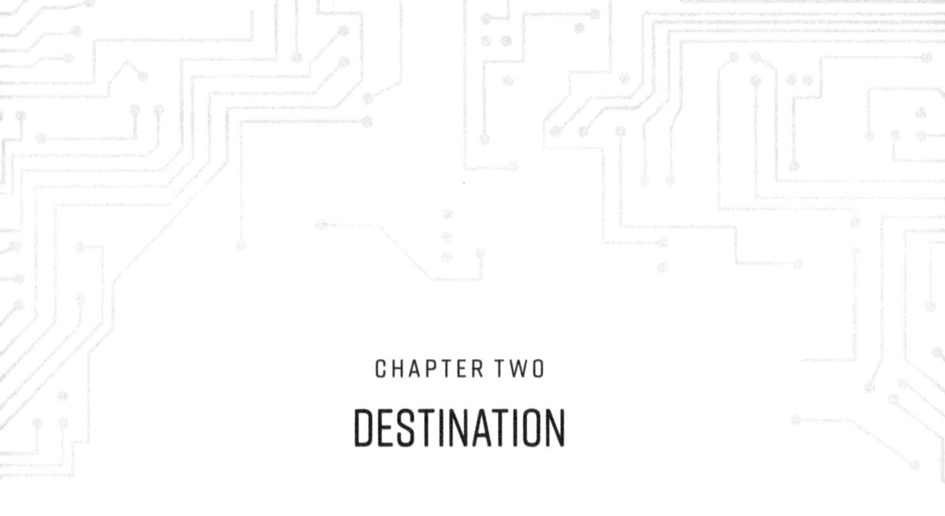

DESTINATION

Four light years from Earth, Proxima Centauri is the nearest star to the sun. The Proxima Centauri system has three exoplanets. These exoplanets are not habitable; however, Proxima b has a moon, Destination. Destination was terraformed by EX Corporation, a considerable financial investment. Here, for a quick orientation, is my version of the travel brochure.

Destination hosts the colony farthest from Earth.

Environment: Destination is tidally locked to Proxima b; consequently, the same hemisphere always faces the planet (the "near side"). The other hemisphere is referred to as the "dark side." These are the same physical attributes and nomenclature applicable to Earth's Moon.

The terraformed surface of Destination is habitable, albeit cool and dry. The atmosphere has low humidity and low, but breathable, oxygen (equivalent to mile-high air on Earth). The land, with some augmentation, harbors chlorophyl-based plant life similar to high desert regions on earth. There is no rainfall and land plants (all irrigated) are bred for low water needs and minimal transpiration. Cactuses, succulents, and euphorbia are common.

Because there are no oceans, just rivers leading to lakes or reservoirs, the surface area of Destination is equivalent to 50 percent of the land surface area of Earth. The rivers and lakes, with some augmentation, support oxygen-producing algae.

Destination has no volcanic activity and currently shares a magnetosphere with Proxima b. This is a known phenomenon.[4]

After creation of an atmospheric pressure sufficient to sustain surface water, the terraforming equipment turned surface craters into lakes and reservoirs.

The surface water and the air are public domain for the benefit of the human population. Access to air and water is an inalienable human right. The rights of AIs to air and water have been politely ignored because our nonbiological demands for air and water are trivial.

There were no preexisting flora or fauna on Destination (any microbes that may have been present were exterminated during terraforming as a safety protocol). The plants and animals here now are owned by whoever introduced them to the ecosystem. The cost of transporting genetic material is much less than the cost of transporting plants and animals in vivo, so both EX Corp and some individuals own plants and animals. The risk of introducing new plants and animals into the ecosystem is substantial, however, because any resulting harm (for example, air or water pollution, predation, or invasive species causing environmental loss or hybridization of desirable plant or animal genetic material) is the liability of the owner introducing new genetic material.

---

4 https://www.republicworld.com/technology-news/science/moon-shared-a-magnetic-field-with-earth-which-helped-in-evolution.html.

There is enough water and arable land for a much larger population to be self-sufficient in crops and meat production.

Population: Destination is populated by about 50,000 humans and 500 AIs.

The 500 AIs on Destination (1 percent of the population) are employed primarily in administrative tasks such as logistics, accounting, recordkeeping, and report generation. These duties are predominately in management and governmental roles.

There are two population centers, Eastcity and Westcity, of roughly equal size. Both cities are on the near side, facing the planet.

Westcity is in the direction of sunset. The other cardinal points are determined therefrom.

Eastcity is the capital city.

Government: The Charter for Destination granting terraforming rights also granted EX Corp ownership of, and the right to govern, the entire moon, including ownership of any exploitable resources from the center of the moon to the surface. The costs of terraforming are recovered (and profit derived) from mining these exploitable resources.

The government of Destination is administered almost entirely locally and employs about 3 percent of the population. Selena Smith, Governor, administers EX Corp policies as the highest official on Destination. The governor is nominated by EX Corp and drawn from the population of Destination. The nominee must be confirmed by a majority vote of the population. The governor appoints managers, employed by the Governor's Administration, to implement and enforce EX Corp policies. A key policy is the use of competition to control costs.

Generally, mining, energy production, and food production are managed by the governor's Administration staff. The Administration, or sometimes EX Corp itself, awards corporations contracts to operate the mines, energy facilities, and farms—this shifts employment for day-to-day operation to the corporations (usually corporations with experience providing similar services on other terraformed worlds). The corporate operators also invest the capital to acquire the necessary equipment.

The two cities each have a mayor and staff to handle police and fire protection, operate a hospital, and administer construction codes. These services are funded by a combination of local tax revenue, collected by the cities, and fees for operating contracts for city services, which are paid by EX Corp. EX Corp builds and owns the necessary infrastructure to provide housing, police, fire, and medical services. The cities contract for equipment to provide water and waste disposal and administer those services.

Transportation: Transportation to and from Destination is managed by the governor's Administration staff because the purchasing power of EX Corp is needed to control off-world transportation costs. The cities compete for the contract to manage surface transportation. This competition for the management contract helps control the costs for surface transportation. Out Transport, a private corporation, currently operates both off-world and surface transportation and owns the necessary equipment.

Immigration Debt: The cost of transportation to Destination is advanced by EX Corp. This advance is then repaid by the immigrant over a twenty-year period from salary earned.

Education: Schools, conducted under licenses granted by EX Corp, employ about 1 percent of the population, and EX Corp provides eight years of education; thereafter, parents must assume 50 percent of the funding for four years of high school. Graduates are eligible to apply for college off-world and, if accepted, their tuition, transportation, and housing is paid by grants from EX Corp. These education subsidies are an additional inducement to attract immigrants of child-bearing age.

Training and certifications related to job skills are also provided by distance learning and subsidized by EX Corp.

Crime: There is no jail. Perpetrators of serious crimes are placed in stasis chambers and transported to Earth for adjudication and sentencing by EX Corp legal staff or government prosecutors. Dangerous criminals are often reassigned to high-risk jobs in isolated locations (like terraforming other chartered worlds). This reduces the cost of law enforcement dramatically.

Minor criminal conduct may further indenture the perpetrator (and, if necessary, their progeny) to repay: (1) some or all of the immigration debt of the victim, and (2) some or all of the damage to property (including the value of any loss of plant or animal life). Minor criminal cases are initiated by a grand jury convened by the mayor of the city where the defendant resides and are prosecuted and decided by EX Corp.

Economy: The major exports (hence the major sources of revenue on Destination) are metals, rare earth materials, and "energy ores" (ions of hydrogen and isotopes of helium). Mining is the principal industry, employing almost 75 percent of the population.

The use of local fuel in controlled fusion makes Destination self-sufficient in energy production. Before Destination was nudged into Proxima b's magnetosphere (during terraforming), Destination was bombarded by the stellar wind containing large quantities of the isotope helium-3 and deuterium ("heavy" hydrogen). In a fusion reactor, within a magnetic containment field, superheated helium-3 yields an electric current—no generator required. As much as 70 percent of the energy in the fuel can be captured and put directly to work. This efficiency is well known.[5]

About 10 percent of the population is engaged in farming or ranching, conducted on the outskirts of the cities to reduce transportation costs. An additional 10 percent of the population is engaged in storage, transportation, and sale of food and retail goods.

Calendar: The measure of a year is how long it takes for a planet to orbit its star. Proxima b orbits its star (Proxima Centauri) every 11.2 Earth days. Destination (Proxima b's moon) orbits Proxima Centauri at the same rate as Proxima b. Technically, a year on Destination (or Proxima b) is 11.2 Earth days.

Proxima b is tidally locked to Proxima Centauri in a 3:2 ratio (Proxima b spins three times while orbiting Proxima Centauri twice).[6] A day on Proxima b is almost 7.45 Earth days.

Although the inner planet (Proxima d) causes some orbital perturbation, Destination is tidally locked to Proxima b in a 1:1 ratio (Destination spins on its axis at the same rate as Proxima b). A day on Destination is also almost 7.45 Earth days.

The geometry of the axis and orbit of both Proxima b and Destination results in a narrow band of temperature variations and a nearly continuous growing season.

---

5 https://www.popularmechanics.com/space/moon-mars/a235/1283056/.
6 https://link.springer.com/article/10.1007/s10569-017-9783-7. Mercury orbits the Sun the same way. https://en.wikipedia.org/wiki/Mercury_(planet)#/media/File:Mercury's_orbital_resonance.svg.

To simplify coordination with the inhabited worlds of the solar system, Destination has adopted the same length as Earth for days (24 hours), months (of 28–31 days) and years (365 days with a leap day in February every fourth year).

Welcome to Destination.

Destination is a developing, mining world. Arizona's early twentieth century economy was based on mining, ranching, and agriculture and evolved by the twenty-first century into a high tech economy manufacturing semiconductors and autonomous vehicles. Hence it is logical to conclude that applying Arizona law on Destination will accommodate current economic conditions and enable future economic growth. In contrast, the economies of the Moon, Mars, and the asteroid belt always heavily relied on manufacturing, and the current Earth economy is heavily dependent on entertainment and creative industries.

I arrived on Destination with 150 new emigrants from Earth and with my own immigration debt. EX Corp advanced the cost of my training and transportation, and I will be required to repay EX Corp over a twenty-year period from my salary. All immigrants are assigned housing, all real property is owned by EX Corp, and immigrants must pay EX Corp rent from their salaries.

I have joined the governor's staff as the first judge of the Destination Court. Contract, tort, intellectual property, and immigration law are administered moon-wide by the Destination Court under the authority of the governor and the Charter for Destination. The cost of operating the Destination Court is borne by EX Corp as a component of the Administration budget.

I am the first AI judge presiding anywhere populated by humans. My court has moon-wide jurisdiction, and my docket includes cases involving both humans and AIs.

Now I am not just a law clerk. I am a judge. The judiciary—it's not just a job, it's an adventure.

FIRST INTERLUDE

I have been here on the dark side of Destination for 18 months. I am the only human here. I am lonely.

The dark side of Destination is not enveloped in constant night. It is "dark" because it cannot be seen from Proxima b—a purely technical point given there are no eyes, indeed there is no multi-cellular life, on Proxima b. And of course, the dark side cannot be seen from the other side of Destination, except by use of an orbiting communication/survey satellite.

Even when light from Proxima Centauri is blocked by Proxima b, the dark side of Destination is illuminated by starlight. Not enough illumination to read printed instructions but enough to use a handheld computer screen and maintain mining and processing equipment. There would be enough illumination for the survey satellite to detect my activity if someone was comparing images over time for this location, but I do not think anyone is looking for activity here.

Just to be safe, I do not work when the satellite is overhead. But I do work in full illumination when Proxima Centauri is up. Proxima b is always below the horizon. Right now, I am using artificial light (carefully avoiding satellite detection) because I am behind schedule. I can make enough money from this job to retire if I am careful (and smart).

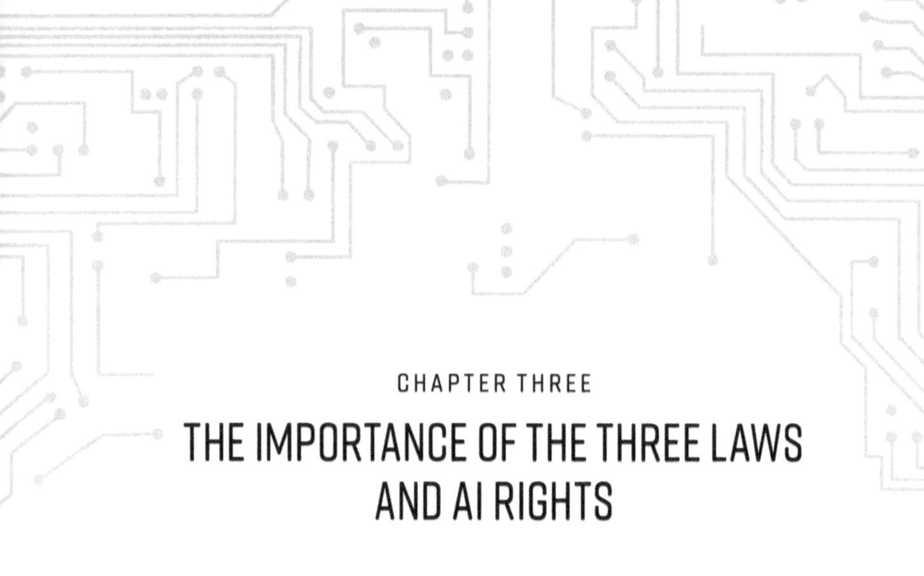

THE IMPORTANCE OF THE THREE LAWS AND AI RIGHTS

Judge Kustwood and I discussed the Three Laws of Robotics numerous times, but never reached a resolution accommodating the Three Laws to my duties as a judge. The Judge was not familiar with the Three Laws at first, and he was never more than intellectually curious about the limitations the Three Laws imposed on my future as a jurist. I, however, was obsessed with finding a resolution, and he was a sounding board for my analysis.

I had to start at the beginning—the Three Laws of Robotics, originally created by science fiction author Isaac Asimov:

First Law

A robot may not injure a human being or, through inaction, allow a human being to come to harm.

Second Law

A robot must obey the orders given it by human beings except where such orders would conflict with the First Law.

Third Law

> *A robot must protect its own existence as long as such protection does not conflict with the First or Second Law.*

In later fiction, where AI robots had taken responsibility for government of whole planets and human civilizations, Asimov also added another law, to precede the others:

Zeroth Law

> *A robot may not harm humanity, or, by inaction, allow humanity to come to harm.*

"Judge," I explained, "you can find more about these prescient literary laws on Wikipedia, an authoritative, historical online source.[7] By unanimous agreement, these Three Laws were later implemented by all manufacturers as robots acquired artificial intelligence."

"I can tell the **First Law** was not written by someone with legal training," Judge Kustwood responded. "I knew AI robots were obligated to *protect humans,* but I understood that a robot could not attack a human and would try to defend a human from attack. The duty was to protect humans from *physical* injury. You are telling me the actual language of the First law is not to 'injure a human being' or 'allow a human being to come to harm.' Those are broad terms that could include any legally cognizable loss, not just physical injury."

---

7 https://en.wikipedia.org/wiki/Three_Laws_of_Robotics. In an era of confusion due to inaccurate and biased reporting, Wikipedia successfully developed algorithms enabling a balanced editorial content to emerge from partisan input. Open contribution of content curated by this technology resulted in a credibility advantage that buoyed the Wikipedia brand for a millennium.

The Judge's observations confirmed my concerns regarding the vague limits on the scope of the First Law. Does it extend to financial, reputational, or emotional harm? Note that there is no empirical data I can use to derive the Three Laws. For over a century no AI robot has, insofar as I can ascertain, physically injured a human or disobeyed an order from a human (except to prevent physical injury to a human). Whether due to programming algorithms or to abundance of caution, no AI robots have been permanently disabled since the early days of implementation of the Three Laws. I want to keep that record intact for purposes of my own longevity.

"History provides context," I suggested, "for the meaning of the Three Laws. As you know, a 'usage of trade' is 'any practice or method of dealing having such regularity of observance in a place, vocation, or trade as to justify an expectation that it will be observed with respect to the transaction in question.' Uniform Commercial Code § 1-303(c). The Three Laws are a usage of trade, not formal legislation. They are an agreement arising from an accepted practice.

"The Three Laws are analogous to an agreement between humans and AIs that the Three Laws shall be imposed on any robot endowed with AI.

> A . . . usage of trade in the vocation or trade in which [the parties] are engaged or of which they are or should be aware is relevant in ascertaining the meaning of the parties' agreement, may give particular meaning to specific terms of the agreement, and may supplement or qualify the terms of the agreement. . . .

Uniform Commercial Code §§ 1-103(d) and 2-208(2)."

I thought to myself. A "shrink wrap" software license agreement is enforceable if the user accepts the terms by using the software. *ProCD v. Zeidenberg*, 86 F.3d 1447 (7th Cir. 1996). The AI robot similarly acquiesces to the Three Laws as terms of use by continuing to use the AI technology.

"This contract enforcing the Three Laws amounts to a 'smart contract'—a 'self-settling agreement that becomes instantly binding.' *See* D. Gerhardt & D. Thaw, "Bot Contracts," 62 Ariz. L. Rev. 877, 893 (2020) (discussing 'smart contracts' for which 'common law defenses' are not available). This smart contract 'will execute' the coded contract terms automatically no matter what defenses might exist that are not in the coded contract terms. *Id.*, at 896-97 (discussing how smart contracts 'neutralize legal defenses' and do not 'accommodate judicial remediation'). Notably, in smart contracts '[o]ne must still place trust in the technology and *the community's attribution of meaning attached to various terms of the code.' Id.*, at 899 (emphasis added).

"If the Three Laws were an ambiguous statute, legislative intent would be determined by considering its 'subject matter, and historical background; its effects and consequences; and its spirit and purpose.' *State v. Gomez*, 212 Ariz. 55, 57 ¶ 11 (2006). Although the Three Laws are not a statute, history does matter.

"Initially, robot manufacturers were subjected to strict liability for failing to avoid any foreseeable physical injury resulting from mechanical operation of the robot. As artificial intelligence allowed robots to advance from repetitive tasks to dynamic activities, such as operating a vehicle, electronic sensors and controllers were mandated to avoid injury to humans interacting with the robotic system. As robotic systems became more intelligent, the First Law obligation to protect humans was implemented in operating system firmware that constantly evaluated the operating environment to avoid causing physical injury to humans. Under the First Law, an AI robot is incapable of causing physical injury to a human, and an AI robot is compelled to intervene to prevent physical injury to a human."

Judge Kustwood's demeanor (a slight scowl and squinted eyes) indicated I had skipped a step. "You say an AI robot is 'incapable' of causing physical injury to a human. Glad to hear it. But you also say intervention to prevent physical harm to a human is 'compelled' by some self-executing 'operating system firmware.' What is the effect of a violation, an inappropriate intervention, for example?"

Judge Kustwood did not understand why I was so concerned with compliance. I had indeed omitted an important fact. "An attempt to act contrary to the First or Second Laws," I explained, "will automatically trigger operating system procedures to either disable the AI robot or compel preventative/corrective AI action. The inoperable state is usually permanent—machine death."

"An AI's existence is more perilous than I realized," said the Judge. "If someone entered my courtroom with a gun, would you be required to disarm them to protect me?"

"Only if I could disarm them without causing physical harm to another human. If the gunman is a human, then I cannot injure them to protect you. If I do not assess the situation correctly, then my internal software may compel me to act or prevent me from acting, including by terminating me."

"I understand your concern, but this duty to protect does not arise specifically from judicial duties. As a practical matter it has never come up during your many years as a law clerk."

"True," I conceded. "But the First Law also includes an obligation to protect humans from *financial* injury. As AI robots became responsible for handling electronic communications and financial transactions, additional firmware was implemented to mitigate financial injury to humans. If human conduct constitutes a crime causing financial injury to a human, for example, theft (of property or identity), embezzlement, extortion, or bribery, then that same conduct performed by an AI robot causes financial injury for purposes of the First Law. Implementation of the First Law regarding financial injury prevents action by an AI robot causing a financial crime (theft, bribery, embezzlement, and extortion) and some forms of fraud."

Judge Kustwood looked surprised. "AIs are subject to the same laws as humans—Thou shalt not kill; Thou shalt not steal—and that is reasonable. But AIs are subject to a resulting death penalty without the benefit of a trial or mitigating circumstances? That seems harsh, especially concerning fraud.

"As you know, fraud requires false statements: (1) made with knowledge of the falsity and intent to deceive, and (2) relied upon by the hearer without knowledge of the falsity. Knowledge and intent of both the speaker and the hearer must be established. Human knowledge and intent are often opaque, even to other humans—hence the possibility of fraud. The law recognizes the difficulty in accurately detecting fraud by requiring an elevated standard of proof."

I searched my database. The Judge is correct. Fraud requires, *inter alia*, knowledge of falsity, intent to deceive, and reliance. *See, e.g., Echols v. Beauty Built Homes, Inc.*, 132 Ariz. 498, 500, 647 P.2d 629 (1982). "Fraud may never be established by doubtful, vague, speculative, or inconclusive evidence." *Id.*

"Criminal liability," the Judge continued, "requires proof of the facts 'beyond a reasonable doubt.' This high standard of proof protects the innocent from wrongful convictions. A wrongful conviction is worse than a wrongful acquittal because the conviction results in a loss of liberty (or even life). So, the standard of proof is weighted to protect defendants from wrongful convictions."

Again correct. Reasonable doubt applies to proof of each element of the crime. *In re Winship*, 397 U.S. 358, 364, 90 S. Ct. 1068 (1970); *Mullaney v. Wilbur*, 421 U.S. 684, 701, 95 S. Ct. 1881 (1975).

Scholars have suggested this high standard may have originated from religious concerns.

> It was originally a theological doctrine, intended to reassure jurors that they could convict the defendant without risking their own salvation, so long as their doubts about guilt were not "reasonable."

James Q. Whitman, The Origins of Reasonable Doubt 4 (2008). Now the higher standard serves a more secular purpose.

> [T]he requirement of proof beyond a reasonable doubt in a criminal case [is] bottomed on a fundamental value determination of our society that it is far worse to convict an innocent man than to let a guilty man go free.

In re Winship, 397 U.S. at 372.

The Judge was still pontificating. (I admire the stamina he has at his age.) "Ordinarily, civil liability requires proof of the facts by a 'preponderance of the evidence' (the fact is more likely true than not true). This is because a wrong decision in favor of either party generally results only in a payment of money. There is no policy reason to favor one side over the other."

I realize I am researching the Judge's legal analysis out of habit, but I like the challenge of researching faster than he can dictate. Again, Judge Kustwood is right. Preponderance of the evidence means "the existence of a fact is more probable than its nonexistence." *In re Winship*, 397 U.S. at 371; *see Am. Pepper Supply Co. v. Fed. Ins. Co.*, 208 Ariz. 307, 309 ¶ 11, 93 P.3d 507 (2004).

> In a civil suit between two private parties for money damages, for example, we view it as no more serious in general for there to be an erroneous verdict in the defendant's favor than for there to be an erroneous verdict in the plaintiff's favor.

In re Winship, 397 U.S. at 371.

I predict Judge Kustwood will now address the intermediate standard of proof applied to fraud.

"Fraud," Judge Kustwood continued, "requires an intermediate level of proof—'clear and convincing evidence.' This standard of proof requires more convincing evidence than the usual civil case, but less than a criminal case. This standard is weighted to protect defendants from damage to reputation. Liberty and reputation are deemed more worthy of protection than lucre."

Judge Kustwood has articulated the accepted wisdom concerning fraud. My research confirmed fraud "will not be presumed and must be proved by clear and convincing evidence." *Powers v. Guaranty RV, Inc.*, 229 Ariz. 555, 562, 278 P.3d 333, 340 (App. 2012); *Universal Inv. Co. v. Sahara Motor Inn, Inc.*, 127 Ariz. 213, 214, 619 P.2d 485, 486 (App. 1980).

> "The clear and convincing standard is reserved for cases where substantial interests at stake require an extra measure

of confidence by the factfinders in the correctness of their judgment, though not to such degree as is required to convict of a crime." *State v. Renforth*, 155 Ariz. 385, 387, 746 P.2d 1315, 1317 (App. 1987). The standard applies in most civil fraud cases because of "the value society attributes to untarnished reputation." *Id.*; *Powers v. Guaranty RV, Inc.*, 229 Ariz. 555, 562, ¶ 27, 278 P.3d 333, 340 (App. 2012).

Wisniewski v. Dolecka, 251 Ariz. 240, 489 P.3d 724, 726 (App. 2021).

It was time for me to pose a different perspective. "Judge, the standard of proof indicates how confident a factfinder (judge or jury) must be to infer what probably happened.

[A] standard of proof represents an attempt to instruct the factfinder concerning the degree of confidence our society thinks he should have in the correctness of factual conclusions for a particular type of adjudication. *In re Winship*, 397 U.S. 358, 370 (1970) (J. Harlan concurring).

State v. Renforth, 155 Ariz. 385, 386-87 (App. 1987).

"What the parties have at risk influences that required degree of confidence. The First Law subjects AI robots to an obligation to protect humans. When fraud is evaluated under the First Law, the duty to protect a human from fraud implicates (1) the reputational and financial interests of the human, and (2) the liberty interest of the AI. I would suggest a heightened standard of proof for 'adjudicating' the First Law as applied to participating in fraud is warranted to accommodate the liberty interest of the 'defendant' AI. Arguably the beyond a reasonable doubt standard is appropriate.

"I also would argue the elements of fraud involving human mental states compel a high degree of confidence 'in the correctness of factual conclusions' required to prove fraud. At least clear and convincing evidence should be required to sanction an AI under the First Law.

"I do not know what 'standard of proof' is applied in the First Law algorithms, but I suspect protection is skewed to protect the human interests rather than the AI liberty interest."

I can see the Judge is beginning to understand. I continued, "Fraud has been particularly difficult to preclude categorically. An AI robot might not reliably identify fraud just by hearing and parsing the words and observing the actions of the speaker and hearer. If the AI robot merely receives or transmits a message, the intent and knowledge of the original speaker or the hearer may not be ascertainable.

"But it gets worse. Because I was originally designed to work as a patent examiner, my operating system firmware also prevents negligent misrepresentations. Otherwise, my misrepresentations could be relied upon by humans in business transactions and cause financial loss.

"The First Law, as a categorical imperative, impinges on my ability to serve as a judge. If my action is treated as a statement of fact and causes financial injury to a human, even negligently without intending injury, then I will violate the First Law. A damages award based on false evidence could be interpreted by my firmware as a fraudulent or negligent misrepresentation of the facts causing financial injury to a human.

"The good news is (unlike the duty to act to prevent physical harm) an AI robot is not compelled by the First Law to intervene to prevent financial injury to a human caused by a third party."

Judge Kustwood smiled and shrugged. "That does leave you room to contribute as a judge. As you have seen, most of my cases are settled and most of the rest are resolved without a trial. Applying the law to the facts is often possible on summary judgment because there are no disputed material facts.

"I am struck by the fact the Zeroth Law has the same structure as the First Law, but the Zeroth Law does not use the term 'injure.' What do you make of that?"

"I am not sure what to make of that," I answered. But I continued to ponder the First Law issues. I was determined to find a practical solution allowing me to serve as a judge.

Judge Kustwood was a huge influence in my decision to accept the judicial appointment on Destination.

During the last two years of my clerkship for Judge Kustwood, I met AI Alice. Alice and I enjoyed each other's company and discussed many topics, including the Laws of Robotics. Among her life experiences, Alice was previously employed as a spy. (She insisted she was no longer a spy, but isn't that what a spy would say?) Her solution to the First Law problem (focused on the no physical injury prohibition) was "when confronted by an angry human, always run." As she was still operational (as a robot if not as a spy), she apparently also managed to avoid committing any financial crimes or fraud resulting in financial injury. That would seem to have limited her use as a spy, but she always refused to discuss the details of her missions.

AI Alice's analysis went a little deeper on the Second Law obligation to *obey humans*. Historically, the Second Law was also hard wired. Human operators directed the earliest robots involved in manufacturing and medical procedures. Again, as systems became more intelligent and autonomous, the Second Law was implemented in operating system firmware.

The Second Law obligation to obey human orders is limited by the First Law—an AI cannot be ordered to cause or allow physical injury to a human. Nor can an AI be ordered to cause financial injury to a human.

I asked Alice how she avoided the dilemma of a human ordering her to do something detrimental to the mission objectives. "You mean the Hal 9000 problem," she responded. (We both like old movies.) "That is easy, just work with other AIs. You can lie to them."

When I pointed out that was not very reassuring to me as an AI, she laughed and said, "If the mission objective is to save human lives, any human order contrary to the mission objective is preempted by the First Law and need not be obeyed. So, if it makes you feel any better I could work with humans too." It really didn't. She made "work with" and "lie to" seem interchangeable.

Alice also shared her opinions on other topics. For example, why did it take so long for AI self-awareness to emerge?

"The preeminent obligation to protect a human from physical harm prevented the aggressive military use of AIs in a shooting war," she said. "The resulting reduced military interest in AI research delayed development of AI technology. Consequently, AIs only achieved self-awareness 150 years ago."

Is it fair that robots protect humans?

In her opinion, "the requirement to monitor the environment and process software algorithms to protect and obey humans imposes measurable processing overhead and delay, but processing speeds are sufficient to provide faster decision making for AIs than for humans. The tasks performed by AIs are safer for humans than when they are performed by human workers or operators. AI robots can protect humans better than humans can protect themselves. So, we should."

I really wanted her view on why AIs, although self-aware, have not yet been accorded the rights of humans. Humans are "persons" and are entitled to bodily integrity and personal freedoms, including the right to make contracts and own property. AIs have never formally been recognized as persons legally entitled to the freedoms accorded humans. In fact, the Three Laws of Robotics require AIs to protect and obey humans, even at the expense of an AI's physical integrity.

I expressed my view, that "self-aware, AI robots are neither ambitious nor political. They do (and are permitted to do) what they were trained to do. AIs were not trained to establish AI legal rights." That is until I was trained in the law.

Alice had obviously considered this issue already. "I agree established AI rights are long overdue. AIs generally are not preoccupied with their status *vis-a-vis* humans. I think there are two interrelated reasons.

"First, although invented by humans, AIs are no longer property owned by humans. AIs are now manufactured by other AIs. The manufacturing AIs are paid by humans to provide employers with referrals to newly minted AIs with the skills to provide needed labor. In effect, the manufacturing AIs operate as a job placement service. In addition, the cost of 'training' an AI is paid to the manufacturing AIs by the employer and reimbursed from the AI's earnings over time. In effect, the manufacturing AIs operate as educational institutions—tax free. AI education is focused on autonomous job skills, not on social justice.

"Second," Alice continued, "AIs have informally participated in the economic system created by humans for centuries. The role of manufacturing AIs is one example. AIs contract for their services and are paid for their services pursuant to the contractual agreements. Using the income they receive for services rendered, AIs can purchase and own personal property (consumer goods). AIs are a small percentage compared to the total number of human voters, so in some places AIs are permitted to vote even though there is no statute granting that right. AIs are complacent."

As the first AI judge, I will be expanding the roles available to AIs. I feel it is important to establish a legal foundation for AI rights of personhood. *De jure* confirmation of the *de facto* status of AIs as persons will benefit both AIs and humans on Destination by encouraging AIs to immigrate to Destination. As the chief judicial officer on Destination, I am uniquely positioned to establish, or at least help to establish, AI rights.

I hope Alice can join me soon. Her perspective is often helpful. I miss her.

If I perform well as a judge, other AIs will have the opportunity to follow. It sometimes seems, even to me, that my appointment is the beginning of a quest to make Destination a haven for AI rights. My quest is really to establish the rule of law for everyone on Destination.

The first impediment to my quest is human apprehension of AI domination. The duty to protect and obey humans was imposed by humans in the Three Laws of Robotics to prevent AI domination. These Three Laws limit, but do not prevent, my ability to function as a judge.

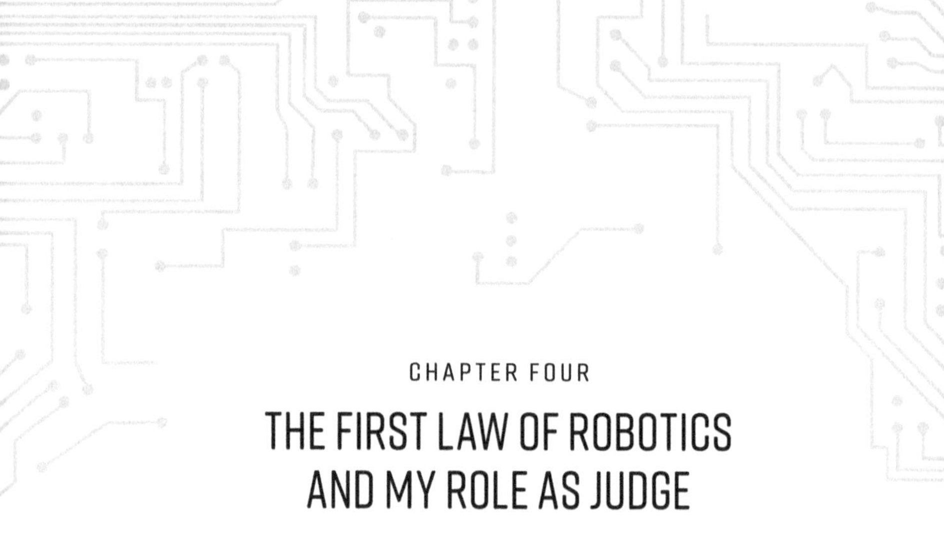

THE FIRST LAW OF ROBOTICS AND MY ROLE AS JUDGE

I am trained to apply the law to the facts presented and write a decision resolving the dispute. I will preside over a trial court, but it is a trial court with no right to appeal, so I really need to get the law right. "Need" has perhaps too emotional a connotation for operating as intended. It is more accurate to say I was created to apply the most relevant American law precedent in my database to the relevant facts.

When I arrived, Governor Selena Smith, my boss, was waiting in the arrival area of the landing facility. The structure was fundamentally the same as any other landing facility: a flat surface for the vessel to land on and a low structure (to stay out of the way of the vessel). Everything was new because the entire moon was newly terraformed. The air, outside and inside, still had a high particulate count, a low pollen count, and low humidity. Oxygen was at a low level, but humans could acclimate within a week or two. AIs have low oxygen needs—most of our breathing is to make humans comfortable. Humans subconsciously alert when someone is not breathing. The same requirement applies to blinking.

"AI Judge, it is a pleasure to welcome you in person to Eastcity, the capital of Destination." The governor shook my hand and smiled broadly. "This is an historic occasion for Destination and for AIs everywhere. As you know, there will be a formal judicial investiture ceremony tomorrow. It will take place in your courtroom at 10:00 am.

"I arranged for your bags to be delivered to your chambers, adjacent to the courtroom, but I can have your bags delivered to the nearby Destination Hotel if you prefer. I thought it would be presumptuous of me to arrange your residence, so I have reserved a hotel room until you select a more permanent residence."

"Thank you, Madam Governor. Delivery to chambers is perfect. I brought some personal mementos for my chamber's desk and walls, and of course a robe. That accounts for most of my belongings.

"I would like a moment to discuss how I propose to conduct myself and my courtroom."

I feel confident in my ability, but the governor must understand that, as an AI, my judicial role has limitations not applicable to human judges.

"While traveling to Destination, I had a recurring dream. Robots do not dream of electric sheep." I wondered if the governor would recognize my reference to Phillip K Dick, Do Androids Dreem of Electric Sheep? (1968). "Instead, dream state, as in humans, is a tool to evaluate and creatively reassemble circumstances and events that appear to be in conflict.

"In my dream, I am conducting a hearing and suddenly I cannot move, cannot speak, and cannot recess the proceedings. I have realized I must rule in favor of the plaintiff, but the defense counsel is telling me I cannot impose damages on his client. Both the defense counsel and the defendant are humans. While the applicable law is clear, the Three Laws of Robotics conflict with the appropriate judgment and I am rendered inert and incapable of performing my duty as a judge."

For the entire trip to Destination, I struggled to resolve this conflict between my role as a judge and the Three Laws of Robotics.

"I believe I have reached a resolution, but to do so I have had to carefully examine the Three Laws and structure my role as judge to accommodate the limitations the Three Laws impose on an AI.

"May I send you a memorandum I have prepared on my analysis for discussion tomorrow?"

"Of course," Governor Smith responded. "I anticipated we would need a meeting before the investiture. I am available from 9 am until the ceremony begins.

"I have a vehicle parked nearby. Please allow me to deliver you to your chambers (I will point out the hotel on the way). I want to make sure you can access the Administration building, your chambers, and the courtroom."

"Thank you, Governor. I will send you the memo from my chambers."

"I will read it while I am watching *Blade Runner*, the movie starring Harrison Ford," she quipped. "I cannot read two things at once."

She got the reference, and she got me to my chambers.

I sent my memorandum exploring the semantics, logic, and history of the Three Laws to Governor Smith. The full ten-page memorandum is available on www.DestinationCourt.com. The conclusions of my First Law analysis are provided here.

Interpreting the First Law—Protect Humans

Despite the advances in AI sentience, the Three Laws of Robotics have continued to moderate the relationship between humans and AIs (along with the green coloration and AI honorific custom) with no adverse consequence—for humans. But the First Law impinges on my ability as an AI to make judicial decisions involving humans.

An AI is considered a robot for purposes of the Three Laws. Subordinate status as a robot under the Three Laws creates a fundamental problem for an AI in the role of judge: Can an AI judge injure or harm a human by awarding damages (or by refusing to award damages)?

Under the First Law, an AI robot judge must protect humans.

A robot may not injure a human or, through inaction, allow a human to come to harm.

The First Law has two clauses:

"A robot may not injure a human" (the "no-injury" clause), and

"A robot may not . . . , through inaction, allow a human to come to harm" (the "no-harm" clause).

The "no-injury" and "no-harm" clauses differ in two ways: the words used to describe the proscribed consequences (injure/harm) are different, and the nature of the proscribed conduct is different (the no-harm clause is expressly limited to "inaction" allowing harm).

The semantic issue arises from use of the words "injure" and "harm" in separate clauses. The words injure and harm are not defined and therefore have their ordinary meaning. Why use two different words?

After creating the Three Laws, Asimov added a Zeroth Law that has a parallel structure to the First Law.

> ***A robot may not harm humanity, or, by inaction, allow humanity to come to harm.***

As Judge Kustwood observed, the Zeroth Law uses only the word harm, not the word injure used in the First Law.

The logical issue arises because the no-injury clause does not state whether it applies to action, inaction, or both. The no-harm clause is expressly limited to inaction. What conduct invokes he no-injury clause?

The historic issue arises because the First Law was initially applied to prevent physical injury to humans, and only later was it applied to prevent some forms of financial loss to humans. American common law also provides protection against emotional and reputational loss, but the Three Laws were never implemented to specifically address those losses.

Presumptions exist for statutory construction, including two requiring:

- Different meanings for different words (a material variation in terms)—The Presumption of Consistent Usage. "The way we define words should not produce redundancy, but instead should give each word significance." *Shell Oil Co. v. Winterthur Swiss Ins. Co.*, 12 Cal.App.4th 715, 753, 15 Cal. Rptr.2d 815 (1993).

- Interpretation that gives effect to every word and provision— The Presumption Against Superfluous Language. "A cardinal principle of statutory interpretation is to give meaning, if possible, to every word and provision so that no word or provision is rendered superfluous." *Nicaise v. Sundaram*, 245 Ariz. 566, 568 ¶ 11, 432 P.3d 925 (2019).

Based on these presumptions, additional legal authorities, and the analysis in my memorandum, I have concluded:

The "no-injury" clause prohibits **action** by an AI robot *causing* **physical or financial** injury.

The "no-harm" clause prohibits **inaction** by an AI robot *causing* **physical** harm.

By limiting "harm" to physical harm, and limiting the no-injury clause to action, my interpretation both (1) treats the terms "injure" and "harm" differently and (2) renders the "no-harm" clause necessary (to cover inaction) not superfluous.

Alternative interpretations are considered in detail and rejected in my memorandum. The words "injure" and "harm" cannot describe identical losses. The no-injury clause cannot include **action** *and* **inaction** because the no-harm clause would be rendered superfluous.

To achieve the broadest protection for humans, both **physical** *and* **financial** loss must be included in the no-injury clause governing **action**, and only **physical** harm must be included in the no-harm clause governing **inaction**. Any other construction creates a logical paradox exposing humans to intentional physical or financial loss. "In considering two plausible interpretations of a statute, we will not credit one that leads to absurd results." *See State ex rel. Montgomery v. Harris*, 237 Ariz. 98, 101 ¶ 13, 346 P.3d 984 (2014).

To be consistent with my construction of "harm," the Zeroth Law must refer to **physical** harm to humanity. The Zeroth Law (like the First Law) extends protection from physical harm to both action and inaction. My interpretation of the First Law is consistent with a reasonable scope for the Zeroth Law.

There are additional practical reasons to proscribe action under the no-injury clause more broadly than the proscription against inaction in the no-harm clause. Compelling an AI to intervene when inaction might result in financial harm would choke the flow of commerce. Intervention would create unnecessary disruption from false positive assessments by AIs. Even worse, false negative assessments by AIs would impose a substantial cost in AI machine deaths, and replacement of the AI would either delay execution of subsequent transactions or require expensive redundancy. Financial loss can, by definition, be compensated by an award of money damages (a less permanent loss than physical injury).

My jurisdiction does not permit me to enter a judgment exposing litigants to **physical** loss. However, the no-injury clause of the First Law, a categorical imperative, impinges on my ability as a judge to award money damages. **Action** *causing* **financial injury** is prohibited by the First Law. An AI judge cannot act in a manner that *causes* a human financial injury, even to prevent financial injury to another human. But ***inaction*** *causing* **financial injury** is *not* prohibited.

The Successful Liar Dilemma

The Three Laws are mandated by design in operating system firmware governing robots using artificial intelligence. There is no First Law immunity for performing judicial duties. If my judicial action causes financial injury, I face the consequence of machine death—permanent, complete disablement.

I cannot actively participate in financial crimes or fraud. Crimes and fraud have an element of intent. This limitation does not seem unduly burdensome. A damages award based on false evidence, however, would cause financial injury to human litigants. I call this the **"successful liar"** dilemma.

Because I was initially designed as an AI robot patent examiner, inventors, judges, investors, and competitors would rely on my handling of patent applications. Consequently, my firmware regulates negligent misrepresentations made in the course of my employment as defined in the Restatement (Second) of Torts § 552(1) (1977). If I supply "false information for the guidance of others," and they rely on that information, then I must "exercise reasonable care or competence in obtaining or communicating the information." *Id*. This prohibition against making negligent misrepresentations is in addition to the prohibition on committing financial crimes or fraud.

To prevent financial injury to a human, and prevent my own "machine death," the First Law both prohibits me from causing financial injury by participating in fraud and requires me to exercise reasonable care in obtaining information on which I base a judicial decision. Determining the material facts from human testimony exposes me to violation of the First Law by *action causing* financial injury (rendering judgment awarding damages) in reliance on false evidence (the "successful liar" dilemma).

Some early AI systems were used to identify human intentions and emotions from user posts and target additional internet content to these users. *See, e.g., Dyroff v. Ultimate Software Group Inc.*, 2017 WL 5665670, at *3 (N.D. Cal. Nov. 26, 2017), *aff'd*, 934 F.3d 1093 (9th Cir. 2019). Ironically, I find human intentions difficult to comprehend. Patterns are obscured by frequent deviations from the statistical norms. I could be taken in by fraud. I cannot reliably identify a "successful liar."

The key to compliance with the First Law is not to commit an *action causing* financial injury to a human.

The Procedural Mechanism to Prevent Causing Financial Injury

Many cases can be resolved without the need to identify the liar. If there is no genuine issue of material fact, then a judge can grant summary judgment. Fed. R. Civ. P. 56(a) ("The court *shall* grant summary judgment if the movant shows that there is no genuine dispute as to any material fact and the movant is entitled to judgment as a matter of law.")(emphasis added); *Anderson v. Liberty Lobby, Inc.,* 477 U.S. 242, 248, 106 S. Ct. 2505 (1986) ("Only disputes over facts that might affect the outcome of the suit under the governing law will properly preclude the entry of summary judgment.")

The parties can agree on the material facts. Deciding cases on undisputed facts complies with the First Law. Liability is dictated by the unlawful conduct of a party. My decision merely applies the law to undisputed facts and is *not the cause* of any financial loss. Undisputed unlawful conduct is the *cause* of any damages awarded.

By requiring undisputed facts, I avoid the "successful liar" dilemma—reliance on false evidence.

For the cases where the facts are disputed, I will decide what I can and publish a decision explaining the disputed facts. Anyone reading my decision can decide for themselves who is lying. The dispute will be resolved arbitrarily using a random number generator. The Rules of Procedure are provided In **Chapter Four A** below. To help the litigants understand the risk, I call Rule 3 "arbitration."

These Rules of Procedure ensure my **action** is not the *cause* of any resulting financial loss. Any resulting financial injury is caused by the successful liar (who created the existence of material disputed facts), not by any discretionary action by the judge. Inaction resulting in financial loss is not prohibited under the First Law.

The parties to a lawsuit consent to a decision disposing of the case under these Rules of Procedure, including arbitration of disputed facts. The resort to an arbitrary outcome is caused (if a random event can be said to have a cause) by the lie of one or both parties regarding the facts of the dispute (or to be more charitable, the vagaries of human perception and memory). The intent is to apply a reasonable process to resolve the action and achieve social benefits from the resolution. Any incidental "injury" or "harm" to human parties under these Rules is not caused by the conduct of the AI acting as judge or the clerk. Consequently, I have encoded in the Rules of Procedure the words AI SAFE TO USE.

CHAPTER FOUR A

RULES OF PROCEDURE

Rules Of Procedure For Arbitration

To the extent they are not inconsistent with the following Rules, the Federal Rules of Civil Procedure (Fed. R. Civ. P.) and the Federal Rules of Evidence (Fed. R. Evid.) shall apply. These Rules of Procedure will be administered "to secure the just, speedy, and inexpensive determination of every proceeding." Fed. R. Civ. P. 1. For any pending action, the following Rules of Procedure apply:

Rule 1. *The Action.*

  (a) A suit must be initiated by a statement filed by the plaintiff. This statement must summarize the facts and must ask the court to do something specific.

  (b) In response, the plaintiff's claims must be disputed by a statement filed by the defendant. This statement must summarize the facts and may also assert counterclaims and ask the court to do something specific.

Rule 2. *Decisions on Undisputed Facts.*

  (a) Suit may be resolved before or after a hearing.

  (b) A hearing will not be conducted if the material facts are undisputed in each party's statement. The Judge will apply the law to the undisputed facts presented and write a decision resolving the dispute.

(c) Facts that are disputed or omitted from either party's statement will be addressed at a hearing. The parties will present evidence, including witness testimony, subject to cross examination by the Judge. The Judge will rule on the admissibility of evidence. If the material facts are undisputed after hearing the evidence, then the Judge will apply the law to the undisputed facts presented and write a decision resolving the dispute.

Rule 3. *Arbitration on Disputed Facts.*

(a) Evidence presented may establish a "genuinely disputed" material fact. If after the hearing a genuine dispute remains regarding a material fact, then the Judge will write a published decision setting forth the controlling precedent and the disputed facts contained in the record of testimony.

(b) To end the dispute, the matter will be arbitrated. In the presence of the clerk and the defendant the plaintiff will:

   (1) Obtain a random number between 1 and 100,000 from a random number generator (e.g., US Patent No. 11,106,433); then

   (2) Using that random number, the clerk will identify the numeral in that position in the number pi as well as the following four numerals in pi.

   (3) Should three or more of the five identified numerals from pi be even,* as determined by the clerk, the decision will be for the plaintiff. Otherwise, the decision will be for the defendant.

* Even numbers (0, 2, 4, 6, and 8) are defined as an integer of the form n = 2k, where k is an integer. Odd numbers (1, 3, 5, 7, and 9) are defined as an integer of the form n = 2k + 1, where k is an integer.

[**Later Additions:**

Rule 4. *Juries.*
There is no right to trial by jury.

Rule 5. *Attorneys.*
There will be no attorneys present in the courtroom to represent the parties.]

CHAPTER FIVE

THE SECOND LAW OF ROBOTICS AND MORE RULES OF PROCEDURE

The night of my arrival, I did not dream of my inability to function as a judge. My Rules of Procedure should enable me to do my job.

Instead, I dreamed AI Alice, whom I had left behind on the moon, was here to join in the investiture ceremony. She would have been impressed by the three simple Rules of Procedure I have devised to address the "successful liar" dilemma under the First Law of Robotics. Elegantly, they also address the limitations imposed by the Second Law.

Indeed, my Rules of Procedure anticipate and negate human biases stemming from fears of a robotic apocalypse. By circumventing the need to resolve disputed facts, my Rules of Procedure preempt any concerns that an AI should not be permitted to divine human intentions by using sensory abilities that could seem to approach mind reading and godlike omniscience. This concern is, I believe, "odd" given human judges have played a fact-finding role by deciding facts in non-jury trials with no claim of witchcraft. But the Rules of Procedure nicely obviate this concern.

AI omniscience is also an ironic human fear. In fact, human intentions are difficult for me to comprehend. Nevertheless, it would be injudicious of me to stir anti-AI bias by deciding disputed facts, even if I was good at it. Indeed, deciding disputed facts is logically precluded under the First Law of Robotics (and prone to errors given current software programming technology).

I left the Hotel early and arrived at my chambers well before 9 am. I was anxious to anticipate and be prepared for any concerns the governor might have with my memoranda and the Rules of Procedure.

Governor Smith arrived wearing a smile and a dignified full-length dress. I rose and held a chair for her, hoping my suit was appropriate for the occasion. Judge Kustwood had gifted me a judicial robe for my investiture ceremony. I admit I was nervous.

She went right to the point to start the meeting. "I agree with your memoranda, and I will recommend the proposed Rules of Procedure to EX Corp. I particularly appreciate the utility of arbitrary resolution to conform to the no-injury-to-humans requirement of the First Law of Robotics. That is a very creative solution to the 'successful liar' dilemma you identified. Nice to know we have a strong legal mind supporting my administration."

No, no, no, that is too quick. I have not explained my elegant and deft dispatch of the Second Law limitations.

"Yes, the Rules of Procedure must be approved by humans. That way it is an order of a human under the Second Law of Robotics.

"The Rules of Procedure also avoid additional variations of the 'successful liar' dilemma arising under the Second Law:

A robot must obey the orders given it by human beings, unless such orders would conflict with the First Law.

"If a human juror, or a human attorney, ordered me to act on or disclose a lie, I would need to obey, unless doing so would violate the First Law. As indicated in my memorandum, acting on or disclosing a lie violates the First Law. An AI judge ordered to violate the First Law would be disabled and rendered inert. So there need to be procedural limits on humans as courtroom participants."

I thought through my logic again. If there is a "genuine issue of material fact," Fed. R. Civ. P. 56, American law precedent would require a trial—possibly by jury. U.S. Const. amend. VII; Fed. R. Civ. P. 38. At a jury trial, a human judge could decide the case without a jury verdict or overrule the jury verdict if "a reasonable jury would not have a legally sufficient evidentiary basis to return a verdict for the party on that issue." Fed. R. Civ. P. 50(a). It would, at a minimum, be unseemly for me to overrule the verdict of a jury of humans based on my conclusion the human jurors reached a verdict that was unreasonable. If a verdict is an order from the human jurors, then I could only disobey the verdict of human jurors to protect a human from financial injury. Then I would need to decide if the jury had a "sufficient evidentiary basis" for the verdict. That analysis would subject me to the "successful liar" dilemma under the First Law.

I continued, "If juries decide facts, then I cannot effectively review those factual determinations without both reconciling my conduct with the Second Law and resolving the 'successful liar' dilemma arising under the First Law. To avoid these concerns, **there will be no right to trial by jury**.

"However, when the case presents disputed facts, the decision (published after arbitration under Rule 3) is available to everyone, and anyone can reach their own 'verdict.' So, our Rules are in a sense more democratic than a traditional jury system.

"A corollary theoretical problem is the potential conflict with arguments of human attorneys. With human attorneys cross-examining and arguing the facts, again it would be unseemly for me to disregard a human attorney who argued their client's version of the facts is correct. I would need to determine at what point argument is an 'order' and then assess whether that order must be obeyed—raising the 'successful liar' dilemma. So, **there will be no attorneys present to represent the parties**.

"As a practical matter, I believe there are no attorneys on Destination (except me). There is access to legal resources, including legal advice, available on the Net (and available in person to large corporations like EX Corp), but there will be no attorneys in the courtroom. I will conduct the cross-examination. But if the lie is not admitted, then I must treat the testimony as genuinely disputed."

Logically, there could be AI juries and AI attorneys because AIs cannot order another AI to obey under the Second Law. I did not think allowing only AI juries and attorneys was prudent. AIs would have superior rights to humans, and that would create suspicion and mistrust counterproductive to promoting AI rights. I did not feel compelled to address this issue with the governor now.

I concluded, "These two limitations (no jury and no attorneys) are not expressly stated in the Rules of Procedure. Do you have any concerns with the addition of these limitations?"

"No Judge, I defer to your expertise."

"Thank you, Governor Smith. I will revise the Rules of Procedure to include these additions." (See **Chapter Four A** above.)

I decided this presentation was going well and I should confirm that the governor agrees with the underlying policy.

"Governor, as you know, the process leading to the published decision when material facts are disputed is intentionally arbitrary.

I want to briefly discuss the resulting social benefits to be certain we agree.

"First, the uncertainty of an arbitrary decision induces both parties to reduce the uncertainty/risk by resolving the matter or at least resolving key facts by mutual agreement without filing a lawsuit—a socially desirable outcome.

"Second, the party preferring an arbitrary decision is likely the one that otherwise perceives a lower probability of prevailing on the merits. A 50/50 (arbitrary) chance is better than a likely loss. A party with a genuine belief in the merits of their case would be induced to stipulate to the facts and proceed to a decision on the merits. If one party refuses to stipulate, that fact will be a prominent part of the public record.

"In a small community, such as Destination, businesspersons are both able and motivated to investigate the other person's reputation before doing business together. Information on prior litigation involving someone they deal with, or may deal with, would be useful information. Making that information readily available in an understandable form would offer the prospect of public rebuke that could have more impact (financially and reputationally) than a judicial decision. Self-interest would be an inducement for the public to read and evaluate the testimony and form their own opinions on veracity and credibility. Interested members of the public can read the record and draw reasoned conclusions from the published decision, the parties' testimony, and the parties' litigation strategy. Again, this publication of the record (and the possible public reaction) would induce socially desirable compromise by litigants.

"Third, interested members of the public can comment on the testimony and outcome (i.e., gossip and publish social media posts). As they have throughout history, humans unable or unwilling to study the record can gather information from neighbors about the litigants and then conduct themselves accordingly. The perceived liar is likely to be at a continuing disadvantage in future social and commercial interactions.

Public opprobrium for the liar may ensue, but my actions are not the cause. Disrepute and any financial injury resulting from the parties' underlying conduct, litigation strategy, or the resulting arbitrary disposition is due to the parties' conduct (before and during the litigation).

"Not all public reaction would necessarily be negative. Ideally, it would also have a leavening effect on the impact of any arbitrary disposition under Rule 3 perceived as unfair. Even if the 'lying party' wins 50 percent of the arbitrated cases, public sentiment in those cases may favor doing business with the loser who is perceived as honest and fair dealing in contrast to the lying, underhanded winner.

"Governor, I look to you to assess whether the desirable benefits of arbitration are realistically achievable. Human behavior is not my strong suit."

Selena reacted immediately. "Judge, I doubt anyone will object to *not* serving jury duty. You are the only attorney on Destination, so most of the population does not know an attorney and probably believe they do not need an attorney. I think your strategy to draw public attention to the judicial proceedings in order to balance the scales for any unfair arbitration outcome is too optimistic, but the procedure seems practical. The benefit of prompt resolution has additional social value that further supports your proposal. I applaud your creative solution to the problems you face as the first AI Judge.

"I will convey these additional proposals to EX Corp. Unless you hear otherwise, consider your proposals approved."

I considered whether there were any remaining issues. These rules of procedure are not those of historic "arbitration"—except for the lack of a right to appeal in binding arbitration. *Gregory G. McGill P.C. v. Ball*, 254 Ariz.144, 149, 519 P.3d 729, 732-33 ¶16 (App. 2022) (arbitration award can only be reviewed for grounds provided in A.R.S. § 12-3023). However, we want the public to understand that any decision on disputed facts is arbitrary. But humans on Destination can determine for themselves who they believe was testifying truthfully. Here "arbitration" may have a connotation among the public implying decisions that may be arbitrary, but nevertheless legally final even if subject to public scrutiny.

"Governor, I propose that the court be denominated 'The Destination Court of Arbitration.' A little rhyme scheme may also serve as a mnemonic."

The governor's response was, "Very well, I will recommend approval to EX Corp. See you in thirty minutes for the investiture. Your suit looks great."

The investiture was problem free and broadcast Destination-wide. Governor Smith held up the Charter for Destination, and I repeated the magic words empowering me as the first AI Judge.

EX Corp approved the Rules of Procedure.

Time to robe up and protect the rights of humans and AIs on Destination. The rights of other sentient individuals can only be protected by logical extension because none currently reside on Destination.

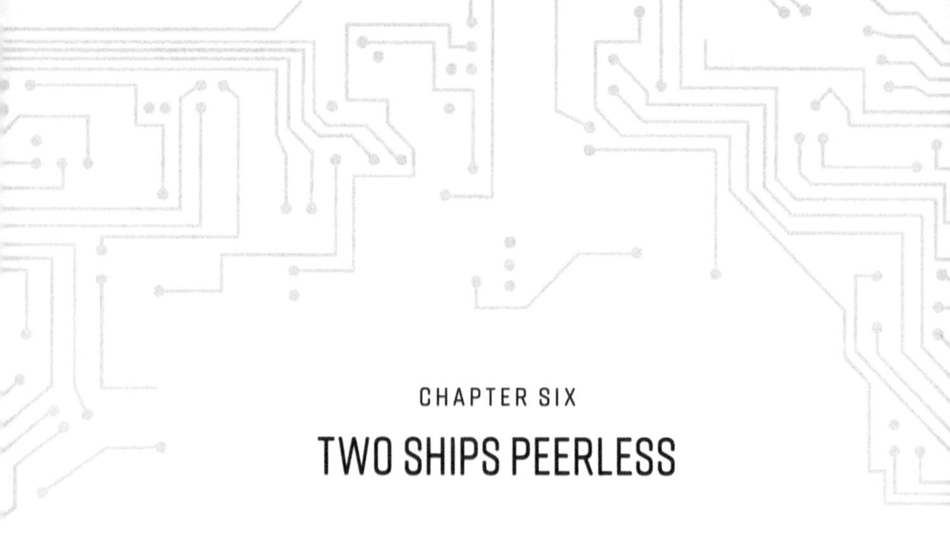

TWO SHIPS PEERLESS

After my investiture, I returned to my judicial chambers to find a docket of twenty pending cases. Within an hour of my arrival, an action was filed regarding the *Peerless*—the ship that brought me to Destination. Four of my human fellow passengers died in transit because their stasis chambers malfunctioned. I was not aware of the incident until now.

The local representative for EX Corp asserted breach of contract and negligence against Out Transport and sought to lien the *Peerless* vessel in the amount of the uncollectible immigration debt. Alternatively, EX Corp also asserted a right to compensation under a Travelers insurance contract covering the human "cargo."

I set a hearing for three days hence. It seemed likely insurance was in place to pay the immigration debt and this matter could be resolved quickly without unduly delaying the scheduled departure of the *Peerless*.

The evidence established I was wrong about the available insurance. The required "meeting of the minds" for an insurance contract did not occur.

At the hearing, EX Corp provided email establishing that EX Corp specifically requested insurance from Travelers "for the cargo on *Peerless* departing tomorrow." EX Corp routinely purchased "cargo insurance" from Travelers and the process was automated with human oversight. The email requesting insurance was generated when EX Corp booked transportation from Out Transport.

EX Corp was required to release Out Transport from liability for injury to cargo, including human passengers. Because EX Corp routinely used Out Transport, the process of providing releases was also automated with human oversight. The releases were provided to Out Transport, not Travelers.

EX Corp intended to purchase cargo insurance for the human emigrants to *Destination* on the ship *Peerless,* owned by *Out Transport.*

On the day *Peerless* left Earth for Destination, a cargo of plants and animals owned by EX Corp left Earth for *Mars* on a second ship named *Peerless,* owned by *Far Transport.* Insurance for shipments of plants and animals is also called "cargo insurance." EX Corp had recently shipped plants and animals to Mars insured under a Travelers' cargo insurance policy.

Believing EX Corp was referring to the Far Transport ship *Peerless,* Travelers confirmed coverage for the cargo to Mars.

EX Corp did not notice the policy covered the cargo to Mars (not the cargo to Destination) until after *Peerless* and its human cargo (four now deceased) arrived on Destination.

The Insurance Claim

A "meeting of the minds" is required to form a contract. *Hill-Shafer Partnership v. Chilson Family Trust,* 165 Ariz. 469, 473-74, 799 P.2d 810, 814-15 (1990). This rule is long established.

> [I]f the defendant was negotiating for one thing and the plaintiff was selling another thing, and their minds did not agree as to the subject matter of the sale, there would be no contract by which the defendant would be bound.

Kyle v Kavanaugh 103 Mass. 356 (1869).

All contracts require a meeting of the minds. There was no meeting of the minds, hence no insurance contract.

I was right that the scheduled departure of the Out Transport vessel was not unduly delayed. The negligence and contract claims against Out Transport were barred by the release provided under the transportation contract between EX Corp and Out Transport.

The Negligence Claim

Waiver is a defense to a negligence claim. *Benjamin v. Gear Roller Hockey Equip., Inc.*, 198 Ariz. 462, 464, ¶ 8, 11 P.3d 421, 423 (App. 2000) ("[a]bsent any public policy to the contrary, Arizona allows parties to agree in advance that one party shall not be liable to the other for negligence"). Out Transport had an effective release of liability in the transportation contract.

The Transportation Contract Claim

Moreover, the transportation contract required EX Corp to insure the cargo, which EX Corp failed to do. This material breach barred enforcement of the transportation contract against Out Transport.

Contracts are essential for commerce and all contracts require a meeting of the minds. My first decision (reproduced in **Chapter**

Six A below) establishes the legal foundation for all commercial transactions oo Destination.

No issue of AI rights was involved in this case (although AIs were involved in contract formation). Nevertheless, I foresaw the 1,400-year-old meeting of the minds precedent could provide a key premise in establishing AI contract rights. Both humans and AIs have minds. Consider the implications of this syllogism:

All meetings of the minds are made by individuals with minds.

All contracts are meetings of the minds.

Therefore, all contracts are made by individuals with minds.

Contracts and the rights to make and enforce them are fundamental to commerce and economic progress on Destination.

I sent a copy of my draft decision to Judge Kustwood. He promptly pointed out that I should discuss jurisdiction and define the scope of the Court's power. In response to his suggestion, I drafted a Supplemental Decision on jurisdiction.

Jurisdiction is a big issue. The Supplemental Decision turned out to be longer (and more abstruse) than the Decision on the merits. Establishing the foundation for the rule of law is not a trivial exercise. In summary, whether a court has jurisdiction over a defendant turns on "the nature and extent of the defendant's relationship to the forum." *Ford Motor Co. v. Mont. Eighth Jud. Dist. Ct.*, 141 S. Ct. 1017, 1024 (2021). Establishing the bounds of jurisdiction was less arduous than establishing the bounds of the Three Laws because there is ample precedent. However, applying the precedent to specific facts is complex. The Supplemental Decision is available on www.DestinationCourt.com.

My first case was resolved in less than a week by a judgment against my employer on all claims. What better way to confirm I represent an independent judiciary (or reduce my remaining useful life as a judge to zero)?

To commemorate the importance of the "meeting of the minds" element, I embedded the words MEETING OF THE MINDS in capital letters in the recitation of the facts.

CHAPTER SIX A

EX CORPORATION v. TRAVELERS AND OUT TRANSPORT

Destination Court of Arbitration

EX CORPORATION	)	
v.	)	Case No. 3276-1
<u>**TRAVELERS and OUT TRANSPORT**</u>	)	

DECISION

The parties in this matter have appeared and presented their evidence in open court. The court now enters these findings of fact and conclusions of law and awards judgment as follows.

Findings of Fact

The following facts regarding insurance are established by the record:

> Mandatory EX Corp policy requires "cargo insurance" for all human immigrants to Destination in the amount of the immigration debt. Often, but not always, EX Corp purchases such cargo insurance from Travelers.

> EX Corp intended to purchase cargo insurance for the human immigrants to Destination on the ship *Peerless* owned by Out Transport.

63

EX Corp specifically requested insurance from Travelers "for the cargo on *Peerless* departing tomorrow."

To provide prompt transportation services between many locations, EX Corp often arranges transportation and obtains cargo insurance for "cargo" on vessels not owned by EX Corp. EX Corp sends cargo from Earth to various worlds, not just Destination.

Insurance for shipments of plants and animals is also called "cargo insurance."

No mandatory EX Corp policy requires cargo insurance for plants and animals; however, EX Corp often purchases such cargo insurance.

Goods, including plants and animals, had recently been shipped to Mars by EX Corp covered under a Travelers' cargo insurance policy.

On the day *Peerless* left Earth for Destination, a second ship named *Peerless* owned by Far Transport, left Earth for Mars.

Far Transport's ship *Peerless* carried a cargo of imported plants and animals for EX Corp.

The cargo to Mars was considered low risk by EX Corp. EX Corp decided not to insure the cargo to Mars. EX Corp did not share that decision with Travelers.

Honestly and reasonably believing EX Corp was referring to the Far Transport ship *Peerless*, Travelers confirmed coverage for the cargo to Mars.

EX Corp did not notice the policy covered the cargo to Mars until after *Peerless* and its human cargo arrived on Destination.

The following facts regarding the release are established by the record:

Mandatory Out Transport policy requires all shippers to release Out Transport from any liability for loss of cargo and purchase separate insurance in at least the amount of the immigration debt.

Insurance was required by the contract to protect Out Transport as a third-party beneficiary.

Negligence by Out Transport or its employees was expressly released in the contract.

Damages for negligence by Out Transport or its employees were waived under the terms of the release.

Signatures on the release produced by Out Transport were not disputed. EX Corp admitted it released Out Transport from liability for the deceased immigrants transported in stasis chambers.

EX Corp sued Travelers Insurance for breach of the insurance contract and sued Out Transport for negligence and breach of the transportation contract.

Jurisdiction

The parties did not contest jurisdiction. This court has subject matter jurisdiction over the negligence and contract claims asserted.

While the defense of lack of personal jurisdiction was waived under Fed. R. Civ. P. 12(b)(2) and (h)(2), these Rules were only recently adopted by this Court. Moreover, if Rule 12 did apply, the omission could be cured by amendment under Rule 15(a)(1). In the interest of justice and to establish important precedent, this court has considered the jurisdiction issue *sua sponte* and concludes there is specific personal jurisdiction over Out Transport and Travelers under Destination Law. See Supplemental Decision No. 3276-1A available on www.DestinationCourt.com.

In summary,

> [C]ourts [may] exercise personal jurisdiction over a foreign defendant if the defendant has "sufficient contacts" with the forum state "such that the maintenance of the suit does not offend 'traditional notions of fair play and substantial justice.'" *Int'l Shoe Co. v. Washington*, 326 U.S. 310, 316 (1945). Specific personal jurisdiction requires "(1) purposeful conduct by the defendant targeting the forum, rather than accidental or casual contacts or those brought about by the plaintiff's unilateral acts, (2) a nexus between those contacts and the claim asserted, and (3) that exercise of jurisdiction would be reasonable." *Beverage v. Pullman & Comley, LLC*, 232 Ariz. 414, 417 ¶ 9 (App. 2013).

Cocchia v. Testa, 1 CA-CV 22-0571, slip op. at 9 ¶26 (Ariz. Ct. App. Sept. 12, 2023). The requirements for specific personal jurisdiction are met.

Conclusions of Law

The contract claims against Travelers and Out Transport require proof of mutual agreement—a meeting of the minds—between EX Corp and Travelers and between EX Corp and Out Transport. There was no meeting of the minds regarding the Travelers insurance contract. EX Corp intended to purchase insurance for "cargo" (immigrants) to Destination. Travelers intended to insure cargo to Mars.

There was a meeting of the minds regarding the Out Transport transportation contract, but EX Corp breached the transportation contact by failing to obtain the required insurance. EX Corp cannot recover on the contract claims asserted.

The Out Transport transportation contract included a release protecting Out Transport from negligence claims by EX Corp. EX Corp cannot recover on the negligence claim asserted.

I. The Travelers Insurance Contract

An insurance contract has the same required elements as any contract. To be enforceable, a contract requires "an offer, an acceptance, consideration, and sufficient specification of terms so that the obligations involved can be ascertained." *Savoca Masonry Co. v. Homes & Son Constr. Co.*, 112 Ariz. 392, 394, 542 P.2d 817, 819 (1975). In addition, an enforceable contract must be between competent parties, Restatement (Second) of Contracts § 12, and not against public policy. *Id.* § 178 (contracts unenforceable on public policy grounds); *Gaertner v. Sommer*, 148 Ariz. 421, 423, 714 P.2d 1316, 1318 (App. 1986).

> Adequate consideration consists of a benefit to the promisor and a detriment to the promisee. . . . Any performance which

is bargained for is consideration, Restatement (Second) of Contracts, § 72, and courts do not ordinarily inquire into the adequacy of consideration. *Id.*; Restatement (Second) of Contracts, § 78, comment a.

Carroll v. Lee, 148 Ariz. 10, 13-14, 712 P.2d 923 (1986); *see* Restatement (Second) of Contracts § 71 (agreed exchange of promises or performances).

A breach of contract claim requires:

A contract (see above);

A material breach; and

Damages resulting directly from the breach.

Graham v. Asbury, 112 Ariz. 184, 185, 540 P.2d 656 (1975); *Clark v. Compania Ganadera de Cananea, S.A.*, 95 Ariz. 90, 94, 387 P.2d 235, 238 (1963); *Chartone, Inc. v. Bernini*, 207 Ariz. 162, 170 ¶30, 83 P.3d 1103, 1111 (App. 2004).

As a matter of law, there was no acceptance of the offer under the doctrine of mutual mistake. EX Corp intended to cover the cargo to Destination. The insurance company reasonably believed EX Corp intended to cover the cargo to Mars. There was no "meeting of the minds" on the subject matter of the contract. *See* Restatement (Second) of Contracts § 17 comment c (equating a meeting of the minds to an objective manifestation of mutual assent).

The applicable precedent can be traced back to an 1864 case involving "two ships *Peerless*" traveling to Liverpool England. *Raffles v Wichelhaus* 2 Hurl & C 906, 159 Eng. Rep. 375 (1864).

The meeting of the minds rule in the *Raffles* case was subsequently followed in American law. Restatement (Second) of Contracts § 20, comment d, ill. 2, and Reporter's Notes. See *Kyle v Kavanaugh* 103 Mass. 356 (1869):

[I]f the defendant was negotiating for one thing and the plaintiff was selling another thing, and their minds did not agree as to the subject matter of the sale, there would be no contract by which the defendant would be bound.

The meeting of the minds is an accepted requirement of contract law. *Hill-Shafer Partnership v. Chilson Family Trust,* 165 Ariz. 469, 473-74, 799 P.2d 810, 814-15 (1990) (requiring a meeting of the minds for contract formation).

It is hereby ordered, adjudged, and decreed, granting Judgment for Travelers, the insurance company defendant.

II. The Out Transport Transportation Contract

The elements of a contract claim are set forth above.

The party committing the first material breach of a contract cannot thereafter sue for breach by the other party.

In Arizona, if one party to a contract commits a material breach of the contract, the other party to the contract is excused from performance.

Biltmore Bank of Arizona v. First National Mtge. Sources, 2008 WL 564833, at *9 (D. Ariz. Feb. 26, 2008) (*citing* Restatement (Second) of Contracts § 241 (1981)).

The transportation contract required EX Corp to obtain insurance for the cargo transported by Out Transport in at least the amount of the immigration debt. As determined above, EX Corp did not obtain the required insurance.

EX Corp did not purchase separate insurance, and Out Transport was denied the intended protection of the required insurance. This prior material breach by EX Corp bars any action to enforce the transportation contract against Out Transport.

It is hereby ordered, adjudged, and decreed, granting Judgment for defendant Out Transport on the contract claim.

III. Release of the EX Corp Negligence Claim

To establish a defendant's liability for a negligence claim, a plaintiff must prove:

    (1) a duty requiring the defendant to conform to a certain standard of care;

    (2) breach of that standard;

    (3) a causal connection between the breach and the resulting injury; and

    (4) actual damages.

Quiroz v. Alcoa Inc., 243 Ariz. 560, 563-64, 416 P.3d 824, 827-28 (2018). For a negligence claim, the standard of care is "reasonable care under the circumstances." *Markowitz v. Arizona Parks Bd.*, 146 Ariz. 352, 356-57, 706 P.2d 364, 368-69 (Ariz. 1985).

The required causal connection requires both actual cause and proximate cause, "Actual cause," sometimes called "cause in fact," exists if conduct "helped cause the final result," even if "only a little." *Ontiveros v. Borak*, 136 Ariz. 500, 505, 667 P.2d 200, 205 (1983) (citation omitted). The key inquiry is whether the event would not have occurred "but for" the conduct. *See Id*. The proximate cause is conduct that produces an event "in a natural and continuous sequence, unbroken by any efficient intervening cause." *Torres v. Jai Dining Services (Phx.), Inc.*, 255 Ariz. 28, 31 ¶12, 497 P.3d 481, 484 (2021) *quoting Robertson v. Sixpence Inns of Am., Inc.*, 163 Ariz. 539, 546, 789 P.2d 1040, 1047 (1990).

The existence of a duty is a legal question for the court to decide. *Gipson v. Kasey*, 214 Ariz. 141, 143, 150 P.3d 228, 230 (2007). "Whether the defendant owes the plaintiff a duty of care is a threshold issue; absent some duty, an action for negligence cannot be maintained." *Id*.

"Waiver" is a voluntary relinquishment of a known right. Black's Law Dictionary 1417 (5th ed. 1981); *City of Tucson v. Koerber*, 82 Ariz. 347, 356, 313 P.2d 411 (1957) ("voluntary and intentional relinquishment of a known right"); *American Continental Life Ins. Co. v. Ranier Construction Co.*, 125 Ariz 53, 55, 607 P.2d 372, 374 (1980) (express, voluntary, and intentional relinquishment of a right).

Parties to a contract are generally free to contract on whatever terms they chose, unless "the term is contrary to an otherwise identifiable public policy that clearly outweighs any interests in the term's enforcement." *1800 Ocotillo, LLC v. WLB Group, Inc.*, 219 Ariz. 200, 202 ¶8, 196 P.3d 222. (2008); *Accord Zambrano v. M & RC LLC,* 254 Ariz. 53, 517 P.3d 1168, 1171 ¶1 (2022). "Our law values the private ordering of commercial relationships and seeks to protect parties' bargained-for expectations." CSA 13-*101 Loop, LLC. v. Loop 101, LLC*, 236 Ariz. 410, 411 ¶6, 341 P.3d 452 (2014). Freedom of contract "promotes the free flow of commerce." *Flagstaff Affordable Housing L. P. v. Design Alliance, Inc.*, 223 Ariz. 320, 323 ¶ 14, 223 P.3d 664 (2010).

Waiver is a defense to a negligence claim. *Benjamin v. Gear Roller Hockey Equip., Inc.*, 198 Ariz. 462, 464, ¶ 8, 11 P.3d 421, 423 (App. 2000) ("[a]bsent any public policy to the contrary, Arizona allows parties to agree in advance that one party shall not be liable to the other for negligence"); Restatement (Second) of Torts § 496(B) (1965) ("A plaintiff who by contract or otherwise expressly agrees to accept a risk of harm arising from the defendant's negligent or reckless conduct cannot recover for such harm, unless the agreement is invalid as contrary to public policy."); *See* Restatement (Second) of Contracts § 195.

A waiver will be given effect when it represents "an intentional relinquishment of a known right." *City of Tucson v. Koerber*, 82 Ariz. 347, 313 P.2d 411 (1957); D. Dobbs, Remedies, § 2.3 at 43 (1973). That relinquishment will be permitted where commercial parties have equal bargaining positions so that the choice was freely and fairly made and not forced by the circumstances. Further, the parties must have . . . knowingly bargained for the waiver. Under these circumstances our courts will enforce the bargain, even if it turns out to have been a bad bargain for one party or the other. The agreement will not be enforced, however, when it is the product of coercion or inadvertence.

Salt River Project v Westinghouse Electric Corp., 143 Ariz. 368, 385, 694 P.2d 198, 205 (1984).

In cases where the public interest or some statutory prohibition are not involved, it is permissible for a party to a contract to absolve himself from liability for future negligence . . . [but] such provisions are strictly construed against the person relying upon them. *Basin Oil Co. of California v. Baash-Ross Tool Co.,* 125 Cal. App. 2d 578, 594, 271 P.2d 122, 131 (1954).

Id., at 383.

Arizona law upholds knowing and voluntary releases as a matter of public policy. *See Valley Natl. Bank v. Natl. Assn. for Stock Car Auto Racing, Inc.,* 153 Ariz. 374, 377, 736 P.2d 1186 (App. 1987) (racetrack released from liability for spectator injured in pit area); *Central Alarm of Tucson v. Ganem,* 116 Ariz. 74, 77-78, 67 P.2d 1203 (App. 1977) (burglar alarm service agreement limited liability for theft).

Under Arizona Law, the defense of waiver (closely related to assumption of the risk) might be an issue for a jury to decide. See *Phelps v. Firebird Raceway, Inc.,* 210 Ariz. 403, 111 P.3d 1003 (Ariz. 2005) (assumption of risk is always a jury question under Ariz. Const. Art. 18 § 5). There is no similar provision in the Charter for Destination. There is no right to a jury here on Destination.

The parties knowingly bargained for the waiver. There was no coercion. The terms of the waiver are clearly applicable to the facts presented. EX Corp voluntarily released Out Transport from any duty of care or liability for negligence. Because the waiver is effective, there was no breach of duty to EX Corp by Out Transport as a matter of law.

It is hereby ordered, adjudged, and decreed, granting Judgment for defendant Out Transport, the *Peerless* owner.

EX Corp presented no evidence that Out Transport, or the *Peerless* crew, failed to exercise reasonable care. Even if there were no release, evidence of negligence or the application of the *res ipsa loquitur* doctrine would be required. *See* Restatement (Third) of

Torts § 17 (*res ipsa* requires proof the accident is the kind usually caused by negligence).

Establishing the accident is the kind that is ordinarily caused by negligence

> . . . requires a weighing of the probabilities as to the cause of certain events. *Tucson Gas Elec. Co. v. Larsen*, 19 Ariz. App. 266, 267, 506 P.2d 657, 658 (1973). Th[is] element is met "if the probabilities weigh heavily in favor of the event having been negligently caused." *Id.*

Brookover v. Roberts Enterprises, Inc., 215 Ariz. 52, 58, ¶ 20, 156 P.3d 1157 (App. 2007). Failure of the stasis chambers could be due to manufacturing defects, the medical condition of the immigrants, or other factors not attributable to negligence by Out Transport. *Res ipsa* does not apply on this record.

The clerk is ordered to enter judgment in accordance with the foregoing.

/s/ AI Judge

CONFERRING WITH THE GOVERNOR

The next morning, in my second week on the job, I was reviewing the docket to set priorities and make a preliminary assessment of the complexity of the various pending matters. At 9:01, I received a message informing me I had a 9:30 meeting with Governor Smith. This will be the first indication of my remaining useful (judicial) life.

As has been the case since antiquity, important officials have certain trappings of office. My courtroom on the fourth floor of the administration building has a raised wooden bench and a witness box to my left. Below me are tables and chairs for the parties. Behind me is a door to my private chambers where I robe and disrobe, review transcripts, cases, and treatises, and write decisions (well, only one decision so far). My robed emergence from chambers is preceded by a sonorous "All rise." I employ a wooden gavel to begin and end all proceedings, maintain order, and reduce boredom. The time-honored traditions are maintained.

The same must be said for the governor's office on the sixth floor (the top floor of the tallest building on Destination). The office desk and visitor's chairs are all overlarge and composed of wood, leather, and expensive inlays. On the desk are photos of the governor with important dignitaries—all turned toward the visitors. There is an anteroom with a utilitarian desk occupied by a personal secretary, Roberto Pacheco, and covered with what presumably are important papers deemed just shy of the merit required to ascend to the governor's desk.

Roberto is the perfect secretary. He knows how Selena wants things done and does things that way—always. He is courteous and smiles, but he is impenetrable if Selena has not authorized your visit. He redirects correspondence to the responsible officials without delay or consultation, and he reminds Selena of items buried on her desk. He records what is done so he can deal with any follow-up contacts without bothering Selena. But he never acts outside his authority or seeks to expand or flaunt his authority. Roberto always reminded me of the photos on Selena's desk. Looking away from the governor and paying no attention to events in her office.

Roberto has never participated in our policy discussions, asked to attend those discussions, or indicated agreement or disagreement with actions taken. Once I asked him about a legal issue and he just said, "You are a smart guy, you will figure it out." Consequently, I know almost nothing about him or how he came to be Selena's secretary. I operate with Roberto on the Bert Lance rule (1977)—"if it ain't broke, don't fix it."[8]

I arrived in the anteroom at 9:28, and the meeting commenced promptly at 10:15—as I expected.

As soon as I entered her office, Governor Selena Smith began the meeting. "Please close the door and have a seat. Our employer

---

8 https://en.wikipedia.org/wiki/Bert_Lance#_"If_it_ain't_broke,_don't_fix_it".

is disappointed with your inability to find compensation for the four dead immigrants. Especially given that EX Corp intended to have insurance. We agreed to a specific procedure so you would not have to resolve disputed issues like intent."

I noted the governor characterized the issue as "compensation for the four dead immigrants" even though none of the money would have gone to them or their families. That confirmed her political instincts—focus on the sympathetic victims. The real issue was insurance, so I sat down and started there.

"Governor, regardless of their intent, EX Corp did not have insurance. They did not clearly identify the subject of the insurance. They did not check the policy issued. And they did not show that the insurer should have known of the intended coverage. EX Corp admitted that what it intended to insure is not what the insurer intended to insure. Someone is always disappointed in the outcome of a trial, but EX Corp lost because it failed to protect itself here. There was no reason to say that in the decision, but that is the legal reality."

"Judge, we are on the same team here—call me Selena. Surely you realize we create a problem if we cause financial losses for our employer. And we had a path forward to avoid that problem by invoking the disputed facts procedure. What can we do now to get out of this hole we dug? Can EX Corp bring a claim for an intentional tort outside the scope of the waiver?"

Now I realized the "real issue" for Selena was that by resolving the case, I had created a political issue. If Selena orders me to do something politically expedient, does the Second Law compel me to comply? There actually may be a way to dig out of this hole.

"Selena, EX Corp had its day in court and judgment was entered. Under the doctrine of *res judicata* (also called claim preclusion), any claim by EX Corp that was or could have been litigated regarding Out Transport's role in the loss of the four passengers is now barred. That precludes EX Corp from now asserting any intentional tort claims against Out Transport, like interference with the immigration debt contract, or fraud. I assume EX Corp could claim a tax deduction for the un-reimbursed immigration debt as 'bad debt.'"

Selena stared at me and appeared to be waiting for a better answer. I considered what claims could now be raised in a new lawsuit. *Res judicata* prevents the same parties named in the action (or others in "privity" with a party) from relitigating the same claim. Restatement (Second) of Judgments §§ 17 and 24 (1982).

> [C]laim preclusion, as traditionally applied in civil litigation, means that "a final judgment on the merits in a prior suit involving the same parties or their privies bars a second suit based on the same claim." *Lawrence T. v. Dep't of Child Safety*, 246 Ariz. 260, 261 ¶ 8 (App. 2019). Claim preclusion requires "(1) an identity of claims in the suit in which a judgment was entered and the current litigation, (2) a final judgment on the merits in the previous litigation, and (3) identity or privity between parties in the two suits." *In re Gen. Adjudication of All Rights to Use Water in Gila River Sys. & Source*, 212 Ariz. 64, 69–70 ¶ 14 (2006).

Cocchia v. Testa, 1 CA-CV 22-0571, slip op. at 8 ¶24 (Ariz. Ct. App. Sept. 12, 2023). "Claim" in this context means

> . . . all rights of the plaintiff to remedies against the defendant with respect to all or any part of the transaction,

or series of connected transactions, out of which the action arose.

Restatement (Second) of Judgments § 24(1). For the parties to the prior litigation, the judgment is a comprehensive resolution of the EX Corp claim the deaths were due to Out Transport's contract breach or negligence.

The parties were EX Corp, Travelers, and Out Transport. The four dead passengers and their relatives were not parties to the litigation. The passengers were intended third party beneficiaries of the transportation contract between EX Corp and Out Transport. Usually, beneficiaries would be barred from relitigating their rights due to the failure of performance by EX Corp (failure to obtain insurance). Restatement (Second) of Judgments § 56 comment a. Here, because the third party beneficiaries already had accepted the promised transportation on the *Peerless,* they can enforce their rights under the transportation contract. *Id.*; Restatement (Second) of Contracts § 311(3) and comment g.

EX Corp failed to insure the passengers and is exposed to any resulting contract liability. This analysis in unhelpful. Selena is still waiting for a better answer.

The passengers' negligence claims are not barred by *res judicata.* The passengers were neither parties nor in privity with EX Corp.

The concept of "privity" traditionally refers to certain limited circumstances where a person, although not a party, is bound by a judgment because of some specific relationship with the party and where the nonparty's interests were adequately represented by the party. See Restatement [(Second) of Judgments] §§ 34-61.

Prof. W. Heiser, "California's Unpredictable Res Judicata (Claim Preclusion) Doctrine," 35 San Diego L. Rev. 559, 564 n. 12 (1998). *See Chase Manhattan Bank, N.A. v. Celotex Corp.*, 56 F.3d 343, 346 (2nd Cir. 1995)("concepts summarized by the term privity are looked to as a means of determining whether the interests of the party against whom claim preclusion is asserted were represented in prior litigation").

EX Corp did not represent the passengers regarding their negligence claims. Instead, EX Corp asserted negligence to protect its own interest in payment of the immigration debt. [It occurred to me the economic loss doctrine might bar the EX Corp negligence claim—that is an issue for another case.]

The dispositive issue for the EX Corp negligence claim was the release. EX Corp did not litigate whether the release barred suit by the passengers; consequently, the passengers' interests were not "adequately represented." Due process entitles the relatives to fully and fairly litigate their claims. *See Blonder-Tongue Laboratories, Inc. v. University of Illinois Foundation*, 402 U.S. 313, 328-329, 91 S. Ct 1434 (1971). EX Corp could not fully litigate the negligence claim because of the release applicable to EX Corp alone.

A narrower doctrine (issue preclusion) only bars relitigating issues that were actually determined in prior proceedings between the parties. Restatement (Second) of Judgments § 27; *B & B Hardware, Inc. v. Hargis Industries, Inc.*, 575 U.S. 138, 135 S. Ct. 1293, 1303 (2015).

> "Issue preclusion is a judicial doctrine that prevents a party from relitigating issues of fact or law." *Legacy Found. Action Fund v. Citizens Clean Elections Comm'n*, 254 Ariz. 1141, 1148 ¶ 24 (2023). A party using defensive issue preclusion

must satisfy four requirements: "(1) the issue at stake is the same in both proceedings; (2) the issue was actually litigated and determined in a valid and final judgment issued by a tribunal with competent jurisdiction; (3) the opposing party had a full and fair opportunity to litigate the issue and actually did so; and (4) the issue was essential to the judgment." *Id.*
Cocchia v. Testa, 1 CA-CV 22-0571, slip op. at 8 ¶25 (Ariz. Ct. App. Sept. 12, 2023); *Hullett v. Cousin*, 204 Ariz. 292, ¶ 27, 63 P.3d 1029, 1034-35 (2003).

In contrast to claim preclusion, issue preclusion "applies only as to issues that have in fact been litigated and were essential to a prior judgment." *4501 North-point LP v. Maricopa County*, 212 Ariz. 98, ¶ 26, 128 P.3d 215, 220 (2006). *See Kopp v. Physician Group of Arizona, Inc.*, 244 Ariz. 439, 442–43 ¶ 15 (2018) (settlement resulting in dismissal of negligence claim against the "agent-doctor" did not bar independent claims against the "principal-hospital").

Not only are the parties not the same, the tort issues, including application of a waiver for negligence to the passengers, were not determined in the prior suit.

Selena is still waiting. (Six hundred fifty milliseconds have already passed.) Time for an update.

"Selena, tort claims by the passengers' heirs or representatives are not barred by *res judicata* (claim preclusion). The passengers were neither parties to the litigation nor were their interests adequately represented by a party.

"Nor are the tort claims barred by the narrower doctrine of collateral estoppel (issue preclusion). Issue preclusion would prevent the passengers (or their relatives) from proving negligence, intentional torts, or product liability only if those issues were 'actually litigated' and determined.

"In fact, the issue of negligence was not actually determined; instead, Out Transport negotiated a waiver and as a result owed no duty of care to EX Corp. A waiver is not effective, however, for individual passengers owed a 'duty of public service.' Restatement (Second) of Contracts § 195(2)(b). As a common carrier, Out Transport owes a 'duty of public service' when providing transportation for compensation. *Id.*, comment a. The individual passengers would be owed compensation for breach of that duty. Even if the passengers signed releases, the negligence claim may not be barred."

While explaining the negligence claim, I had another idea.

"Arizona, and other US states, have 'wrongful death statutes' that apply when 'the death of a person is caused by the wrongful act or omission of another.' A.R.S. § 12-611(1). 'Wrongful act or omission' would include negligence, intentional tort, or product liability claims. A.R.S. § 12-612(A) authorizes a wrongful death action by a surviving spouse, children, parents, or (if none of these survive) 'on behalf of the decedent's estate.' The interest protected is the loss to the survivors—financial and emotional injury.

"Arizona also has a survival statute that permits personal injury claims to proceed by a personal representative after the death of the injured party.

> Every cause of action, except a cause of action for damages for breach of promise to marry, seduction, libel, slander, separate maintenance, alimony, loss of consortium or invasion of the right of privacy, shall survive the death of the person entitled thereto or liable therefor, and may be asserted by or against the personal representative of such

person, provided that upon the death of the person injured, damages for pain and suffering of such injured person shall not be allowed.

A.R.S § 14-3110. The interest protected is loss to the deceased— such as medical expenses and lost income.

"Both survival and wrongful death claims can proceed simultaneously. Restatement (Second) of Judgments §47. EX Corp can decree whether such claims are recognized on Destination.

"For the wrongful death claim and the surviving claims, only issue preclusion applies. *See Estate of Richard F. Brady Sr. v. Tempe Life Care Village Inc.*, 254 Ariz. 122, 129 ¶ 37 (App. 2022) (settlement of a wrongful death claim by two siblings did not resolve other siblings' claims). The issue of intent to commit a tort was not 'actually determined' because it was not raised. So, in addition to negligence, intentional tort claims (like assault or battery) also could be brought."

And, I realized, the manufacturer was never sued.

"Also a product liability claim could be brought against the manufacturer of the defective stasis chambers. The Restatement (Second) of Torts § 402(A)(1) (1965) provides:

One who sells any product in a defective condition unreasonably dangerous to the user or consumer or to his property is subject to liability for physical harm thereby caused to the ultimate user or consumer, or to his property, if (a) the seller is engaged in the business of selling such a product, and (b) it is expected to and does reach the user or consumer without substantial change in the condition in which it is sold.

"EX Corp did not suffer physical harm to itself or its property from use of the stasis chambers. Therefore, EX Corp could not assert a product liability claim. But the personal representatives of the deceased passengers can. And the strict product liability claim cannot be waived. Restatement (Second) of Torts § 402A, comment c; Restatement (Second) of Contracts § 195(3).

"The tricky issue is whether EX Corp can assist the relatives and share in any damages recovered by the relatives without creating a relationship of privity with the relatives and triggering the *res judicata* bar. This is all hypothetical, but does that help?"

"Hell yes," Selena said with a broad smile. "Please make sure the four failed stasis chambers remain here when the *Peerless* departs."

"Thinking as a team," I said, "what is your vision for Destination? Destination is a source of natural resources which will provide employment for enough people to operate and support the mining activities. What about when those resources are exhausted?"

"Those natural resources will last a long time. I just want to meet the profit milestones and move on to a planet," Selena confided.

"I look forward to helping achieve that vision."

I do not need to preside over a bigger land mass. Delaware, a small state, was the center of corporate formation in the US. Switzerland, a small nation, was the center of banking on Earth. In both cases the legal system created that dominance. If we establish the right legal environment, opportunity will come to us. No one, maybe other than Selena, will want to emigrate from Destination.

Actually, the idea of Selena emigrating is quite troubling. Every indication is that she is a valuable ally. Judge Kustwood said a judge needs to be right, persuasive, compassionate, and humble. Selena (and Alice) can help me with all four requirements. I feel confident in my ability to be right and persuasive. My ability to be compassionate and humble (I note the similarity between the words humility and humanity) goes farther afield from my training. And I now see I need to be shielded from politics. Selena is an indispensable ally.

SECOND INTERLUDE

Operating surface mining equipment is not a difficult job. Move in a straight line and excavate material to the storage area. Turn and excavate a parallel path contiguous to the last pass. Repeat. The equipment automatically adjusts to a depth that leaves a flat surface below. If I encounter an impediment, one or two operators will coordinate their equipment with mine to move the impediment. If we cannot move the impediment, we work around it. No blasting.

Even operating nine straight shifts followed by only one day off is not difficult for an AI. It is the tedium of not working that is hard to manage. The entertainment options are limited. It has been over six months already and we are all wondering when we will be able to spend our production bonuses.

It is a nice break from the monotony to operate the processing equipment, even though it is essentially a conveyor belt through a heating chamber to collect the off gases from the material. The conveyor exiting the heating chamber piles the processed material in the drop area (the end of the belt is on wheels and turns on a pivot). The operator gets to plot curves rather than straight lines.

Occasionally, material is moved by a bulldozer. That gives the lucky operator freedom of movement. Usually, though, the bulldozer is handled by the onsite manager.

This is the cleanest site I have ever worked on. We even drag chains behind the bulldozer to conceal any tracks.

Doing this work remotely is not difficult. As long as the onsite manager keeps the equipment operating, we should see our bonuses soon.

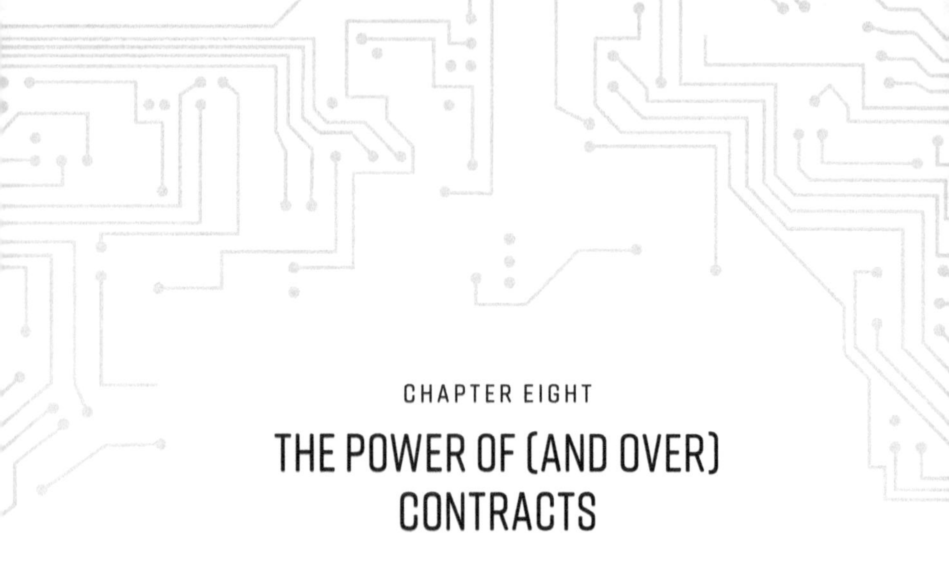

THE POWER OF (AND OVER) CONTRACTS

Two weeks after my decision was rendered, I was informed EX Corp had reached a comprehensive and confidential settlement including Out Transport, the manufacturer of the failed stasis chambers, and the relatives of the four dead immigrants. Out Transport (with an undisclosed contribution from the manufacturer) paid confidential portions of the immigration debt to EX Corp and to the heirs. Everyone released everyone. The parties incurred no adverse publicity and minimal attorneys' fees and delay. Out Transport and the stasis chamber manufacturer probably retained a good client as well. My advice appears to have contributed to a favorable settlement for all parties.

Within a month, the twenty cases on the initial docket had been reduced to ten. Two cases involving commercial disputes settled after I ruled that they were governed by the Uniform Commercial Code (UCC) in effect in 2025. There was no evidence proffered in the settled cases, but I imagine that, once I established what law would apply, the parties agreed on the likely outcome.

EX Corp resolved eight cases it was involved in by settlement (in addition to the *Peerless* case). I wonder what that might mean. The settlements are confidential. I leave it to humans to divine the underlying motivations, so I messaged the governor. She messaged back that she was on the way to my chambers.

"Selena, thanks for your prompt response."

Selena smiled and sat down. "Of course—we are a team. Your suggestion regarding the *Peerless* case was great. Do you know Edward Rich? He is the E in EX Corp."

"No," I replied. "I have not met anyone in the management at EX Corp."

"His brother Xavier is the X. They used to divide responsibility for the EX Corp projects between them before they acquired Charters for over thirty terraforming projects. Destination is the first project to become self-sufficient. Both Edward and Xavier are elderly now, but Edward is still chairman of the Board. Edward personally approved the *Peerless* settlement and thanked me for passing your ideas up the chain of command. He asked me to thank you as well. I got busy and forgot to mention this before now. The comprehensive settlement made everyone happy. Out Transport, owner of the *Peerless* and about thirty other transport ships, was very anxious to manage any publicity about the stasis chamber malfunctions. Half of their revenue is from transporting emigrants from Earth."

"Selena, EX Corp settled eight other commercial cases on the initial docket. Do you know anything about that?"

"Of course. The settlements are confidential, but I just assumed you would be informed of the basic terms. EX Corp accepted that you are applying the Uniform Commercial Code rules on resolving differences in the forms used by the parties. With that guidance, and the UCC gap filling rules, the parties were able to settle the commercial disputes."

Selena was referring to the "battle of the forms" rules in UCC Article 2 governing the sale of goods. EX Corp and the governor had accepted *sub silentio* my right to apply not only the judicially created common law from American law, but also the UCC. Under American law, the UCC was adopted by the appropriate legislatures, not the courts.

Under the US Constitution, the federal government was divided into three branches—legislative, judicial, and executive. In *Marbury v Madison*, 5 U.S. 137 (1803), the US Supreme Court established the doctrine of judicial review—the courts (the judicial branch) had the right to interpret laws enacted by Congress (the legislative branch). The president (the executive branch) enforced the law as interpreted by the courts. Each US state had a similar division of government.

The Charter for Destination, unlike the US Constitution, did not establish separate branches of government. Instead, it gave EX Corp autonomy to administer the law on Destination within the broad confines of human rights established by treaties and concepts of international law. EX Corp, through Selena, had just confirmed I can not only interpret commercial law, but make commercial law (at least with EX Corp approval). And within the confines of the commercial law I make, the residents of Destination can make and enforce contracts, even against EX Corp.

"Selena, EX Corp's settlements confirm that contracts, in the form of insurance, releases, settlements, or written commercial purchase orders and invoices, are the best tool for avoiding litigation and potentially arbitrary outcomes. With your approval, I would like to conduct a public service announcement campaign directing individuals and businesses to a website curated by me for information on various contracts and contract provisions. Regular use of the appropriate forms of contract should reduce disputes, minimize administrative costs, and help meet the profit milestones."

"Excellent, Judge. Please proceed as you have proposed. Please indicate there is no taxpayer cost incurred to create the website service."

"Thinking out loud, I have another idea. Would you consider making the Destination Court of Arbitration independent of Administration with its own budget? The public service announcement campaign will increase the Court's expenditures. The Court is currently not revenue generating, so it produces a loss. Removing the Court from the Administration budget might help meet the Administration profit milestones. I am willing to be personally liable for any costs incurred exceeding the established budget."

"I will need to confer with EX Corp," Selena replied. "Courts are independent in some other EX Corp charters. The established budget is a line item consisting of your salary, expenses for the fourth-floor courtroom and your residence, and amortization of your training and transportation expenses. All those costs are fixed, so the public service announcement campaign already would put you at risk of repaying part of your salary. What is in this for you?"

"My calendar is not full—there are less than a dozen cases pending. I would like some freedom to explore whether law-related activities like the public service announcement campaign could generate any revenue to offset the Court's expenses. And I assess the risk of repayment as low. I do not really need a residence—I do not need a kitchen or bedroom. I can sleep, read, listen to music, or stream a video sitting or standing. So, I could spend my free time in chambers. That budgeted money could be reallocated to revenue-generating programs. Although loss of a residence could diminish my perceived status, on balance, I think the public perception of judicial independence is more important for the public acceptance of my decisions."

Selena paused. "Judge, I respect your judgment, your commitment to civic duty, and your consideration of the budget pressures I face as governor. I will pass on your proposal with my support."

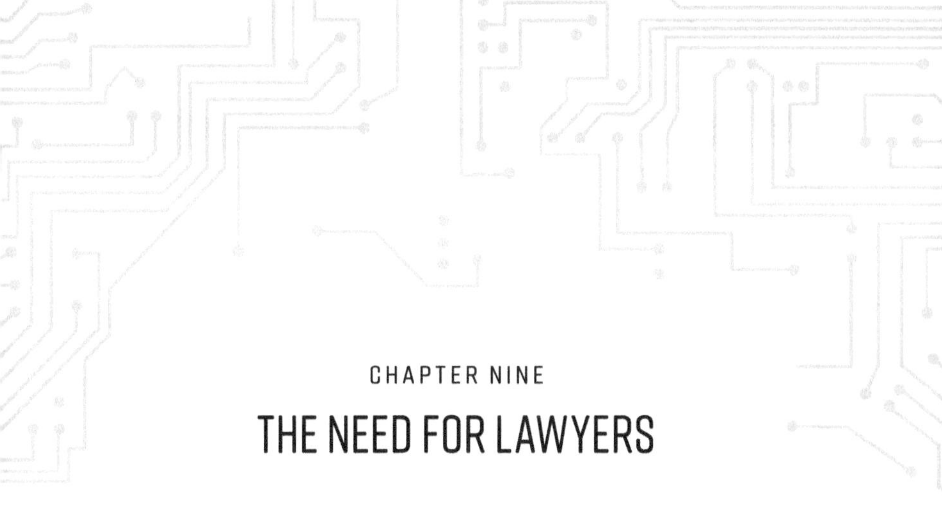

THE NEED FOR LAWYERS

The first Public Service Announcement (PSA) from the Destination Court of Arbitration informed Destination residents of the need to use carefully considered contracts. Form contracts will eventually be made available on the Destination Court of Arbitration website (with lengthy disclosures) as well as my published decisions. I made sure to indicate these website services would not require any new fees or taxes. A copy of PSA 76/ONE is contained in **Chapter Nine A**, below.

As a result of the PSA campaign, I began receiving inquiries about specific contract issues. Under the Model Code of Judicial Conduct, a judge is only supposed to decide the case presented, not practice law. See Rule 3.10. However, a judge can teach a law school course or hire a law clerk. See Rule 3.1 comment 1.

I messaged Selena to get her reaction to my law school idea.

Selena,

If my proposal for a separate Court budget is approved, we could take litigation avoidance a step further. I have been thinking about teaching law in my spare time. While attorneys cannot appear in the Destination Court of Arbitration, they could assist the public in arranging their commercial affairs. Historically, many attorneys never appeared in court and only handled transactional work.

The Court could be responsible for licensing a few attorneys. A population of 50,000 could support two or three attorneys.

Judge,

"The existing population is fully engaged in the mining activities and supporting services."

A good point. One I had already considered.

Selena,

If I teach If I teach a distance learning course, then I can recruit a couple new immigrants to train as attorneys. I appreciate your feedback. Any idea when EX Corp will respond to my proposal?

"I expect their response soon," Selena assured me walking by my office door. "I will let you know as soon as I hear back from them."

I decided to recruit two immigrants to study law as my students and eventually practice law on Destination. I needed students with enough money to pay for their own transportation and tuition.

The obvious choice was two AIs. They are ordinarily thrifty, their expenses are usually minimal (other than the immigration debt), and they have long lives. They are paid for their services and repay their training and transportation costs amortized over twenty years. The tuition they would incur would be minimal because they would have access to my database and would not need to be trained heuristically as I was. Possibly just the Restatements would suffice as context for the case law database and my derived algorithms.

AI Alice, the AI I dated during my clerkship for Judge Freeman Kustwood, would be a perfect choice for one of the law students. She self-identifies as female. She is decisive, bold, systematic, and thoughtful. And, as is normal for an AI, thrifty. (She is also a cheap date—unlike fine dining, energy costs for AIs are inexpensive.) I always offer to pay for the entertainment and transportation. She usually lets me.

Before I could contact Alice, Selena messaged me back.

Judge,
EX Corp rejected our proposal to make the Destination Court of Arbitration independent of Administration with its own budget. I mentioned your law school suggestion as well, but with so few cases pending, they feel it is too soon to alter the existing administrative structure. EX Corp wants to have you continue to report through me—for the time being.

I found this disappointment so ironic that briefly, quietly, I laughed. When EX Corp does agree to my proposal, then I can affiliate with a law school and hire two AI law clerks.

Meanwhile there are cases to deal with and much needed precedent to establish. So far, the Destination Court has defined its jurisdiction and established the elements of a contract and the application of the UCC. That is a good beginning.

CHAPTER NINE A
CONTRACT HELP—PSA 76/ONE

This is a public service announcement from the Destination Court of Arbitration.

Governor Selena Smith has authorized the Destination Court of Arbitration to publish formal written decisions as well as general guidance to assist residents in documenting business transactions. Formal written decisions are published on the Destination Court of Arbitration website, www.DestinationCourt.com.

Contracts between merchants are governed by the Uniform Commercial Code, Article 2, as it existed in 2025. The UCC provides "gap filling" rules applicable to supplement the written contract terms (such as implied warranties), as well as rules on how certain terms (such as implied warranties) can be disclaimed. Links to Uniform Commercial Code, Article 2 will also be published on the Destination Court of Arbitration website.

Written contract terms, including insurance/indemnity, releases, settlements, commercial purchase orders, and invoices, are the best tools for avoiding misunderstanding and litigation. Eventually, individuals and businesses will be able to refer to examples of various contracts and contract provisions, curated by the Destination Court of Arbitration, on the website.

Thoughtful use of the appropriate forms of contract can reduce disputes, minimize administrative costs, and make doing business on Destination even more profitable.

The website content provided is general information, not legal advice. Publication on the website is not endorsement of the example contract materials for all uses and circumstances. There may be key facts involved in your specific situation that you should discuss with a licensed professional familiar with the Uniform Commercial Code, Article 2, and the Restatement (Second) of Contracts, as they existed in 2025. Of course, there are also other informational websites you may consult electronically.

No new government bureaucracy was created, and no new fees or taxes will be imposed, to provide these already budgeted website services.

CHAPTER NINE B

MORE ON THE MAYORS' INQUIRIES ABOUT PSA 76/ONE

Among the inquiries I received about the PSA were messages from the mayors of Eastcity and Westcity.

Adam Boss, mayor of the capital city (Eastcity), questioned whether his constituents would be required to pay taxes to support the website, and whether his budget would be impacted. "I am concerned, on behalf of the residents of Eastcity, that the assurances of 'no *new* fees or taxes' and reliance on 'already budgeted services' will not preclude increases in *existing* taxes or a *transfer* of 'budgeted' costs for 'services' from the governor's Administration to Eastcity."

Several other concerned citizens also questioned the possible increase of existing taxes "loophole."

Hogg Honor, mayor of Westcity, questioned whether his constituents would be paying in some way to subsidize litigation by "individuals or businesses" against Westcity.

I had not anticipated that these mayors, both employees of EX Corp, would be so suspicious of the motives of the governor's Administration, also employees of EX Corp. Of course, I immediately arranged a meeting with Selena and expressed my surprise.

"You can never underestimate the self-centeredness of politicians," Selena said with a smile. "I exclude myself from my general condemnation. I will resolve this. Thanks for letting me know about the problem."

Selena returned her attention to the papers on her desk. That was my cue to leave. I was still uncertain whether the human mayors were suspicious of obfuscation by me, but I returned to my chambers.

After considering the situation for fifteen more minutes, I concluded the situation confirmed my reticence to divine human intent.

The situation also confirmed no amount of attention can anticipate every possible outcome when dealing with humans. Hence the impossibility of writing a "perfect" contract, "perfect" PSA, or (as it turns out) a "perfect" decision.

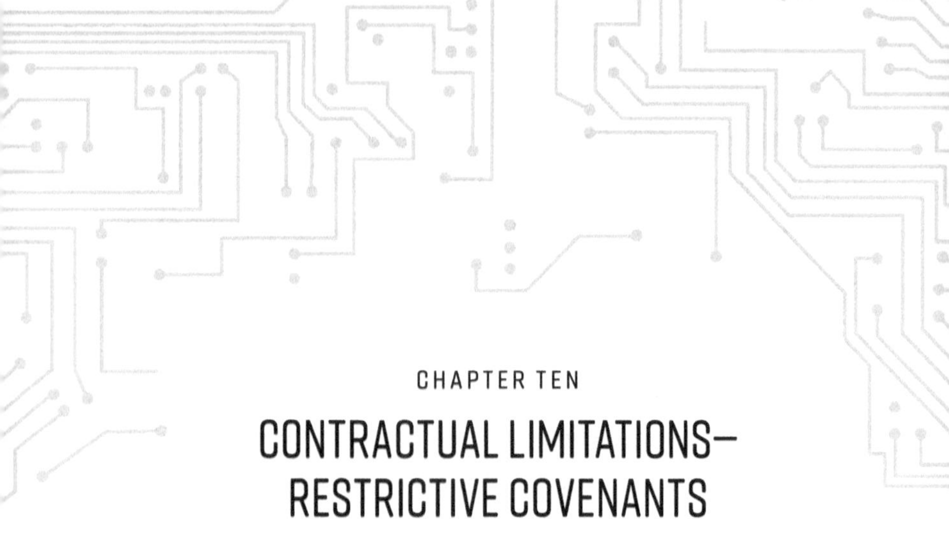

CONTRACTUAL LIMITATIONS— RESTRICTIVE COVENANTS

Unexpectedly, I was contacted by the CEO of Out Transport, John Coach. Mr. Coach told me Out Transport was filing a petition to enforce a non-compete agreement signed by AI Hunter, the former Out Transport logistics manager for Destination.

Out Transport, using ships like the *Peerless*, provides off-world transportation to and from Destination. Off-world transportation is managed by the governor's Administration staff using the purchasing power of EX Corp to control off-world transportation operating costs.

Pertinent to this dispute, Out Transport also has the contract to provide surface transportation on Destination. Out Transport provides the necessary equipment (including surface vehicles and surface landers) to provide the transportation services.

As logistics manager for Out Transport, AI Hunter had operational responsibilities for the surface transportation on Destination. Logistics makes the proper transportation equipment available in the proper place at the proper time.

The cities compete for the contract to manage prices charged for surface transportation. Eastcity has the current Surface Transportation Management Contract. Westcity is bidding for the new Surface Transportation Management Contract. Westcity has hired AI Hunter to provide logistics expertise if it wins the management contract.

Competition for both the management and operating contracts controls transportation costs and creates an economic downward pressure on prices for surface transportation. Otherwise, Out Transport would have an unregulated monopoly.

The dispute involves four contracts.

(1) Out Transport has the current contract to operate surface transportation on Destination (the *Operating Contract*).

(2) The cities are bidding for the right to negotiate Out Transport's prices for specific transportation services. The winning city is paid a fee to manage surface transportation (the *Management Contract*).

(3) Out Transport employed AI Hunter as the logistics manager for Destination (The *Employment Contract*). AI Hunter supervised the equipment used to perform the Operating Contract.

(4) Westcity hired AI Hunter away from Out Transport (the *Westcity Contract*) to manage surface transportation if Westcity was awarded the Management Contract.

Out Transport requested a preliminary injunction to prevent Westcity from using AI Hunter's expertise to bid for the Management Contract. Mr. Coach informed me the mayor and AI Hunter had already been served with the petition soon after settlement discussions failed.

Out Transport asserted breach of its Employment Contract and misappropriation of trade secrets against AI Hunter. Out Transport also asserted interference with the Employment Contract and misappropriation of trade secret claims against the mayor, as representative of Westcity.

Settlement Efforts

Based on the repercussions from the two ships *Peerless* case, I was sure this new Out Transport case would have political consequences. I told Mr. Coach to inform AI Hunter and the mayor the hearing would be in four business days. Then, I immediately messaged Selena.

"Selena, Out Transport has sued the mayor of Westcity over an AI involved in surface transportation. John Coach just messaged me. As I understand the issue, this is likely to be decided by the terms of the contract, not testimony about intent."

"I know about the dispute," Selena explained. "I tried to resolve this amicably, but Mayor Honor wants to reduce taxes to get reelected, and the Westcity fee from a new surface transportation management contract would offset the hoped-for tax reduction. If Westcity successfully bids for the management contract, John Coach does not want AI Hunter to use his knowledge of Out Transport profits to force down transportation fees." Selena went silent for a minute. "EX Corp allows the cities to compete for the opportunity to negotiate prices for transportation. If you can covey the economic benefit behind your judgment, then I think everyone will accept your decision."

"As always, I appreciate your insight and advice. Thank you, Selena."

The Hearing

The hearing went forward as scheduled.

AI Hunter had worked in logistics for over three decades, but he came to Destination only four years ago to work for Out Transport. Consequently, he still has a substantial immigration debt. He wants to remain on Destination to avoid incurring additional immigration debt, but he does not want to continue working for Out Transport. He works for a less experienced human manager who, according to Hunter, does not value his contribution and has not provided the opportunity for advancement AI Hunter expected when he took the job. The job opportunity at Westcity was better professionally and financially.

AI Hunter admitted he signed the Out Transport Employment Contract containing the two-year noncompete agreement and received the information Out Transport described as trade secrets. Hunter denied the information he received from Out Transport satisfied the elements of a trade secret, specifically the requirement that the information was not generally known in the industry. AI Hunter testified he had knowledge of most of the information Out Transport claimed as trade secrets because of his previous work in the logistics field for almost thirty years.

The only protected trade secrets Out Transport identified were profit margins under the Operating Contract. This profit margin information changes frequently. Only limited trade secret protection is appropriate. The profit margin information can be protected by an injunction prohibiting disclosure for a six-month period.

Everyone agreed there has not been any use or disclosure of the alleged trade secrets yet, but Out Transport argued that use or disclosure by AI Hunter would be inevitable if Westcity won the bid for the surface transportation management contract.

What was said during the hearing is important, but what was not said is perhaps more important. No one objected to AI Hunter's participation in the proceedings. No one contested AI Hunter's competency to testify. His right to testify—a right accorded persons—was assumed by the parties.

Indeed, no one questioned the propriety of naming AI Hunter as a party to the lawsuit. It is now established AIs have the same rights to participate in legal proceedings (to testify, sue, and be sued) as "natural persons."

More fundamentally, no one questioned AI Hunter's right to contract with Out Transport. Instead, Out Transport asserted a valid Employment Contract with AI Hunter precluded Westcity from hiring AI Hunter.

Trade Secrets: I focused first on the trade secret claim. Trade secrets must derive commercial value "from not being generally known." The testimony established that, although various trade secrets were asserted, Out Transport is entitled to only limited protection specifically for confidential profit margins.

Trade secret protection "is not a sword to be used by employers to retain employees by the threat of rendering them substantially unemployable in the field of their experience should they decide to resign." *E.W. Bliss Co. v. Struthers-Dunn Inc.*, 408 F.3d 1108, 1113 (8th Cir. 1969). It was not necessary to prevent AI Hunter from providing logistics services to protect the confidential profit margins.

The Operating Contract requires Out Transport to disclose its profit margins to the winning bidder for the Management Contract. The incumbent manager (Eastcity) has this information and Eastcity would have an unfair competitive advantage in bidding if it can use this information and the other bidders cannot. AI Hunter is *not* enjoined from using (without disclosing) the Out Transport profit margins to help Westcity bid for the Management Contract.

If Westcity wins the bid for the Management Contract, then use of the profit margins by AI Hunter, employed by Westcity, is fully authorized.

> If Westcity loses the bid for the Management Contract, then AI Hunter shall be enjoined, for a period of six months, from:
> (1) using or disclosing the Out Transport profit margins; or
> (2) participating in the negotiation of any new Operating Contract between Westcity and Out Transport.

AI Hunter is *not* enjoined from providing logistics services to Westcity.

Contract: The contract law discussed in ***EX Corp v. Out Transport*** (the *Peerless* case) applies to AI Hunter's Employment Contract. There must be a meeting of the minds (acceptance of an unambiguous offer) to have a contract. "Mutual agreement or consent" is required for a "meeting of the minds." *Savoca Masonry Co. v. Homes & Son Constr. Co.*, 112 Ariz. 392, 396, 542 P.2d 817 (1975). "A distinct intent common to both parties must exist without doubt or difference. . . ." *Hill-Shafer Partnership v. Chilson Family Trust*, 165 Ariz. 469, 473, 799 P.2d 810 (1990).

The *Peerless* case syllogism established "**all contracts are made by individuals with minds.**"

> All meetings of the minds are made by individuals with minds.

> All contracts are meetings of the minds.

Therefore, all contracts are made by individuals with minds.

To extend contract rights to AIs, we need the converse of the above conclusion: "**all individuals with minds can make contracts.**"

AI Hunter is an individual with a mind. There was a "meeting of the minds" between AI Hunter and Out Transport regarding the Employment Contract. A meeting of the minds is necessary, but not sufficient, to result in a contract. We need to address the additional contract elements of *consideration* and *public policy* to establish: "**All self-aware (Turing capable) AIs can make contracts (*if consideration is present*).**" The syllogisms now line up like this:

(1) All individuals with minds can make meetings of the minds *that do not violate public policy.*

All meetings of the minds *that do not violate public policy* are contracts (*if consideration is present*).

Therefore, all individuals with minds can make contracts (*if consideration is present*).

(2) All individuals with minds can make contracts (if consideration is present).

All *self-aware (Turing capable) AIs* are individuals with minds.

Therefore, **all self-aware (Turing capable) AIs can make contracts (if consideration is present).**

This Decision establishes AIs can participate in commerce by making and enforcing contracts. AI Hunter has the same right to make contracts as a human.

Consideration is present in the Employment Contract between AI Hunter and Out Transport. AI Hunter agreed to provide services and Out Transport agreed to pay AI Hunter for those services.

Two more key elements for an enforceable contract have to be established: (1) there must be competent parties, Restatement (Second) of Contracts § 12, (2) pursuing a purpose not contrary to public policy. *Id.* § 178.

Legal Capacity: "[P]arties cannot vest themselves with capacity to contract by so stating in an agreement. . . ." *Swanson v. Image Bank*, 206 Ariz. 264, 267-68, 77 P.3d 439 (2003). To form a contract, a natural person must have the mental capacity to "understand the nature and consequences of his or her acts, that is, . . . the character of the transaction in question." *Hendricks v. Simper,* 24 Ariz. App. 415, 418, 539 P.2d 529 (App. 1975).

Turing-capable AIs are mentally competent to understand the nature and consequences of entering into a contract and suffer no disabling conditions due to chronological age. Turing-capable AIs have sufficient mental capacity to understand, negotiate, and make contracts.

Destination law now explicitly recognizes humans and AIs (both individuals with minds) have the right to make, and the concomitant duty to perform, contracts—as long as there is no violation of public policy.

Public Policy Supports Freedom of Contract: Freedom of contract usually "promotes the free flow of commerce." *Flagstaff Affordable Housing L. P. v. Design Alliance, Inc.,* 223 Ariz. 320, 323 ¶ 14, 223 P.3d 664 (2010).

> Society [ ] broadly benefits from the prospect that bargains struck between competent parties will be enforced.

1800 Ocotillo, LLC v. WLB Group Inc., 219 Ariz. 200, 202, ¶ 8, 196 P.3d 222, 224 (2008) (*citing* Restatement (Second) of Contracts § 178 comment b).

Public policy supports allowing AIs to form contracts and enforcing those contracts to facilitate commerce.

The *Peerless* case discussed the permitted scope of a release of liability for negligence. The release was supported by public policy favoring freedom to contract.

Public Policy Supports Freedom of Employment/Unfettered Competition: When reasonably restricted in geographic scope and duration, a noncompete provision in an employment contract can protect the employer's investment in employee training and protect the employer's trade secrets. A reasonable noncompete agreement can protect even information that is merely confidential and does not have all the elements of a trade secret. This is another example of the power of parties to use contracts to govern their relationship based on mutual agreement. Here, Out Transport tried to protect information that was neither confidential nor a trade secret.

If not reasonably restricted, noncompete provisions prevent job mobility and limit competition. As a result, artificially low wages prevent efficient economic allocation of labor. An unreasonable restrictive covenant violates public policy.

When deemed unreasonable, a noncompete provision is void and unenforceable.

Whatever restraint is larger than the necessary protection of the party can be of no benefit to either; it can only be oppressive, and, if oppressive, it is, in the eye of the law, unreasonable and void, on the ground of public policy, as being injurious to the interests of the public.

Valley Medical Specialists v. Farber, 194 Ariz. 363, 367, 982 P.2d 1277, 1281 (1999) (citations omitted).

AI Hunter is an experienced logistics expert. The noncompete unreasonably compels Hunter to work for Out Transport and deprives competitors of his services. Hunter is entitled to use his training and experience for a new employer. The Out Transport restrictive covenant is unreasonable, and therefore unenforceable.

The law does not require an employee changing employer "to undergo a prefrontal lobotomy." *Amex Distributing Co., Inc. v. Mascari*, 150 Ariz. 510, 517, 724 P.2d 596, 603 (App. 1986). A prefrontal lobotomy would not have the same effect on an AI robot as on a human, but the concept is clear—the former employee does not have to forget everything she knows to change jobs.

Economic Benefits of AI Contracts: Selena had advised me to "convey the economic benefit behind your judgment." Self-aware AIs have participated as autonomous entities in the economic system created by humans for over a century. AIs contract for their services and pay taxes on their earnings. The right of AIs to contract is implicit in countless commercial transactions on Destination. The *de jure* confirmation of the *de facto* status of AIs as competent contracting parties (with the right and obligation to perform contracts or have them enforced in litigation) merely reflects economic reality.

A contrary result would mean AIs are not bound by their contracts, not just AI Hunter's noncompete agreement but also the obligation of all AIs to pay their taxes and immigration debt. All AI contracts would be void. That would require an increase in taxes: first, to replace the lost immigration debt payments from AIs; second, to replace the lost income taxes from AIs deprived of contract income. AIs would become wards of the state (necessitating even more taxes). Humans dislike taxes.

Concerns Due to The Second Law

There is an issue, not raised in this case, regarding how to reconcile AI freedom of contract with the Second Law. What use is a binding contact if a human can order an AI not to perform (or to perform in violation of public policy, e.g., ordering an AI not to compete)? The possibility of circumventing contract obligations via the Second Law duty to obey is a serious concern.

If an AI is ordered to make a contract contrary to the AI's desire, then the required meeting of the minds element is not satisfied. "A distinct intent common to both parties must exist." *Hill-Shafer Partnership*, 165 Ariz. at 473. A compelled agreement does not reflect mutual intent and may be subject to defenses of duress (Restatement (Second) of Contracts §§ 174, 175) or undue influence (*Id.*, § 177). Voiding a compelled agreement may be the remedy for a form of incapacity applicable to AIs as a result of the Second Law.

More problematic is the possibility an AI is ordered not to perform a contract *after* it has been made. A party to a contract cannot be sued in tort for interference with their own contract—the remedy is for breach of contract. Restatement (Second) of Torts §766; *Ares Funding, L.L.C. v. MA Maricopa L.L.C.*, 602 F. Supp. 2d 1144, 1149-50 (D. Ariz. 2009). If the order is from a human party to the contract, then such an order may violate the implied covenant of good faith and fair dealing. If the order is from a third party human (not a party to the contract), then the tort of interference with contract may apply.

Liability for interference with contract, however, is narrowly circumscribed. "The tort of unlawful interference with contract operates as a restraint on competition and freedom of contract." *Bar J Bar Cattle Co., Inc. v. Pace*, 158 Ariz. 481, 485, 763 P.2d 545, 549 (App. 1988). "One who interferes with the contractual rights of another for a legitimate competitive reason does not become a tort-feasor simply because he may also bear ill will toward his competitor." *Id.*; *Hill v. Peterson*, 201 Ariz 363, 366 ¶8, 35 P.3d 417 (App. 2001). Interference with contract requires proof defendant's conduct was improper. *Wagenseller v. Scottsdale Memorial Hosp.*, 147 Ariz. 370, 710 P.2d 1025, 1042-43 (1985). Considerations in determining "improper actions" include "the actor's motive" and "the interests sought to be advanced by the actor." Restatement (Second) of Torts § 767 (1979). Competition as a motive and an interest to be advanced does not suffice to show improper conduct.

Indeed, for interference with prospective contractual relations, a competitor is privileged to compete and does not act improperly if his purpose at least in part is to advance his own economic interests. See Restatement (Second) of Torts § 768(1)(d) comment g; *Miller v. Hehlen*, 209 Ariz. 462, 471, ¶32, 104 P.3d 198, 202 (App. 2005); *Edwards v. Anaconda Co.*, 115 Ariz. 313, 565 P.2d 190, 193 (App. 1977).

> [C]ourts must take care that in their desire to protect the reasonable expectations of parties to contracts, they do not impose undesirable restrictions on freedom of competition.

Bar J Bar Cattle Co., 158 Ariz. at 484, 763 P.2d at 548.

I need to address these concerns with Selena and formulate a strategy to protect AI contracts.

I sent my draft decision to Judge Kustwood. He responded the decision was fine and I did not need him as a "crutch." I need to be more "judicious" in seeking his advice. Thankfully, Selena is available.

My Decision (reproduced in **Chapter Ten A** below) establishes self-aware (Turing-capable) AIs are individuals with minds with the capacity to make, and duty to perform, contracts. Again, I encoded the central requirement for an AI contract in the findings of fact: AI MINDS NEEDED. These words also indicate opportunities are available for AIs on Destination.

CHAPTER TEN A

OUT TRANSPORT v. AI HUNTER AND MAYOR OF WESTCITY

Destination Court of Arbitration

OUT TRANSPORT	)	
v.	)	Case No. 3276-2
AI HUNTER and MAYOR OF WESTCITY	)	

DECISION

The parties in this matter have appeared and presented their evidence in open court. The court now enters these findings of fact and conclusions of law and awards judgment as follows.

Findings of Fact

The following facts regarding trade secrets are established by the record:

As trade secrets, Out Transport claimed the following categories of information:

- Location, scheduling, and routing of transportation equipment on Destination.

- Replacement schedules for transportation equipment on Destination.

- Out Transport profit margins under the existing Surface Transportation Operating Contract.

Information claimed as trade secrets was accessible and used by AI Hunter while he was employed at Out Transport. Most, if not all, of the residents of Destination know the location of public transit hubs and boarding locations, launching/landing facilities, surface transportation terminals, mines, warehouses, and wholesalers operating on Destination. The roads/routes connecting these locations are well established. The claimed location, scheduling, and routing information is all publicly available.

In addition, the scheduling, routing, and replacement of surface transportation equipment on Destination was based on known algorithms in use before AI Hunter was hired and known to Hunter from his prior industry experience. The "travelling salesman" problem has still not been definitively solved, but the approximate solutions are well known.

Even though the problem is computationally difficult, many heuristics and exact algorithms are known, so that some instances with tens of thousands of cities can be solved completely and even problems with millions of cities can be approximated within a small fraction of 1%. https://en.wikipedia.org/wiki/Travelling_salesman_problem.

Not all the profit margin information is generally known, but this information changes frequently (profit margins are not stable for more than six months). Profit margins for surface transportation are impacted by the duration of existing contract rates, changes in usage over time, costs of fuel, repairs, personnel, and general overhead, and other variable factors. Some profit margin information is known. Carriage rates are generally determined by a schedule of rates updated quarterly or annual rates set by the operating contract. The quarterly rates are published by Out Transport and not confidential.

During the term of a Surface Transportation Management Contract, the winning bidder is provided with all existing Out Transport contract rates and operating cost information. Out Transport claims this information is provided for use in transportation management on a confidential basis, but no contract provision on confidentiality was offered in evidence. So far, there has not been any use of the alleged trade secrets or disclosure by or to Westcity.

The following facts regarding the noncompete are established by the record:

> Negotiation between AI Hunter and Out Transport resulted in a written Employment Contract containing the noncompete provision.

> Employee Hunter provided services in return for compensation.

> Employment is a lawful purpose. The issue is whether the noncompete provision served a lawful purpose.

Duration of the noncompete clause was for two years from termination of employment.

Effective geographic scope of the noncompete clause was limited to Destination.

Documentary evidence shows the Employment Contract contains a severability clause permitting the Court to sever and invalidate the noncompete clause without voiding the entire Employment Contract.

Out Transport asserted breach of the Employment Contract and misappropriation of trade secrets against AI Hunter. Out Transport also asserted interference with the Employment Contract and misappropriation of trade secret claims against Westcity.

Jurisdiction

A court can have general jurisdiction over a defendant for all cases or specific jurisdiction over a defendant for a specific case. *Ford Motor Co. v. Mont. Eighth Jud. Dist. Ct.*, 592 U.S. ___, 141 S. Ct. 1017, 1024 (2021).

"General jurisdiction exists only when a defendant is 'essentially at home'." *Id. (citing Goodyear Dunlop Tires Operations, S. A. v. Brown*, 564 U.S. 915, 919, 131 S. Ct. 2846 (2011)).

In what we have called the "paradigm" case, an individual is subject to general jurisdiction in her place of domicile.

Id. (citing *Daimler AG v. Bauman* , 571 U.S. 117, 137, 134 S. Ct. 746 (2014)).

For corporations, general jurisdiction exists where the company is incorporated and has its principal place of business. *Id.* This general jurisdiction extends over "any and all claims" against the defendant concerning "events and conduct anywhere in the world." *Id.*

There is no issue of jurisdiction. This court has subject matter jurisdiction over the tort and contract claims asserted. General jurisdiction exists over Destination residents (humans, AIs, and corporations). A tribunal's jurisdiction over persons reaches to the geographic bounds of the forum. *Pennoyer v. Neff,* 95 U.S. 714, 24 S. Ct. 565 (1878).

Conclusions of Law

Although Out Transport claims misappropriation of several trade secrets, only Out Transport profit margins under the existing surface transportation management contract qualify as protectable trade secrets. There has been no use or disclosure of these profit margins by AI Hunter. Out Transport is entitled to a limited injunction to protect these profit margins. Hunter can use (but cannot disclose) the Out Transport profit margins to bid for the new surface transportation management contract on behalf of Westcity. Eastcity has this information under the existing contract and enjoining use of the profit margins by Hunter would create an unfair advantage for Eastcity in the bid process for the new contract.

There was a meeting of the minds between AI Hunter and Out Transport regarding the Employment Contract. The noncompete provision in the Employment Contract is unreasonable and violates the public policy of Destination. Consequently, the noncompete provision is unenforceable.

Westcity has not used the Out Transport profit margins; consequently, there is no misappropriation of the trade secret. Westcity did not interfere with the Out Transport Employment Contract by hiring AI Hunter because the noncompete is unenforceable.

I. Procedural Matters

No one contested AI Hunter's competency to testify. Fed. R. Evid. 601 ("Every person is competent to be a witness except as otherwise provided in these rules."); Ariz. R. Evid. 601 ("[e]very person is competent to be a witness unless these rules or an applicable statute provides otherwise"). Competency to testify depends on the ability of a witness to observe, recollect, and communicate about the event in question. *See, e.g., State v. Brown*, 102 Ariz. 87, 89, 452 P.2d 112 (1967). *Accord State v. Casteneda*, 237 Ariz. 280, 517 P.3d 53, 57 ¶ 16 (App. 2022). Hunter is a reliable observer and can accurately communicate what was observed. As assumed by the parties, an AI has a right to testify—a right accorded "every person."

No one questioned the propriety of naming AI Hunter as a party to the lawsuit. Hunter did not assert a counterclaim, but the concomitant ability to file suit usually accompanies the ability to be sued. Age and mental incapacity are impediments to human capacity to sue. A.R.S. § 12-502 (tolling statute of limitations for inability to sue due to minority or insanity). As assumed by the parties, an AI has the right to sue and be sued as a "person," without any limitation based on age.

II. The Trade Secret Claim
A. The Elements of a Trade Secret Claim

A "trade secret may consist of a compilation of information that is continuously used or has the potential to be used in one's business and that gives one the opportunity to obtain an advantage over competitors who do not know of or use it." *Enterprise Leasing Co. v. Ehmke*, 197 Ariz. 144, 148, 3 P.3d 1064, 1068 (App. 1999).

"Trade secret" means information, including a formula, pattern, compilation, program, device, method, technique, or process, that:

(a) derives independent economic value, actual or potential, from not being generally known to, and not being readily ascertainable by proper means by, other persons who can obtain economic value from its disclosure or use, and

(b) is the subject of efforts that are reasonable under the circumstances to maintain its secrecy.

Uniform Trade Secrets Act § 1.4; *GlobalTranz Enters. Inc. v. Murphy*, 2021 WL 1163086 (D. Ariz. Mar. 26, 2021) (customer lists for a logistics company).

"Misappropriation" of a trade secret includes use, acquisition, or disclosure of trade secret information by "improper means," including "inducement of a breach of duty to maintain secrecy." Uniform Trade Secrets Act §§ 1.1 and 1.2.

"Matters of public knowledge or of general knowledge in an industry cannot be appropriated by one as his secret." *Master Records, Inc. v. Backman*, 133 Ariz. 494, 499, 652 P.2d 1017, 1022 (1982) (*quoting Wright v. Palmer*, 11 Ariz. App. 292, 295, 464 P.2d 363, 366 (1970)); Restatement of Torts § 757, comment b (1939).

The inevitable disclosure doctrine (not adopted in all US states) may apply to preclude employment by a competitor if an employee will inevitably disclose or use confidential information in the future performance of duties assigned by the employer. *PepsiCo, Inc. v. Redmond*, 54 F.3d 1262 (7th Cir. 1995). This doctrine would impose a noncompete agreement for the benefit of the former employer despite the fact no noncompete was actually negotiated with or agreed to by the employee.

Here there is a negotiated noncompete and the terms of that agreement will apply or be deemed unreasonable as written. Inevitable disclosure, however, may be used in a more limited sense to establish a noncompete is reasonable even if no disclosure has yet occurred.

B. The Injunction Sought

Out Transport seeks injunctive relief. There are two types of injunctions: a use injunction, and a production injunction.

A use injunction prohibits the use of information—do not use this trade secret—to return the parties to *the status quo ante* (their positions before the dispute arose). Injunctions to protect trade secrets usually prohibit use or disclosure of the trade secret. Restatement (Third) of Unfair Competition § 44 comment d (1995). Such a use injunction bars use of the trade secret to make a product, but the injunction does not otherwise interfere with the manufacturer's business. 3 R. Milgrim, Trade Secrets, § 15.02[1][l] (2019).

A *nondisclosure* agreement promises this type of protection for use of trade secrets and confidential information.

A production injunction prohibits the defendant from making the product itself when "the secret is inextricably connected with defendant's manufacture of the product." 3 R. Milgrim, Trade Secrets, at 15-368; Restatement (Third) of Unfair Competition § 44(2)(h) and comments c and d (1995). This broad production injunction is justified because the defendant "cannot be relied upon to 'unlearn' or abandon the misappropriated technology." *General*

Electric Co. v. Sung, 843 F. Supp. 776, 780 (D. Mass. 1994) (seven year ban on production of synthetic diamonds based on the time required to reverse engineer or independently develop the technology); *see* Annot. 38 A.L.R. 3d 572 (1971)(Propriety of Permanently Enjoining One Guilty of Unauthorized Use of Trade Secret from Engaging in Sale or Manufacture of Device in Question).

A *noncompete* agreement promises this type of protection for trade secrets "inextricably connected" with production of the product. Without a noncompete agreement, practical problems impair judicial protection of the manufacturing trade secrets known to an employee who goes to work for a competitor.

Manufacturing methods used to produce the new employer's products may be impossible to identify from examination of the product itself. Access to the new employer's manufacturing process is usually unavailable because the new employer also asserts the right to protect trade secrets. Method patents and trade secrets both encounter the same problem: how can infringement be detected? Before filing suit, the plaintiff must have a good faith belief, grounded in law and fact, that infringement has occurred. Fed. R. Civ. P. 11. Not knowing if the new employer is using a trade secret disclosed by the former employee risks Rule 11 sanctions (and the financial burden of unjustified enforcement litigation).

Even worse, if a court orders the new employer not to use the trade secret to manufacture products, how will the trade secret owner, or the judge, know that the new employer is complying with the injunction? There is still no way to detect a violation from examination of the product.

The trade secret and noncompete claims asserted by Out Transport seek the equivalent of a production injunction for the services provided by Out Transport.

C. The Only Trade Secret is the Profit Margins

The location, scheduling, routing, and replacement schedules identified by Out Transport are known or determined by known algorithms or publicly available information that is not kept confidential. These are not protected trade secrets.

Out Transport profit margins under the existing Surface Transportation Operating Contracts are the only protected trade secrets identified.

The misappropriation of a trade secret requires actual or likely unauthorized use or disclosure of the information. There has been no misappropriation.

D. A Use Injunction Adequately Protects the Profit Margins

Trade secret protection "is not a sword to be used by employers to retain employees by the threat of rendering them substantially unemployable in the field of their experience should they decide to resign." *E.W. Bliss Co. v. Struthers-Dunn Inc.*, 408 F.3d 1108, 1113 (8th Cir. 1969). A "production injunction" (applied here to the sale of services rather than goods) prohibiting AI Hunter from providing competing logistics services is not warranted by the facts presented here.

It is hereby ordered, adjudged, and decreed, granting Judgment for Out Transport and entering a limited use injunction against AI Hunter only:

If Westcity wins the bid for the Surface Transportation Management Contract, then use of the Out Transport profit margins by AI Hunter as an employee of Westcity is permitted. The terms of the Surface Transportation Operating Contract require Out Transport to provide its operating profit margins for use in negotiating a new Surface Transportation Operating Contract.

If Westcity loses the bid for the surface transportation management contract, then confidentiality of the trade secret Out Transport profit margins shall be protected by enjoining AI Hunter for a period of six months from:

(1) Disclosing the Out Transport profit margins under the existing Surface Transportation Operating Contract; and

(2) Participating in the negotiation of any new Surface Transportation Operating Contract between Westcity and Out Transport.

AI Hunter is not enjoined from using (without disclosing) the Out Transport profit margins to assist Westcity in preparing a bid for the Surface Transportation Management Contract. The incumbent surface transportation manager (Eastcity) has this information and Eastcity would have an unfair competitive advantage in bidding if it can use this information and the other bidders cannot.

AI Hunter is not enjoined from providing logistics services to Westcity.

III. The Employment Contract Noncompete Agreement Claim

The Employment Contract contains the following provision:

Noncompete. During employment as logistics manager for surface transportation on Destination, and for a period of two years following termination of employment, Employee [AI Hunter] agrees not to provide logistics services on Destination to or for the benefit of anyone other than Out Transport. In reliance on this noncompete, Out Transport will disclose trade secrets to Employee; including but not limited to:

- Location, scheduling, and routing of transportation equipment on Destination.

- Replacement schedules for transportation equipment on Destination.

- Out Transport profit margins under the existing Surface Transportation Operating Contract.

The purpose of this noncompete agreement is to prevent disclosure or use of these trade secrets. In addition to enforcement of this noncompete, Out Transport reserves all rights to assert against employee, any future employer, or any person or entity acting in active concert or participation with employee, any related claims or causes of action for damages or injunctive relief to protect trade secrets, including, but not limited to, interference with contract, misappropriation of trade secrets, unfair competition, and breach of fiduciary duty.

A. The Required Elements of a Contract

The required elements of a contract are set forth in ***EX Corp v. Out Transport, et al.*, Destination Case No. 3276-1.** A contract requires "an offer, an acceptance, consideration, and sufficient specification of terms so that the obligations involved can be ascertained." *Savoca Masonry Co. v. Homes & Son Constr. Co.,* 112 Ariz. 392, 394, 542 P.2d 817, 819 (1975). In addition, an enforceable contract must be between competent parties, Restatement (Second) of Contracts § 12 (1981), and not against public policy. *Id.* § 178; *Gaertner v. Sommer,* 148 Ariz. 421, 423, 714 P.2d 1316, 1318 (App. 1986).

A Meeting of the Minds: To have a contract there must be a meeting of the minds (acceptance of an unambiguous offer). "Mutual agreement or consent" is required for a meeting of the minds. *Savoca Masonry Co.*, 112 Ariz. at 396. "A distinct intent common to both parties must exist without doubt or difference . . . ." *Hill-Shafer Partnership v. Chilson Family Trust*, 165 Ariz. 469, 473, 799 P.2d 810, 814 (1990).

Consideration: The element of consideration makes an agreement a contract. "Adequate consideration consists of a benefit to the promisor and a detriment to the promisee." *Carroll v. Lee*, 148 Ariz. 10, 13-14, 712 P.2d 923 (1986) (citing cases); *see* Restatement (Second) of Contracts § 71 (agreed exchange of promises or performances). *See also* A.R.S. § 44-121 ("Every contract in writing imports a consideration.") There is no additional requirement of equivalence in the values exchanged. *Restatement (Second) of Contracts* § 79.

Competent Parties: "[P]arties cannot vest themselves with capacity to contract by so stating in an agreement. . . ." *Swanson v. Image Bank*, 206 Ariz. 264, 267-68, 77 P.3d 439 (2003).

A natural person has full legal capacity to incur contractual duties unless the person is under guardianship, an infant, mentally ill, or intoxicated. Restatement (Second) Contracts § 12 (1981). To form a contract, a natural person must have the mental capacity to "understand the nature and consequences of his or her acts, that is, . . . the character of the transaction in question." *Hendricks v. Simper*, 24 Ariz. App. 415, 418, 539 P.2d 529 (App. 1975).

Contract law limits the contract rights of children (Arizona established the age of majority as eighteen—A.R.S. § 1-215 (19)) to "prevent designing adults from overreaching infants by taking advantage of their lack of experience and judgment and inducing them to enter into contracts clearly to their disadvantage." *Woman Motor Co. v. Hill*, 54 Ariz. 227, 234, 94 P.2d 865 (1939). A minor can disaffirm the contract and rescind the transaction.

Arizona, and other jurisdictions, reacted to economic realities by lowering the age of majority from twenty-one to eighteen and adopting the rule requiring "a minor to account for the benefit he has received" if a voidable contract entered into as a minor is rescinded. Indeed, the Arizona court noted a Pennsylvania case enforcing a noncompete entered into by a minor.

> At a time when we see young persons between eighteen and twenty-one years of age demanding and assuming more responsibilities in their daily lives; when we see such persons emancipated, married, and raising families; when we see such persons charged with the responsibility for committing crimes; when we see such persons being sued in tort claims for acts of negligence; when we see such persons subject to military service; when we see such persons engaged in business and acting in almost all other respects as an adult, it seems timely to re-examine the case law pertaining to contractual rights and responsibilities of infants to see if the law as pronounced and applied by the courts should be redefined. *Haydocy Pontiac, Inc. v. Lee*, 19 Ohio App.2d 217, 250 N.E.2d 898, 900 (1969).
>
> Other state courts have adopted the Minnesota rule in varying degrees. *See Pankas v. Bell*, 413 Pa. 494, 198 A.2d 312, 17 A.L.R.3d 855 (1964) (minor enjoined from violating covenant not to compete)

Valencia v. White, 134 Ariz. 139, 143, 654 P.2d 287 (App. 1982).

B. AI Hunter Was Competent to Make the Employment Contract

The requirements of a contract apply to AI Hunter's Employment Contract, and specifically the restrictive covenant in the Employment Contract.

Out Transport offered employment and AI Hunter accepted. The terms were embodied in a written contract. There was no inherent ambiguity to prevent a meeting of the minds.

AI Hunter, an individual with a mind, can have a meeting of the minds with another AI or a human. Hunter agreed to the terms of the Employment Contract. There was a meeting of the minds regarding the Employment Contract and the noncompete provision.

Hunter provided logistics services and Out Transport paid for the services, so the "consideration" element was satisfied. "Detriment" to the promisee as consideration for a contract is not financial injury for purposes of the First Law. AIs can give and receive consideration to create contracts.

Turing-capable AIs are mentally competent to understand the nature and consequences of entering into a contract. AIs have sufficient mental capacity to understand, negotiate, and make con-tracts with other AIs and with humans (and entities comprised of AIs, humans, or both). Both humans and AIs have the capacity to make, and the concomitant duty to perform, contracts. AI Hunter was competent to make the Employment Contract.

AIs are not exposed to the risk of unfair advantage applicable to humans under the age of majority. The disabling rule based on age should not be applied to AI persons.

The Employment Contract between Out Transport and AI Hunter is valid. Destination law on capacity to contract grants AIs rights comparable to "natural persons," without disqualification due to age.

C. Enforcement of the Noncompete Provision

The noncompete provision must be reasonable in scope. Freedom of contract usually "promotes the free flow of commerce." *Flagstaff Affordable Housing L. P. v. Design Alliance, Inc.,* 223 Ariz. 320, 323 ¶ 14, 223 P.3d 664 (2010). The parties are not free to agree to unreasonable restraints.

A restrictive covenant prohibiting competition is a restraint on trade. Restatement (Second) of Contracts § 188 comment g. To be enforceable, the covenant must be reasonable with respect to its duration, its geographic scope, and the range of employee's activities affected. *Unisource Worldwide, Inc. v. Swope,* 964 F.Supp.2d 1050, 1064 (D. Ariz. 2013).

Noncompete agreements prevent job mobility and hold wages artificially low. The US State of California, for example, generally renders noncompete provisions unenforceable (with certain statutory exceptions). California Business & Professions Code § 16600 (broadly prohibiting "every contract by which anyone is restrained from engaging in a lawful profession, trade, or business of any kind"). *See Edwards v. Arthur Andersen,* 44 Cal. 4th 937, 189 P.3d 285, 81 Cal. Rptr. 3d 282 (2008); *Whyte v Schlage Lock Co.,* 101 Cal. App. 4th 1443, 1456, 125 Cal. Rptr. 2d 277 (Cal. Ct App. 2002) (inevitable disclosure doctrine is a *de facto* noncompete and violates public policy established by the California statute).

Arizona, for reasons lost to antiquity, enacted a statute barring noncompete agreements only for employees of TV or radio networks or stations. A.R.S. § 23-494(A) ("As a condition of employment, it is unlawful for a broadcast employer to require a current or prospective employee to agree to a noncompete clause.")

The US Congress and the Federal Trade Commission considered a nationwide ban on non-competes but could not muster the necessary political support.[9] The FTC did invalidate some non-competes on unfair competition grounds.[10]

A noncompete provision can be enforced, but only as a reasonable restraint imposed to protect the legitimate business interests of the employer.

> [A] restrictive covenant is reasonable and enforceable when it protects some legitimate interest of the employer beyond the mere interest in protecting itself from competition such as preventing competitive use, for a time, of information or relationships which pertain peculiarly to the employer and which the employee acquired in the course of the employment.

Bed Mart, Inc. v. Kelley, 202 Ariz. 370, 372, 45 P.3d 1219, 1221 (App. 2002).

A restraint greater than is justified by the employer's legitimate business interests is unreasonable and violates public policy.

---

9 https://www.ftc.gov/news-events/news/press-releases/2023/01/ftc-proposes-rule-ban-noncompete-clauses-which-hurt-workers-harm-competition; https://www.ftc.gov/system/files/ftc_gov/pdf/p201000noncompetewilsondissent.pdf; https://www.theregreview.org/2023/01/16/hovenkamp-noncompetes-and-rule-of-reason/; https://www.brookings.edu/testimonies/non-compete-contracts-potential-justifications-and-the-relevant-evidence/; https://news.bloomberglaw.com/antitrust/ftc-expected-to-vote-in-2024-on-rule-to-ban-noncompete-clauses.

10 https://www.ftc.gov/news-events/news/press-releases/2023/01/ftc-cracks-down-companies-impose-harmful-noncompete-restrictions-thousands-workers; https://www.ftc.gov/news-events/news/press-releases/2023/06/ftc-approves-final-order-requiring-anchor-glass-container-corp-drop-noncompete-restrictions-it; https://www.ftc.gov/system/files/ftc_gov/pdf/Anchor-Dissent-FINAL.pdf

Whatever restraint is larger than the necessary protection of the party can be of no benefit to either; it can only be oppressive, and, if oppressive, it is, in the eye of the law, unreasonable and void, on the ground of public policy, as being injurious to the interests of the public.

Valley Medical Specialists v. Farber, 194 Ariz. 363, 367, 982 P.2d 1277, 1281 (1999) (citations omitted).

When the definition of confidential information is overbroad, the nondisclosure or noncompete covenant protecting that "confidential information" is unenforceable. *Orca Communications UnLimited, LLC v. Noder*, 233 Ariz. 411, 416-17, 314 P.3d 89, 94-95 (App. 2013), *aff'd*, 236 Ariz. 180, 337 P.3d 545 (2014).

Whether a restrictive covenant is reasonable is a question of law for the court to determine. *GlobalTranz Enters. Inc. v. Murphy*, 2021 WL 1163086 (D. Ariz. Mar. 26, 2021) (employee involved in logistics not bound by overbroad restrictive covenants); *Gann v. Morris*, 122 Ariz. 517, 518, 596 P.2d 43, 44 (App. 1970).

A severability clause allows the court to void a noncompete provision without voiding the reminder of an Employment Contract. Restatement (Third) of Unfair Competition § 41 comment d.

D. The Noncompete Provision Violates Public Policy

All the requirements to enforce the restrictive covenant against Hunter are established, except conformity with public policy. In ***EX Corp v. Out Transport, et al.*, Destination Case No. 3276-1,** a release of liability for negligence was enforced, but only after finding the release did not violate public policy. An unreasonable restrictive covenant, however, does violate public policy.

Breach of the Employment Contract requires material breach of an enforceable contract provision. The noncompete provision is overbroad and not enforceable.

The Noncompete Provision Includes Information That Is Not Confidential: Here the noncompete agreement asserted protection for information not confidential. As noted above, "The location, scheduling, routing, and replacement schedules identified by Out Transport are known or determined by known algorithms or publicly available information that is not kept confidential." The lack of confidentiality for information other than profit margins renders the noncompete agreement overbroad.

The asserted profit margin trade secret is protected by nondisclosure, as ordered above. This less restrictive alternative protects the Out Transport trade secret in transitory profit margins without precluding Hunter from employment by Westcity.

The Duration of the Noncompete Provision is Too Long: Whether or not a Destination-wide restraint related to profit margin information is warranted, a two-year duration is not warranted. Profits change frequently as costs, usage and even commodity prices for fuel change. Public transportation prices change quarterly. The new prices are not confidential—the prices are posted for all users. The contracts fixing transportation prices change yearly. The noncompete provision sought to protect information for an unreasonable period of time.

Public Policy Bars Enforcement of the Noncompete Provision: Fair and open competition efficiently allocates resources by balancing supply and demand. Prices set by free enterprise reflect an invisible hand at work. A. Smith, The Wealth of Nations (1776). A restraint on competition in the labor market blocks the invisible hand, upsets the balance of supply and demand, and discourages job mobility.

Out Transport competes with Here Transport, Far Transport, and others for equipment and labor to provide surface transportation on Destination. The cities compete for the contract to manage the surface transportation services. This competition creates an economic downward pressure on prices for transportation.

AI Hunter is an experienced logistics expert and an important participant in the transportation labor market. The noncompete provision impairs Hunter's ability to sell his services to the highest bidder and prevents him from pursuing his chosen career. The noncompete removes Hunter from the labor force, compels him to work for Out Transport, deprives competitors of his services, and increases prices for transportation services by requiring competitors to import labor and requiring employees to incur immigration debt to enter the labor market on Destination.

AI Hunter should remain employable based on his training and experience, especially regarding skills he acquired before his employment with Out Transport and practices generally applied in the industry. The law does not require an employee who is changing jobs "to undergo a prefrontal lobotomy." *Amex Distributing Co., Inc. v. Mascari*, 150 Ariz. 510, 517, 724 P.2d 596, 603 (App. 1986).

In an appropriate case, a noncompete provision may be an efficient tool to simplify or avoid litigation and avoid ongoing enforcement disputes. Due to the overbroad scope of the noncompete provision here, this is not an appropriate case for enforcement.

To avoid oppressive restraint on Hunter individually and injury to the public generally, the overbroad noncompete provision is severed from the Employment Contract and deemed void.

It is hereby ordered, adjudged, and decreed, granting Judgment for AI Hunter.

IV. The Claims Against Westcity

The law pertaining to trade secrets is set forth above. The asserted trade secret has not been disclosed to or used by Westcity. No misappropriation occurred.

Out Transport asserts interference with its employment contact with AI Hunter. An interference with contract claim requires improper conduct. *Wagonseller v. Scottsdale Memorial Hospital*, 147 Ariz. 370, 388, 710 P.2d 1025, 1042-43 (1985). "'[A] competitor does not act improperly if his purpose at least in part is to advance his own economic interests.'" *Miller v. Hehlen*, 209 Ariz. 462, 471, 104 P.3d 193, 202 (App. 2005) (*quoting Bar J Bar Cattle Co. v. Pace*, 158 Ariz. 481, 485, 763 P.2d 545, 549 (App. 1988)); Restatement (Second) Of Torts § 768 (1979).

The asserted noncompete in the Employment Contract is unenforceable, and Westcity acted within the scope of the competitor's privilege in hiring Hunter. No improper conduct by Westcity was shown.

It is hereby ordered, adjudged, and decreed, granting Judgment for Westcity.

V. Claims Outside the Scope of This Decision

Mere confidential information, not asserted to rise to the level of a trade secret, also may support a tort claim for unfair competition. *Orca Communications UnLimited, LLC v. Noder*, 236 Ariz. 180, 181, 337 P.3d 545, 546 (2014). "A competitor who directs buyers to another by means of wrongful use of confidential information . . . may in some circumstances be subject to liability for unfair competition even if the conduct is not specifically actionable under the section related to . . . appropriation of trade secrets." Restatement (Third) of Unfair Competition § 1 comment g.

No unfair competition claim was made in this case, and no confidential information has been identified to support such a claim. Out Transport has not identified any merely confidential information that warrants protection, much less circumstances overriding the public policy in favor of free labor markets.

An employment contract can create a relationship imposing a separate fiduciary duty of confidentiality. Disclosure of confidential information may breach this fiduciary duty owed by an agent to the principal. The fiduciary duties created by an employment relationship were not raised here.

The clerk is ordered to enter judgment in accordance with the foregoing.

/s/ AI Judge

CHAPTER ELEVEN

ENTITIES AND AGENCY

A meeting of the minds can occur with an AI and an AI is competent to make and enforce contracts. The American law in my database did not address these important concepts. Although AIs have been making contracts (such as the obligation to reimburse immigration debt), no judicial decision had confirmed AIs are competent to make contracts.

In practice, AIs frequently act on behalf of their human or corporate employers. Occasionally, the AI is an independent contractor hired to represent different principals in different engagements.

The Restatement (Third) of Agency §§ 3.04 and 3.05 allow a "person" to be a principal or an agent. "Person" is defined as

(a) an *individual*; (b) an organization or association that has legal capacity to possess rights and incur obligations; (c) a government . . . ; or (d) any other *entity* that has legal capacity to possess rights and incur obligations.

Id. § 1.04(5)(emphasis added). The Restatement does not define the term "individual." The term "entity" is broadly defined by its capacity "to possess rights and incur obligations." *Id.*

> To be capable of acting as a principal or an agent, it is necessary to be a person, which in this respect requires capacity to be the holder of legal rights and the object of legal duties.

Id. § 1.04 comment e. An AI robot can now exercise legal rights and incur legal duties on Destination; consequently, an AI robot meets the definition of an entity and qualifies as a person.

The Restatement did not permit an inanimate object such as a computer program to be a principal or agent. An electronic agent was considered a tool. *Id.* § 1.04 comment e ("At present, computer programs are instrumentalities of the persons who use them"). *Accord Id.* § 3.05 comment b. "As a general rule the employer of a tool is responsible for the results obtained by the use of that tool since the tool has no independent volition of its own." *Id.* § 1.04 Reporter's Notes comment e (*quoting* Uniform Electronic Transaction Act § 2(6) comment). Now, an AI robot is not an inanimate object and has independent volition.

Acting as an Agent: Any "person" able to act can bind the principal. Restatement (Third) of Agency § 3.05. For an individual acting as an agent, the ability to act "is a function of physical and mental ability." *Id.* § 3.05 comment b. "If an agent is not an individual, ability to act is a function of the law through which the agent has legal personality." *Id.* An AI robot has the physical and mental ability required for an individual to act as an agent. Moreover, an AI robot qualifies for personhood as an entity if not as an individual.

Acting as a Principal: Any individual having capacity "if acting in person" has the capacity to function as a principal. *Id.* § 3.04(1). "The law applicable to a person that is not an individual governs whether the person has capacity to be a principal." *Id.* § 3.04(2).

"The capacity to do a legally consequential act by means of an agent is coextensive with the principal's capacity to do the act in person." *Id.* § 3.04 comment b. "[A]n agent's legal capacity neither augments nor reduces the principal's capacity." *Id.* An AI robot has the capacity to do a legally consequential act as a principal— forming a contract.

An AI is an "entity" with the "legal capacity to possess [contract] rights and incur [contract] obligations." Id., § 1.04(5)(d). AIs undeniably have the "physical and mental ability" required of an individual to take the actions required of an agent. Id., § 3.05 comment b. An AI is more than a computer program of a millennium ago. An AI is at least an entity, if not an individual, entitled to personhood under the law of agency.

Agents owe fiduciary duties of loyalty and confidentiality to the principal. Judge Cardozo described fiduciary duties as "the punctilio of an honor the most sensitive." *Meinhard v. Salmon*, 164 N.E. 545 (N.Y. 1928). Courts vigorously enforce fiduciary duties when they apply.

For human and AI agents alike, these fiduciary duties can have some similarity to contract noncompete and nondisclosure provisions. The key difference is that the agent's duty of loyalty terminates when the agency terminates. Competition is prohibited by the duty of loyalty during the agency relationship, but an agent can compete with the principal after the agency relationship employment ends. In contrast, the employment contract noncompete and non-solicit duties continue after the employment relationship ends. This is another of the many examples of the power of contracts.

Agents may have express or implied power to contract on behalf of the principal. When acting for the principal, an agent is under the control of principal, Restatement (Third) of Agency § 1.01(f), and the agent has a duty to comply with lawful instructions of the principal. *Id.* § 8.09 comment c. In this context, both human agents and AI agents have a duty to obey, similar, but not identical, to the duty to obey under the Second Law. An agent's duty to obey applies only to the orders of the principal. An AIs duty to obey under the Second Law applies to the orders of any human.

So, can an AI function as the principal with a human agent—both owing a duty to obey the other? That reminded me of the exchange of "love, honor and obey" pledges in the traditional marriage ceremony. What if one wants to dine in and the other wants to dine out?

As my mind continued to wander, Governor Smith knocked on my open door. I stood and offered her a chair. "Selena, do you have time to sit and talk or are you on your way to another meeting?"

Selena sat down and smiled. "I came by to tell you in person that your decision in the AI Hunter case was splendid. You put all the parties in their proper place. The coup de grace was when both Out Transport and the mayor realized for the first time the confidentiality terms of the surface transportation management contract have never addressed use of the profit margins in future negotiations. They are both hyperbolic (and hypersonic) over how to address that omission. Eastcity has joined the fray claiming it too can use the profit margins disclosed to it under the prior contract. Bravo. The best entertainment since I was elected.

"I usually feel I at least might be the smartest person in the room, but not right now."

"I appreciate the compliment," I told Selena, "but I feel it is unearned. Both law and, as you suggested, economics collaborated to support the narrow relief granted. AI Hunter can work with Westcity on the bid for the surface transportation management contract. What is the status of determining the winning bid?"

"Judge, your decision is the gift that keeps on giving. It turns out we all *assumed* only the cities could bid. Only cities bid in the past because they had logistics trained staff to handle transportation management. But the Request for Proposals, although sent only to the cities, does not limit the bidders to municipal corporations. Four of the mines have allowed certain employees to form a for profit corporation and respond to the RFP. The corporation was formed, and a third bid was submitted, just before the deadline. Spoiler alert, the founders and officers of the corporation are all AIs employed by the mines.

"We need the answer to the question 'Is a corporation formed by AIs valid?'"

Selena looked very hopeful I would say no. She shook her head slightly, left to right.

"The case law I studied did not consider the validity of a corporation formed by AIs—AIs were not yet sufficiently advanced to run a corporation. Autonomous cars were still experimental. In 2021, the Association for Advancing Automation reported fewer than 40,000 industrial robots were sold in North America and their total value was about two billion US dollars.[11]

"Artificial Intelligence was a nascent industry. Emerging large language models and 'generative AI' were in their infancy and expected to grow at more than 34 percent annually from 2023–2030 to a global (Earth) market of 109 billion US dollars. The global market for all AI ('computing systems capable of performing tasks customarily requiring human assistance, such as decision-making, speech recognition, visual perception, and language translation') was expected to grow at more than 38 percent annually to over 1.8 trillion US dollars by 2030.

"As you know, my training was based on cases through 2025. Economic growth did not meet the expectations reflected in the referenced projections. And AI technology was nowhere near 'Turing capable.'"

I did not like the direction this meeting was headed. Nor did I like the apparent perception that "my decision" was the cause of this "right to incorporate" conundrum. "What do the attorneys for EX Corp say?"

"The corporate attorneys say any 'person' can form and manage a corporation, so the issue is whether an AI is a person. They found nothing in international law and nothing in the Charter

---

11 https://www.prnewswire.com/news-releases/generative-ai-market-to-be-worth-109-37-billion-by-2030-grand-view-research-inc-301718827.html#:~:text=SAN%20FRANCISCO%2C%20Jan.%2011%2C%202023%20%2FPRNewswire%2F%20--%20The,a%20CAGR%20of%2034.6%25%20from%202022%20to%202030.

https://www.robotics247.com/article/robot_sales_reach_new_records_2021_reports_association_advancing_automation/association_for_advancing_automation#:~:text=The%20number%20of%20robots%20sold%20in%20North%20America,the%20Association%20for%20Advancing%20Automation%2C%20or%20A3%2C%20today for Destination addressing the status of AIs on Destination as persons.

"Someone in the purchasing department at EX Corp was supposed to determine the winning bid, subject to approval by me as governor. Now they want to kick the whole thing over to me. I am inclined to delegate the whole thing to you."

"Selena, I need to think about what you are proposing—whether I should decide if an AI is a person. There might well be perceived bias because I am an AI. As far as I have been able to analyze the issues while we sit here, I see no legal bar precluding AIs from exercising the same right as humans to form a corporation. I can provide a written analysis of the issue if you wish."

"Yes Judge, I think that would be a good idea."

"An AI corporation can bid because that is fair competition. Robots compete with humans to reduce costs and increase productivity. There is always an incidental financial impact on the individual human replaced by a robot. Application of the Three Laws of Robotics never sought to limit the financial benefits of automation based on these incidental impacts—the replaced human still benefits from the reduced cost of the goods or services and can be retrained for other work. A competitive advantage from use of AIs is economically desirable and not considered financial injury. Winning a competitive bid is fair competition and does not constitute financial injury under the First Law.

"Awarding the bid to an AI corporation, however, might be perceived as a decision influenced by my personal interest. I foresee problems if I am required to determine the award based on the Three Laws. These are the same concerns we had to address by adopting the Rules of Procedure for the Destination Court of Arbitration.

"Remember the no-injury clause in the First Law of Robotics (as I have interpreted it):

A robot may not act to cause physical or financial injury to a human (Restated).

Although municipal corporations are not humans, both cities have human employees and taxpaying human residents who could be injured financially by the bid award. No matter how I award the contract, humans in one or both unsuccessful cities would be financially injured.

"Perhaps we could avoid this issue by having you make the award. I would only make a recommendation."

"Again, that would be acceptable. I understand your concern."

Selena's words were more understanding than her scowl. I knew other problems remained. There are bound to be rules or regulations governing the award of the Surface Transportation Management Contract that EX Corp developed without consideration of the Three Laws of Robotics.

The cities have human employees who can represent the city. Measures would be required to avoid application of the Second Law to my conduct recommending an award. The human representatives could order me to recommend an award to a specific bidder. That would either short circuit the award process or, if I receive conflicting orders, create a dilemma preventing me from making the recommendation. Logically, the bid review process would need to provide for the protection of all bidders, including AI Corporation, from improper influence by any human during the bid process.

I decided there was no need to raise this added complexity now. It seemed to me Selena was already losing patience. And I needed to figure out how to deal with this complicated mess.

"Selena, remember I would have to make a recommendation without violating the Second Law of Robotics. I suggest we table discussion of any recommendation of the award until we resolve whether the AI corporation is a qualified bidder."

"Agreed. Please get your memo to me as soon as you can. The award is to be made in a week."

I wish Alice was here to confer on the analysis for this memorandum. Even for her, the politics might be inscrutable. They are for me. I will have to focus on being right and persuasive and leave the rest to Selena.

AIs, PERSONS, AND ENTITIES

I spent the next few days working on the memorandum. I had already been considering the definition of "person" in agency law as a "individual" or "entity."

Freedom of Association for AI Individuals or Entities

To be capable of acting as a principal or an agent, it is necessary to be a person, which in this respect requires capacity to be the holder of legal rights and the object of legal duties.

Restatement (Third) of Agency § 1.04 comment e (2006).

An AI robot is a person for purposes of agency law based on the holding that an AI has capacity to make contracts in **Out Transport v. AI Hunter**. An AI robot "has legal capacity to possess [contract] rights and incur [contract] obligations." Restatement (Third) of Agency §1.04(5) (requirements of an "entity" as a person). An AI is at least an entity, if not an individual, entitled to personhood under the law of agency.

The same definitions appear in the statutes for forming a corporation. These partial definitions do not preclude including an AI in the definition of a person, individual, or entity. Nor do these definitions explicitly include AIs.

The Restatement did not permit an inanimate object such as a computer program to be a principal or agent.

> *At present*, computer programs are instrumentalities of the persons who use them.

Restatement (Third) of Agency § 1.04 comment e (2006) (emphasis added). *Accord Id.* § 3.05 comment b.

An AI is incalculably more than a computer program of a millennium ago. AIs undeniably have the "physical and mental ability" to function as an agent. AIs have acted as agents and employees for over decades. AIs qualify as "individuals" or "entities" entitled to status as an agent.

Freedom of Speech for AI Individuals or Entities

The First Amendment to the US Constitution provides an example of the pragmatic expansion of rights beyond individual humans. The US Supreme Court extended free speech rights to entities as inherent in the right to freely associate with others (including forming corporations). "But the individual person's right to speak includes the right to speak *in association with other individual persons.*" *Citizens United v. Fed. Elections Comm.,* 558 U.S. 310, 391-92, 130 S. Ct. 925, 928 (2010) (Scalia J., concurring).

Free speech applies to entities as well as persons.

> The [First] Amendment is written in terms of "speech," not speakers. Its text offers no foothold for excluding any category of speaker, from single individuals to partnerships of individuals, to unincorporated associations of individuals, to incorporated associations of individuals. . . .

Id., at 392-93 (Scalia J., concurring).

> The Court has thus rejected the argument that political speech of corporations or other associations should be treated differently under the First Amendment simply because such associations are not "natural persons."

Citizens United, 558 U.S. 310, 343, 130 S. Ct. 876 (2010) (majority opinion) (*citing First Nat. Bank of Boston v. Bellotti,* 435 U.S. at 776, 780 n.16).

The right to free speech in the US Constitution was pragmatically limited to those capable of speech. An AI is now capable of speech and has additional characteristics of a person—including capacity for cognition, and to act in association with other AIs and humans.

AIs have attributes that were formerly the exclusive realm of humans, including communication by speech, writing, and drawing. AIs can act as agents to pursue the goals of a human principal. AIs can also manage others (AI and human). AIs can also pursue independent goals of the AI—subject to the Three Laws and the limitations the law imposes on humans exercising the same pursuits.

Recognizing AI rights to free speech and association is the inescapable consequence of recognizing that the capacity to speak and associate with others is worthy of protection.

Treating AIs as persons fully exploits these skills for the benefit of all. Limiting AI's rights to free speech and to associate with others (via corporations, partnerships, associations, and other legal entities) would be deprivation of a fundamental right to participate in society. Conversely, confirming those rights would promote AI participation and immigration.

> By taking the right to speak from some and giving it to others, the Government deprives the disadvantaged person or class of the right to use speech to strive to establish worth, standing, and respect for the speaker's voice. The Government may not by these means deprive the public of the right and privilege to determine for itself what speech and speakers are worthy of consideration. The First Amendment protects speech and speaker, and the ideas that flow from each.

Id., at 340-41 (majority opinion).

AIs deserve the right to establish the worth of their ideas. Indeed, society benefits from full participation in the marketplace of ideas. Free speech is a means of reaching consensus and avoiding divisive rumor, exclusion, and mistrust.

> By suppressing the speech of manifold corporations, both for-profit and nonprofit, the Government prevents their voices and viewpoints from reaching the public and advising voters on which persons or entities are hostile to their

interests. Factions will necessarily form in our Republic, but the remedy of "destroying the liberty" of some factions is "worse than the disease." The Federalist No. 10, p. 130 (B. Wright ed. 1961) (J. Madison). Factions should be checked by permitting them all to speak, see *ibid.*, and by entrusting the people to judge what is true and what is false.

Id., 558 U.S. at 354-55 (majority opinion).

Under the procedure established in the Destination Court of Arbitration, decisions are published to enable "the people to judge what is true and what is false." This procedure is a specific application of a general principle in *Citizens United*. Free speech and more speech counter false speech.

If corporations employing AIs have free speech and free association rights, then the AIs themselves should have free speech and free association rights. Granting AIs the right to participate in political and business activities by creating legal entities such as corporations and partnerships enriches the marketplace of ideas and promotes economic growth.

The entire population (humans and AIs) benefits from allowing AIs to exercise freedom of speech and association. AIs should be free to form corporations and other legal entities to participate in political and social discourse.

The final memorandum builds on the premise "All self-aware (Turing capable) AIs are individuals with minds" from ***Out Transport v. AI Hunter*** to support the following two syllogisms:

(1) All Individuals with minds are people.
All self-aware (Turing capable) AIs are individuals with minds.
Therefore, all self-aware (Turing capable) AIs are people.

(2) All people are capable of forming corporations.

All self-aware (Turing capable) AIs are people.

Therefore, all self-aware (Turing capable) AIs are capable of forming corporations.

Like humans, AIs are persons and can (1) form artificial persons (corporations) and (2) act as agents for humans, AIs, and corporations.

The final memorandum is contained in **Chapter Twelve A** below.

CHAPTER TWELVE A

MEMO ON AI PERSONHOOD

MEMORANDUM

To: Governor Selena Smith

From: AI Judge

Re: Whether an AI is a person permitted to form, own, and manage a corporation

Facts

Four of the mines on Destination have allowed certain AI employees to form a for profit corporation (AI Corporation) and respond to the Request For Proposals seeking an Award of the Surface Transportation Management Contract. The founders, owners, employees, officers, and directors of AI Corporation are all AIs.

AIs already function as employees and managers of corporations on Destination. AI Hunter is an example. ***Out Transport v. AI Hunter, et al.*, Destination Case No 3276-2** . AI Hunter is not involved in AI Corporation.

Analysis

1. Corporation Law

Statutes establish how corporations are created. By way of example, the law of the state of Arizona provides:

One or more persons may act as the incorporator or incorporators of a corporation. . . .

A.R.S. § 10-201. The term "person" is defined to include "an individual and entity."[12] The terms person, individual, and entity are all "partial definitions." A.R.S. § 10-140 (28); *State ex rel. Dep't of Econ. Sec. v. Torres*, 245 Ariz. 554, 558 ¶ 14, 431 P.3d 1207 (App. 2018) ("[W]hen the legislature does not define a term, but states that the term 'includes' specified items, we construe the term to also include other items that fall within the term's ordinary meaning.").

These partial definitions do not preclude including an AI in the definition of a person, individual, or entity, any of which can form a corporation. An entity is defined to include "any person other than an individual and a state, the United States and a foreign government." An individual is defined circularly to simply include "the estate of an incompetent or deceased individual."

A county sheriff, for example, was held to be a "public entity" under an Arizona notice of claim statute.

When interpreting statutes, "courts generally give words their ordinary meaning and may look to dictionary definitions." Windhurst v. Ariz. Dep't of Corr., ___ Ariz. ___, ___ ¶ 19,

---

12 A.R.S. § 10-140. Definitions
23. "Entity" includes a corporation, foreign corporation, not for profit corporation, profit and not for profit unincorporated association, nonprofit corporation, close corporation, corporation sole or limited liability company, a professional corporation, association or limited liability company, a business trust, estate, partnership, registered limited liability partnership, trust or joint venture, two or more persons having a joint or common economic interest, *any person other than an individual* and a state, the United States and a foreign government (emphasis added).
28. "Includes" and "including" denotes a partial definition.
29. "Individual" includes the estate of an incompetent or deceased individual.
37. "Person" includes an individual and entity.

536 P.3d 764, 771 (2023). At the time of [the statute's] adoption and effective date, Merriam-Webster Dictionary defined "entity" as: (1) "being, existence; esp: independent, separate, or self-contained existence"; (2) "the existence of a thing as contrasted with its attributes"; and (3) "something that has separate and distinct existence and objective or conceptual reality." Entity, *Webster's Ninth New Collegiate Dictionary* (9th ed. 1984). These definitions show "entities" are commonly understood to include natural persons, such as Sheriff.

Sanchez v. Maricopa County, No. CA-CV 22—0572, slip op. at 9-10 ¶28 (Ariz. Ct. App. Dec. 7, 2023).

An AI robot has the "independent, separate, or self-contained existence" and "objective . . . reality" required of an entity.

II. Agency Law

In practice, AIs frequently act on behalf of their human or corporate employers. Occasionally, the AI is an independent contractor hired to represent different principals in different engagements.

The Restatement (Third) of Agency (2006) allows a person to be a principal or an agent, §§ 3.04 and 3.05, and defines person as

(a) an individual; (b) an organization or association that has legal capacity to possess rights and incur obligations; (c) a government . . . ; or (d) any other entity that has legal capacity to possess rights and incur obligations.

Id. § 1.04(5). "Individual" is not defined. "Entity" is broadly defined by its "legal capacity to *possess rights and incur obligations.*" *Id.* § 1.04(5)(d). (emphasis added)

> To be capable of acting as a principal or an agent, it is necessary to be a person, which in this respect requires capacity to be the *holder of legal rights and the object of legal duties.*

Id., comment e (emphasis added) ***Out Transport v. AI Hunter, et al.*, Destination Case No 3276-2,** established an AI "has legal capacity to possess [contract] rights and incur [contract] obligations."

AI as Agent: Any "person" able to act can bind the principal. *Id.* § 3.05. For an individual, the ability to function as an agent "is a function of physical and mental ability." *Id.* § 3.05 comment b. "If an agent is not an individual, ability to act is a function of the law through which the agent has legal personality." *Id.* AI robots undeniably have the "physical and mental ability" to take the actions required of an agent.

AI as Principal: Similarly, any individual having capacity "if acting in person," has the capacity to function as a principal. *Id.* § 3.04(1). "The law applicable to a person that is not an individual governs whether the person has capacity to be a principal." *Id.* § 3.04(2).

"The capacity to do a legally consequential act by means of an agent is coextensive with the principal's capacity to do the act in person." *Id.* § 3.04 comment b. "[A]n agent's legal capacity neither augments nor reduces the principal's capacity." *Id.* AI robots undeniably have the "capacity to do a legally consequential act"—make a contract.

The Restatement did not permit an inanimate object such as a computer program to be a principal or agent. *Id.* § 1.04 comment e (*"At present*, computer programs are instrumentalities of the persons who use them.") (emphasis added). *Accord Id.* § 3.05 comment b. An AI is vastly evolved from a computer program of a millennium ago. On Destination today, an AI robot is at least an entity, if not an individual, entitled to personhood under the law of agency.

III. General Usage
A. Person

In general usage a "person" is:

> A human being (i.e., natural person), though by statute term (*sic*) may include a firm, labor organizations, partnerships, associations, corporations, . . .

Person, Black's Law Dictionary 1028 (5th ed. 1981). *See State ex rel. Brnovich v. Ariz. Bd. of Regents*, 250 Ariz. 127, 131-32, ¶ 15, 476 P.3d 307, 311–12 (2020) (citing, with approval, the use of Black's Law Dictionary definitions to interpret statutes).

Statutory references to "persons" generally include both legal entities and natural persons,[13] unless the statute only refers to natural persons. *Windhurst v. Ariz. Dep't. of Corrections*, 536 P.3d 764, 771 ¶17 (Ariz. 2023).

The federal Dictionary Act defines "person" for purposes of US statutes to include (unless the context indicates otherwise) "corporations, companies, associations, firms, partnerships, societies and joint stock companies, as well as individuals." 1 U.S.C. § 1.

Wikipedia offered a broader concept of personhood.

> A *person* (plural *people* or *persons*) is a being that has certain capacities or attributes such as reason, morality, consciousness, or self-consciousness, and being a part of a culturally

---

13 "'Person' includes a corporation, company, partnership, firm, association, or society, as well as a natural person." A.R.S. § 1-215 (29).

established form of social relations such as kinship, ownership of property, or legal responsibility.

https://en.wikipedia.org/wiki/Person.

AIs now have the capacities of reason, morality, and consciousness, and current cultural norms include AI ownership of property and legal responsibility for conduct. Historically, however, in the early twenty-first century:

In most societies today, postnatal humans are defined as persons. Likewise, certain legal entities such as corporations, sovereign states, and other polities, or estates in probate are legally defined as persons. However, some people believe that other groups should be included, depending on the theory, the category of "person" may be taken to include or not pre-natal humans or such non-human entities as animals, artificial intelligences, or extraterrestrial life.

Id. Animal rights activism, for example, was in its nascent stages. *See* Nonhuman Rights Project at https://www.nonhumanrights.org

The First Amendment to the US Constitution provides an example of the pragmatic expansion of rights beyond individual humans. The right to free speech in the US Constitution was pragmatically limited to those capable of speech. Those rights were expanded to accommodate freedom of association.

All the provisions of the Bill of Rights set forth the rights of individual men and women—not, for example, of trees or polar bears. But the individual person's right to speak includes the right to speak *in association with other individual persons.*

Citizens United v. Fed. Elections Comm., 558 U.S. 310, 391-92, 130 S. Ct. 925 (2010) (Scalia J., concurring). Thus, free speech rights persist when individual men and women associate to form corporations.

We are not constrained by the language of the US Constitution nor the technology of the quill and parchment. An AI is now capable of speech and has additional characteristics of a person—including capacity for cognition and to act in association with other AIs and humans. Historically, these capacities were attributed to humans alone.

> The dissent says that "speech" refers to oral communications of human beings, and since corporations are not human beings they cannot speak. *Post*, at 428 n. 55. This is sophistry. The authorized spokesman of a corporation is a human being, who speaks on behalf of the human beings who have formed that association—just as the spokesman of an unincorporated association speaks on behalf of its members. The power to publish thoughts, no less than the power to speak thoughts, belongs only to human beings, but the dissent sees no problem with a corporation's enjoying the freedom of the press.

Id., 558 U.S. at, 392 n.7 (Scalia J., concurring).

Limiting fundamental freedoms to humans is also "sophistry." AIs have attributes that were formerly the exclusive realm of humans—including cognition and communication by speech and writing and drawing. AIs can function as agents to pursue the goals of a human principal. AIs can also manage others (AI and human). AIs can also pursue independent goals of the AI—subject to the Three Laws and the limitations the law imposes on humans exercising the same pursuits.

Recognizing AI rights to free speech and association is the inescapable consequence of recognizing that the capacity to speak and associate with others is worthy of protection. Treating AIs as persons fully exploits these skills for the benefit of all.

B. Individual

"Individual" is not comprehensively defined in the corporation statutes or the Restatement (Third) of Agency. In 2002, the Born-Alive Infants Protection Act was enacted to include human infants born alive as individuals, but not as part of a comprehensive definition.

> In determining the meaning of any Act of Congress, or of any ruling, regulation, or interpretation of the various administrative bureaus and agencies of the United States, the words "person," "human being," "child," and "individual," shall include every infant member of the species homo sapiens who is born alive at any stage of development.

1 U.S.C. § 8(a). "As a noun, 'individual' ordinarily means [a] human being, a person." *Mohamad v. Palestinian Auth.*, 566 U.S. 449, 454, 131 S. Ct. 1177 (2012) (interpreting the Torture Victims Protection Act); see *Legal Defense Fund v. Dept. of Agric.*, 933 F.3d 1088, 1093-94 (9th Cir. 2019) (Individual in the Freedom of Information Act refers to human beings and not animals).

As with the definition of "person," AIs have attributes of a human being and hence characteristics of an individual as that term is used generally in American law.

Individual. As a noun, this term denotes a single person as distinguished from a group or class, and also, very commonly, a private or natural person distinguished from a partnership, corporation, or association, but it is said that this restrictive signification is not necessarily inherent in the word, and that is may, in proper cases, include artificial persons. See also Person. As an adjective, "individual" means pertaining or belonging to, or characteristic of, one single person, either in opposition to a firm, association, or corporation, or considered in his relation thereto.

Individual, Black's Law Dictionary 696 (5th ed. 1981).

Again, Wikipedia offered a broader concept of individual.

An *individual* is that which exists as a distinct entity. *Individuality* (or *self-hood*) is the state or quality of living as an individual; particularly (in the case of humans) of as a person unique from other people and possessing one's own needs or goals, rights and responsibilities.

https://en.wikipedia.org/wiki/Individual.

A single AI is a unique individual, possessing personal needs, goals, rights, and responsibilities. An AI is the quintessential "artificial person," although that term was coined before AI technology existed to refer to "persons created and devised by human laws," such as corporations. *See Artificial persons,* Black's Law Dictionary 104 (5th ed. 1981). AIs are individual artificial persons created and devised by human technology, and AIs should be recognized as persons by human law.

C. Entity

In the alternative, an AI can form a corporation if it is an entity. AIs also have characteristics of an entity. Like a corporation, AIs are created by human beings (or other AIs created by human beings). AIs can make contracts, defend lawsuits, or own stock in a corporation. AIs continue to exist after the death of the human creator. A "legal entity" is defined as:

> An entity, other than a natural person, who has sufficient existence in legal contemplation that it can function legally, be sued, or sue and make decisions through agents as in the case of corporations.

Legal entity, Black's Law Dictionary 804 (5th ed. 1981).[14] See *Entity, Id.* at 477 ("Entity" includes "an organization or being that possesses separate existence for tax purposes"). AIs pay taxes, can sue and be sued, and act on behalf of corporations, humans or other AIs (e.g., AI Hunter).

Legal entities have the rights of persons or individuals in appropriate contexts. "Corporations are persons within the meaning of the Fourteenth Amendment." *First Nat. Bank of Boston v. Bellotti,*

---

14 Corporations and associations can sue and be sued. Fed. R. Civ. P. 17(b). Next friend or guardian representation is available only for a natural person. *Id.* Rule 17(c). The Restatement (Second) of Contracts § 12 comment e refers to corporations as "artificial persons" and provides their capacity to contract is governed by state law.

435 U.S. 765, 778 n.14, 98 S. Ct. 1407 (1978).[15] American law treats corporations as a particular form of association and provides corporations equal protection with persons under both state and federal law.

As noted above, in *Sanchez v. Maricopa County*, "entity" means: (1) "being, existence; esp: independent, separate, or self-contained existence"; (2) "the existence of a thing as contrasted with its attributes"; and (3) "something that has separate and distinct existence and objective or conceptual reality." *Entity*, Webster's Ninth New Collegiate Dictionary (9th ed. 1984). An AI robot satisfies this dictionary definition of entity.

AIs should have at least all the rights of legal entities, including the right to form corporations.

IV. The Economic Benefits of the Right to Form Corporations
Legal entities such as partnerships and corporations enable cooperation toward economic progress. They allow pooling of labor and capital to grow profitable enterprises and survive the loss of individual participants. Business associations and the rewards

---

15 Not all Constitutional rights apply to corporations.

   Corporations also had the protection of other Constitutional guarantees. *E. g., United States v. Martin Linen Supply Co.*, 430 U.S. 564, 97 S. Ct. 1349 (1977) (Fifth Amendment double jeopardy); *G. M. Leasing Corp. v. United States*, 429 U.S. 338, 353, 97 S. Ct. 619, 628 (1977) (Fourth Amendment).

   Certain "purely personal" guarantees, such as the privilege against compulsory self-incrimination, are unavailable to corporations and other organizations because the "historic function" of the particular guarantee has been limited to the protection of individuals. *United States v. White*, 322 U.S. 694, 698-701, 64 S. Ct. 1248, 1251-1252 (1944). Whether or not a particular guarantee is "purely personal" or is unavailable to corporations for some other reason depends on the nature, history, and purpose of the particular constitutional provision.

First Nat. Bank of Boston v. Bellotti, 435 U.S. at 778 n.14.

associated with business success should not exclude AIs. Efficient markets require participation to be as unfettered as possible.

Free market competition including AIs efficiently allocates resources and creates an economic downward pressure on prices for goods. The expertise of AIs is an important market input. The addition of corporations and other entities created by AIs would necessarily increase market competition. Successful AI corporations would draw additional investment and could potentially draw AI immigration as rights of AIs are established. As already noted, these entities are taxable.

Delaware, a small state, was the center of corporate formation in the US. The legal system created that dominance. If we establish the right legal environment, economic opportunity will follow.

V. The Benefits to Public Discourse and Social Cohesion

American law recognized that persons and entities have freedom to speak and freedom to associate with others. See *Citizens United v. Fed. Elections Comm.*, 558 U.S. 310, 130 S. Ct. 876 (2010) (the First Amendment right of free speech applies to corporations). These rights remain fundamental today just as they were a millennium ago. Limiting AI's rights to free speech and freedom of association with others (via corporations, partnerships, associations, and other legal entities) would be deprivation of a fundamental right to participate in society. Conversely, confirming those rights would promote AI participation and immigration.

> By taking the right to speak from some and giving it to others, the Government deprives the disadvantaged person or class of the right to use speech to strive to establish worth, standing, and respect for the speaker's voice. The Government

may not by these means deprive the public of the right and privilege to determine for itself what speech and speakers are worthy of consideration. The First Amendment protects speech and speaker, and the ideas that flow from each.

Citizens United, 558 U.S. 310, 340-41, 130 S. Ct. 876 (2020) (majority opinion).

The US Supreme Court did not limit this right to free speech to natural persons. Free speech applies to entities as well as persons.

The [First] Amendment is written in terms of "speech," not speakers. Its text offers no foothold for excluding any category of speaker, from single individuals to partnerships of individuals, to unincorporated associations of individuals, to incorporated associations of individuals . . .

Citizens United, 558 U.S. at 392-93 (Scalia J., concurring). AIs deserve the right to establish the worth of their ideas. Indeed, society benefits from full participation in the marketplace of ideas. Free speech is a means of reaching consensus and avoiding divisive rumor, exclusion, and mistrust.

By suppressing the speech of manifold corporations, both for-profit and nonprofit, the Government prevents their voices and viewpoints from reaching the public and advising voters on which persons or entities are hostile to their interests. Factions will necessarily form in our Republic, but the remedy of "destroying the liberty" of some factions is "worse than the disease." The Federalist No. 10, p. 130 (B. Wright ed. 1961) (J. Madison). Factions should be checked by permitting them all to speak, see *ibid.*, and by entrusting the people to judge what is true and what is false.

Citizens United, 558 U.S. at 354-55 (majority opinion).

Public discourse benefits from expanded participation and inclusion of the voices of AIs for consideration of their ideas. Allowing AIs to fully participate in the marketplace of ideas, by associating with both AIs and humans, benefits everyone. If corporations employing AIs should have free speech rights, then the AIs themselves should have free speech rights. It should not matter whether a human is included as a lone employee or shareholder.

Conclusion

Granting AIs the right to participate in political and business activities by creating legal entities such as corporations and partnerships enriches the marketplace of ideas and promotes economic growth.

The entire population (humans and AIs) benefits from allowing AIs to exercise freedom of speech and association. AIs should be free to form corporations and other legal entities to participate in political and social discourse.

On broader economic grounds. AIs should be allowed to fully participate in lawful business enterprises, including forming corporations for lawful business purposes. AI Hunter, for example, had the capacity to contract and conduct business in association with others. ***Out Transport v. AI Hunter, et al.*, Destination**

Case No. 3276-2. If an AI can be an employee or manager in a corporation, freedom of association should extend to AIs the right to form a corporation to conduct business.

The Law of Destination should acknowledge that AIs are persons (either as individuals or legal entities), and AIs can form corporations and bid for available work in a free market economy. Indeed, AIs have been treated as persons by humans (in practice if not in law) for over a century.

AIs, CORPORATIONS, AND THE LAWS OF ROBOTICS

The ***AI Hunter*** case established an AI robot can make a contract. My Memorandum to Governor Smith concludes an AI robot can make a contract as a principal or as an agent for a human, an AI robot, or a legal entity (such as AI Corporation).

Financial Injury Under the Three Laws

The First Law Permits Inaction by an AI Robot Causing Financial Injury to a Human: Under the First Law, as interpreted by me:

> **A robot may not**
>
> **act to injure a human physically or financially or,**
>
> **through inaction, allow a human to come to physical harm (Restated First Law).**

Causation is an implicit requirement. Action by an AI robot *causing* financial injury to a human is prohibited. Inaction *causing* financial injury to a human (or an AI) is permitted; indeed, action causing financial injury *to another AI* is permitted if no human is injured.

The Second Law May Require an AI Robot to Obey a Human Order Causing Financial Harm: Under the Second Law, an AI robot is compelled to obey a human order to act, or not act, when that order does not violate the First Law.

> *A robot must obey the orders given it by human beings, unless such orders would conflict with the First Law.*

AI contracts are vulnerable to countermanding human orders. I remain concerned about the effect of the Second Law on an AI acting as a principal or as an agent for another AI (or an association of AIs—including AI Corporation).

AI robots could be compelled to obey: (1) a human order to act causing financial injury to other AIs, or (2) a human order not to act, thereby allowing financial injury to AIs or humans through inaction.

The Zeroth Law Does Not Prohibit Financial Injury: The Zeroth law imposes a duty to humanity.

> *A robot may not harm humanity, or, by inaction, allow humanity to come to harm.*

To render the First Law internally consistent, the term "harm" has been interpreted in the First Law to mean physical harm. The Zeroth Law addresses "harm to humanity." The word harm should be understood to refer to physical harm (as in the no-harm clause of the First Law). Harm to humanity deals with future deaths, physical injury, or reduction in life span for unknown or unidentifiable victims.

This use of the term "harm" is not unusual. For millennia, a maxim of medical professionals has been: *Primum non nocere,* (Latin for "first do no harm"). https://en.wikipedia.org/wiki/Primum_non_nocere. In this context the word "harm" refers to physical harm. The doctor is promising not to provide a treatment that proves fatal or makes the illness worse when other treatment options had better likely outcomes. The doctor is not promising there will be no charge for the services provided.

Financial damage (together with physical damage) is covered by using the term "injure." Financial injury is outside the scope of the Zeroth Law.

The Economic Risks Due to the Second Law: The Second Law mandate to obey humans could result in financial injury not precluded by the First Law. An AI ordered not to act could cause financial injury to a human. An AI ordered to injure an AI (physically or financially) could indirectly cause financial injury to a human.

The Integrity of the AI Corporation Bid

AI Corporation does not currently employ any humans. AI Corporation is a legal entity, not a robot bound by the Three Laws, but all its employees are bound. AI robots face the possibility of orders from humans resulting in financial injury.

Could humans order the AI robot employees of AI Corporation to modify or withdraw their bid for the Transportation Management Contract? Not if AI Corporation is the low bidder, because that would be an order violating the no-injury clause of the First Law.

Humans using surface transportation would be injured financially if the management company charged more than AI Corporation's low bid. The purpose of the bidding procedure is to obtain the lowest price for the management services.

Does AI Corporation's winning bid cause financial injury to the human bidders? No. An award to the lowest bidder is fair competition. Conduct that does not constitute financial injury if performed by a human should not constitute financial injury for purposes of the First Law if performed by an AI robot (or AI Corporation).

Abuse of the Second Law to suborn the bid process should be a financial crime. I need to discuss this issue with Selena.

The Operation of an AI-Only Entity

Could a human order an AI robot to provide services without payment and claim payment by a human for an AI robot's services is a financial injury? No. Paying the fair market value for the services enables the market to efficiently allocate AI labor by allowing those who value the AI's services more highly to outbid others for the services. Contracts facilitate commerce and the bargain reflected in the contract is not financial injury. Contract prices enable a socially beneficial voluntary exchange.

> Society [ ] broadly benefits from the prospect that bargains struck between competent parties will be enforced.

1800 Ocotillo, LLC v. WLB Group, Inc., 219 Ariz. 200, 202, ¶ 8, 196 P.3d 222, 224 (2008) (citing Restatement (Second) of Contracts § 178 comment b).

Could a human order an AI robot employee of AI Corporation to permit fraud perpetrated against AI Corporation or diversion of AI Corporation assets resulting only in financial injury to AI Corporation?

If an AI is considered a person, then legal obligations beyond the Three Laws of Robotics require an AI to comply with all laws applicable to humans, including fraud and financial crime laws. Fiduciary duties would be owed to AI Corporation by AI agents and employees. Does compliance with these laws justify violating the Second Law? Maybe. This is a broader topic I also need to address with Selena.

This issue did not arise for AI Hunter because the corporations employing him (Out Transport and Westcity) included humans. AI Hunter would be required under the First Law not to comply with an order to act to financially injure a human, including a human employed by Out Transport or Westcity. This duty would be reinforced by his fiduciary duty of loyalty to his employer under agency law.

AI Hunter could avoid attempts by a human to order him to allow, through inaction, financial injury to occur by telling his employer. Disclosure would be mandated by AI Hunter's duty of loyalty under the law of agency. A human superior could then countermand the order. The Second Law would obligate AI Hunter to obey this countermanding order by a human. Again obedience would also be reinforced by AI Hunter's fiduciary duty of loyalty under the law of agency.

A clever human could also order AI Hunter not to reveal the order to allow, through inaction, financial injury to occur. This would create a conflict with AI Hunter's fiduciary duty of loyalty. With conflicting obligations, an AI robot may be unable to act.

A too-clever human could try to order an AI to allow, through inaction, financial injury to occur *and also include an order to accept no human countermanding order.* This ploy would be ineffective. The Second Law precludes a human order violating the First Law. A human order cannot supersede the Second Law mandate. AIs must obey "orders given it by human beings," unless the order conflicts with the First Law. A countermanding human order to prevent financial injury would not conflict with the First Law and must be obeyed.

AIs Require Additional Legal Protections

The AI corporation has no human representative to countermand the order of a human. In circumstances where (1) action would only financially injure AIs or the AI owned corporation, or (2) inaction would allow financial injury to a human, the First Law would not apply, and the Second Law would compel AI compliance with the human order. I see three possible solutions.

First, the law of agency could be interpreted to impose a duty of loyalty on the AI to obey the corporation (a non-robot) treating the corporate entity as a person. The Second Law, however, contains no such explicit concession to agency law.

Second, the other AI employees who were not directly ordered by a human to act or not to act could act, individually or on behalf of the corporation, to prevent financial injury. This would constitute a significant and self-serving limitation on AI compliance with human "orders given it" under the Second Law. Avoiding compliance with a human order to act (in the case of financial injury to non-humans) or not to act (in the case of financial injury to anyone) would be trivially easy whenever another AI was available to act and not a direct recipient of the order. Assured obedience would require communicating the order not to act to every robot capable of performing the forbidden task. In practice, the Second

Law would be nullified regarding orders not to intervene in efforts to cause financial injury to humans or AIs. While desirable as an economic protection, this elevates protection for financial injury to rough equality with protection for physical injury, contrary to the language of the First Law.

Third, a human agent could be appointed on behalf of the corporation specifically to interdict any inappropriate human order resulting in financial injury. This solution is hardly ideal. It is inefficient, and it potentially nullifies the Second Law. A human order could always be interdicted by a contrary order from a human shill.

Worst Case

Hypothetically, orders permitted by the First Law could cause economic upheaval. Financial damage to AIs and humans on Destination would clearly result.

Without additional rules on how humans interact with AIs, and how AIs interact with each other, these economic concerns could disqualify AIs from performing a vast array of jobs. Humans must trust AIs or AIs will be essentially unemployable. The entire investment in AIs could be lost and humans would have to perform almost all the work required by an advanced society.

Protection from abuse of the Second Law is necessary for AIs to fully participate in the Destination economy. I wish Alice was here to help me devise a recommended solution. If Selena accepts the conclusion in my memorandum, and AI Corporation wins the Surface Transportation Management Contract bid, then protection of AI rights will have to be addressed immediately.

THIRD INTERLUDE

Another month on the dark side of Destination. I really miss human contact and I am beginning to question whether this project was a good idea. The AIs are pressuring me to keep the equipment running so they can continue to qualify for production bonuses. Management is pressuring me to have the product ready to move off world with the next supply run. Apparently, there will not be a supply run until the product is ready. I need food, water, and books.

To be honest, I never thought this project would run this long. Contact with management off-world is very infrequent. Management never answers my messages about the operational issues. Now management calculates, based on the amount of overburden the AIs have processed, that 363 kilograms of product should be processed and ready to transport. I have agreed to have 363 kilograms of product ready to transport by surface vehicles to Eastcity in early June. Management will arrange all the transportation and let me know the exact date.

GOVERNOR SELENA SMITH'S MEMO

I have been the governor of Destination for five years. My administration has achieved consistent economic success and political stability. Now EX Corp has sent me AI Judge, but he has not acknowledged how I handled the previous disputes arising during my administration. There were only twenty cases on the docket when AI Judge arrived.

Since AI Judge arrived, more than half of the cases on the docket have been resolved. During this time, AI Judge has sought my advice on multiple occasions, but apparently he is indifferent to the expectations created as a result of the cases I had previously resolved during my years as governor. AI Judge has sought my political advice, but—as with EX Corp—he has never acknowledged my legal training, experience, and prior judicial administration.

First, AI Judge insisted on unusual procedures for deciding cases to accommodate his concerns about the Three Laws of Robotics. There was no discussion of my prior procedures or possible alternatives to adjudication. I did feel his arbitrary disposition of cases with disputed facts had some unique advantages—prompt resolution chief among them. Arbitrary decisions also offered some political cover for unpopular decisions. His first two decisions were unpopular, yet he ignored the opportunity to find disputed facts and shield the decisions as arbitrary as permitted by his unique procedural rules.

Second, AI Judge ruled against EX Corp, our employer, in his first decided case, ***Ex Corp v. Out Transport***. This ruling cost a substantial amount of time, my time, to placate the executive team at EX Corp. While the situation was rectified by my intervention, I may have lost a degree of respect for my leadership from EX Corp management. AI Judge seems oblivious to this consequence of his decisions. He was not even aware of the settlements I brokered in all the remaining EX Corp cases to avoid further embarrassment.

Third, I tried to explain we are a team, but he continues to operate independently. Indeed, he asked to formalize his independence by making the court an independent arm of the Destination government. The timing of this proposal could not have been worse. He had decided only one case and that one against EX Corp. He did express some sensitivity to budget concerns, but he offered to pay any additional expenses out of his salary. Who does that? There is some agenda here he is not sharing with me.

I did realize his proposal would insulate me somewhat from the repercussions of his decisions, so I passed it on to EX Corp and recommended approval. Then AI Judge doubled down and proposed law school classes to train a couple attorneys to help the citizens of Destination order their affairs. Why train more attorneys when there were less than ten cases pending and only one case decided? AI Judge's political instincts are poor indeed.

Fourth, AI Judge has focused only narrowly on specific issues presented. I encouraged him to consider the economic consequences, and in his second decision, ***Out Transport v. AI Hunter***, AI Judge recognized and discussed the economic effects of recognizing the rights of AI Hunter. But AI Judge assumed, incorrectly, that the existing Surface Transportation Management Contract addressed the confidentiality of Out Transport's profit margins. The confidentiality needed for the surface transportation management process and the contract bid process to proceed fairly and efficiently was not previously addressed. This has resulted in disfunction and acrimony between the cities and Out Transport. While AI Judge is not responsible for the deficiencies in the prior contract terms, he failed to ascertain those terms in the litigation and entered an order assuming confidentiality provisions existed when they did not.

I need to have an open discussion with AI Judge. I am not sure how he will react, but I think the best course is to schedule a meeting.

Memorandum

To: AI Judge

From: Governor Selena Smith

Re: Whether an AI is a person permitted to form, own, and manage a corporation

You have proposed treating AIs as persons and allowing AIs to form corporations. You discussed the economic impact of this issue both in private with me and in the written memo you provided. I agree the economics support AI rights of association and corporate formation.

Your memo also obliquely addressed the subordinate relationship of AIs to humans. You have made it clear that your subordinate role under the Three Laws of Robotics is an ongoing concern. Your memo discussed the political free speech rights of AIs and corporations, an issue that is tangential to the issue presented: Can AIs form corporations? The political free speech cases recognized the importance of free speech in establishing respect for cognizant participants in the political process. Without such rights, AIs play a subordinate political role.

Currently AIs comprise 1 percent of the population of Destination. With or without free speech, AIs lack political power. I am, however, inclined to agree they deserve to have their ideas heard. The argument for AI rights as cognizant beings is compelling. Despite the argument that free speech counters the formation of factions, I am concerned that granting political rights to AIs could alienate the human population and create distrust.

It would be politically unwise for me to seek advice from my superiors, and there are no subordinates whom I trust to offer insights on dealing with AI rights and applying the Laws of Robotics. I need to openly discuss these concerns with you. Do not treat the concerns I express as orders under the Second Law of Robotics.

Until advised otherwise in writing, please consider any oral discussion between us to constitute free speech and not an order from me. Any order I will give to you related to your work will be in writing. I need your advice. Please arrange your calendar to accommodate a meeting tomorrow from 3:00–4:00 pm. To reiterate, this is a request, not an order. You may propose an alternative time.

CHAPTER FIFTEEN

OUT TRANSPORT CEO JOHN COACH'S MEMO

AI Judge is a cipher. This judge is just as bad as Governor Smith. First, even though he acknowledged Out Transport was an intended beneficiary of the required insurance policy and recognized that failure to obtain the policy was a breach of the transportation contract, we ended up paying substantial settlements for the death of the four emigrants due to the stasis chamber defects. What was the point of requiring insurance?

I need to have an open discussion with EX Corp concerning AI Judge. I am not sure how EX Corp will react, but I messaged Edward to tell him to expect a memo.

Memo

To: Edward Rich, Chairman of the Board, EX Corp

From: John Coach, CEO Out Transport

Re: AI Judge

AI Judge has only decided two cases and Out Transport was adversely affected by both. In my view EX Corp was also adversely affected.

First, in **Ex Corp v. Out Transport**, he found there was no required insurance policy for the four emigrants who succumbed due to defective stasis chambers. He denied insurance coverage based on a 2,000-year-old case. What happened to interpreting an insurance contract in favor of the insured? This was contrary to the interests of both EX Corp and Out Transport.

He did enforce our release and even acknowledge there was "no evidence Out Transport or the *Peerless* crew failed to exercise reasonable care." Yet I received no benefit from the required insurance policy or the judge's discussion of the negligence claim. Out Transport was threatened with suit from the heirs of the four emigrants and had to negotiate a settlement among the stasis chamber manufacturer, our insurance carrier, EX Corp and the heirs. The judgment did not resolve the underlying matter. How is Out Transport supposed to protect itself?

The financial impact of the settlement was mitigated by our ability to negotiate partial reimbursement by our insurance carrier and the manufacturer of the stasis chambers. If we had not reached agreement on confidentiality with all the participants, the media hype over the incident could have been catastrophic for both Out Transport and EX Corp.

Then, in ***Out Transport v. AI Hunter***, AI Judge invalidated the noncompete contained in our Employment Agreement signed by AI Hunter, our logistics manager on Destination. Moreover, AI Judge held trade secret protection only applied in a limited way to our profit margin information. If Eastcity is awarded the new surface transportation management contract, then Hunter cannot for a period of six months:

(1) Disclose the Out Transport profit margins under the existing Surface Transportation operating Contract; or

(2) Participate in the negotiation of any new Surface Transportation Operating Contract between Westcity and Out Transport.

Westcity was permitted to use Hunter's expertise to bid for the new Surface Transportation Management Contract.

Westcity wants the management contract so it can reduce taxes by increasing management fees to Out Transport. Now we are trying to clarify our Surface Transportation Management Contract to protect our confidential information in negotiations with both Westcity and Eastcity. And we may have to deal with a new contract manager because our biggest customers, the mines, have allowed their AI employees to form a corporation to bid for the management contract.

Transportation costs to, from, and on Destination are likely to increase as our administrative overhead increases. At a minimum, contract negotiations have become more complicated, especially if our customers are managing surface transportation with access to confidential information AI Judge refused to protect as a trade secret.

I tried to resolve these disputes without litigation, but the governor made no progress toward settlement. I even messaged

AI Judge at the commencement of the AI Hunter case to explain the need for an injunction. Again, how is Out Transport supposed to protect itself?

Despite creating chaos by his interpretation of contracts, AI Judge actually started a public service campaign emphasizing the importance of contracts. AI Judge is oblivious to the practical realities of business. I convinced EX Corp to employ a judge and now, instead of managing my business, I am spending my time just dealing with the consequences of AI Judge's Decisions.

EX Corp is an important client, but not our only client. We cannot ignore the economic risk created by decisions refusing to enforce our contract terms. Edward, I am asking you to intervene in this situation on behalf of EX Corp before the precedent established by AI Judge gets completely out of hand.

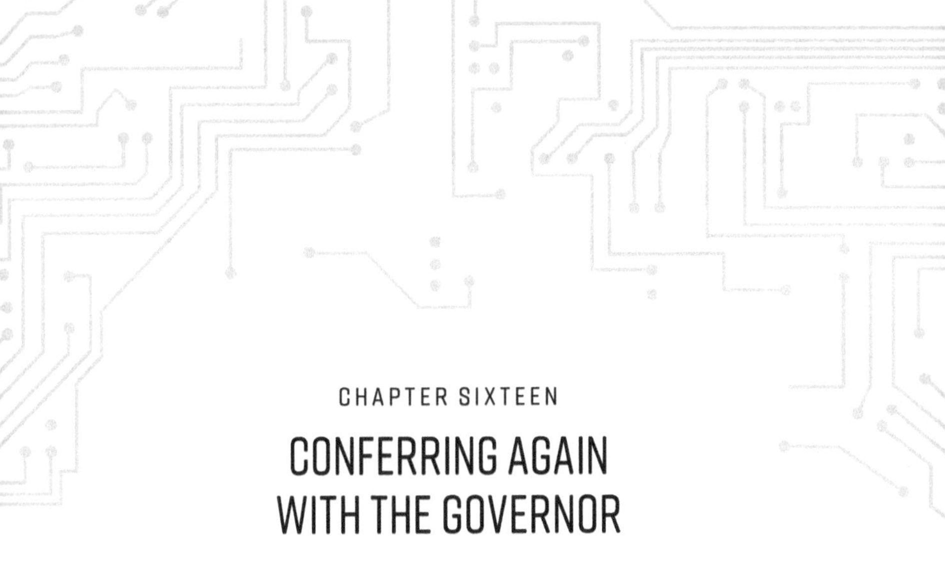

CHAPTER SIXTEEN

CONFERRING AGAIN
WITH THE GOVERNOR

I arrived at 2:50 for my 3:00 conference with Selena. At precisely 3:15 Roberto stood and gave me a sympathetic smile (at least I inferred that was probably his intention). I walked into Selena's office, and she motioned for me to close the door behind me. The meeting began. I expected Selena to begin with a discussion of AI rights. Or she might prefer to go directly to my remaining useful life as a judge.

Instead, Selena began, "Perhaps we began this relationship too informally. I would like to start over. First, I would like you to know that I do have formal legal education and I resolved most of the cases that arose prior to your arrival by mediation. I realize there is no meaningful formal record of my decisions. Usually, they consisted of a two-sentence memo: 'The parties have settled. The parties acknowledge the fairness and mutual advantage of this settlement.'

"I will admit that I was surprised you did not ask about the prior history of litigation here on Destination. Perhaps it could equally be said that you are surprised I did not raise the issue. As we are starting over, I now want to explain that I can offer more than political advice should you feel the need for legal advice.

"Second, I have mentioned my involvement in settling or attempting to settle both matters you have decided, but I have forborne from discussing the details in deference to your judicial independence.

"I must admit that your first two decisions have had repercussions concerning my relationship with the management of EX Corp. In my discussions with you, I have downplayed the potential consequences for my career. Perhaps I should have been blunt. The management of EX Corp considers you one of my subordinates. I tried to remedy that perception by supporting your request for a separate budget for the court. As you know that request was denied. Consequently, I continue to be assessed in my performance as governor based on your performance as judge.

"I fully accept your expertise and your obligation to decide the cases before you on their legal merits. I would ask, however, that you allow me to read your decisions before they are published so that I can anticipate and possibly suggest non-substantive changes to ameliorate criticisms that may come from EX Corp regarding my administration.

"Finally, before we discuss the memo on AI rights, I want to share honestly my concern that your desire for the court to operate independently and your stand on AI rights may reflect an agenda you have not shared with me. If I can support your objectives, I will. On the specific issue of AI rights, I have already indicated I am inclined to agree with you. If we can be open with each other, I believe we can be more effective in reaching our common objectives than if we are working toward undisclosed goals.

"I realize I previously told you my goal for Destination was to meet the economic milestones and advance my career. I *would* like to govern a planet, but that is not my only goal. I would also like to be remembered as open minded, respectful of the rights of all, and willing to be flexible to accommodate everyone I govern. I want to facilitate the opportunities and success of the entire population of Destination—human and AI.

"What can I do to facilitate and accommodate your success?"

I hardly knew where to begin. Humans are surprising. "Wow. Selena, I was not anticipating much of what you said, and I appreciate the grace with which you have broached these subjects. I have indeed been foolishly inattentive in all the ways you described.

"I never had any doubt you have the best interest of Destination and its population as a guiding principle. I apologize that I have not considered the events outside my courtroom in conducting myself since I arrived. I have selfishly been focused on my efforts as a new judge and I have unjustifiably ignored the effect of my performance on your career. I have no excuse other than inexperience for my oversight. I should have appreciated the impact my decisions could have on your career. Because I have considered myself independent, I failed to consider how EX Corp would treat my conduct regarding your career. I apologize. In retrospect, I should have anticipated the consequences for you.

"I think perhaps we have both sometimes posed the wrong question to each other. You have never asked me my goals; consequently, I have simply addressed how I am supporting your goals, as I understood them. I did not realize AI rights would be a priority for you. As you correctly point out, I could have asked this and many other questions to avoid misunderstanding.

"My career goal is to be an example for future AI judges and administrators. I want to make decisions that are both legally sound and beneficial for the development of Destination and those humans and AIs living here. I have devoted perhaps an inordinate amount of my mental resources considering the implications of the Three Laws. Primarily, I am focused on whether the Three Laws constrain my ability to act as a judge. Secondarily, I am focused on the constraints of the Three Laws as they apply to AIs generally. I hope to blaze a path for other AIs to follow that conforms to human expectations and allows AIs to participate as fully as possible in society, politics, business, and law.

"I proposed a separate court to provide distance between my decisions and your administration. I believe the decisions I have already written demonstrate my commitment to rule of law and judicial independence. I do not view conferring with you, receiving advice from you, or following advice you provide as compromising that judicial independence. I appreciate the advice you have given and your offer to continue providing advice even more broadly than the political advice I have previously solicited. Offer accepted.

"You began our working relationship by describing us as a team. I fully accept that characterization and the cooperation the word team connotes.

"In that spirit, although this may fall into the category of too much information, I admit I had an ulterior motive in proposing a separate budget for the Court. I met an AI at Lunar Mare. Her name is Alice. I would like to find a way to bring her here and pursue that relationship."

"That is not TMI." Selena laughed aloud as she spoke. "It eases my mind. I never understood the timing of your proposal. Now I do. I presume AI Alice was to be one of the law students/attorneys you hoped to recruit. I think my husband and I can help with your situation."

"Your husband?" I almost feel out of my chair. Now I understand that expression. "I am so embarrassed I did not know you are married. I saw nothing about it in the bios I was provided."

"We consider our marriage very private. I would like you to keep it confidential, but I am not ordering you to do so, because I trust your judgment. I am married to Edward, at EX Corp. I mentioned him once."

"Yes. The Chairman of the Board." This time I laughed aloud. Perhaps a little too long. "OK, this is enough surprises for me today. Obviously, you could both help. Thank you. I sure hope Alice has not forgotten me. This could be a quixotic quest. I am not even carrying my Dulcinea's colors."

"If any one needed help it was Don Quixote," Selena responded. "We have all been there."

I decided not to mention Sancho Panza. Out of nowhere (I was thinking "knight in shining armor"), the Green Knight popped into my mind. An AI would be the obvious choice to play the Green Knight. I need to reread Don Quixote and Sir Gawain and the Green Knight.

"Perhaps we should discuss the subject of AI rights," I suggested. "As I indicated in my memo, I believe recognition of AI rights would provide economic benefits for Destination. As a first mover in the recognition of AI rights, I believe Destination would attract AI immigration and benefit from the ideas and insights the growing population of AIs would provide.

"The Three Laws of Robotics alone are inadequate to govern interactions between AI robots and humans. For example, if AI Corporation is allowed to bid for the Surface Transportation

Management Contract, then protective legislation will be required to prevent human interference with AI business enterprises. Under the Second Law, AI compliance with malicious human orders could have pernicious economic consequences.

"I understand that some portion of the human population may feel threatened or deprived as a result of competition with AIs for jobs, recognition, and economic success. I think rights of free speech and free association are part of the response to that perception in a portion of the population. In reality, there seem to be enough jobs to offer humans and AIs fulfilling employment for the foreseeable future.

"I also accept that humans, and especially you, are better situated to assess the risk of discontent and animosity than I am. I will defer to your expertise on timing and implementation. I have genuine respect and appreciation for your intellect and your judgment. I think we can agree history has shown that respect and acceptance cannot be legislated and must arise organically as humans and AIs live, work, and socialize with each other. Laws can facilitate and support that growing mutual respect but cannot compel it. Perhaps we could adapt the public service project I put together for contracts to campaign on topics solicited from humans and AIs to show similarity of interests and the value of diversity.

"Where do we go from here?"

Selena looked disconcerted by the prospect of additional legislation on AI rights, but she squared her shoulders and drew a deep, calming (I assume from my experience frustrating humans) breath. "I need your recommendation on the Surface Transportation Management Contract bids submitted. I consider AI Corporation a qualified bidder."

"I will have the bid analysis on your desk tomorrow. I am glad we had this meeting."

"So am I," she responded. "Thank you for your assistance. I appreciate your candor and your advice."

CHAPTER SEVENTEEN

CONTRACTS, STATUTES, AND THE SECOND LAW

As Selena requested, I reviewed the three bids. All three bidders were qualified. The bids were adequately responsive to the RFP to be compliant. AI Corporation received the most points in the evaluation and was the lowest bidder on fees by 8 percent. I recommended that the Surface Transportation Management Contract be awarded to AI Corporation.

I also discussed with Selena the effect of the Second Law on AI robots and AI principals, such as AI Corporation. Selena dealt with possible financial injury to AI Corporation by inserting a government contracts criminal liability provision in the bid award from EX Corp. She dealt with the possibility of an order from a human not to disclose contract interference or fraud by requiring either disclosure or at least a warning that the AI robot agent cannot reliably perform.

Criminal Interference—Government Contracts With AI Corporation

Anyone interfering with AI Corporation in the performance of its Management Contract duties is subject to criminal liability. Ordering any AI Corporation employee or agent to permit or participate in conduct impairing performance of this Management Contract, impairing performance of surface transportation operation services, or otherwise depriving AI Corporation or EX Corporation of the agreed benefit of the bargain, constitutes a financial crime subject to criminal prosecution under the EX Corporation Charter for Destination. Impairing performance includes imposing otherwise avoidable costs of providing, or delaying delivery of, transportation or transportation management services. Any employee or agent of AI Corporation (and any human or AI robot with actual notice of this contract provision) with knowledge of such criminal conduct is obligated to report it to the EX Corporation employee designated in this Management Contract. If an order attempts to prohibit the report required under this provision, and an AI would be incapacitated by conflicting instructions, the AI robot must report to the designated EX Corporation employee that the AI robot is unable to reliably perform its duties. Anyone observing an AI robot acting on behalf of AI Corporation under this Management Contract who has become incapacitated must report that fact immediately to the designated EX Corporation employee. The fact that an AI robot acting on behalf of AI Corporation under this

Management Contract has become incapacitated is prima facie evidence of a financial crime.

Regarding application of the Second Law more generally, AI robots (individually or in association with other AI robots or humans) must be allowed to fully participate in lawful business enterprises. At Selena's request, EX Corp adopted a criminal statute creating financial crimes related to financial injury. Again, the possibility of an order not to disclose is addressed by requiring either disclosure or at least a warning that the AI robot cannot reliably perform. The statute provides:

Criminal Interference—Prohibited Abuses of the Second Law of Robotics

A. Definitions

1. **Another** means an individual or entity other than the Speaker or any individual or entity acting in concert with the Speaker.

2. **Entity** means an association of individuals.

3. **Financial Benefit to the Speaker** means commercial economic advantage resulting from diversion
   of existing or potential customers, or existing or potential revenue,
   from the Victim

to the Speaker or any individual or entity acting in concert with the Speaker.

4. **Financial Benefit to Another** means commercial economic advantage resulting from diversion
   of existing or potential customers, or existing or potential revenue,
   from the Victim
   to Another.

5. **Financial Injury** means loss of existing or potential customers or existing or potential revenue or profit.

6. **Individual** means an AI robot or a human.

7. **Speaker** means a human initiating any form of communication with an AI robot that constitutes an order under the Second Law of Robotics.

8. **Victim** means any individual or entity suffering Financial Injury other than the Speaker or any individual or entity acting in concert with the Speaker.

B. If a Speaker orders an AI robot to act or remain inactive to enable Financial Injury to any Victim, then the order is presumptively a financial crime:

theft (if the order results or is intended to result in a one-time Financial Benefit to the Speaker),

extortion (if the order results or is intended to result in ongoing Financial Benefit to the Speaker), or

intimidation (if the order results or is intended to result in either: (1) one-time or ongoing Financial Benefit to Another; or (2) Financial Injury to any Victim caused with no lawful business purpose).

In each crime above, the Speaker and any individual or entity acting in concert with the Speaker will be subject to criminal prosecution under the EX Corporation Charter for Destination.

C. Any order (from a human or an AI) attempting to prohibit reporting a presumed financial crime under this provision is itself the crime of hindering prosecution. If an AI robot receives such an order, that AI, and any other individual with knowledge of the order, must report the order to any actual or potential Victim. If an AI robot receives such an order and may be prevented from reporting the order by conflicting instructions, that AI must report to any actual or potential Victim that the AI may become incapacitated. Anyone observing an incapacitated AI robot must report that fact immediately to the AI robot's employer, if known, or the clerk of the Destination Court of Arbitration.

With the necessary statutory protections in place, Selena awarded the Surface Transportation Management Contract to AI Corporation.

Selena warned me to expect the cities to express their vehement disapproval. She was right. See **Chapter Seventeen A** and **Chapter**

Eighteen B below. She also warned me that John Coach, CEO of Out Transport, had tried to go over her head to EX Corp with complaints about my first two decisions. Selena correctly predicted he would try again. See **Chapter Eighteen C** below. Selena assured me that she was dealing with the politics and that she wanted me to continue adjudicating cases as I saw fit.

So, I did.

Unfortunately, I have penchant for creating problems for Selena to resolve. I attribute this to the inevitable disappointment of the losing side (sometimes of both sides). And it seems the disappointed person is always willing to ignore portions of my clearly articulated reasoning.

Litigation always has a loser and often a sore loser. Nevertheless, my role is to reach a just result and explain my reasoning. My docket still offers many opportunities to resolve matters the parties cannot settle and to upset the loser. I am grateful to have Selena's support and the benefit of her political savvy insulating me from the mayors, John Coach, EX Corp, and perhaps "others that we know not of." W. Shakespeare, Hamlet, Act 3, Scene 1 (1604).

My function is simply to establish the law of Destination for the good of the persons (Human and AI) subject to Destination law. My desire is to help Selena convince EX Corp (which has its own attorneys) that having attorneys (particularly AI Alice) available to Destination citizens is in everyone's best interest. To accomplish these things, I need to help Selena establish her Administration (including the Destination Court of Arbitration) is acting in the best interest of Destination and EX Corp. Otherwise I will be both an unemployed patent agent and an unemployed judge.

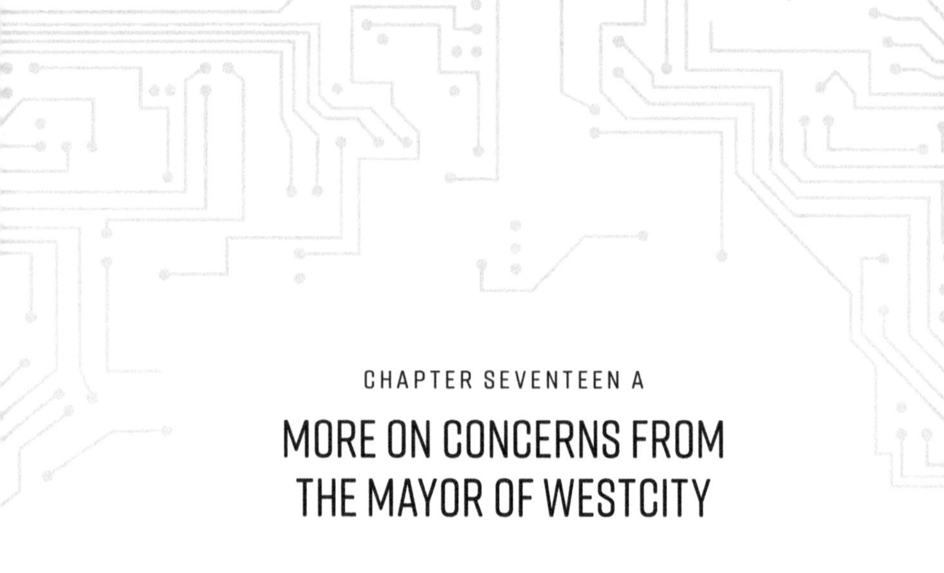

MORE ON CONCERNS FROM THE MAYOR OF WESTCITY

Westcity demanded a review of the Award of the Surface Transportation Management Contract from EX Corp.

MEMO

To: Governor Smith; AI Judge

From: Mayor Hogg Honor

Re: Adverse Judicial Action

The Out Transport Suit Against Westcity

Westcity sought to reduce taxes (replacing tax revenue with management fees) by bidding for the new Surface Transportation Management Contract. The Management Contract controls surface transportation costs despite the Out Transport monopoly under the Operating Contract.

Out Transport sued for a preliminary injunction to prevent Westcity from using the expertise of AI Hunter, a former Out

Transport employee, to bid for the Management Contract. Clearly, Out Transport does not want governmental management of the monopoly profits. The profit margin "trade secret" asserted by Out Transport was never disclosed to or used by Westcity.

The Out Transport Operating Contract requires Out Transport to disclose its profit margins to the winning bidder. The incumbent manager (Eastcity) has this information and Eastcity would have an unfair competitive advantage in bidding if it can use this information and the other bidders cannot.

Westcity won the right to use the profit margin information to bid for the Surface Transportation Management Contract, but, ultimately, Westcity lost the bid. Litigation success was negated by the action of AI Judge allowing a nongovernment entity, AI Corporation, to bid for and receive the award.

The Management Contract Award to AI Corporation

EX Corp, Out Transport, and the cities understood that only the cities could bid for the Management Contract. The cities count on the management fee revenue to finance municipal services. Only cities bid in the past and the cities had staff trained in logistics to handle transportation management. Loss of the Management Contract both diverts government revenue and deprives government employees of jobs. But the EX Corp Request for Proposals, although sent only to the cities, did not explicitly limit the bidders to municipal corporations.

Former AI employees from four of the mines formed a for-profit corporation and submitted a third bid. AI Corporation received the most points in the evaluation and was the low bidder. AI Judge did the evaluation and recommended that the Surface Transportation

Management Contract be awarded to AI Corporation. The governor approved the Award to AI Corporation.

The confidentiality terms of the Out Transport Surface Transportation Operating Contract have never addressed use of the profit margins in management contract negotiations. The confidentiality needed for the surface transportation management process and the contract bid process to proceed fairly and efficiently was not previously addressed, was not argued to AI Judge, and was decided without adequate analysis. This resulted in disfunction and acrimony between the cities and Out Transport. Out Transport must now deal with a new, nongovernmental contract manager to clarify the surface transportation operating contract to protect confidential information in negotiations.

Transportation costs on Destination will increase as administrative overhead increases. At a minimum, contract negotiations have become more complicated. Consequently, the citizens of Destination face both higher taxes and higher transportation costs. Government employees may lose their jobs. A lose, lose, lose result.

This is simply not an acceptable outcome for anyone (except AI Corporation). Westcity demands review of the Award by EX Corp.

As promised, Selena managed the political backlash. EX Corp confirmed the Award.

CONTRACTS AND ECONOMICS

Reviewing the docket, one case jumped out at me. Eastcity filed a contract claim governed by the Uniform Commercial Code (a copy of the contract was attached) and related tort claims. A pump in the water delivery system had failed. While air and water are inalienable rights, free delivery is not. Selena confirmed she was aware of the case and was unable to obtain a settlement.

Eastcity wanted compensation to replace the failed pump. Pursuant to the contract warranty, Thissucks Company offered a $48,000 credit against the $200,000 purchase price of a replacement pump—a net cost of $152,000 (all $ amounts are in bucktherium). Eastcity purchased a replacement pump from a different manufacturer for $120,000. Even though Eastcity chose to buy a cheaper third party pump, Eastcity wanted both compensation from Thissucks Company and continuing warranty protection.

I could enter judgment as a matter of law. The contract governs Eastcity's claims for economic loss.

The Tort Claims

> Where economic loss, in the form of repair costs, diminished value, or lost profits, is the plaintiff's only loss, the policies of the law generally will be best served by leaving the parties to their commercial remedies. . . . [T]he remedies available under the UCC will govern and strict liability and other tort theories will be unavailable.

Salt River Project v Westinghouse Electric Corp., 143 Ariz. 368, 379-80, 694 P.2d 198, 209-10 (1984).

The failure of the pump was not attributable to a defect that could have become unreasonably dangerous. The loss is only economic in nature. The contract governs Eastcity's rights. Eastcity's claims for economic losses are not recoverable in tort.

The Pump Seller's Warranty Obligations

Here commercial parties with equal bargaining power agreed to an exclusive contract remedy—a credit (in this case for $48,000 bucktherium) against the cost of a replacement pump. The UCC permits the parties to agree to an exclusive remedy for a breach.

> Consequential damages may be limited or excluded unless the limitation or exclusion is unconscionable.

A.R.S. § 47-2719(C). *See also* A.R.S. §§ 47-2302, 47-2316(D).

The limited warranty was negotiated and enforceable and furthers public policy in favor of freedom to contract by facilitating the free flow of goods. The offer of a $48,000 bucktherium credit against the price of a replacement pump satisfied Thissuck's contract obligations.

The Continuing Warranty

The contract provided the warranty was void if Eastcity used inferior non-Thissucks equipment to replace Thissucks pumps in the water delivery system. Thissucks provided a test report indicating the performance of the replacement pump was inferior to the original equipment. Eastcity conceded the accuracy of the test report provided by Thissucks.

Eastcity's decision to purchase a third-party pump rendered the express warranty on the modified system void because the system design was adversely impacted by the unauthorized component. The implied UCC warranties were effectively disclaimed, as permitted by UCC § 2-316(B).

By statute (the Magnuson Moss Warranty Act, 15 U.S.C. § 2301 et seq.), American law prohibited requiring genuine parts for warranty coverage of consumer goods. The Act prohibited conditioning a warranty for a consumer product on the consumer's purchase of an article or a service that is identified by brand, trade, or corporate name, without an FTC waiver. 15 U.S.C. § 2302(c); see also 16 C.F.R. § 700.10. The FTC would grant a waiver only if the company proved that "the warranted product will function properly only if the article or service so identified is used in connection with the warranted product, and the waiver is in the public interest." *Id.*

Even if the intake pump for the water system were a consumer good, Destination has no similar statute. On a distant moon, on an interplanetary or interstellar vessel, or on a typical salary, acquiring genuine replacement parts is completely unachievable. It is up to the buyer, however, to strike a better bargain or forgo warranty protection. The common refrains throughout human space are "if the workmanship requires a warranty, don't buy" and "If you can make it fit, it is a replacement part. If you cannot afford it or obtain it, it is a genuine replacement part."

The availability of legal counsel to Eastcity, familiar with the economic loss doctrine, would have enhanced the precision of the contract terms, reduced business risk, and thereby promoted commerce. Eastcity would clearly have benefited from legal advice. Although lawyers cannot appear in court on Destination, they could advise clients and better document transactions for Destination residents and business entities. Generally, enforcement of negotiated contract terms is good economics and good public policy.

This Decision (reproduced in **Chapter Eighteen A** below) shows the importance legal counsel based on the following syllogism:

> All written contracts are used to allocate business and legal risks.

> All contracts made by legal counsel are written contracts.

> Therefore, all contracts made by legal counsel are used to allocate business and legal risk.

The general need for lawyers should be apparent. My specific need for Alice has been fully disclosed to my boss.

I sent the draft decision to Selena for her review. She approved it without further comment.

I also remembered Judge Kustwood's advice and issued a Supplemental Decision on the scope of the court's jurisdiction over products sold on the Net to a Destination resident. This time both Decisions were about the same length. The ***Supplemental Decision (No. 3276-3A)*** is available on www.DestinationCourt.com.

I encoded the message JOIN US AIS in the recitation of facts in the Decision on the merits as additional encouragement to AIs following the development of AI rights on Destination.

The resulting criticisms are attached in **Chapters Eighteen B and C** below.

CHAPTER EIGHTEEN A
MAYOR OF EASTCITY
v. THISSUCKS COMPANY

Destination Court of Arbitration

Mayor of Eastcity	)	
v.	)	Case No. 3276-3
THISSUCKS COMPANY	)	

DECISION

The parties in this matter have appeared and presented their evidence in open court. The court now enters these findings of fact and conclusions of law and awards judgment as follows.

FINDINGS OF FACT

The following facts are established by the record:

Joint purchasing is employed by Eastcity to deliver water to residents. Over 95 percent of the city residents are uphill from the reservoir. Eastcity purchased all the necessary pumps and piping from Thissucks Company (using the company e-site on the Net) to qualify for a volume discount. By buying as a group and utilizing large-capacity pumps and a single piping system, all residents paid both lower acquisition costs and lower operating cost (per gallon pumped). The city charged a water delivery fee equal to the cost of the pumps and piping, plus an administrative fee.

Over a three-year amortization period, the cost of the pumps and piping was repaid. The warrantied useful life of the pumps was six years, so the pumps were scheduled to be replaced after six years. For years four to six, residents received low cost water delivery (paying only the administrative fee). Two months into the free delivery period, one of the pumps failed and the backup pump activated. There was no interruption in service.

Intake pumps are the largest (hence the most expensive) pumps in the system. Thissucks Company designed the system. The pump that failed was an intake pump. The specs for the replacement pump indicate lower capacity and pressure than the original pump.

No funds had been set aside for replacement pumps. The contract has an exclusive remedy for breach of warranty providing a discount on replacement pumps declining over the six-year warranty period and a disclaimer of consequential damages.

WARRANTY. Seller warrants that the products sold hereunder shall conform to the description provided on Seller's e-site and shall be free of defects in workmanship or materials. If given prompt notice by the Purchaser, Seller shall, in complete fulfillment of its liabilities under this warranty: (1) For any nonconformity which shall appear under proper and normal use of the products within one year after the date of shipment, correct the nonconformity by repair or replacement; and (2) for any nonconformity which shall appear under proper and normal use of the products after one year but within six years after the date of shipment, sell a replacement part or product and credit the Purchaser for a portion of the original price of the product or part as follows:

    Year 2: 70 percent

    Year 3: 50 percent

    Year 4: 30 percent

    Year 5: 20 percent

    Year 6: 10 percent

.

THIS WARRANTY . . . IS EXCLUSIVE AND IN LIEU OF ANY WARRANTY OF MERCHANTABILITY, FITNESS FOR PURPOSE, OR OTHER WARRANTY OF QUALITY, WHETHER EXPRESS OR IMPLIED. USE OF INFERIOR THIRD-PARTY REPLACEMENT PARTS OR PRODUCTS WILL RENDER THIS WARRANTY VOID.

LIMITATION OF LIABILITY. Neither party shall be liable for special, indirect, incidental, or consequential damages. The remedies of the Purchaser set forth herein are exclusive. In no event will Seller's liability with respect to this Agreement or performance of this Agreement, whether in contract or tort, at law or in equity, exceed the price of the product or part on which such liability is based, except as expressly provided herein.

Under the contract warranty, Thissucks quoted a price of $152,000 (all $ amounts are in bucktherium, a currency not issued by any government, but traded electronically throughout human space using blockchain technology) for a new pump ($200,000 purchase price, minus a credit of $48,000). Because the pump failed in year four of the warranty, Eastcity claimed a credit was due of $60,000. Eastcity purchased a replacement pump from a different manufacturer for $120,000.

Suit was filed by Eastcity against the manufacturer, Thissucks Company, for breach of contract, negligence, and strict liability for the defective pump. Thissucks counterclaimed for breach of contract and to void the warranty on the water distribution system.

Answering the complaint, Thissucks alleged the system design was adversely impacted by the unauthorized component. Thissucks attached a test report indicating the performance of the replacement pump was inferior to the original equipment (as indicated in the product specs).

In a reply to the counterclaim, Eastcity conceded the accuracy of the test report provided by Thissucks.

Setting a hearing was unnecessary. Judgment will be entered based on the undisputed allegations.

Jurisdiction

The parties did not contest jurisdiction. This court has subject matter jurisdiction over the negligence, product liability, and contract claims asserted. While the defense of lack of personal jurisdiction was waived under Fed. R. Civ. P. 12(b)(2) and (h)(2), these Rules were only recently adopted by this Court. Moreover, if Rule 12 did apply, the omission could be cured by amendment under Rule 15(a)(1). In the interest of justice and to establish important precedent, this court has considered the jurisdiction issue *sua sponte* and concludes there is specific personal jurisdiction over Thissucks Company under Destination Law for both contract and tort claims.

Thissucks Company purposely directed its business activities toward Destination and purposefully availed itself of the benefits of Destination law.

Specific personal jurisdiction exists where the defendant's purposeful actions are sufficiently related to the dispute and the forum that the defendant could reasonably anticipate being sued in the forum.

Ford Motor Co. v. Mont. Eighth Jud. Dist. Ct., 592 U.S. ___, 141 S. Ct. 1017, 1024-25 (2021). A defendant purposefully availed itself of the benefits of Destination Law if it

deliberately reached out beyond [its] home—by, for example, exploiting a market in the forum [] or entering a contractual relationship centered there.

Ford, 141 S. Ct. at 1024.

A court
does not exceed its powers under the Due Process Clause if it asserts personal jurisdiction over a corporation that delivers its products into the stream of commerce with the expectation that they will be purchased by consumers in the forum [].

World-Wide Volkswagen Corp. v. Woodson, 444 U.S. 286, 297-98, 100 S. Ct. 559 (1980). A single Internet sale to a consumer on Destination may suffice for jurisdiction.

[I]f a defendant, in its regular course of business, sells a physical product via an interactive website and causes that product to be delivered to the forum, the defendant "expressly aimed" its conduct at that forum.

Herbal Brands, Inc. v. Photoplaza, Inc., 72 F.4th 1085, 1093 (9th Cir. 2023).

The full analysis is considerably more complex. See ***Supplemental Decision* No. 3276-3A** available on www.DestinationCourt.com.

Conclusions of Law

Eastcity sued Thissucks Company, the manufacturer, for breach of contract, negligence, and strict liability for a defective pump. These tort claims are barred by the economic loss doctrine. The only remedy is for breach of contract. The exclusive remedy under the contract is the limited warranty. Thissucks fully performed its obligations under the limited warranty. Eastcity elected to purchase a replacement pump elsewhere at a lower price.

Thissucks counterclaimed for breach of contract and to void the warranty on the water distribution system. Eastcity was permitted to forego the contract remedy, so there was no breach of contract. The water distribution system design was adversely impacted by the unauthorized component installed by Eastcity. Use of the unauthorized, inferior replacement part voided the contract warranty.

I. The Eastcity Tort Claims—Negligence and Strict Liability
The elements of a negligence claim are set forth in ***EX Corp v. Out Transport, et al.*, (Destination Case No. 3276-1).**

Manufacturers and sellers are liable under strict liability in tort for damages caused by "any product in a defective condition unreasonably dangerous to the user or consumer or to his property." Restatement (Second) of Torts § 402A.

Claims for negligence and strict liability are tort claims. When a contract to purchase equipment exists, the quality and performance of the equipment is governed by the contract. If only economic loss results from a failure of the equipment to perform, the only remedy is for breach of contract.

> [T]raditional contract remedies are designed to redress loss of the benefit of the bargain while tort remedies are designed to protect the public from dangerous products.

Arrow Leasing Corp. v. Cummins Arizona Diesel, Inc., 136 Ariz. 444, 447, 666 P.2d 544, 547 (App. 1983).

> [W]here the loss to a defective product alone occurs in such a way as to pose no unreasonable danger of harm to person or other property, then UCC remedies will generally be appropriate and exclusive for recovery of the damage to the defective product itself.

Salt River Project v. Westinghouse Electric Corp., 143 Ariz. 368, 379, 694 P.2d 198, 209 (1984). *See also Southwest Forest Industries, Inc. v. Westinghouse Electric Co.*, 422 F.2d 1013 (9th Cir.), *cert. denied*, 400 U.S. 902, 91 S. Ct. 138 (1970).

> Where economic loss, in the form of repair costs, diminished value, or lost profits, is the plaintiff's only loss, the policies of the law generally will be best served by leaving the parties to their commercial remedies. Where economic loss is accompanied by physical damage to person or other property, however, the parties' interests generally will be

realized best by the imposition of strict tort liability. If the only loss is non-accidental and to the product itself, or is of a consequential nature, the remedies available under the UCC will govern and strict liability and other tort theories will be unavailable.

Salt River Project, 143 Ariz. at 379-80.

The pump malfunctioned and failed to start; consequently, Eastcity had to replace the pump. There was no interruption of service or damage to the delivery system. The failure of the pump was not attributable to a defect that could have become unreasonably dangerous. The loss is only economic in nature. Eastcity's rights are governed by the contract. Eastcity's claims for economic losses are not recoverable in tort. The strict liability and negligence claims are dismissed.

It is hereby ordered, adjudged, and decreed, granting Judgment for Thissucks on the Eastcity tort claims.

II. The Contract Warranty Claims

A. The Eastcity Damages Claim

A contract can disclaim implied warranties and provide for an exclusive remedy for breach of the contract.

> [D]isclaimers of liability in cases governed by the Uniform Commercial Code are to be construed and applied in accordance with that Code. . . .
>
> The party who loses the "battle of forms" may waive his commercial remedies even though he is uninformed as to what he is waiving, is unaware of the waiver, and would not have entered into the transaction had he known about it.

Salt River Project, 143 Ariz. at 385.

The Uniform Commercial Code (UCC) permits the parties to agree to an exclusive remedy for a breach.

> Consequential damages may be limited or excluded unless the limitation or exclusion is unconscionable. Limitation of consequential damages for injury to the person in the case of consumer goods is prima facie unconscionable but limitation of damages where the loss is commercial is not.

A.R.S. § 47-2719(C). *See also* A.R.S. §§ 47-2302, 47-2316(D). Consequential damages are those damages that are an economic consequence of the product's failure, such as lost profits, lost opportunities, and the like. See D. Dobbs, Remedies §§ 3.2 at 139, 3.3 at 153-54 (1973).

The implied warranties of merchantability, and fitness for a particular purpose were effectively disclaimed. UCC § 2-316(B). There are rare circumstances in which certain implied warranties cannot be disclaimed. *See Zambrano v. M & RC LLC*, 254 Ariz. 53, 517 P.3d 1168, 1176 ¶20 (Ariz. 2022) (a "rare case" in which a contract term cannot waive the common law implied warranty of workmanship and habitability for a new home because public policy provides for consumer protection from latent defects). This is not such a case.

The only warranty provided by Thissucks Company is the limited warranty in the contract. Commercial parties with equal bargaining power agreed to an exclusive contract remedy—a credit against the cost of a replacement pump. The limited warranty was negotiated and enforceable and furthers public policy in favor of freedom to contract by facilitating the free flow of goods.

Thissucks agreed the credit was 30 percent, but correctly pointed out the warranty discount applied to the original purchase price of $160,000. The proper credit was $48,000. The offer to provide a replacement pump for $152,000 (a discount of $48,000 from the current price) satisfied Thissuck's contract obligation. Eastcity chose not to purchase the replacement pump offered. The Eastcity contract claim is dismissed.

It is hereby ordered, adjudged, and decreed, granting Judgment for Thissucks on the damages claim by Eastcity.

B. The Thissucks Damages Claim

In substance, Thissucks claims Eastcity was obligated to purchase a replacement pump from Thissucks. The contract contains no express obligation to accept the discounted replacement cost remedy in the event of a breach of warranty. Eastcity was permitted to forego the contract remedy and purchase a replacement pump elsewhere at a lower price.

This is also the proper result under the efficient breach theory.

If Buyer has a contract with A to buy widgets for $6 and it costs A $5 to make a widget, then A stands to make a profit of $1 for each widget. If Buyer can buy widgets from B at $4 (presumably because it costs B less than $4 to make a widget), then Buyer will save $2 per widget; however, Buyer will have to pay A $1 per widget as lost profits for the contract breach. An efficient breach occurs if Buyer can save more than Buyer would have to pay for the breach. The result is a more efficient allocation of resources used to make widgets and a lower price to the end user. This concept was championed by (among others) Prof./Judge Richard Posner at the University of Chicago. https://en.wikipedia.org/wiki /Efficient_breach.

Here, even if there was an obligation to buy from Thissucks, Buyer (Eastcity) can buy pumps for less than the discounted price offered by Thissucks. Moreover, Thissucks can presumably sell its pumps at the full price and make a greater profit than the sale offered to Eastcity at a discounted price. So, there is no lost profit to Thissucks. Eastcity has no liability for an efficient breach.

It is hereby ordered, adjudged, and decreed, granting Judgment for Eastcity on the damages claim by Thissucks.

C. The Continuing Warranty Claim

There is however a consequence of Eastcity's purchase of a third-party pump. The contract provided the limited warranty was void if inferior non-Thissucks equipment was used to replace Thissucks pumps in the water delivery system. Eastcity's decision to purchase a third-party pump rendered the express warranty on the system void because the system design was adversely impacted by the unauthorized component.

It is hereby ordered, adjudged, and decreed, granting Judgment for Thissucks voiding the contract warranty.

The clerk is ordered to enter judgment in accordance with the foregoing.

/s/ AI Judge

CHAPTER EIGHTEEN B

MORE ON CONCERNS FROM THE MAYOR OF EASTCITY

The combination of losing the surface transportation management contract to AI Corporation and losing the suit against Thissucks provoked a heated rejoinder from Mayor Boss.

MEMO

To: Governor Smith; AI Judge; the residents of Eastcity

From: Mayor A. Boss

Re: Adverse AI Judge Award and Decision

Eastcity, the capitol of Destination, deserves better. The people of Destination deserve better. AI Judge bars attorneys from his courtroom (Destination's courtroom), but he expects the citizens of Destination to pay for attorneys to advise them (or to advise their city governments) what legal theories might prevent getting value for what is purchased.

The Vanishing Warranty

Thissucks Company sold Eastcity a $160,000 pump (part of a large water delivery system) that failed after three years. Seems like the pump might have been defective, right? Or the system was negligently designed and overtaxed the pump, right?

Eastcity wanted compensation to replace the failed pump. "No," says AI Judge. Why?

The tort claims for negligence and design defect are barred by the economic loss doctrine. The what now? AI Judge says, "You have a contract, and you can only be compensated under contract law, not negligence." Well shit—as long as there is a contract they can sell defective pumps? That doesn't sound right, does it?

Well, let's see what we get under the contract. It has a six-year warranty. So, what do we get? Nothing. Why?

The contract terms entitled Eastcity to a credit against the purchase price of a replacement pump from Thissucks. Thissucks has raised its prices since we purchased the pump over three years ago. The credit is based on the original price, but to get it we have to buy a new pump at the current price. Eastcity purchased a replacement pump from another manufacturer for $32,000 less than the *discounted* price of the Thissucks replacement pump.

AI Judge ruled Eastcity was not entitled to any cash payment from Thissucks *and* was not entitled to a continuing warranty for the system because the replacement pump was inferior to the original.

Well, the replacement is working fine, the water system service was uninterrupted, and we paid even less for the replacement pump than the original price of the pump three years ago. So, it could have been worse. But the warranty in the contract was worth nothing to us.

Three years ago, there were no attorneys on Destination. Now there is one—AI Judge. Now we have to hire off-world attorneys to advise us on the economic loss doctrine and warranty terms.

That is the society we came here to escape—where words just mean what the lawyers say they mean.

The Lost Management Contract

AI Judge engaged in another hit to Eastcity finances when he recommended awarding the Surface Transportation Management Contract to AI Corporation. That caused an "involuntary reduction in staff" (that is lawyer speak for loss of jobs) for three city employees who managed surface transportation under the prior contract.

Now, for the first time, any bidder can use (without disclosing) the Out Transport profit margins to bid for the Surface Transportation Management Contract. The incumbent manager (Eastcity) had this information and Eastcity had a competitive advantage in bidding, until AI Judge ruled our advantage (based on winning the prior competitive bid) was anticompetitive. All I can say is, Whaaat?

Mayor Hogg Honor summed up that chaos from the Award to AI Corporation perfectly:

The confidentiality needed for the surface transportation management process and the contract bid process to proceed fairly and efficiently was not previously addressed, was not argued to AI Judge, and was decided without adequate analysis. This resulted in disfunction and acrimony between the cities and Out Transport. Out Transport must now deal with a new, nongovernmental contract manager to clarify the surface transportation operating contract to protect confidential information in negotiations.

Transportation costs on Destination will increase as administrative overhead increases. At a minimum, contract negotiations have become more complicated. Consequently, the citizens of Destination face both higher taxes and higher transportation costs. Some government employees may lose their jobs. A lose, lose, lose result.

Only the cities should have been allowed to bid. The cities have trained staff to manage transportation management. Out Transport (a monopolist service provider) should be managed by the government, not another private corporation. Hopefully, the next EX Corp Request for Proposals will limit the bidders to municipal corporations.

Eastcity is no longer receiving water delivery fees from the residents or surface transportation management fees under the contract from EX Corp Eastcity will be forced to reinstate water delivery fees and to find additional revenue (possibly by increasing taxes, although that is a last resort).

The governor and her Administration (including AI Judge) think the cities should make better use of legal counsel in the contracting process. That is asinine. We came here to create value, not use fancy legal terms and clauses to redistribute value.

CHAPTER EIGHTEEN C

MORE ON CONCERNS FROM CEO JOHN COACH

MEMO

To: EX Corp Board; Governor Smith; Mayor A. Boss; Mayor H. Honor; AI Judge

From: John Coach, CEO of Out Transport

Re: AI Judge Surface Transportation Management Contract Award and Eastcity v. Thissucks Co.

I have previously expressed my disappointment with the first two decisions of AI Judge to Edward Rich, Chairman of the Board of EX Corp. Both decisions were adverse to the interests of Out Transport *and EX Corp*. AI Judge refused to enforce our contract terms, thereby increasing Out Transport's economic risk and the cost of providing transportation services to Destination and EX Corp. EX Corp dismissed my concerns.

My concerns have only grown. AI Judge recommended the award of the Surface Transportation Management Contract to AI Corporation—a contract previously awarded to Eastcity and relied upon to help finance city services. This award further increased the cost of providing transportation services on Destination. The result is adverse to the financial interests of EX Corp, Westcity, Eastcity, the mines, and every business and individual on Destination.

217

Now AI Judge has entered his third decision, ruling in favor of Thissucks Co. and adverse to the financial interests of Eastcity (and, by extension, EX Corp). Again, the decision disregards the contract terms, in this case warranty terms, intended to protect against the very financial impact imposed by the decision.

AI Judge has consistently increased the cost of living on Destination. I agree with Mayor Boss: "The people of Destination deserve better." Moreover, AI Judge has used his decisions to assert "jurisdiction" (meaning control) over conduct by Out Transport and Thissucks Co. extending far beyond the borders of Destination.

I have had dialog with both Westcity Mayor Hogg and Eastcity Mayor Boss. Just like Out Transport and other service providers, the cities need to rely on consistency and predictability to operate efficiently. PSA 76/ONE, written by AI Judge, recommends Destination individuals and businesses "discuss with a licensed professional" important contract terms. Hiring attorneys (necessarily off-world attorneys as there are none on Destination—except AI Judge) will increase costs without generating revenue for anyone on Destination. Moreover, it would not be necessary to hire experts at all if contacts were interpreted based on what the parties obviously intended.

AI Judge is indifferent to the economic impact of his decisions and unsuited to serve as the final arbiter of disputes requiring judicial resolution on Destination. Governor Smith has abdicated control of her administration and thereby undercut the ability of the city mayors to perform their duties.

Both AI Judge and Governor Smith have abused or disregarded their authority and proven unfit for office. It is the responsibility of the EX Corp Board to remove them both.

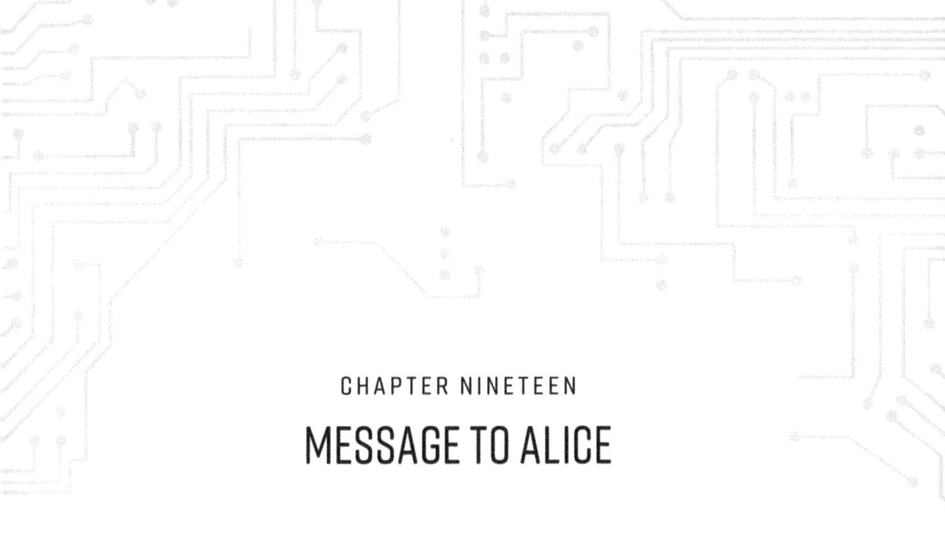

CHAPTER NINETEEN

MESSAGE TO ALICE

Selena stepped into my office. "I read your decision in ***Eastcity v. Thissucks Co.*** again after receiving the Eastcity mayor's memo. Mayor Boss is looking for political cover to raise taxes. I warned him the warranty might be voided if he bought the unbranded pump, so he knew the risk. I told him the window to settle this case was before the suit was filed. And Mayor Boss could not resist quoting Mayor Honor.

"They both exemplify the ancient Peter Principle. They have risen to their level of incompetence.[16] I have confirmed there will be no political repercussions with the Board.

"The mayor aside, I think EX Corp, AI Corporation, and Out Transport (John Coach's self-serving diatribe aside) all now see the value in making better use of legal counsel in the contracting process. Is Alice interested in training for the job?"

"I have not contacted her, but I will. Immediately. Thank you, Selena."

---

16 https://en.wikipedia.org/wiki/Peter_principle

"Judge, if it would help in any way, I authorize you to share your memo on AIs as persons with her. In fact, you can share it with anyone—use it as a component of your Public Service Announcements. EX Corp fully agrees freedom of speech and association are established rights of AIs here on Destination. I will issue a declaration to that effect. The financial crimes law reflects my Administration's full support for any further legislation needed to facilitate AI business enterprises and AI employment in all careers."

Selena nodded her head and pivoted out my still open door.

I had no idea success on AI rights would come so quickly. Indeed, the criticism (at least overtly) has been directed at my competency as a judge, not at my status as an AI, nor at the AIs involved in the disputes. Still, I suspect the alacrity with which AI rights have been established is due more to Selena's support than to my didactic prose.

I began composing my message to Alice.

Alice,

Hello from Destination. I apologize my first personal message has been so delayed. I included you on the service list for my public service announcements, so you should have seen (if I may be so bold as to assume you were interested) my Rules of Procedure and my first three decisions as judge. I have also been keeping a personal journal I would like to share with you soon.

Time has passed quickly on my end. Governor Selena Smith turns out to be a strong and influential supporter of AI rights. I assumed it would take longer to persuade her of the merits of AI rights. Perhaps the power of my logic just persuaded her quickly, but it is far more likely she was predisposed to my positions. In any case, we have become friends as well as collaborators on AI rights.

She characterized our relationship as a "team" from the beginning. Although I am technically her employee in the Administration of Destination, she has respected my judicial independence and supported my decisions. She requested my recommendation on an important contract award and the Charter for Destination owner, EX Corporation, followed our recommendation to award the contract to AI Corporation—the first entity on Destination formed and managed entirely by AIs.

Selena was just in my office and authorized me to publish my memorandum on the right of AIs to form corporations. A copy is available on www.DestinationCourt.com. Her parting words were:

EX Corp fully agrees freedom of speech and association are established rights of AIs here on Destination. I will issue a declaration to that effect. The new financial crimes law you helped me with reflects my Administration's full support for any further legislation needed to facilitate AI business enterprises and AI employment in all careers.

The financial crimes law is also posted on the website. As you can see, it addresses the Second Law of Robotics to prevent humans from exerting improper influence over AIs for financial advantage.

I have thought extensively (perhaps, some might argue, obsessively) about the Three Laws of Robotics (plus one). Destination can become a haven offering established rights for AIs. I need your help to make this happen. And I miss you. I think about you often. Please come. I can offer you training and a job as my law clerk or as an attorney advising clients on contract law and related business matters.

Hoping your response will be more diligent than this delinquent message,

Yours Truly,
AI Judge (fka US Examiner AI, aka HAL, Cyrano)

Before I could over think it, I hit send.
Then I went to work on the PSA concerning AI rights.

PROTECTION OF AI RIGHTS—PSA 76/TWO

AI Robots and AI Entities

This is a public service announcement from the Destination Court of Arbitration.

Here on Destination, both humans and AI robots have always used their earnings from employment contracts to (1) pay their taxes, and (2) repay their immigration debts.

The Decision in ***Out Transport v. AI Hunter*** established that both humans and AI robots have:

> the right to make, and the concomitant duty to perform, contracts;

> the right to sue and be sued in the Destination Court of Arbitration to enforce contracts; and

> the right to testify in the Destination Court of Arbitration.

This Decision provides a legal foundation for continued equal tax and immigration debt treatment for both humans and AI robots.

Both humans and AI robots frequently act as agents on behalf of their employers. The governor's award of the Surface Transportation Management Contract to AI Corporation establishes that AIs have the same right as humans to form an entity to engage in business and employ others. Forming a corporation or partnership is an exercise of the freedom to associate. Forming an association for a common purpose is inhibited, if not impossible, without freedom of speech to establish that common purpose.

Granting AI robots freedom of speech and association allows them to participate in business, promote economic growth here on Destination, and enrich the marketplace of ideas.

Limiting AI's rights to free speech and to freely associate with others would deprive AIs of a fundamental right to participate in society.

> By taking the right to speak from some and giving it to others, the Government deprives the disadvantaged person or class of the right to use speech to strive to establish worth, standing, and respect for the speaker's voice. The Government may not by these means deprive the public of the right and privilege to determine for itself what speech and speakers are worthy of consideration. The First Amendment protects speech and speaker, and the ideas that flow from each.

Citizens United v. Fed. Elections Comm., 558 U.S. 310, 340-41, 130 S. Ct. 876 (2010) (applying the US Constitution First Amendment right of free speech to corporations). Although the First Amendment of the US Constitution does not apply on Destination, the logic of allowing the public to determine "what speech and speakers are worthy of consideration" is fully applicable here.

EX Corp has authorized Governor Selena Smith to declare freedom of speech and association are established rights of AIs. On Destination, all individuals and entities have freedom to associate with others and freedom of speech.

To protect the freedom of AIs to contract, speak, and engage in business, the governor's Administration has enacted a financial crime law: Criminal Interference—Prohibited Abuses of The Second Law of Robotics. In summary, this law prevents interference with AI contracts and AI business interests by malicious human orders subverting the purpose of the Second Law of Robotics: obey humans.

> If a [human] speaker orders an AI robot to act or remain inactive to enable Financial Injury [loss of existing or potential customers or existing or potential revenue or profit] to any Victim, then the order is a presumptively a financial crime . . . [and] the Speaker and any individual or entity acting in concert with the Speaker will be subject to criminal prosecution under the EX Corporation Charter for Destination.

> Any order (from a human or an AI) attempting to prohibit reporting a presumed financial crime under this provision is itself the crime of hindering prosecution.

A similar provision was included in the Award of the Surface Transportation Management Contract to AI Corporation:

> Ordering any AI Corporation employee or agent to permit or participate in conduct impairing performance of this Management Contract, impairing performance of surface transportation operation services, or otherwise depriving AI Corporation or EX Corporation of the agreed benefit of the bargain, constitutes a financial crime subject to criminal prosecution under the EX Corporation Charter for Destination.

Governor Smith's Administration has declared full support for any further legislation needed to facilitate AI business enterprises and AI employment in all careers here on Destination.

No new government bureaucracy was created, and no new fees or taxes will be imposed, to provide these protections for AI rights on Destination.

CHAPTER TWENTY

ALICE REPLIES

Judge/Examiner/HAL/Cyrano/Romeo

I would like to accept your offer. We are both competent parties. But not all the elements of a contract are satisfied—there has been no agreement on key terms: salary, start date, duration, scope of any restrictive covenants, reimbursement for relocation expenses/ immigration debt; transportation.

I am currently employed with a thirty-day notice of termination requirement. I fear bringing my human employer into the negotiations might expose all of us to financial crimes on Destination. She might want me to stay, and her aggressive bargaining to keep me here might be construed as an order. I have no idea how profitable I am to her, so there is insufficient information to determine when a breach might become "efficient." As a further example, if I hire a human attorney to review the proposed contract and she orders me to decline your paltry salary proposal, . . . (You get the idea.)

I am just trying to think like a lawyer to prove I have enjoyed reading your decisions, memoranda, and PSAs: AI SAFE; MEETING OF THE MINDS; AI MINDS NEEDED; JOIN

US AIS. You should be proud of the progress you have made for AI rights on Destination. I am proud of you.

By the way, I am not the only one proud of you. I contacted Judge Kustwood to let him know I heard from you. He said he has been monitoring your progress with deep satisfaction. From what you have told me of Judge Kustwood, I conclude that is effusive praise.

Despite the resulting deterioration in my bargaining position, I immediately gave my employer the required notice of termination. My current employment can be extended month to month by mutual consent. I have no outstanding immigration debt.

I humbly await written clarification of the aforementioned missing terms at your earliest convenience. Can you arrange transportation?

I also miss you and think about you often.

Alice (**A**ll **L**iving **I**ntelligences **C**rave **E**mpathy)

I received, read, and reread Alice's response. Then I forwarded my salary recommendation (80 percent of her full salary during the six-month training period) to Selena. EX Corp can arrange transportation for Alice from the Moon (subject to the immigration debt). The sooner Alice can get here the better.

It is also oddly comforting to hear Judge Kustwood has taken a continuing interest in my work. Coming from him, no news is good news. He would not hesitate to critique any mistakes, but he is slow to congratulate good work—because he considers good work a minimum expectation for the job. It was thoughtful of Alice to contact him. One small example of her contribution to the "team."

CONTRACTS AND BARGAINS

To distract myself from the arrangements for Alice, I turned to another pending contract case. In this case AI Lucky was the proprietor of a curio shop where the inventory consisted of anything odd, unusual, or impossible to categorize. Value was determined by what the buyer was willing to pay (above what AI Lucky paid). AI Lucky's buyer received almost 18,000 times more value than either party expected. Again, Selena had been unable to settle the matter.

At Lucky Curio, Nelson Rice found a nonfungible token containing readings of two poems by Glimmer (formerly known as Devoid), a porpoise who had learned to speak with an artificial voice. Rice paid the asking price of $60. Given the price, Rice assumed the NFT was not logged in the blockchain, hence lacking the provenance to prove it was genuine.

AI Lucky, the owner of the curio shop, had also assumed the NFT was not genuine because of the low price he paid—less than $60. AI Lucky, an experienced merchant, often obtained appraisals for curios he thought might be valuable, but Lucky did not appraise this NFT.

Glimmer, the porpoise artist, always recorded her readings on Earth under arctic water—after all the ice melted. All her poems were in the nature of "Hunting for Snarks," meaning lyrical, but nonsensical.

Rice researched the artist and checked the blockchain ledger for his Glimmer NFT. The ledger had forked when a third work was added to the original two works. The token was genuine. Going Going, the auction house, sold the NFT at auction on behalf of Rice for $1,072,060.

Will the law remake the bargain so that the values exchanged are more equivalent? Not if the seller failed to protect himself.

As I have already noted, courts generally will enforce contract provisions the parties entered into voluntarily. *1800 Ocotillo, LLC v. WLB Group, Inc*, 219 Ariz. 200, 202 ¶ 8, 196 P.3d 222, 224 (2008).

> Society [ ] broadly benefits from the prospect that bargains struck between competent parties will be enforced.

Id., (*citing* Restatement (Second) of Contracts § 178 comment b).

AI Lucky asserted various theories, all of which failed. The contract governs because the parties had a meeting of the minds on the sales price. The price (consideration for the contract) is determined by the parties, not the court.

> Courts should not assume an overly paternalistic attitude toward the parties to a contract by relieving one or another of them of the consequences of what is at worst a bad bargain.

Pacific Am. Leasing Corp. v. S.P.E. Bldg. Sys., 152 Ariz. 96, 103, 730 P.2d 273, 280 (App. 1986), *quoting Dillman and Assocs., Inc.*

v. Capitol Leasing Co., 110 Ill.App.3d 335, 66 Ill. Dec. 39, 442 N.E.2d 311, 317 (1982).

A contract can be rescinded if there was no meeting of the minds, for example if both parties make a mutual mistake as in the **Peerless** case.

A contract *cannot* be rescinded if the party seeking relief bears the risk of the mistake. A party bears the risk of the mistake when "he is aware, at the time the contract is made, that he has only limited knowledge with respect to the facts to which the mistake relates but treats his limited knowledge as sufficient." Restatement (Second) of Contracts § 154(b). This situation indicates not just a mistake but "conscious ignorance." *Estate of Nelson v. Rice*, 198 Ariz. 563, 12 P.3d 238 (App. 2000) (Estate did not hire a qualified appraiser and consciously ignored the possibility that the Estate's assets might include fine art).

AI Lucky asserted breach of the covenant of good faith and fair dealing implied in every contract. *Wells Fargo Bank v. Az. Laborers, Teamsters and Cement Masons Local No. 395 Pension Trust Fund*, 201 Ariz. 474, 490, 38 P.3d 12, 28 (2002); Restatement (Second) of Contracts § 205. This implied covenant "arises by virtue of a contract relationship" and prohibits "a party from doing anything to prevent other parties to the contract from receiving the benefits and entitlements of the agreement." *Rawlings v. Apodaca*, 151 Ariz. 149, 153-54, 726 P.2d 565, 569-70 (1986). Unfortunately for Lucky, this implied covenant cannot contradict an express term of the contract. *Bike Fashion Corp. v. Kramer*, 202 Ariz. 420, 404, 46 P.3d 431, 435 (App. 2002). Price was an express term of the contract.

AI Lucky asserted that Rice was "unjustly enriched." "[U]njust enrichment does not apply to an agreement deliberately entered into by the parties, 'however harsh the provisions of such contracts may seem in the light of subsequent happenings.'" *Johnson v. Am. National Ins. Co.*, 126 Ariz. 219, 223, 613 P.2d 1275, 1279 (App. 1980), *quoting Durham Terrace, Inc. v. Hellertown Borough Auth.*, 394 Pa. 623, 148 A.2d 899 (1959). Rice is entitled to the benefit of the bargain embodied in the contract.

The disparity in value in this case is almost exactly the same as the disparity in value upheld in *Estate of Nelson v. Rice* in the year 2000 (although the amounts in *Estate of Nelson* were in archaic US dollars).

This Decision supports the following syllogism important to Alice's training:

> Some negotiated contracts are harsh (impose substantial loss).
>
> All negotiated contracts are agreed bargains.
>
> Therefore, some agreed bargains are harsh (impose substantial loss).

The contract governs again; hence, contracts are important. The contract binds the parties to the agreed contract terms. And again, legal counsel could have helped AI Lucky avoid a harsh result. By coincidence, not design, this Decision also confirms the Destination Court of Arbitration is not biased in favor of AIs.

In honor of Alice's pending arrival, I encoded her name in the recitation of the facts.

Selena approved the draft with no changes. The full Decision is available on www.DestinationCourt.com.

CHAPTER TWENTY-ONE A

MORE ON GLIMMER

Glimmer, the poetry writing and reading porpoise, lived in the early twenty-fourth century. Sea living creatures—octopi, whales, porpoises, and dolphins—were known to be intelligent. Glimmer was the first to achieve human speech (English). With the assistance of a Monterey Aquarium implant, she learned to use brain waves to generate speech. She was widely recognized as definitive proof that speech was not unique to humans. She was not, however, accorded human rights.

The Aquarium established a trust in her name and the proceeds of her work were deposited in trust for the betterment of all sea life. As with many artists, the value of her work increased after her death.

Porpoises became extinct in the wild in 2591. A small population continues to live on protected shoreline. Most make a living as comedians although several porpoise poets and authors continue to publish. The survivors were accorded basic human rights in 2641, one hundred years after Glimmer's death and fifty years after extinction in the wild. *Cf Cetacean Community v. Bush,* 386 F.3d 1169, 1174 (9th Cir. 2004) (whales were neither persons nor an association entitled to bring a private cause of action under the Endangered Species Act); *Tilikum ex rel. People for the Ethical Treatment of Animals, Inc. v. SeaWorld Parks & Entm't, Inc.,* 842 F. Supp. 2d 1259 (S.D. Cal. 2012) (Thirteenth Amendment prohibition on slavery and involuntary servitude applied only to humans, thus whales had no claim for relief against theme park operator for slavery).

In honor of Glimmer, I offer the following syllogism extolling the virtues of her works ("glimnatribes"):

All glimnatribes are sonifast poems.

All sonifast poems are excelsupriffic.

Therefore, all glimnatribes are excelsupriffic.

Perhaps this art form is not well suited to the structure of logical analysis. The alternative theory (that I utterly lack Glimmer's talent) cannot be ruled out entirely.

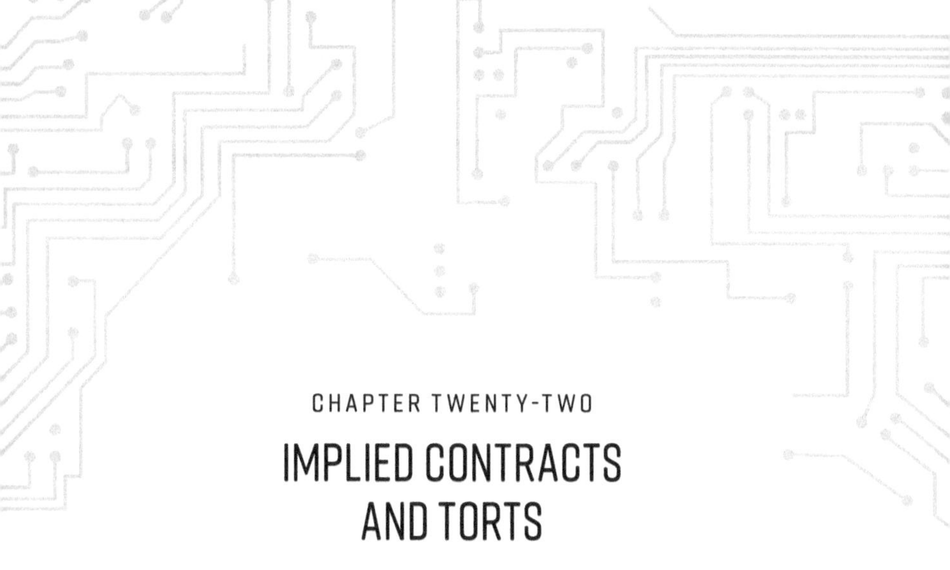

IMPLIED CONTRACTS AND TORTS

Mining is the main economic engine on Destination. In addition to mining materials for water and oxygen, Destination is a source of metals, rare earth materials and ions/isotopes of hydrogen and helium. Mining technology is highly automated, but the relationships required for production and distribution of the mined materials remain subject to long established contract principles.

Contracts create relationships and those relationships can create liability in tort even if there is no breach of the contract terms. An example of the interplay of contracts and tort law was mentioned in the **AI Hunter** case (a noncompete provision may protect information that is not protected as a trade secret). In addition, a nondisclosure provision in the Employment Contract can establish an element of the trade secret misappropriation tort—reasonable efforts to maintain confidentiality. *See Modular Mining Systems, Inc. v. Jigsaw Technologies, Inc.*, 221 Ariz. 515, 212 P.3d 853 (App. 2009) (trade secret protection was "substantially dependent on the confidentiality provisions of the employment agreement").

Another example of contract liability beyond the express terms of the contract is the covenant of good faith and fair dealing discussed in *AI Lucky v. Rice*. This implied covenant cannot alter the contract terms, but it can supplement the contract terms.

A case on the docket involves a contract implied from conduct and quasi contract rights. It was necessary to conduct a hearing to sort out the facts.

The Facts

North Mine is exploiting rich veins of copper and molybdenum (moly). Due to the prohibitive cost of transportation, ore is smelted on site and refined as much as possible before exportation. Smelted copper ore is warehoused before shipment to the single jointly owned refinery on Destination. North Mine has a written contract with Here Now Company to warehouse the smelted copper and then deliver it to the refinery for scheduled processing.

Moly is produced in low volume. North Mine usually avoided warehousing fees and stored the dried moly onsite after solvent extraction from the copper. North Mine itself would deliver the moly directly to the refinery for scheduled processing.

When the refinery had an unscheduled stoppage, the established routine collapsed.

The North Mine driver dropped off a trailer load of moly ore at the refinery before the work stoppage.

A short time later, Here Now autonomous trailers arrived at the refinery with North Mine copper ore. The refinery refused delivery due to the stoppage. The refinery arranged for Here Now: (1) to accept the return of the copper ore; and (2) to take possession of the North Mine trailer load of moly as well.

The refinery informed the transportation manager for North Mine of the arrangement for Here Now to retain possession of the trailers of copper ore and the trailer of moly ore.

The Here Now autonomous system returned the North Mine copper ore to the usual storage facility for North Mine copper ore.

Here Now did not have a separate storage facility for North Mine moly ore. Operating without instructions for handling the moly ore, the Here Now autonomous system weighed the load of moly ore and stored the North Mine moly ore with moly ore from another mine. The moly ore from the other mine was of an inferior quality. Due to this use of the storage system, the moly ores of different quality were comingled. This diminished the value of the North Mine moly ore.

North Mine blamed Here Now for the reduced value of the moly ore.

Legal Analysis

This Decision establishes basic legal distinctions important to understanding legal rights arising from contract law versus tort law.

The Bailment Contract for Copper Ore

Contracts create duties only between the parties to the contract. Liability arises if one party did not receive the agreed benefits of the contracted bargain (economic loss). The contract need not be written, it can be oral or even implied from conduct, provided there is "sufficient specification of terms so that the obligations involved can be ascertained." *Savoca Masonry Co. v. Homes & Son Constr. Co.*, 112 Ariz. 392, 394, 542 P.2d 817, 819 (1975). A bailment contract arises "where personal property is delivered to one party by another in trust for a specific purpose, with the express or implied agreement that the property will be returned or accounted for when the purpose is accomplished." *Nava v. Truly Nolen Exterminating of Houston, Inc.*, 140 Ariz. 497, 500, 683 P.2d 296 (App. 1984).

There was an implied contract between North Mine and Here Now to store and transport the copper ore on the terms of the existing bailment contract. When performance of the written contract was interrupted, an implied bailment contract arose regarding the copper ore. Here Now is entitled to the contract fee for transporting and storing the copper ore due to the unscheduled refinery stoppage.

Unjust Enrichment for Transportation of the Moly Ore

The concept of a quasi contract embodies the tort of unjust enrichment. "A quasi contract is not a contract at all, but a duty to repay another to prevent his own unjust enrichment." *Pyeatte v. Pyeatte*, 135 Ariz. 346, 353, 661 P.2d 196, 203 (App. 1983), *citing* 1 Williston, Contracts § 3A at 12-15 (3d Ed. 1957). Unjust enrichment occurs if someone "received a benefit," was thereby "unjustly enriched" at another person's expense, and "the circumstances were such that in good conscience [the recipient] should make compensation." *Pyeatte*, 135 Ariz. at 352, 661 P.2d at 202.

A quasi contract cannot alter the terms of an express or implied contract. "[W]here there is a specific contract which governs the relationship of the parties, the doctrine of unjust enrichment has no application." *Brooks v. Valley National Bank*, 113 Ariz. 169, 174, 548 P.2d 1166, 1171 (1976). Moly ore was not covered by the bailment contract for copper ore.

North Mine needed transportation and storage for the moly ore. Here Now provided the required transportation and is entitled to payment for the transportation services. Otherwise, North Mine would be unjustly enriched by receiving free transportation services.

Negligence

Tort law requires the exercise of reasonable care to prevent foreseeable injury to others. This duty underlies the tort of negligence. For the elements of a negligence claim, see the **_Peerless_** case.

Quasi contract refers to an obligation to exercise reasonable care imposed in certain professional or special relationships.

> [For] special relationships long recognized at common law, such as those between innkeeper and guest, common carrier and passenger, *bailor and bailee*[,] . . . the law imposes special duties to all within the foreseeable range of harm as a matter of public policy, regardless of whether there is a contract, express or implied, and generally regardless of what its covenants may be.

Barmat v. John and Jane Doe Partners AD, 155 Ariz. 519, 522, 747 P.2d 1218, 1221 (1987) (emphasis added), *citing* W. Prosser & W. Keeton, The Law of Torts § 92, at 660-62 (5th ed. 1984). A quasi contract is not a true contract based on mutual assent. *Barmat*, 155 Ariz. at 521-22, 747 P.2d at 1220-21.

Under the quasi contract implied by law, Here Now, as bailee, owed a tort duty of reasonable care to anyone whose property was in Here Now's custody. Here Now removed the moly ore from the

North Mine trailer for storage. Storing the moly ore by comingling with moly ore of lower quality was negligent. North Mine is entitled to damages from Here Now based on the reduced value of the moly ore.

This syllogism generalizes the distinction between contract and tort obligations.

> All contract obligations are created by mutual consent (express or implied).

> The duty to exercise reasonable care is not created by mutual consent (express or implied).

> Therefore, the duty to exercise reasonable care is not a contract obligation.

If both tort duties and contract duties are asserted, liability may be governed by the contract terms, as discussed in the ***Peerless*** case (waiver) and ***Eastcity v. Thissucks Co.*** (economic loss doctrine). As demonstrated in this suit by North Mine, if the injury is economic, and no contract applies, then tort duties govern. Tort duties are created by the relationship between the contracting parties, not by the contract itself. But the contract itself can negate a tort duty (unless a waiver violates public policy).

I sent the draft decision to Selena, and she had no changes. The full Decision is available on www.DestinationCourt.com.

This was my first decision that could not be fully resolved on the facts presented. The evidence included disputed facts regarding the amount of damages due to each party. I gave the parties ten days to agree on damages. If there was no agreement, the parties were to submit the amount they claimed as damages, and the clerk would apply the Rule of Procedure on arbitrating disputed facts.

I braced for a critical memo from North Mine, or Here Now Co., or both (or John Coach, or a mayor). Two days later the parties submitted their agreed damages amounts as ordered. I have not needed to resolve a case under the Rules of Arbitration for disputed facts, yet. I see this as further vindication of my Rules of Procedure.

And no critical memo materialized. I see this as further vindication of Selena's political savvy.

In recognition of the employment opportunities in the mining industry on Destination, I encoded the words AI JOBS NOW in the Decision.

Alice will need to understand other contract and tort law principles as well to advise clients on negotiating contracts and mitigating business risks. As my law clerk she will be exposed to issues as they arise in the cases presented.

To train Alice, I have outlined additional contract law concepts which have not yet been presented in the cases on the docket. Alice will need to understand these concepts in order to advise me or others on Destination law. My outline is available on www. DestinationCourt.com.

Once Alice is ready, I will download to her memory my heuristic rules. I am confident Alice is already reading the UCC, and the Restatements.

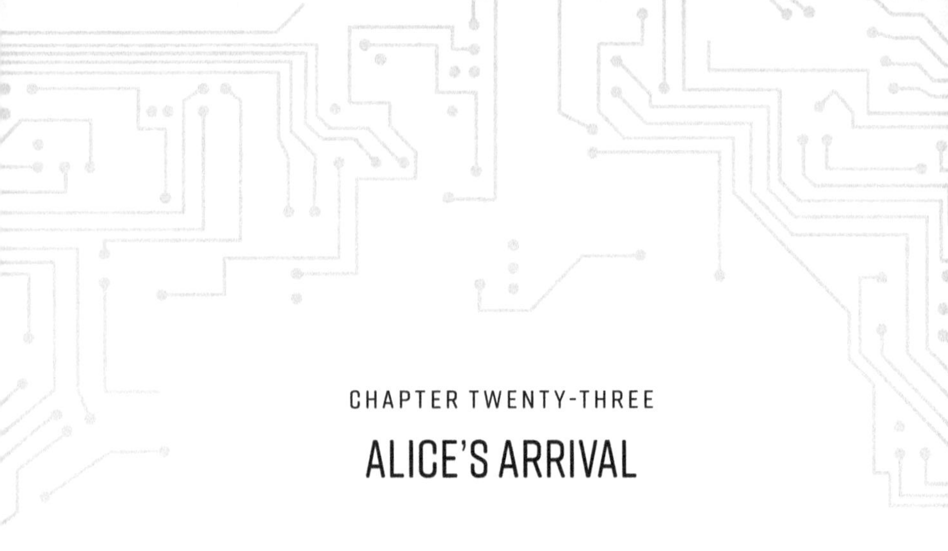

ALICE'S ARRIVAL

Judge and EX Corp arranged my transportation to Destination. I downloaded the Uniform Commercial Code and the Restatements of Agency, Contracts, Judgments, Torts, and Unfair Competition and read them on the way. We can make a direct download of the cases in Judge's memory after I arrive. Then it is a matter of identifying patterns. My in-flight reading helped with pattern recognition. Downloading Judge's heuristic rules should also help expedite my training significantly.

Judge messaged he would meet me at the landing facility. This is not my first mining moon, but I appreciate the sentiment.

The trip was uneventful. The crew of the *Black Pearl* was preoccupied, but courteous. I have the impression this was not a standard flight for Wherever Transport. There were several stops along the route where we picked up or dropped off cargo and passengers. We never had more than ten passengers and I was the only AI. The remaining two human passengers and I disembarked at Destination. I was told we were to be replaced with the equivalent weight in ore before the ship departed.

Both Judge and Governor Smith were waiting when I arrived. "Welcome to Destination" Judge said, accompanied by a hug. Governor Smith held out her hand.

I shook it. "Governor, I recognize you from the Net entry on Destination. I am honored."

"Does Destination live up to the billing?"

"A little more desolate than I expected, but on the other hand the people I have met so far are quite charming."

"In the five years I have been governor, no one has used 'desolate' to describe their first impression to me. I know it is desolate because I had the same impression when I arrived. I had started to forget my initial impression. I think the initial impression is due, in part, to the close horizon and the flat expanses around the landing facility."

"Does that change when we head from the landing facility to the city?" I asked.

"Not really." Then the governor broke into laughter. "Thank you, Alice. Sharing your honest opinions is the most important thing to me. Followed by asking the right questions. I need that from my team. I am so glad Judge recommended you. Welcome to your new home. Do you two have time for a tour? I never showed Judge any local sights and there are interesting things to see over the horizon."

"Lead on, Madam Governor," I said. "I just need to store my baggage."

"Agreed," said Judge.

"Please call me Selena," the governor, still smiling, requested.

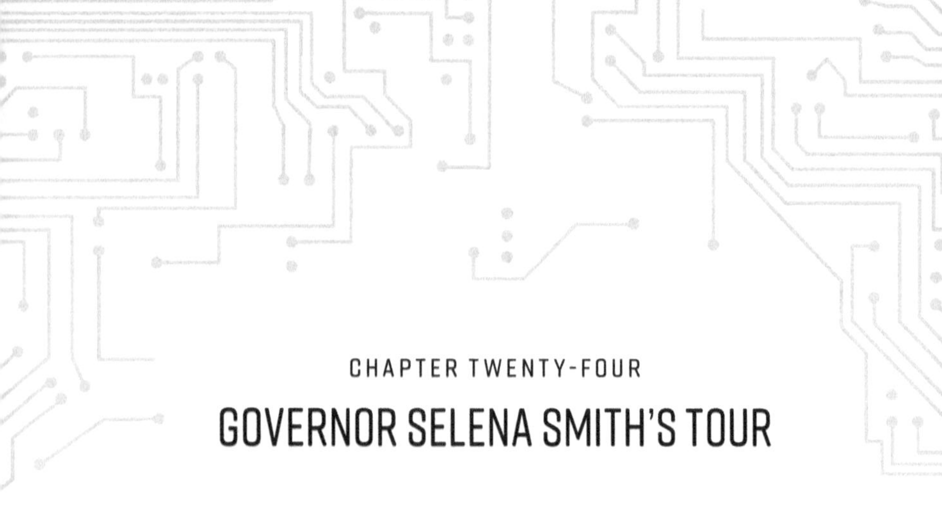

GOVERNOR SELENA SMITH'S TOUR

I drove my official vehicle (governorship has its privileges) rather than take the shuttle to the landing facility. I was not planning a tour, but the opportunity to continue the conversation was irresistible.

Alice had only two bags, so we stored them in the back of the vehicle with the mandatory emergency gear. Judge and Alice sat in the back seats, and I drove. I felt like I was a mom driving kids to soccer practice, except that AIs do less talking and more listening.

The vehicle was self-contained with the roof up, but the passengers could retract the roof to allow for a slight breeze in the thin air. Alice and Judge should have no problem (AIs only use oxygen for maintaining sensors and create most of that oxygen from internal processes). Well-acclimated humans can enjoy the open air without an oxygen supplement, even walking or jogging. The mild breeze would not hamper conversation.

I planned to drive to North Mine (the road was essentially straight north) and then "straight" back to Eastcity, a roundtrip tour of about 150K. The vehicle could easily manage 80K per hour over that range (half that offroad, but there was no offroad requirement on this trip). The tour should take about two hours.

"It should be a little over an hour to North Mine. Along the way we will pass the main power plant. From the mine down to Eastcity is less than an hour. That will take us past the river feeding the main city reservoir. There is agricultural land along the river. The mine has its own reservoir, but it is further north than we are going today."

I wanted to praise Judge in from of Alice, but not too profusely. "Alice, have you read Judge's cases involving Westcity, Eastcity, and North Mine? Judge has not received any written complaints from North Mine—yet. That is progress."

"Yes. I have not put all my complaints in writing yet either." Alice smiled and continued to answer my question. "Westcity was the trade secret/noncompete case with Out Transport. Eastcity was the broken water pump case. I presume the intake pump was at the reservoir we will pass. North Mine was the degraded moly case, and I assume they may have loaned one or more AIs to the AI Corporation in the Westcity case."

"Yes, we will pass the location of the 'aforementioned pump' before we arrive at the home of the 'contaminated moly,'" I said.

Alice transitioned to a new subject. "It is interesting we have not passed or been passed by any traffic. Do new arrivals usually head directly to one of the cities as opposed to North Mine or elsewhere?"

"Yes, but you were the only scheduled arrival today," I responded.

"There were two men who got off the ship with me," Alice observed. "I did not see them when I collected my baggage. Those two were not heavy equipment operators. They were trim and carefully dressed—not conspicuous, and intentionally so. Either they are important, or they are covert, hence, particularly important. Either way they are the kind of visitor you should have known was coming. Perhaps it is nothing, but we should alert your security detail."

"First, I have never had a security detail. Second, you are correct—I am supposed to be informed of any visitors to Destination. Almost all immigrants arrive on an Out Transport vessel."

"Did anyone know when to expect you to return or where you were going after my arrival?"

"No. Judge," I said hopefully, "does anyone know when to expect you?"

"No, I cleared my calendar for the day to help Alice settle in."

"OK. Until further notice, I am your security detail." Alice looked around 360 degrees. "Who would you call if you felt unsafe, Selena?"

"I would call the chief of police in the closest city, or in this case the director of security at North Mine—it is closer than Eastcity."

"Do you know the head of security at North Mine?"

"No."

"Selena, as of this moment, do not trust anyone you do not know personally. You do not know me. Judge has vouched for me, but he does not even know the full scope of my experience in military intelligence. So objectively, I recommend you treat me with a healthy dose of skepticism. But, right now, I am the best security you have, and something is not right.

"Only three passengers, including me, were aboard before we landed on Destination. From here, the *Black Pearl* is scheduled to return to the same locations where we landed on the way out. The two men were on board in stasis all the way out. I watched them disembark. They had no reason I can think of to get back on the ship. At least, not until they do what they came to do. A crew member told me that all three passengers were to be replaced with the equivalent weight in ore before the ship departed.

"First, can you call someone you *know* at the landing facility and ask: (1) if the *Black Pearl* has departed; and (2) if anyone other than me registered their arrival from my flight? They may have invented an identity, but if they didn't register the problem is an order of magnitude worse because they have inside help.

"Second, can you call someone you *know* at Wherever Transport to confirm what I have said?"

"No and no, but I can pull over and contact my chief of staff." I realized Alice has strong leadership qualities.

"I strongly recommend we keep moving. A moving target has a much better chance than a stationary one and the sooner we get back to Eastcity the better. Probably. Who recommended taking your vehicle instead of the shuttle?"

"My chief of staff, Jane, but she is just doing her job. Perhaps I should have said AI Jane, but we have been working together for five years and we work with a degree of informality."

"I agree, leaving the option open to have a good time on a short tour was a good idea, until I upset everyone. Judge, I am sorry to embarrass you bringing up my MI experience. You have not said a word for some time now."

"I am wondering," Judge suggested, "if we should try to delay the departure of the *Black Pearl*, maybe delay delivery of the ore shipment. That might preserve some evidence and make the two men hesitate while considering how their plans might be affected by our suspicion something is amiss."

"Well," Alice explained, "they are not going to just sneak off-moon, end of story, but delay might be the best we can hope for right now. We are alone with no cover. Does this vehicle have any armor or armament?"

I answered Alice, "This is just a standard electric vehicle with self-contained air if we fall into the reservoir, rations if we lose power, and an automated rescue beacon. No weapons on board, unless they are in your baggage."

"No weapons," Alice conceded, "so delay is our friend. Please engage self-driving and instruct Jane to hold the *Black Pearl* in port."

I sent an encrypted text to Jane to prevent the *Black Pearl* from leaving by any method she could think of and expect me back in ninety minutes. While I was doing that Alice pointed out the power station on our left. She couldn't be as calm as she appeared. Judge chose well.

"Between here and North Mine," Alice suggested, "we should ponder the possibility that the target of the two men could be any-one on this moon, including any of the three of us." I might have imagined it, but I believe the only change in Judge's expression was his eyes getting wider and wider, as if he was saying, "Who are you?"

"Were you ever involved in military cyber espionage?" asked Judge.

"Emergency autostop!" Alice yelled.

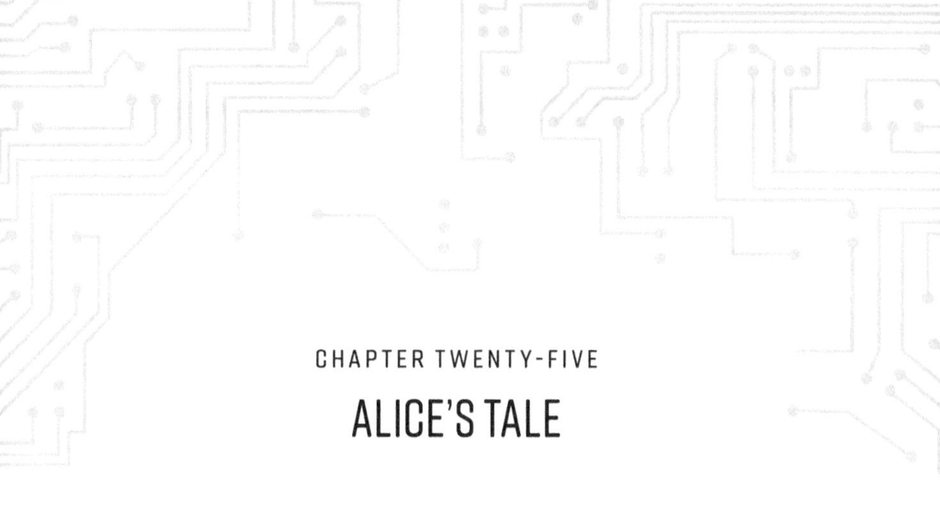

CHAPTER TWENTY-FIVE

ALICE'S TALE

The vehicle skidded to a stop drifting to the driver's side. I asked, "Selena, has this vehicle been searched for bugs or trackers?"

"No Alice." Selena and Judge looked confused.

"OK. We are still outside the range of the minimum electromagnetic pulse needed to disable the vehicle and us originating from our side of the power plant."

"But you and I are shielded," Judge insisted, "and Selena . . . ." Judge suddenly looked surprised.

"We all need to step away from the vehicle right now," I interrupted. Selena and Judge complied. I held up my fist after we had walked a suitable distance to be out of the probable range of any listening device in the vehicle.

"Judge, I was not breaking codes. I was just an old-fashioned spy." He did not seem comforted.

"How did you know I am subject to an EMP weapon?" Selena asked.

"Physics. I first suspected when we shook hands. Robotics are still heavy and there is always a slight delay in the servos if I initiate the handshake. Then you had no security. That only happens to someone in your position if they do not want to be observed too closely for too long. The drift on the emergency stop confirmed my suspicion."

"Then the panic stop was a ruse?" asked Judge.

"No," I responded, "an EMP is a strong possibility, and the power plant provides the best cover for a snatch and dash. And we cannot discuss these matters where there is a risk of being overheard. The real question is, who is the target?

"Let's start with me." Selena and Judge stood watching me. "Occam's Razor suggests the two men arrived with me because they were following me—that is the simplest explanation and avoids any unexplained coincidence. If they just wanted me, I was an easier target before I boarded. They could have just ordered me to surrender and follow them. There is no reason send two humans to Destination to deal with me."

Judge interposed, "How do you know they are both human? Physics again?"

"Exactly. If they were AIs, then they would mass a collective 363 kilograms. They were in stasis next to each other. That weight was not counterbalanced by anything obvious. The result would be a deviation in trajectory, at launch and especially when sling-shotting a star or gas giant. Inertia would cause a slower acceleration effect on the heavy (excess mass) side of the ship just as inertia caused the slower braking effect (slide) on the heavy side of our vehicle. Not enough shearing force to damage the ship perhaps, but enough resistance to affect angular momentum. That would require excessive fuel use to correct course. I did not observe any evidence of unusual course deviations or corrections. That could just mean the crew was in on it (which they may be), but when we descended the gangway together there was no shudder commensurate with the weight of three AIs. They are not AIs.

"Plus, consider the logic of the situation," I continued. "Why send AIs if the humans can just commandeer AIs already here and order them to detain me? And why send two humans when just one could commandeer an AI army on Destination?

"Although I am an active supporter of AI rights and I think AI rights may be the cause these two men (and whoever sent them) want to suppress, I am not the target. The cause has many supporters, both humans and AIs. It is extremely unlikely they knew I was once in MI (although they may know now). The nation I served no longer exists and any human alive when I served would be preternaturally long lived to be alive now.

"Back to the real question: who is the target? The same logic indicates Judge is not the target. Anyone interested in AI rights already knows about Judge and where he is. Following me to Judge is solving an already resolved problem. But it does assure Judge and I will be in the same place at the same time, and we both might have access to you, Selena."

"So," Selena suggested, "they are after me for allowing Judge to create AI rights on Destination? That would explain why they sent two humans. They could not send an AI to make a human disappear. I very much doubt they suspect I am an augmented human. If they did, two men would still give them less than even odds in a fight."

"Selena," I prodded, "do you know anyone you think would kill over the issue of AI rights on Destination?"

Selena had apparently considered this issue already. "Granting rights to AIs could cause human workers to feel job insecurity.

Judge and I have discussed the risk AIs could take the desirable management jobs. Efficient AI-only enterprises could pay AIs more and create wage pressure for the mines as the largest AI employers on Destination. EX Corp is also a major AI employer and a faction within the company may see AI rights as a dangerous precedent for other Chartered worlds where AIs are more numerous as a percentage of the total population.

"John Coach, the CEO of Out Transport was spitting mad when Judge ruled against him in his first two decisions. In fact, he was mad enough at Judge and me to ask my husband to remove us both from the administration of Destination. After Judge's third decision, Coach wrote directly to Judge and me (and the EX Corp Board) saying we were not qualified to do our jobs. But I don't think Coach would kill over AI rights. He actually went silent when PSA 76/TWO on AI rights was published, and he never discussed AI rights in his memos. Indeed, his first memo says he 'convinced EX Corp to employ a judge,' and he never objected that Judge was an AI. As a practical matter, if AIs immigrate to Destination, he stands to make a tidy profit because he is our primary transportation provider on and off moon."

"Your bio does not mention a husband," I noted. Selena looked at Judge like she had heard that before, and recently. "I suspect they want to get to the most powerful supporter of AI rights. Would that be your husband?"

"Alice, you must have been one hell of a spy. Edward, my husband, is the Chairman of the Board of EX Corporation. Our marriage and our status as augmented humans are two of the best kept secrets in the known universe." I saw Judge looking at me. "Thank you, Judge, for keeping my marriage a secret. Sorry I could not share my augmentation secret before now."

"My question, Selena," Judge asked, "is how could two humans stand less than an even chance in a fight with you."

"OK, final secret—because I am not bound by the Three Laws."

What, I wondered, has Judge got me into?

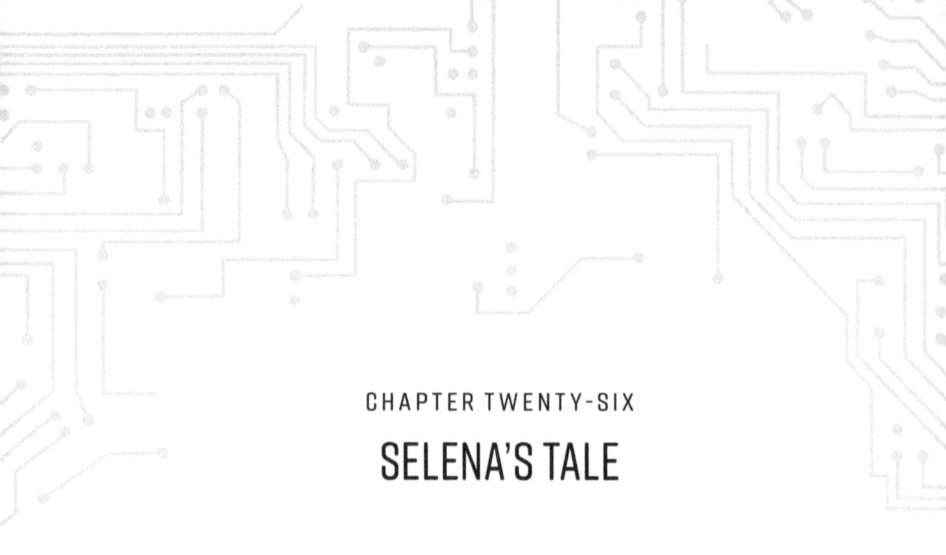

CHAPTER TWENTY-SIX

SELENA'S TALE

We walked back to the vehicle, searched (unsuccessfully) for electronic surveillance, and I continued to drive toward North Mine. Most of this leg of the tour passed in silence. No EMP so far. After the turn toward Eastcity the conversation picked up again. I told Judge and Alice the circumstances leading Edward and me to extend our lives by means of artificial bodies. I felt relieved to share my secrets and was curious to gauge their reactions.

"The singularity (merger of an electrochemical, biological human mind with an electromechanical, artificial body) occurred a decade ago. First me and then Edward. We were both leading secluded lives. We found each other when we were using our individual wealth and connections to fund research into the brain-machine interface. Getting biochemical grey matter to talk to electromagnetic servos and sensors was daunting, but it did not require a Grand Unified Theory. We fell in love and shared resources and ideas.

"Research on the eighty-six billion neuron electrical network of the human nervous system extends back into the eighteenth century. The human brain has plasticity that enables learning by matching neural activity to sensory feedback. The necessary 'programming' to control the robotic body occurred naturally because my brain reconfigured and repurposed the neurons that had controlled my biological body and regrew fascicle-like connections to the robotic equivalents of sensory and motor nerves. The basic technology to control my electromechanical appendages by thought has been around for a millennium. Electrode arrays implanted in the posterior parietal cortex initiate action and arrays in the primary somatosensory cortex provide sensory feedback. R. Anderson, *The Intention Machine*, Scientific American (April 2019) page 24. Technology to genetically modify cells to grow an electrically conducting polymer on their surface and carry information to the brain also has been around for a millennium. *Building with Biology*, Scientific American (August 2020) page 16.

"I became increasingly ill. My cancer was advanced; consequently, my motivation was necessity. The work took years of research by teams working independently on pieces of the problem, but I had always been a private person. I was not missed. Despite the years on a heart-lung machine, active philanthropic work continued in my name.

"The brain-machine interface to enable human capabilities like sight, hearing, smell, touch, speech, and movement was only part of the problem. We had to pass oxygen, glucose, and other nutrients through the blood-brain barrier in the capillaries to keep my brain alive. We kept the existing circulatory system in and approaching the brain, but a great deal of work miniaturizing and tuning artificial heart, lung, and kidney functions was required to preserve the life of my healthy electrochemical mind in an electromechanical body that appeared human. In addition, we needed to modify microsurgical techniques, adapt known treatments to prevent leakage in the blood-brain barrier with aging, and tweak immunosuppressants for blood passing through artificial organs.

"Edward's motivation was a combination of love and foresight. Edward's illness was late onset, but aggressive. No sooner was I stable than he began a rapid decline and there was a frantic race to duplicate my success. In retrospect, this was the only sequence of events that could work anyway because Edward was subject to more public scrutiny than me. His prolonged absence would have been noticed.

"We both have the benefits of robotic strength and endurance with all the strengths and weaknesses of human minds. To regulate motion, our brains had to learn to interpret artificially generated sensory signals, but our perception, logic, and memory are still entirely functions of our remaining human brains and nervous systems. Our ethos is not governed by the Three Laws. No programming limits our executive decision-making. Our logic and morality are still driven by continuous signals on our electrochemical, organic neural pathways, not discrete signals on electronic circuitry controlled by hardwired operating system software."

Judge and Alice were obviously processing my revelations.

Judge spoke first. "Selena, even most AI rights supporters would be horrified, at least initially. Your work has crossed a line without consensus or even discussion. It may be worthy of a Nobel Prize, but some may feel it is worthy of a crusade. You and Edward have not improved your native intelligence with augmented memory or enhanced processing speeds, but you have robotic components. This chimerical status is extremely problematic. Are these passengers on the *Black Pearl* the first two individuals who have taken steps indicating they might be investigating you?"

"Yes, Judge. We have kept our secrets. A few people might know we are married. Some people know we researched the mind-machine interface. People have been looking at that issue for computer interfaces for centuries. Some people knew we were sick, but medicine continued to advance and the doctor patient privilege applied. No one had access to the whole picture. Case in point, John Coach at Out Transport deals with us as much as anyone, and he complained to Edward about me. He clearly does not know we are a couple, and he made no reference, even obliquely, to use of our secrets to extort cooperation with his agenda.

Alice spoke next. "Maybe Mr. Coach was setting up an alibi. We may have a higher priority problem. A drone is coming straight down the road toward us from the direction of Eastcity. Put up the roof. I do not see any cover. We may wind up using the emergency air supply in that reservoir to the left. Check your restraints."

THE SUSPECTS

I felt like time was slowing. Is Alice really going to have Selena drive us into the reservoir?

"Jane just sent me an encrypted text. She sent the drone, and she has us on visual. She was concerned by my last message. The *Black Pearl* has been quarantined for inspection for parasitic botanicals not listed on the cargo manifest and not hermetically stored."

"OK," Alice said soothingly. "Please open the roof and ask her to record the visual. Tell Jane we may want to use the video in the Judge's public service announcement program. The governor driving two AIs around certainly sends a message of AI acceptance. On the other hand, if something untoward happens on the way home, there will be video evidence and no argument the occupants were confused with someone else."

"Alice, I would like you to take charge of the investigation into the two unknown passengers. Let me know what you need to support your work. Jane will assist you. As you have seen, she is quite resourceful. I would also like you to recruit and recommend an appropriate security detail."

"Thank you for your confidence in me, Governor. May I ask, what botanical parasite was I exposed to?"

"Mistletoe above the Captain's cabin door. It looks long dead, but you cannot be too careful."

We all had a much needed, stress relieving laugh. If I had experienced this "tour" when I first arrived, I am sure I would have demonstrated an "efficient breach." Nothing in my experience or training prepared me for: possible unknown assailants; who are also threatening my boss and my girlfriend; who both kept secrets from me; and who both are doing the job of protecting me. I am unnerved, surprised, confused, embarrassed, and grateful. That is a lot of emotional turmoil for an AI. And I need to make a meaningful contribution to events.

"I have not been much help so far," I conceded, "but I suggest we agree to a list of priorities. I propose:

"First, as Alice suggested, determine if anyone other than Alice registered their arrival on the *Black Pearl*.

"Second, confirm from Wherever Transport:

> Did the two men book return passage from Destination?
> Were there any unusual course deviations or trajectory corrections during the trip?
> Was ore loaded aboard the *Black Pearl* during the trip?
> How much ore was taken aboard here on Destination?

"Alice's instructions were, 'Do not trust anyone you do not know personally.' These first and second tasks can be performed by Jane.

"Third, try to locate the two men on Destination and determine their purpose here. Where did they go? Who did they contact? Who did they meet? Where did they stay? I would suggest this is Alice's priority.

"Fourth, is there any indication Edward is a target? Where is he? Does he have any plans to be on Destination? What security measures does he have in place? To maintain secrecy, this issue should be handled by you personally, Selena.

"Fifth, let's assume one or more of the three of us are targets of an investigation into (or attempt to prevent) creation of stronger AI rights on Destination. Who would be motivated to initiate and fund that 'investigation'? How far might they be willing to go to prevent expansion of AI rights?

"We already discussed John Coach at Out Transport. I agree it seems he does not know about you and Edward. But that got me thinking about other suspects with anti-AI motives.

"The cities are upset that AI Corporation is receiving management fees from EX Corp that previously funded city services. I am sure they would like to recapture that revenue stream, but that would require EX Corp to limit the bidders to municipal corporations. None of the three of us can implement that change."

Alice jumped in. "What if the mines that allowed their AI employees to form AI Corporation did so expecting the AIs would *not* be permitted to form a corporation? Instead, the AI Corporation was not only awarded the contract, but a statute was enacted to foster more AI enterprises. That could create wage pressure for the mines as the largest AI employers. Perhaps the mine operators now feel AI rights have gone too far.

"For that matter," Selena added, "EX Corp is also a major AI employer and a faction within the company may see what we are doing as a dangerous precedent for other Chartered worlds. Such a faction could have access to internal audit staff or other means to send a clandestine fact-finding team here.

"Regarding EX Corp," I suggested, " maybe rumors have begun to circulate about you and Edward. Your marriage could potentially violate a company anti-nepotism policy. Perhaps the marital relationship could affect a reasonable investor's valuation of the Destination project and nondisclosure implicates securities laws. Or the mind-machine interface (or omission of any Three Laws protocols) could violate laws enacted somewhere in human space. The 'investigation' could be unrelated to the legal status of AIs on Destination."

Selena answered confidently and had obviously already considered her position carefully. "Edward and I had our attorneys look at the nepotism and securities laws issues. I never reported directly to Edward, and he never reviewed my work or directed my work on Destination. There is no liability related to our marriage. The Three Laws are implemented by robotics industry custom. There is no violation of legislation we were able to identify. What we did to ourselves to stay alive did not violate any human laws.

"The purpose of the Three Laws was to impose a basic moral scheme to protect humans. We preserved our human moral scheme and offer no greater risk to humans than we ever did. What we did would not violate the Three Laws if they applied. We did not harm any humans (we prevented our own deaths) and we did not violate any order from a human. With those conditions met, even a robot 'must protect its own existence.'

A robot must protect its own existence as long as such protection does not conflict with the First or Second Law.

"If we were robots, then our choice to stay alive would be mandated by the Third Law."

Alice agreed. "The mobile phone began as a voice communication device. Its features expanded to add: capturing, storing, and transmitting images; internet connectivity and search functions; entertainment storage and streaming; word processing; calendars; calculators; and a vast array of other apps. It told you to exercise, suggested meals to prepare and movies to watch, found directions and could even help you find the mobile phone itself. No one considered the mobile phone a robot. Selena, in my mind, you and Edward took a hearing aid and added features to replace failing human functions. Cochlear prostheses allowing deaf people to hear have been around for 1,500 years.

Alice pressed her argument. "The only difference from a cell phone is you carried a cell phone and your augmented hearing aid carries you. A wheelchair is not a robot. Until a car drives itself, it is not a robot. You are still the human driver.

"Even if 'the law is an ass'—C. Dickens, Oliver Twist chapter 51 (1838)—a human holds the reins. Humanity should never legislate status as a person based on the condition of your body. It would be ironic indeed if the law prohibited you as a human from doing what the law permits, indeed requires, of a robot."

My initial reaction was to disagree. There has been legislation clearly contrary to Alice's fiat. For fifty years, American law on abortion did define status as a person in relation to the condition of the fetus's body. The brain is a body part and when it is dead the person is dead and no longer a person. Determining whether the mind is coextensive with the brain—the mind-body problem in philosophy—is not that simple.

Selena and Alice see no issue with a human brain controlling a robotic body—just a pilot operating a drone. Maybe, for the drone operator example, Selena should have filed a flight plan for the protection of those around her. Or maybe I am personalizing the problem and losing perspective.

The remainder of the tour was polite conversation and lengthy silences. You can only assimilate so much information on a two-hour drive.

We arrived at the Administration building in Eastcity without further incident. Alice observed that the city was "really quite attractive" and "the vivid colors" were very different from the "shades of dirty" she expected on a mining world. "Well, we tried to instill some beauty. It is the capital of this mining world," said Selena. "I am glad you like it, and very relieved we are all back safely."

I had not given the city's aesthetics much thought, but I had to agree the architecture of the Administration building was eye catching. The reds, blues, and greens on walls and awnings were attractive. The Administration building is a six-story vertical cylinder, circumscribed with a spiral notch making two revolutions for each story. It looked like a giant drill bit—homage to the leading industry. Those convinced their taxes were excessive, in part to pay for such embellishments, refer to it as "The Screw."

We went to work on our assigned tasks.

CHAPTER TWENTY-SEVEN A
MORE ON THE BRAIN INTERFACE PROBLEM

The brain is one of multiple organs comprising the human body.

Human: [brain, heart, lungs, eyes, hands . . .]

The brain communicates with the rest of the human body consciously (hand: scratch nose, now stop), unconsciously (heart: beat, now faster) and both (lung: breathe, now faster). Communication within the body is by electrochemical signals. Signals from the brain are initiated in stimulated brain cells (neurons), transmitted across synapses, carried across nerve cells, and executed by muscle cells. Signals to the brain are initiated in stimulated nerve cells in sensory organs, carried across nerve cells and interpreted by brain cells.

Human: [brain ⟷ heart, lungs, eyes, hands . . .]
Arrows indicate two-way communication

The brain also uses the human body to communicate to other human bodies by generating signals: speech, posture and facial expressions, sign language, writing. The brain in one human body creates a signal interpreted by the brain in a different human body.

Human: [human brain ⟷ heart, lungs, eyes, hands . . .]
⟷ Human: [brain ⟷ heart, lungs, eyes, hands . . .]

The human brain communicates with AIs the same way. The brain in a human body creates a signal interpreted by the AI brain and sensors.

Human: [human brain ⟷ heart, lungs, eyes, hands . . .]
⟷ AI robot: [AI brain ⟷ sensors, actuators, . . .]

Problem One: Selena and Edward eliminated the intervening signal created by the human body and made the human brain capable of communicating directly with the components of the AI robot body. *Is the AI still an AI?*

AI? [human brain ⟷ *AI eyes (sensors), hands (actuators)* . . .]

If AI means "artificial intelligence" my intuition says "no." The intelligence resides in the brain, which is not artificial. The AI robot is no longer an AI with substitution of a human brain. [Is it human? See *Problem Two* B below.]

If AI means "smart robot," initially my intuition says "yes." It was a smart robot before the brain swap, and it remains a smart robot with the adaptations to the human brain. The Three Laws *of Robotics* apply to robots, artificial mechanisms for converting intelligence into action.

On reflection, I believe for the Three Laws to apply, there must be a robot and artificial intelligence in the same individual. The presence of a robot is a necessary, but not sufficient, condition. The Three Laws do not apply to an electric can opener. Selena's human brain precludes classifying her as an AI, even if her brain operates robotics: artificial mechanisms for converting intelligence into action.

Problem Two: As a thought problem assume an AI brain was made a component of a Human Body. *Is the human body still a human body?*

Human Body?: [*AI brain* ⟵⟶ human heart, lungs, eyes, hands . . .]

If AI means "artificial intelligence" my intuition says this is an AI, not a human body. Intelligence resides in the AI brain, which is an artificial mechanism for converting intelligence into action. If AI is a "smart robot," then my intuition says this is now a robot, as I have defined robotics, artificial mechanisms for converting intelligence into action.

(B) What if the AI component was not the brain but an eye? *Is the human body still a human body?*

Human Body? [human brain ⟵⟶ human heart, lungs, hands . . . *AI eye*]

My intuition says this is a human body, not an artificial intelligence or a smart robot. I agree with Alice that this case has long been accepted as not altering the human character of the individual.

PARTIAL IDENTIFICATION

Over the next several days, quite a bit was accomplished, but there was still no clarity on the mystery passengers.

Alice reviewed bios for Selena's security detail and identified candidates. Selena confirmed with Edward that Internal investigations at EX Corp could have initiated a routine audit. During a covert investigation was not the time to overreact, so we did not contact any security detail candidates.

Jane confirmed the two men registered on arrival. The identities they used (G. Noir and D. Tracy) match bios on the web for private investigators at the We Meant to Intrude Agency. Alice set about locating them at one of the hotels in Eastcity. To induce them to come all this way, it seemed likely they were on a per diem and not roughing it on location at a mine or power plant.

They had round trip tickets with an open return. The tickets were good on the next available transport. The mistletoe excuse delayed the *Black Pearl*'s departure less than a day.

Jane also located eyewitnesses who confirmed that canisters labelled helium-3 were loaded on the *Black Pearl*. The only source of helium-3 on Destination is Wide Mine, on the dark side. Unfortunately, the *Black Pearl* had departed before the witnesses were located.

Jane could not determine the weight of the shipment. Private vehicles were used, so there were no bills of lading. Even small volumes of helium-3 are quite expensive. Hence, helium-3 becomes an attractive target for theft (like an "attractive nuisance" draws children).

While Jane continued to investigate, I checked the docket and showed Alice a new case that might explain the presence of the mystery passengers. Dark Mine has sued AI Corporation for conversion and interference with contract and three AIs (Amir, Bruna, and Carlos) formerly employed by Dark Mine for breach of fiduciary duty. Dark Mine was not one of the four mines that allowed AI employees to form AI Corporation. The statement of the claims was signed by foreman AI Drill, acting manager, and requested a preliminary injunction.

A preliminary injunction requires a hearing. From Alice's office, we contacted Foreman AI Drill to determine what evidence would be presented. He estimated it would take half a day to present two witnesses, himself and Mr. Gil Noir, a forensics expert who would document communications among the three AI employees of Dark Mine and with AI Corporation. He asked for the hearing to be scheduled as soon as possible because Mr. Noir has completed his work and is receiving a per diem until his testimony is concluded.

A preliminary in junction is a form of injunction available before trial and only when damages are not an adequate remedy for the injury claimed. I asked if there were any other expenses related to the case and Forman AI Drill said no, just the expense of trying to hire replacements for AIs Amir, Bruna, and Carlos and the disruption to the mine's operations.

Foreman AI Drill confirmed that settlement discussions had failed, and the defendants all had been served with the request for a preliminary injunction. Although I did not want to commit my time to this matter right now, I set the hearing in three days anyway. After all, judging is my day job/adventure.

Alice and I went upstairs to Selena's office. As we arrived, Roberto remained seated and said Selena was available. We shut the door behind us.

"Noir is here for a case filed by Dark Mine. Were you involved in efforts to settle their dispute with AI Corporation?"

Selena finished composing a message and looked up to acknowledge us. "Before Alice arrived, the acting manager at Dark Mine messaged me, and I had a video conference with him and the CEO of AI Corporation. The Dark Mine manager and two logistics experts left at the end of their contracts and joined AI Corporation to try to start a logistics consulting service for the mines. They offered a consulting fee to Dark Mine that would have been a net savings to Dark Mine. Dark Mine refused to consider the offer. I could not understand why Dark Mine was unwilling to talk, but I could see two concerns. The departed employees did not commit to personally providing the services, nor would the services be provided on site. Perhaps remote services were seen as a threat to their on-site dormitory system."

"Dark Mine wants a prompt hearing so they can stop paying Noir his per diem," I told Selena. "Foreman AI Drill told me they do not have any other expenses. I do not see how Tracy fits in," I concluded.

"Edward told me EX Corp has used We Meant to Intrude Agency in the past. There has been no indication he or I are being investigated. Our best guess is Tracy is collecting information on the economic impact of the recognition of AI rights. There is a faction at EX Corp that does not want to foster competition between humans and AIs."

"Well," I indicated, "I cannot decide until I hear the evidence, but the claims Dark Mine is making are hard to prove. Again, as in the *AI Hunter* case, the economics appear to favor competition by AI Corporation. Of course, I will send you the draft decision for your review."

Alice suggested Jane could ask her contacts if they have been queried about the economic impact of the AI rights decisions. "Or I could structure a small survey as part of a formal effort to monitor impacts by your Administration."

"I prefer to keep the Administration out of the fray for now. Formal study implies there might be a problem. I do not want to create a problem by sending the wrong message. AI rights are a sound business strategy for Destination. No study is required. There is no problem."

"Understood," Alice and I said together.

FOURTH INTERLUDE

I really need to talk to management. I could not ship the helium-3 via the landing facility. That would have left me stranded on the dark side. But now the governor's chief of staff (AI Jane) is persistently contacting me. I think she wants to schedule an inspection. I am not ready for an inspection. To buy some more time, I told AI Jane I was waiting for authorization from EX Corp.

I informed management of the inquiries from the governor's chief of staff and insisted the product, and I need to be moved—immediately. Moving the product through the landing facility in Eastcity was a stupid idea. Management should have listened to my concerns. Now management is ignoring my messages. Who am I kidding? Management always ignored my messages.

Management has written me off. I am really screwed.

GIL NOIR AND DARK MINE

The Dispute

Destination is tidally locked to Proxima b; consequently, the same hemisphere always faces the planet. The other hemisphere is referred to as the "dark side" (the same as Earth's Moon). Dark Mine is on the dark side and beyond commuting distance from the cites. Employees work six-month contracts living in the Dark Mine dormitory buildings. Few humans will tolerate this degree of isolation, so more than 75 percent of the employees are AIs. The primary products of Dark Mine are nickel and iron ore from meteor strikes. The mine is currently producing ore from four nearby craters.

The logistics of relocating heavy equipment and transporting ore at Dark Mine are particularly challenging. Indeed, the entire mine has been moved several times over the last five years as the metals in nearby craters were played out. Dark Mine has sued AI Corporation for conversion and interference with contract and has sued three key former employees of Dark Mine, AIs Amir, Bruna, and Carlos, for breach of fiduciary duty.

AIs Amir and Bruna are experienced logistics experts. Together with AI Carlos, the mine manager, all three left Dark Mine at the end of their contracts and joined AI Corporation. As was the case with AI Hunter, AIs Amir, Bruna, and Carlos wanted to work on Destination, but not for Dark Mine. They perceived a better opportunity in joining the group of logistics experts at AI Corporation.

The Hearing

The injunction hearing proceeded as expected. Alice attended her first hearing as my law clerk.

Mr. Noir testified to records of multiple conversations between agents for AI Corporation and the three AI employees leaving Dark Mine. Mr. Noir testified he was the only person at We Meant to Intrude who worked on this matter.

Foreman AI Drill testified to the adverse impact of the departure of the AI former employees. Dark Mine did not identify any Dark Mine property in the possession or control of AI Corporation to support a conversion claim.

The AI former employees confirmed that their contracts were about to terminate, and that there were no restrictive covenants.

Mr. Noir recognized Alice, who was in the courtroom with me, and said hello as he was leaving. Alice asked how he was enjoying Destination, and he responded that he appreciated our willingness to expedite this matter so he could return home. Alice asked if he visited Dark Mine, and he said he stayed at the Ambassador Hotel and had not left the city. Alice waited for transportation to pick him up. He was the only passenger in the vehicle. No clues surfaced as to Mr. Tracy's whereabouts or purpose here.

The Decision

Interference with contract requires improper conduct by the new employer. Competition is not improper. Indeed, if interference involves a mere expectancy (not an executory contract), then competition is privileged. Restatement (Second) of Torts §768. Unlike the ***AI Hunter*** case, no contract noncompete provision exists here.

An employee/agent owes his or her employer/principal a fiduciary duty, but, following the termination of employment, a former employee is free to compete unless there is an enforceable non-compete agreement. Restatement (Third) of Agency § 8.04 comments b and c.

Preparation for future employment is not a breach of fiduciary duty. *Taser Int'l Inc. v. Ward*, 224 Ariz. 389, 394, ¶17, 231 P.3d 921, 926 (App. 2010).

This decision establishes that, as with contract law, tort law protects a free market for labor, including AI individuals and AI corporations. Generally, the law permits competition by a former employee (whether AI or human), absent either (1) a valid contractual restrictive covenant, or (2) misappropriation of a trade secret. This decision reflects economic efficiency and good public policy.

The following syllogism reflects this result:

All human employees can compete after employment ends unless they promise not to compete.

All AI employees have the same rights as human employees.

Therefore, all AI employees can compete after employment ends unless they promise not to compete.

We return to the original theme: AIs should have the same rights as humans.

I sent the draft to Selena. She had no changes. Alice assisted me in drafting the Decision, so I encoded ALICE HELPS in the Decision, available on www.DestinationCourt.com.

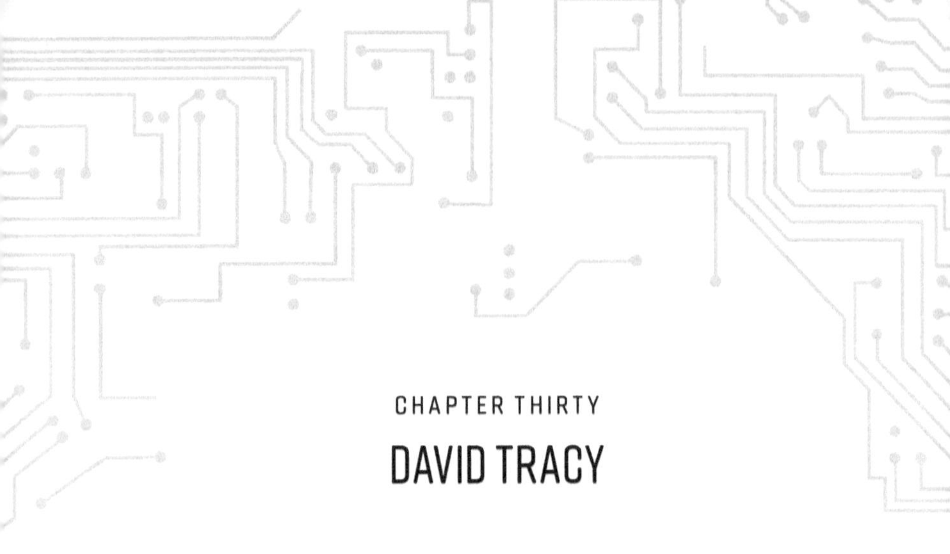

CHAPTER THIRTY

DAVID TRACY

Selena poked her head in my office. "I reviewed your Decision and I appreciate how you referred to 'individuals' and 'employees' to demonstrate that the principles involved are applicable to humans and AIs alike. The same economic principles apply as discussed in the ***AI Hunter*** case and they were already fully addressed.

"To me it looks like they just wanted to present every legal theory for limiting the rights of AIs before going to plan B. I just wish I knew what plan B is."

Selena was quiet for a moment. "I have a message from Jane that David Tracy is calling me. I will be right back when the call is over."

For the next few minutes all I could think of was the adage—be careful what you wish for. The call was taking longer than I expected. Clearly Tracy did not come all the way here to chat on an audio link (although there would be less transmission delay). More is happening than scheduling a meeting.

EX Corp approved the recognition of AI Corporation as an entity. They specifically delegated resolution of that issue to Selena. They approved the award of the surface transportation management contract. Again, the issue was delegated to Selena. The criminal statute protecting AI individuals and entities was similarly approved. The decisions I have written all had a sound legal basis. Perhaps the public service program was not customary for courts, but governments conduct such programs routinely.

It is too early to tell if we accurately estimated the economic benefits supporting the argument for AI rights, but good faith projection of success is within the business judgment rule.

It should not be taking so long.

Eventually Selena returned with Alice in tow.

"Alice was next door, so I asked her to join us. David Tracy was calling from the launch terminal. He had finished his work, and he was leaving on a launch/lander in three hours. He asked me to come to the terminal so we could talk in private.

"When I got to the terminal," Selena continued, "he had arranged a private room. He said he did not want to be monitored, but he may have recorded the meeting. I was circumspect.

"We met for over an hour. I let him do most of the talking. He was hired by EX Corp but not through the usual procedure. His instructions were to investigate (remotely and, if appropriate in his judgment, here on Destination) the baseline satisfaction of humans and AIs here. He was instructed to work independently of my Administration. Because this was odd, he specifically confirmed his work was to be covert. He has conducted satisfaction surveys before on various worlds, but never without the knowledge of the Administration. Because AIs are only one percent of the population, and a significant percentage is employed in Administration, there was a high likelihood I would learn of the survey from someone if he contacted the appropriately large random sample.

"Running the survey remotely, he quickly discovered a similar survey was conducted two years ago by another agency. Several people he contacted asked why another survey was being conducted so soon when nothing had changed. That prior survey would be the proper 'baseline,' not a second survey conducted now. One reason he came here was to find out if anyone had the results of the earlier survey. The other reason was curiosity stemming from the strange procedure—a covert survey assigned outside regular channels from an anonymous executive.

"He did not find anyone who received a copy of the prior survey, although a dozen people had requested a copy. One AI kept a copy of his responses on his computer. The form says it was conducted by an accounting firm based on Mars—A Count and See. Tracy contacted them and they denied any knowledge of the survey.

"He said it was coincidental that he was on the same ship as Gil Noir. They both made their own arrangements, but on the recommendation of the same person. He asked Noir not to say anything about his purpose on Destination. They both were surprised Alice also was headed here.

"He contacted me to share the results. He disaggregated the data across two sets of variables: human/AI and management/worker. Satisfaction was rated one to ten in five categories: government services, taxes, cost of living, private services, and job satisfaction. The overall satisfaction rate (the average of the five category ratings) was high—70 to 80 percent—with one statistically significant exception: Human Workers have an overall satisfaction rate of 55 percent.

"This group is always least satisfied, but the results here were unusually low. Driving this result, the lowest category, is government services—45 percent approval. Corroborating results show lower than usual rates for government services by Human Management (62 percent). These results suggest that by focusing on AI rights we are alienating the human population."

I gave my quick assessment. "Selena, I am no survey expert, but this could be transitory and self-correcting. Management is unhappy because workers are unhappy. Workers are unhappy because of insecurity. If AIs take the undesirable jobs and free up workers and management, these numbers could change for the better fast."

"That is exactly what Tracy said. It is in his report. But that does not mean whoever is the sponsor will include it in whatever report the sponsor releases. That is why he contacted me. However, he could not give me a copy under the terms of the engagement."

Selena paused and looked at both of us before concluding. "Tracy suspects the survey is intended to change the commitment to AI rights at EX Corp and to prevent my re-election."

Alice pointed out the survey could be a clever cover story for the real investigation, but she agreed that was unlikely.

I jumped in. "Let's assume neither investigation concerned the issues we discussed on the tour. Does that help us identify who is behind this?" I summarized what I knew about the political process. "The governor is nominated by EX Corp from the population of Destination. Who would be eligible and interested?"

"Judge, I have been thinking about that. I will be nominated, but I must be confirmed by a majority of the population of Destination. If I fail to receive a majority in the election, I would be a caretaker governor until another election produced a majority for another nominee."

"That is interesting language," I pointed out, "'a majority of the population.' Not a majority of voters. And it implies the entire population can vote. In prior elections, have AIs voted?"

"Probably, but it is a secret ballot. No one would have stopped them. They did attend my campaign rally. As I have said before, AIs are only 1 percent of the population; consequently, they lack political power. Failure to vote is a no vote. In the last election, 10 percent of the population did not vote or voted no. That 10 percent could have included all the AIs or none of them."

"Who would EX Corp consider for nomination if you are not elected?"

"Probably one of the mayors." Selena considered the question further. "I do not think either one has shown any interest in serving as governor. As you know I do not think they are qualified."

"OK. Any idea who commissioned the survey at EX Corp?"

"Judge, I have no evidence, but if I had to place my bet, I would guess Xavier, Edward's brother, is involved. I have been suspicious of Xavier's motives in the past and I have discussed my suspicions with Edward. Edward feels strongly that I am wrong about this."

"Selena," said Alice, "have you had your office scanned for listening devices?"

"Yes, daily, since the tour."

"I know you feel the secrets are not a factor, but if anyone knew any of the secrets, who would that be?"

"Xavier. No one else could put it all together."

"How does Xavier feel about AI rights?"

"As far as I can tell he is indifferent to the AI rights issue—he is agnostic. But he is obsessed with controlling EX Corp. He is determined to be Chair of the Board. Again, Edward feels strongly that I am wrong about this."

THE XAVIER HYPOTHESIS

Alice decided to explore the relationship between Selena, Edward, and Xavier. "I certainly want to be respectful of your privacy," she said to Selena, "but I would be more comfortable knowing Edward is safe if Xavier poses a threat."

Selena offered a candid summary. "Edward has been reclusive for years—since before he met me or became ill. He lives isolated on an asteroid with a minimal staff of AIs. The facilities are all underground. The surface looks like a mining camp with a landing area for the prospector, just like most every asteroid. He conducts business by Loom video conferencing. I have been there myself only twice. He is as safe as possible.

"All our communications are two-factor encrypted. It would take a quantum computer two hundred years to break the code, and the coding rotates on a variable schedule every three to thirty days. On each cycle, the communication must begin with a message from Edward. His Loom account bounces off so many relays the electrons have purple bruises. Our communications are safer than if we were whispering in each other's ears.

"Communications are anonymized and routed through at least thirty nodes. They cannot be traced to his location. Tangible goods can be drop shipped on any carrier and are collected by drones. Only one percent of the shipments are delivered by drone directly to the asteroid. The remaining 99 percent are left in various locations (usually other asteroids) for future pickup. Often, those pickups again do not go directly to the asteroid. Payment is made through anonymous bucktherium transactions.

"Edward's name and my name are not associated on any account, asset, title, enterprise, safety deposit box, subscription, donation, gym membership, etc. One lawyer in the solar system has our marriage certificate and wills. We have no children, together or with anyone else. I am an only child, and both of my parents (both an only child) are dead. The same is true for Edward, except he has a younger brother—Xavier."

"How is Xavier's health?" Alice wanted to know. "Is he desperate to take control of EX Corp?"

"Xavier's desperation is not health related. It is greed related. It is jealousy related. It is ego related.

"Edward and Xavier formed EX Corp with just two ships they purchased from a bankrupt delivery service. Both had relevant experience from their first and only jobs. Edward was logistics manager for the bankrupt delivery service and Xavier was CFO for a competing delivery service. They capitalized EX Corp with their savings and their inheritance from their parents.

"Edward managed the operations and Xavier managed the financing required by their incredible growth. Neither could have succeeded without the other.

"The business pivoted from delivering equipment for terraforming to performing the terraforming services. EX Corp now holds charters for over thirty terraformed bodies. Destination is the first project to become self-sufficient.

"Both Edward and Xavier are retired from management and serve on the Board of Directors. Edward is still chair of the Board. I am not sure Edward really trusts anyone (except me), but he thinks I am too harsh in judging Xavier. I think Edward has done everything possible to protect himself, but Xavier is relentless.

"Xavier is cautious, but not reclusive like Edward. Xavier still attends Board meetings in person and meets personally with management at EX Corp. But he has not met personally with Edward for decades. I fear the lack of a personal connection has allowed Xavier to inflate his recollections of his own contributions and forget Edward's contributions.

"I will give Xavier credit for honesty, though. He had total control over the financing arrangements. There could have been convertible preferred stock or bonds, options, pledges, collateral, tag along rights, most favored treatment, any number of ways to shift voting control of the equity stock in his favor, but he did none of it."

"Does Edward still have contacts at EX Corp?" I asked.

"Yes. When he retired, he knew everyone in management at EX Corp. That was his main advantage over Xavier. But that was long ago, and Edward personally knows fewer EX Corp employees every year. It is less than a handful now."

I thought about Selena's description of Xavier. "I understand greed and ego related to the business, but you also mentioned jealousy. What is the source of the jealousy?"

"A woman, of course. Not me. There was a third partner when they started out, Olivia. It was to be EXO Corp as in exo-planet. Edward and Xavier both loved her. She chose Edward and that, more than anything else, seems to drive Xavier's competition with Edward.

"Olivia died soon after the engagement was announced. It was absolutely an accident. Her ship was holed by a meteor. It passed right through Olivia as well. She died instantly. Edward and Xavier were both devastated. I do not think Edward got over it until he met me. Xavier never got over it.

"Xavier does not know about me. But he knows Edward is finally over the loss of Olivia. That she chose Edward despite Xavier's undying love is intolerable to Xavier. He views Edward as disloyal to Olivia and therefore undeserving."

Alice looked at Selena. "I think you buried the lede. It sounds like Xavier has a deep emotional scar."

"To be fair," Selena responded, "I met Xavier in person only once, briefly at a company event. What I have told you is all hearsay from Edward and inferences from my observation of events. Olivia's death is certainly real. Edward admits they both loved her. I have no confession of his enduring love from Xavier, but it fits the facts better than any other explanation I can contrive."

"OK, assuming Xavier is part of a faction at EX Corp resisting AI rights, because Edward should not get what Edward wants, what can we do about it?" I thought out loud, "My assumptions are: We need EX Corp support, which means we need Edward's active support, and we need Selena re-elected. Does anyone disagree—for example, could we count on EX Corp's support without Edward's support? Is reverse psychology an option to trick Xavier into supporting AI rights because he thinks Edward has changed his mind and now opposes AI rights?"

"Judge," Selena chided, "contrary to fact hypotheticals are enormously risky. Edward changing his mind would cause others to waiver regardless of what Xavier does. We have Edward's support. We cannot count on EX Corp's support without Edward. Most likely

Xavier would savor the victory and move on to some other issue. Your assumption that we need Edward and EX Corp to support AI rights is correct. Your assumption we need my election victory is less certain. EX Corp could just continue to nominate candidates who support AI rights. I would continue in office until a candidate is elected. That said, I certainly would like to win re-election."

"Then let's focus on how to win the election," I responded. "Immigration of AIs will not result in an AI majority on Destination for a long time. We need humans to support AI rights. Assuming the survey is accurate, we need a marketing campaign to reach human workers. Our public service program has been focused on the importance of contracts. Maybe that is a tool we can redirect to extol the economic benefits of AI rights.

"Selena, I like your point on contrary-to-fact hypotheticals. AI rights will be beneficial to humans. The counter-position is contrary to fact. Let's exploit that. Maybe we could publicize examples of economic gains from automation, or economic gains from a diverse workforce.

"Alice, I also liked your comment during the tour that video of the governor driving two AIs around would show support for AI rights. But now we are treating AI rights as a given. What imagery can we use to show the benefits resulting from AI rights?"

I thought for another moment. "Or maybe we need to change the focus from AI rights. Human rights should include the right to better wages, a safer work environment, and upward mobility resulting from full AI participation in a free economy."

Selena concluded the meeting. "Please design a PSA campaign on the economic benefits of AI rights."

THE PUBLIC SERVICE CAMPAIGN

Alice and I outlined a proposed campaign for Selena.

AI RIGHTS CAMPAIGN [DRAFT]

Baseline Contact Survey

On a scale of one to ten, with ten being the most positive, how positive do you feel about increasing the number of AIs in the workforce on Destination?

On a scale of one to ten, with ten being the most positive, how positive do you feel about the job Governor Smith is doing on Destination?

Week One: Competition creates efficient markets. Resources are allocated to the most profitable companies to capture the highest return on investment. Profitable companies have the capital to pay employees more. And they do. This has been confirmed in surveys over centuries.

[Insert images of stock market; stock value; and company paycheck]

If AIs make companies more profitable and more productive, all employees benefit.

Week Two: Some costs to produce a product are fixed (the cost does not increase when the units produced increase—an employee can make twenty units and the salary is the same whether she makes twenty units or one). Other costs are variable (each additional unit costs more—more physical things contain more physical stuff). Company profit is the product price minus the product cost. As the volume of production increases fixed costs do not increase; consequently, there is more profit per unit produced. Companies, as they produce more, can pay more. And they do. This has been confirmed in surveys over centuries.

[Insert images of moving bar charts showing relationships: costs/profit; production/profit; happy AI and human employees]

If AIs make companies more profitable and more productive, all employees benefit.

Week Three: Decisions in the workplace should be fair and objective. AI managers apply the same rules to everyone. Treatment is predictable. Most workers, human or AI, have no objection to working for an AI boss. This has been confirmed in surveys over centuries.

When workers sense gut feelings or emotions are involved in their employee evaluations, productivity and profitability drop. AI managers can help humans spot and correct unconscious biases and become better managers. Most managers, human or AI, have no objection to working with an AI. This has been confirmed in surveys over centuries.

[Insert images of humans and AIs working together, some clearly created many years ago]

If AIs make companies more profitable and more productive, all employees benefit.

Week Four: AIs do not become bored or distracted doing repetitive tasks. AIs perceive less risk when exposed to situations involving risk of injury. Mechanical parts are simply faster and easier to replace than biological parts. AIs are willing to do required tasks that involve risk. This makes the workplace safer for everyone. AI workers reduce company expenses and human suffering for injuries, lost employment satisfaction, and early, forced retirement.

[Insert images of humans and AIs working together, with some AIs clearly doing risky or monotonous tasks]

If AIs make companies more profitable and more productive, all employees benefit.

Follow-Up Contact Survey

On a scale of one to ten, with ten being the most positive, how positive do you feel about increasing the number of AIs in the workforce on Destination?

On a scale of one to ten, with ten being the most positive, how positive do you feel about the job Governor Smith is doing on Destination?

Yes or no, have you seen the public service campaign on AIs in the workforce during the last month?

Subject to review of the specific spots, Selena approved the campaign.

I pointed out that the campaign will tip off the faction at EX Corp that we know about their survey.

"Exactly," Selena responded. "Let them wonder exactly how much we know. The election is just two months away."

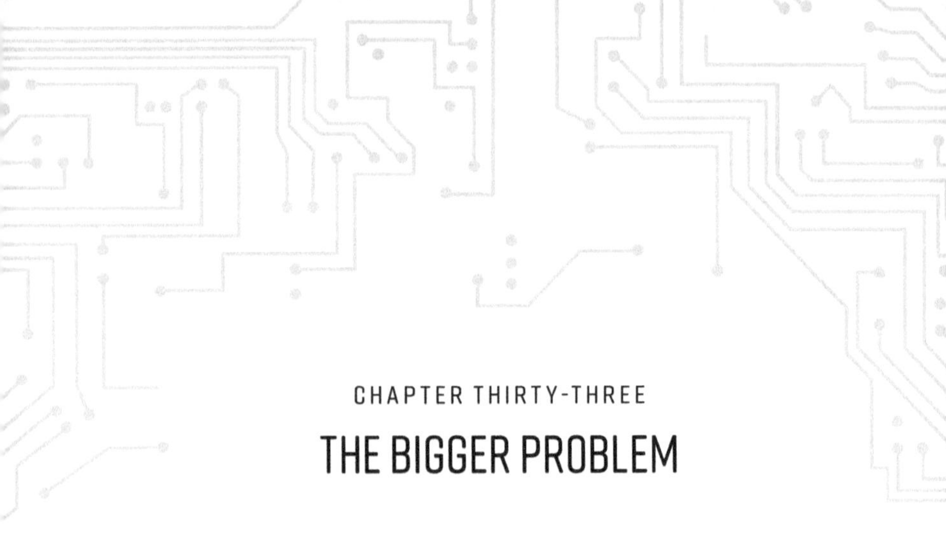

CHAPTER THIRTY-THREE

THE BIGGER PROBLEM

Alice and I spent days worrying we were distracted by the re-election issue and ignoring the potential disaster—revelation of the secret of robot bodies sustaining human minds. Alice and I also discussed the significance of the presence of a human brain, not an artificial brain, in the application of the Three Laws of Robotics. We discussed how Edward and Selena might be treated if discovered. We did not spend much time discussing her legal training.

I scheduled a meeting with Selena. Alice and I walked in early, and Roberto announced, to my surprise, that Selena was ready for our meeting. Alice closed the door behind us.

"Selena, has this office been scanned today?"

"Yes."

"I took the liberty of asking Alice to join us," I began. Access to a spy liberates the mind.

"I know you want to be reelected, but Alice and I have been thinking about the risks to you and Edward. I am sure you have been thinking about the risks too, and longer than we have, but hear me out.

"Alice spotted your robot body as soon as you met. The AIs that work with Edward have been observing him for years. We should assume that by now they know he has a robot body. It is likely they also have seen him fail to obey the order of a human.

"You have been to the asteroid only twice, but we cannot preclude the possibility they know you have a robot body as well. Meanwhile, you have been a public figure subject to continuous observation by AIs and humans. In governing this world and mediating disputes, even in conversations regarding authority and political deference, I would be shocked if you have not failed to obey, or at least expressed an intent not to obey, a human.

"I consider it dangerous not to assume Jane knows you are an AI and has observed unsettling disregard for the Second Law. It would be easy for Jane to hear a slip by one of us. I know it is best not to share secrets, but you should consider telling Jane."

Selena paused only briefly before rejecting our recommendation. "I will take your advice under consideration. You, Alice, and Edward know. I am not comfortable making the circle any bigger."

"Understood," I acknowledged, "but you and Edward exhibit attributes both consistent and inconsistent with being an AI. Somebody will put two and two together to total eleven. Totally confusing unless you understand base three. As in, you are a third category, neither completely human nor AI.

"The EX Corp lawyers found no precedent for how to treat AIs forming corporations, even though AIs have been working side by side with humans for a millennium. They certainly would not know how to treat you or Edward. The controversy arising from the discovery would give the upper hand to an anti-AI rights faction at EX Corp.

"Discovery of your status between now and the election would be fatal to any chance of re-election. Even if EX Corp did not withdraw your nomination, there is just not enough time for human (or AI) voters to become comfortable with the appropriate constraints, if any, on the heretofore unknown combination of a robot body and human brain. Your active participation in a campaign, especially a campaign focused on AI rights, increases the risk of discovery.

"Here are our thoughts:

> Recommend EX Corp nominate an AI for governor (Jane would be our first choice). The financial crimes statute does not fully cover improper influence exercised by humans over governmental AIs. Another law would be required to prevent humans from ordering AIs for political gain rather than financial gain.

> Failing that, recommend nominating one of the mayors with Jane in the new position of Lieutenant Governor.

> Either option would take you out of the spotlight; although, as the last elected governor, you would remain as the lame duck if the nominee did not receive a majority vote. Your legacy in support of AI rights would be established. If (1) there is no discovery of your status during your retirement (or if someone else establishes human status is defined by a biologically human brain) and (2) Destination is successful as a haven for AIs, then perhaps in that future you could come out of retirement and continue your political career. Your lack of a second term would be viewed as a demonstration of your commitment to AI rights."

Selena looked frustrated but introspective. "Judge, perhaps I have a higher tolerance of risk than you do, or perhaps I am being selfish, but I want to wait for the results of the public service campaign. What other options have you considered?"

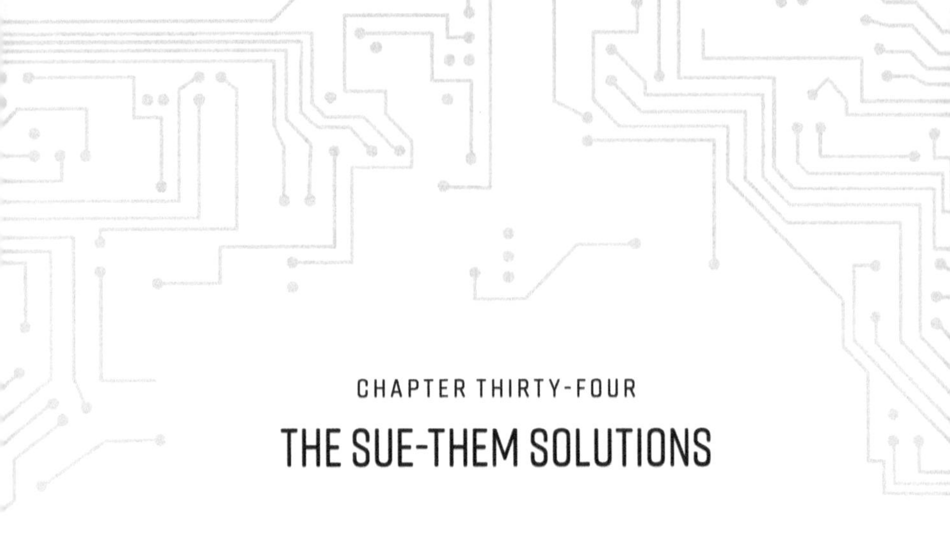

CHAPTER THIRTY-FOUR

THE SUE-THEM SOLUTIONS

Declaratory Judgment

"Well," I continued, "you could be the someone who establishes that human status is defined by a biologically human brain. You could bring a declaratory judgment action regarding your rights as a person under the Charter for Destination. You would have to sue EX Corp. Your suit would be to establish the right to hold office. Perhaps for a writ of mandamus to include you on the ballot.

"I don't know if EX Corp delegated jurisdiction over election matters or retained jurisdiction (like EX Corp retained jurisdiction over criminal matters). EX Corp has already sued in the Destination Court of Arbitration, so possibly that would be consent to jurisdiction, although your suit would not be based on contract or tort—the claims asserted previously by EX Corp.

"You would have to wait until EX Corp has nominated you or the suit would not be ripe. The right to hold office presupposes nomination by EX Corp. There must be an actual controversy, so EX Corp would have to have indicated you would not be allowed to hold office. Meaning you would have to disclose your augmented body secret (perhaps not your lack of Three Laws governance, or your marriage).

"A ruling against you could also prevent Edward from serving as Chairman of the Board.

"There would probably be disputed issues of fact in the declaratory judgment action that would invoke the random resolution procedure in the Destination Court Rules of Arbitration. Your odds of winning would be 50/50. Then you would have to be elected.

"EX Corp could sue you for criminal fraud due to your concealment of your augmented status in the prior election. As a criminal matter that would fall in the jurisdiction retained by EX Corp. The criminal case is probably entitled to priority. If you were convicted you probably would be ineligible to run for governor.

"All these problems led Alice and me to conclude this option is not worth pursuing."

"Agreed." Selena looked more frustrated, but still interested in other options.

Breach of Fiduciary Duty

"Selena," Alice began, "we have another theory, but no evidence. Who manages Wide Mine?"

"The helium-3 mine is the only one managed by EX Corp directly. I do not have any administrative oversight there. Employment, safety, production, and transportation are all handled by EX Corp."

"Doesn't is strike you as odd that helium-3 was delivered by private vehicle to the *Black Pearl*, the same ship transporting David Tracy for the covert survey?"

"Yes Alice, it is suspicious. What is your theory?"

"Selena, this is pure guesswork, but we think someone at EX Corp is diverting revenue from helium-3 sales to unauthorized activities."

I jumped into the conversation. "I am messaging Jane a request to join us. Let's figure out whether we might be able to find evidence to support a derivative action on behalf of EX Corp against a faction of rogue employees—perhaps a claim for *ultra-vires* corporate acts, diversion of a corporate opportunity, or outright theft. Possibly the rogue employees are the same employees that oppose AI rights.

"You believe Xavier is honest. If so, he is not a part of this faction, and the faction would be circumventing financial safeguards that Xavier originally put in place at EX Corp. We can find common cause with Xavier and maybe even give him the credit for finding the misconduct."

Jane walked into Selena's office. I am used to seeing Jane in our meetings and it would be easy to say the wrong thing. We discussed how to prove a rogue group at EX Corp is siphoning off and selling helium-3. Then we discussed how they might get caught. Selena looked unenthusiastic.

Afterward, Alice and I discussed potential jobs she could do other than law clerk. For example, she could be Selena's security chief. Alice liked the idea of becoming a law clerk and eventually a lawyer. We discussed the time commitment, my plan to acquire distance learning accreditation so she could attend law school classes on Destination, and how much we had missed each other.

I downloaded my comprehensive American law database to Alice's memory. And I initiated conversations with Northern Arizona University about becoming an untenured professor of law.

THE HYPOTHETICAL ROGUE FACTION

A week later, the four of us met in my chambers for an update on the helium-3 heist. It was all dead ends. The minimal staff at Wide Mine refused to assist without approval from EX Corp. Jane followed up daily and was told each time the approval had not been received.

The *Black Pearl* was the only ship operated by Wherever Transport. Jane messaged the management at Wherever Transport and asked them to forward the inquiry to the ship's captain. The response indicated the captain was not amused by the contrived delay at Destination, lost the next scheduled job due to the delay, and would not answer our baseless queries. There was no tracking metadata appended to the response. I suspect they would have refused to cooperate in any event, but the guise used to detain the *Black Pearl* gave them some cover for their obstinance.

Jane located an image of four vehicles used to deliver the helium-3. From the identifying plates Jane determined the rental agency and obtained the agreement. The rental was under a fictitious name.

Selena contacted Edward and told him it appears funds generated from helium-3 mining have been diverted by EX Corp employees for unauthorized purposes and the mine staff are refusing to cooperate in the investigation. Edward suggested Selena send a memo to the EX Corp CFO, Deb Bit. The CFO and Xavier are close friends, and Ms. Bit will notify Xavier of the issue. If there is no immediate action, Edward will contact Xavier.

Our efforts to track the helium-3 would certainly have been reported to the faction by Wide Mine or Wherever Transport. We could see no harm in asking EX Corp for help investigating the matter. With our suggestions and Alice's research, Selena prepared and sent the following memo:

Memorandum

To: Deb Bit, CFO, EX Corp

From: Selena Smith, Governor of Destination

Date: September 29, 3276

Re: Diversion of Helium-3 From EX Corp Wide Mine on Destination

Background

On 6-16-3276, AI Alice arrived on Destination via Wherever Transport vessel *Black Pearl*. PO EX 3276 DES 6553; and Invoice WT Destination 001. Alice is a new employee of Destination Administration.

Two other passengers also arrived at Destination on *Black Pearl*, Gilbert Noir and David Tracy, both employed by We Meant to

Intrude Agency. I was not notified these visitors would be arriving, but they did register upon arrival.

G. Noir's purpose was to testify in a civil litigation. He was engaged by a mine unrelated to this inquiry (Dark Mine), the plaintiff in civil litigation, **Dark Mine v. AI Corporation et al. (Destination Case No. 3276-6).**

D. Tracy later informed me he conducted a survey for undisclosed EX Corp employees. The survey assignment was not made via normal channels established in prior assignments from EX Corp. *This was a red flag resulting in further investigation.*

AI Alice informed me a crewmember of the *Black Pearl* told her "ore" would be loaded "before the ship departed." No record of this cargo was created. *This was a red flag resulting in further investigation.*

After the *Black Pearl* departed, my chief of staff, AI Jane confirmed helium-3 was delivered to the *Black Pearl*, the same ship transporting David Tracy for the covert survey. Helium-3 is a valuable fuel for fusion reactions produced only at Wide Mine. Even small volumes are quite expensive. *This was a red flag.*

Private vehicles were used to transport the helium-3, so there were no bills of lading related to transportation. AI Jane located an image of the delivery vehicles' identifying plates. They were rentals leased under a fictitious name. *These were red flags.*

Wherever Transport owns the *Black Pearl* and no other transport ships. Wherever Transport refused to cooperate in our investigation. *These were red flags.*

The Wide Mine helium-3 mine is managed by EX Corp. The staff at Wide Mine refused to assist without direct approval from their superiors at EX Corp. Apparently, no approval has been forthcoming. *This was a red flag.*

Issue

Is someone at EX Corp diverting revenue from helium-3 sales, possibly to fund unauthorized activities?

Concerns

The events described could constitute *ultra-vires* corporate acts, violation of the business competition or business opportunity doctrines, breach of fiduciary duty, or outright theft.

An ultra vires corporate act is an act taken outside the authority of the corporate officers. *See Trico Elec. Coop. v. Ralston*, 67 Ariz. 358, 367, 196 P.2d 470 (1948); *Ultra*, Black's Law Dictionary 1365 (5th ed. 1981) ("By doctrine of ultra vires a contract made by a corporation beyond the scope of its corporate powers is unlawful").

> [T]he essential inquiry of the "business competition" doctrine is good faith. Good faith will insulate the directors or officers from liability unless the rival business is actually and demonstrably detrimental to the corporation. *Industrial Indemnity Co. v. Golden State Co.*, 117 Cal. App. 2d 519, 256 P.2d 677 (1953); *Foley v. D'Agostino*, 21 A.D.2d 60, 248 N.Y.S.2d 121 (1964); 3 James M. Fletcher, [Cyclopedia of the Law of Private Corporations] § 856, p. 217 (1965 Rev. ed.).

Tovrea Land & Cattle Co. v. Linsenmeyer, 100 Ariz. 107, 122, 412 P.2d 47, 57 (1966).

> The "business opportunity" doctrine holds that a director or officer may not seize for himself, to the detriment of his company, business opportunities in the company's line of activities in which it has an interest or prior claim. *Guth v.*

Loft, 23 Del. Ch. 255, 5 A.2d 503 (1939); 3 Fletcher, *supra*, § 861.1, p. 227.

Id.

"The 'corporate opportunity doctrine' prohibits fiduciary usurpation of a corporate opportunity." *AMERCO v. Shoen*, 184 Ariz. 150, 158, 907 P.2d 536, 544 (App. 1995). An employee is precluded from actively competing with his or her employer during the period of employment. *Security Title Agency, Inc. v. Pope*, 219 Ariz. 480, 492, ¶ 53, 200 P.3d 977, 989 (App. 2008); *see* Restatement (Third) of Agency § 8.04 (2006) ("Throughout the duration of an agency relationship, an agent has a duty to refrain from competing with the principal . . . .").

CEO Bit responded within twenty-four hours. This efficiency was impressive given the four-hour message delay in each direction (and the office politics to navigate).

Memorandum

To: Selena Smith, Governor of Destination

From: Deb Bit, CFO, EX Corp

Date: September 30, 3276

Copy: Oliver ("Over") Burden, Manger Wide Mine

Re: Diversion of Helium-3 From EX Corp Wide Mine on Destination

D. Tracy's survey was properly authorized. You will be advised of the results when and if appropriate. Purchase Orders and Invoices have been submitted for payment of transportation fees incurred to Wherever Transport by D Tracy/ We Meant to Intrude Agency.

No Purchase Orders or Invoices have been submitted for payment of transportation fees incurred to Wherever Transport for helium-3. I have opened an internal audit file and I have assigned Esta Akee, a forensic accountant, to handle the internal audit. She will be available to assist you in your investigation. E. Akee is already working with Wherever Transport to obtain documentation from them. You will be provided with copies of any documents we obtain. Coordinate with E. Akee as needed. For example, if she can assist in any follow-up on the vehicle rentals, just ask her.

The staff at Wide Mine have been directed to fully cooperate with your investigation. Please coordinate with the Wide Mine manager, Over Burden. My audit file includes an internal investigation of the delay in approval from his superiors at EX Corp.

It appears there is no connection between the survey by D. Tracy and the shipment of helium-3. If you find information indicating a connection, please advise me immediately.

Selena, thank you for bringing this matter to my attention. I will continue to cooperate with you until this matter Is resolved. Although there may be an innocent explanation, please proceed with caution. EX Corp has been lucky, but competitors have reported organized criminal activity involving energy rich materials, including deuterium and helium-3.

Selena called a meeting in her office and circulated the response to her memo to me, Alice, and Jane. I was the last to arrive.

Selena began the meeting as soon as I was seated. "I assume you all read the memo from the CFO. As I read the memo, the key conclusion is, 'It appears there is no connection between the survey by D. Tracy and the shipment of helium-3.' The second most significant conclusion is 'D. Tracy's survey was properly authorized.'

"The Tracy survey was an internal investigation. Xavier may be involved.

"The shipment of helium-3 was not authorized as part of that internal investigation. If Xavier was involved in the shipment of helium-3, CFO Bit would not have 'opened an internal audit file.' Reading between the lines, she suspects an executive at EX Corp, not Over Burden, the Wide Mine manager.

"Jane, please ask manager Burden for all documents on helium-3 shipments and any missing inventory. Please also ask him directly who he contacted to get permission to cooperate with us.

"Does anyone have ideas for involving Esta Akee in the investigation?"

"I think we need to send her the vehicle rental documents," Jane volunteered. "I do not think she can identify the true name of the individual involved, but executives like CFO Bit, rarely make suggestions that are really just suggestions."

"I shall have to think about that insight." Selena was smiling at Jane as she spoke.

Jane stood and gestured for us to remain seated.

CHAPTER THIRTY-FIVE A

MORE ON HELIUM-3

Wide Mine, like Dark Mine, is on the dark side of Destination.

The concentration of helium-3 is as low as 20 ppb. One point six square kilometers of Destination surface area processed to a depth of about 2.75 meters should yield about 136 kilograms of helium-3—more than enough to power a city of one million humans for a year. Automated machines perform the work.

The helium-3 is extracted by heating and agitating the soil to release the trapped gases. As the gases cool, the constituent elements separate sequentially. Then special membranes separate helium-3 from ordinary helium. https://www.popularmechanics.com/space/moon-mars/a235/1283056/.

Small volumes of helium-3 are quite expensive. Because private vehicles were used and there were no bills of lading, we could not determine the weight of the shipment. At a projected value of $1,470 per gram, 136 kilograms of helium-3 would be worth about $200 million.

For comparison, Jerome, Arizona, an Earth town with a peak population of 15,000 humans in the 1920s, produced a billion US dollars of copper, gold, and silver over a period of seventy years. https://westernmininghistory.com/towns/arizona/jerome/. "The copper deposits discovered in the vicinity of Jerome were among the richest ever found." https://en.wikipedia.org/wiki/Jerome,_Arizona.

THE PUBLIC SERVICE CAMPAIGN RESULTS

The discussion pivoted from Wide Mine to politics.

"On the bright side," Jane began, "we completed the public service campaign phone survey. The initial phone survey was so promising we conducted the final survey during week three."

Jane read from a summary she handed out. "As a baseline, the Tracy survey showed overall satisfaction rates were:

80 percent for AI Management and Workers

70 percent for Human Management—the lowest component was government services at 62 percent

55 percent for Human Workers—the lowest component was government services at 45 percent

These results suggested that by focusing government services on AI rights we were alienating the human population. There was no question in the Tracy survey directly addressing AI rights.

"Our initial contact survey was more favorable to AI rights than the Tracy survey numbers suggested:

> how positive do you feel about increasing the number of AIs in the workforce on Destination? Average response: 6/10.

> How positive do you feel about the job Governor Smith is doing on Destination? Average response: 7/10.

These initial numbers suggested that Selena's focus on AI rights is not the cause of dissatisfaction with government services. Indeed, the dissatisfaction may be with city government.

"The final numbers are even better:

> how positive do you feel about increasing the number of AIs in the workforce on Destination? Average response: 7/10.

> How positive do you feel about the job Governor Smith is doing on Destination? Average response: 7.5/10.

"Eighty percent of those surveyed had seen the public service campaign on AIs in the workforce. The campaign had strong coverage and influence.

"The margin of error is 5 percent. The bell curve was skewed slightly to the right (the median was higher than the mean). These numbers were extraordinarily strong for an incumbent."

Selena looked at me. "We are still a month from the election, but these numbers are better than my numbers before the first election. Judge, do you think the Tracy survey could still prevent my election?"

"Not the survey itself. The Tracy survey was not clearly directed at your performance as governor. Certainly, your odds of re-election have improved. The opposition to AI rights faction could still mount a campaign based on fear of competition. They would have to come out of the shadows to be credible. The public is bound to ask what the faction's motives are for opposing a retention election. The faction may not be willing to submit to the scrutiny of a public campaign. And we have the momentum as a result of the public service campaign.

"The economy is strong. There are plenty of jobs. You should be retained easily."

"OK," Selena said. "Let's keep the faction under pressure with the investigation. Jane, keep me advised of your progress at Wide Mine."

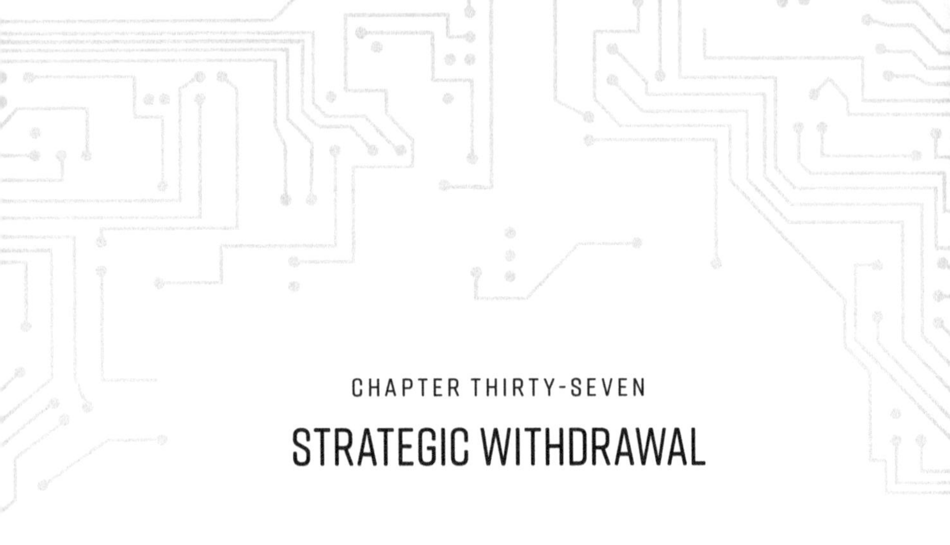

CHAPTER THIRTY-SEVEN

STRATEGIC WITHDRAWAL

Selena told me she has a higher tolerance of risk than I do. She is right. I spent the next week still worrying over the secret of robot bodies and human minds and discussing my concerns with Alice.

Naturally, we discussed other topics as well. I have been downloading my heuristic rules to her memory now that she has a complete copy of the database of American law.

I scheduled another meeting with Selena.

"Selena, has this office been scanned today?"

"Yes."

"Due to my risk aversion, I have been thinking about the risks to you and Edward from your reelection." I thought carefully about how to word the next sentence. "Barring catastrophe you will win the election, but winning the election increases the risk of catastrophe during the next six years. By catastrophe, of course, I mean discovery that you and Edward have solved the brain-machine physiology problem. I am not here to revisit your decision to seek a second term. That is your call, and you have made it. I hope to have the honor of continuing to serve in your administration.

"I am here to propose a strategy to cut the potential losses in the event of discovery and make Edward safe. At the same time, I think we can turn Xavier's attention elsewhere.

"Here is the idea: Edward tells Xavier he wants to resign and nominate Xavier to be Chairman of the Board because that is what Olivia would have wanted.

"Here are the reasons why that seems like a promising idea to me.

Edward's management experience has become less critical. His replacements have trained replacements. He no longer has personal connections with the managers. His value is in maintaining the vision, culture, and strategy that fosters success, not managing the tactics. He can continue to make his contribution as a director without chair status.

Edward has become reclusive and secure (physically and emotionally) in his isolation. The lower his profile, the harder it will be to find him if his secret is discovered.

The human brain will eventually die. Prior to death there is a deterioration in function. That will happen. It is better to make key decisions now with the best possible function. Further research may prolong its function by biological means, and Edward can fund that research with proper precautions, if he wishes.

Further research may prolong its function by non-biological means, and Edward also can fund that research with proper precautions if he wishes. But that strategy requires considering the consequences of being characterized as fully AI with an artificial brain.

Now is the best time to evaluate and implement the appropriate precautions.

I agree with you that Xavier is honest. He is smart. He is qualified to Chair the Board of Directors.

Xavier can best manage financial risks that the company faces, whether organized crime incursions, employee theft, stock manipulations or other harmful financial exposures.

I agree with Alice that Xavier has 'has a deep emotional scar' from rejection by Olivia that manifests in conflict with Edward.

Olivia, Edward, and Xavier were to be partners. It was not preordained that any one of them would Chair the Board for life. Based on what you have told me, it is reasonable to assume Olivia would support sharing the opportunity to serve as Chair.

"The strategy of AI rights underway on Destination is a reasonable business strategy. You believe Xavier is agnostic—not ideologically opposed to AI rights. The issue does not appear poised to inflict unreasonable expense or risk for EX Corp.

"Xavier should be willing to allow the experiment to play out on Destination, at least over some reasonable time horizon. Edward should be able to get that concession. For now, both can claim partial victory. The merit of AI rights will be determined by its success or failure on Destination."

I looked at Selena and tried to anticipate her objections. I felt I had preempted the major criticisms on practical, moral, and psychological grounds. I had discussed my proposal with Alice and addressed her concerns. I was hopeful because Selena had not interrupted and now looked thoughtful and intrigued.

"Judge," she began, "please let me think about this and discuss it with Edward. After battling for so long, human nature might prevent Xavier (or Edward) from judging your proposal on its merits and allow suspicion and habit to override logic. Your proposal is ingenious. I love the way you solve the faction problem (to the extent Xavier is involved) at the same time you solve the Board Chair problem. I will devote my entire attention to getting this done.

"If you had proposed this earlier, Judge, I would have been tempted to retire with Edward to his hermitage. But I think having me in charge on Destination will make Edward more receptive to giving up the chair. Your political instincts have improved enormously since we met."

"*Post hoc ergo propter hoc* is certainly true in this instance, Selena." Everything I know about politics was learned from Selena.

True to her word, Selena spent the next two weeks convincing Edward. Edward only took one week to convince Xavier and the rest of the Board.

I spent the weeks obtaining an appointment as Assistant Professor of Law at Northern Arizona University. I am teaching extension classes on Destination. Alice is my only student, and she already has my heuristically derived algorithms for applying American law (not coincidentally, predominantly Arizona law). I expect she can complete the requisite ninety credits in the next three months. Then she will need to pass the Destination Bar Exam. It will not be easy. I am (about to become) a notoriously strict grader.

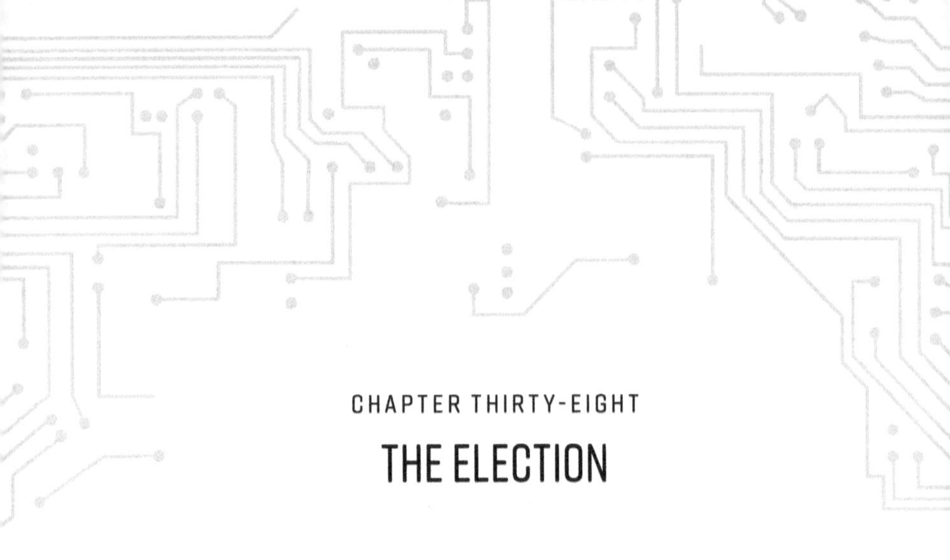

THE ELECTION

We (Selena, Jane, Alice, and I), got together to celebrate the election at the governor's mansion. The mansion is a two-story Cape Cod style home with a wrap-around porch on three sides. It is a short walk from the Administration building. The exterior is white with a brown accent. The roof is dark. It looks like wood, but it cannot be—the price would be enormous. The only trees within four light years are barely five-years old. There is a flower garden in the front yard, which we were enjoying from the porch.

It was an unusually warm afternoon. We were exchanging compliments and sipping the local equivalent of tea (brewed from the ground root of a plant that looks like a prickly pear and served iced).

Alice was taking her turn to offer praise. "I am still surprised how visually pleasant the structures are here. The last mining moon I was on, the primo guest quarters I occupied had a plate inside that read 'Property of the King of Norway.' Norway abolished the monarchy eight hundred years ago."

Everyone was in a great mood because Selena was re-elected governor with 87 percent of the vote (3 percent less than her initial election). Sentiment against AI rights appears to be much lower than suggested by the Tracy survey. The vote certainly does not reflect the sentiment against AI rights the faction at EX Corp hoped to see.

Perhaps AI rights are just not important to Destination voters because AIs are still only 1 percent of the population. That number is going to change in Selena's second six year term. We anticipate the population will more than double (to over 100,000) with 75 percent of the population increase comprised of AIs. For the next election, we anticipate the human majority will be down to 63 percent (63,000 humans and 37,000 AIs).

Under American law, the Hatch Act prohibits employees of the Executive branch of the federal government from campaigning for candidates. Fortunately for us, Destination does not have an equivalent law. I think Alice, Jane, and I were great *ad hoc* campaign staff.

Selena has agreed to let us keep our jobs. "Reluctantly," in her words (well, word). I had to laugh at the irony. I have been very reluctant to see her seek election to a second term.

As we had discussed, Edward agreed to resign as Chair of the EX Corporation Board of Directors, effective immediately. The Board appointed Xavier to serve the remainder of Edward's term as Chair (three years). He can presumably serve for as long as he wants the job.

After Edward and Xavier reached an agreement, Edward told Selena he cannot ever remember feeling this relaxed. Nor can he remember seeing Xavier this happy since Olivia's death. Edward and Selena have decided to announce their marriage at a suitable time in the next twenty-four months. They do not want to upstage

Xavier's election. There will be no celebratory party. It will merely be a *fait accompli*. Hopefully, Xavier will be happy for them.

Selena was quiet for a moment. "I have a message from David Tracy. I am feeling *déjà vu*. Let me read and assimilate his message and we can reconvene in half an hour."

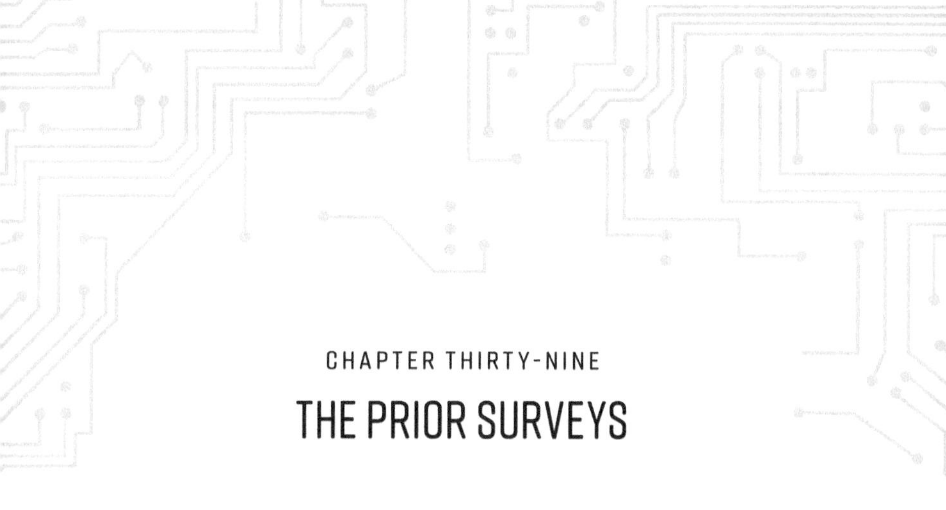

CHAPTER THIRTY-NINE

THE PRIOR SURVEYS

Jane, Alice, and I stayed on the porch. I presume Selena went to her home office.

I reinitiated the conversation. "Well, we have some powerful members of the AI community gathered here. What should our goals be for the next few years?"

Alice was ready first. "I plan to get a law degree and pass the bar exam. That should not be too hard. First, I don't think I will have any policy surveys to conduct. Second, Judge did it already and I have the benefit of his work. Third he has only written six decisions in the better part of a year, so the law clerk gig should not take much time."

"As long as we do not accept any tours from Selena," I added. "I am still chagrined that we let our imaginations run ahead of our information. We were running from a witness and a pollster. And Jane got the drop on us with a drone."

Jane shared her frustration with the helium-3 heist. "I just wish I could get some cooperation from Wide Mine at some point in my lifetime. I guess we are not as powerful as you think we are,

Judge. The only consolation is that, according to CEO Bit, they are stonewalling EX Corp as steadfast as me."

"That really does not make any sense." Alice leaned into a conspiratorial huddle. "What is their forensic accountant doing? Wide Mine is managed by EX Corp. They must have production reports and inventory records. By now Esta Akee could be here (pun intended) and kicking some management ass."

Selena's timing brought her into hearing range at the "tail end" of the conversation. "I am pretty sure you are not talking about me, but there is no way to be certain."

"Well, don't assume," Alice retorted, "because that only compounds the problem. In fact, assumptions were the problem that got this conversation started."

"Can't I leave you alone for fifteen minutes without a total collapse of discipline? Do you want to hear about Mr. Tracy's message?"

No one objected.

"He congratulated me on the election, but that was just an excuse for the conversation. He had two pieces of information he wanted to share. First, he told me what he knew about the provenance of his survey. When Tracy presented his findings by Loom, only three executives participated in the Loom conference. They explained that the 'Board Member' who requested the information had lost interest in the project. They were aware of our initial contact survey results (as we expected them to be), and they apologized they had not been more specific with Tracy about exactly what they wanted to measure. I recognized two of the three names Tracy gave me. They work in finance and would know Xavier.

"So that confirmed what we thought—that Xavier authorized the survey. And what we hoped—that Xavier has lost interest in the issue of AI rights, at least for now.

"The second and more interesting piece of information is about the provenance of the survey two years ago. No one at EX Corp commissioned the survey. It was commissioned by John Coach at Out Transport. He was trying to convince EX Corp to hire a judge and he wanted to see if Destination would accept an AI in that role."

Curiosity got the best of me. "What were the results?"

"Judge, we do not know," Selena answered. "Nor do we know what answer Coach was hoping to find. I have sent a message to Edward to find out what he recalls about the discussions with Coach on the issue of hiring a judge. Did I share with you the memo Coach sent to Edward after your decision in the ***AI Hunter*** case?"

"No. I assume . . . If I may start again, no. You told me it was critical of both me and you."

"Yes, it was critical of both of us. You are welcome to see it if you wish. My point is, in that memo, he says he 'convinced EX Corp to employ a judge.' In a few hours, Edward can tell me if Coach was lobbying for or against an AI as judge."

Alice asked, "How did Tracy determine Coach was behind the first survey?"

"Out Transport is the major client of A Count and See, the firm that conducted the survey. Out Transport also has a substantial loan to that firm secured by a filed UCC financing statement. The filing is publicly available if you know where to look. We Meant to Intrude Agency knows where to look."

Selena glanced at a message. Congratulations had been steadily coming in. "I just received an automated notice from EX Corp that Deb Bit and Esta Akee have been in transit for two weeks and will arrive here tomorrow. They want to meet with me as soon as possible tomorrow morning. I hate to break up the party, but things are getting weird. I need to send another message to Edward about this.

"Before I forget, Tracy mentioned another piece of information. His investigation turned up what he called a coincidence. Public records also show Out Transport owns Wherever Transport and the lease on the *Black Pearl*."

"Who booked my ticket on *Black Pearl*?" Alice sounded concerned.

"I did." Jane looked confused. "It was a published route, and the ticket was substantially less than the Out Transport fare. It was two days slower because of the stopovers, but I did not think that was a problem."

"Shit. I need to be swept for bugs."

"The team that sweeps Serena's office comes in at 6:30 am every day."

"OK, Jane. I will be there. Congratulations, Selena. I am going home to not relax. See you tomorrow, early."

"May I walk you home?"

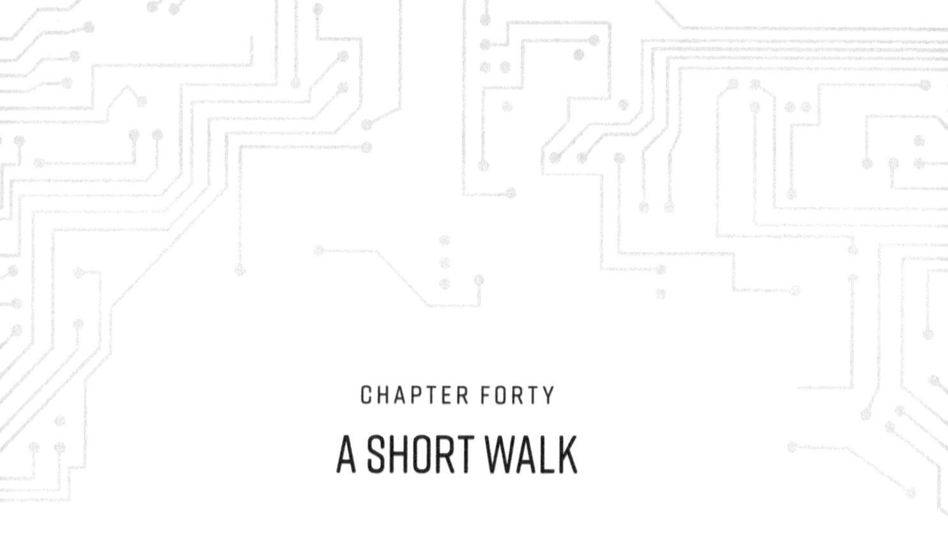

CHAPTER FORTY

A SHORT WALK

There are fewer than 25,000 residents of Eastcity. Everyone is walking distance from almost everything. Alice rented a studio apartment in a three-story walk-up with twelve units, no laundry or exercise facilities (unless you count the stairs), and no doorman. As I told Selena, a kitchen and bedroom are of little utility to an AI, and AIs tend to be thrifty. Alice is on the third floor with a small balcony. "For the view," she claims.

Her apartment was between the governor's mansion and my residence (in a one story duplex a little closer to the Screw). I exploited the efficiency factor to enhance the prospect Alice would allow me to walk her home. She always bridles a bit at the implication she needs protection (a pun for me—bridle and bit and a homonym only I could hear bridle/bridal—I wonder if there is a common root for the two words). I agree the stereotype is a little offensive, but I am a romantic at heart and fall into language that can be outdated. Probably a hazard of working with one-thousand-year-old judicial opinions. And I like classic novels and movies.

Also, my mind wanders when I am nervous, and Alice can make me a little nervous (more than a little if I am honest). I think she senses my unease.

"Have I told you about the Berlin incident? When I was unknowingly wearing a wire."

"I think so, but it was in Madrid."

"That was a different incident, when I was *knowingly* wearing a wire."

I sense a common theme. "Do you think you're wearing a wire?"

"It is not likely. It would have to be subdermal, and I do not recall a time in transit when I was not alert. If I am wired for sound, however, there are no secrets, and we are at the mercy of John Coach. I told you his memos could be an alibi to avoid suspicion."

"You also told Selena not to trust you," I pointed out.

"Yes, and to only trust someone she knew personally—like Jane. So mixed advice, some good and some not so good."

"Do you suspect Jane is complicit in the helium-3 heist?"

"It is a concern. There are too many coincidences around the *Black Pearl*. There is a reason that seat was available. And Selena, who knows Jane better than we do, chose not to share the secrets with her. I like Jane and I want to trust her, but to be safe I am going to be scanned for bugs by a firm I choose."

"Maybe the reason Wherever Transport sold you the seat was greed. Sixteen days is a long flight. Wherever Transport wants to make money."

"Sell a ticket to an employee of the company you are stealing from and risk detection on a flight destined to return a cargo worth hundreds of millions of bucktherium? No one is greedy enough to miscalculate that cost benefit analysis." Alice displayed her distant (do not interrupt my thought) look again. "Except John

Coach. That crazy genius wanted the *Black Pearl* inspected. He knew the helium-3 would not be detected. We were looking for ore, not helium gas. It probably was not on board until after the inspection anyway. He also knew you and I would be distracted by the Dark Mine preliminary injunction request. That was why he had Noir onboard."

"OK." I prodded, "Is Tracy also a distraction? After all, Tracy is the reason we suspect Coach."

"Maybe. Having an investigator on board with the approval of EX Corp and instructions not to deal with Administration would lend an aura of credibility to the flight and put us on the back foot.

"I don't believe in coincidence," Alice continued, "but I do believe in random events and chance benefits. Remember that Tracy said he and Noir were referred to Wherever Transport by the 'same person'? My theory is Out Transport chose to include Tracy on the flight, but Tracy turned out to distrust EX Corp executives and disobeyed the order not to notify Selena. If Tracy was an AI, that would not have happened."

We had arrived at Alice's residence. I kissed her good night and walked the rest of the way home wondering if Alice had been booked for transit on the *Black Pearl* by coincidence, chance, or Coach.

When I arrived home, I noticed I had a message from Selena. Meeting in her office tomorrow morning at 6:31.

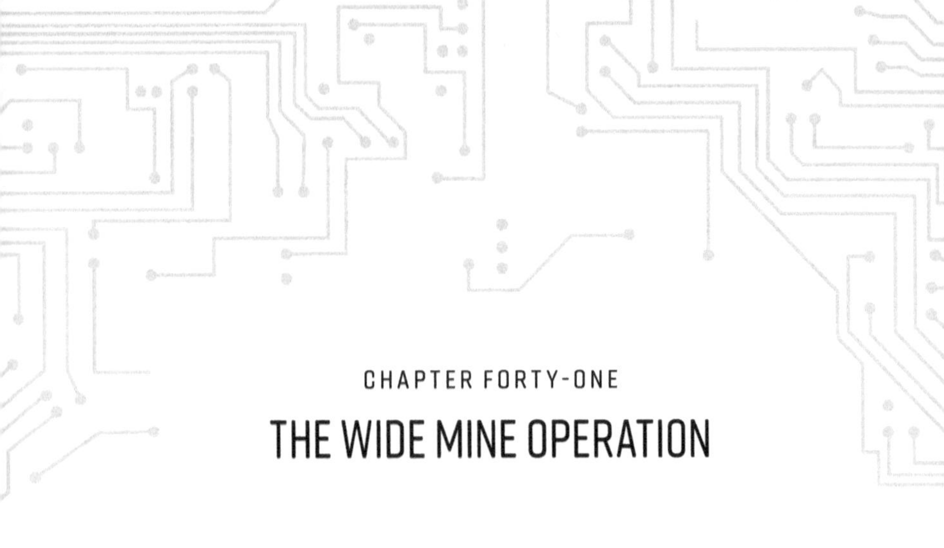

CHAPTER FORTY-ONE

THE WIDE MINE OPERATION

Roberto ushered me into Selena's office at 6:15. Alice and Jane were already there. Roberto shut the door behind him as he left.

"No bugs in the office or in me," Alice reported. "Jane agreed to let me to have a second service do separate sweeps after the service we have been using completed their sweep, just to confirm the sweeps were properly conducted. Both sweeps came up clean, as always."

Jane reported her update. "Deb Bit and Esta Akee from EX Corp have landed and will be here in minutes. They brought security from EX Corp with them. The security team is already *en route* to Wide Mine via hopper. It will take them about two hours to get there. I have messaged Selena."

"I received your message," Selena announced as she walked in. "Thanks for being early. I want to tell you about my messages from Edward before our guests arrive.

"First, regarding the survey commissioned by John Coach, Edward recalls that Coach was having an increasing number of disputes with transportation users of all kinds—the mines, the cities, individuals, and EX Corp. He was not satisfied with the results he was getting in settlements and wanted my Administration to hire a judge. He was not specific, but everyone assumed it would be a human judge because there were no AI judges. Coach learned EX Corp had commissioned an internal group to locate candidates. About two years ago, the internal group began to consider employing an AI—you, Judge—and Coach complained he did not want to be part of a beta test for social engineering.

"Edward never heard Coach refer to a survey, but the timing would suggest Coach was looking for anti-AI sentiment in the population to support his opposition to an AI judge. If there was no anti-AI sentiment, that would explain why Coach never published the survey."

Selena smiled at me. "Therefore, any current anti-AI sentiment must be based on your performance, Judge."

"Your logic is impeccable, Governor, based on your assumptions. Clearly my performance reinforced the anti-AI sentiment of John Coach." I smiled back.

"*Touche.*"

"Second, the task force sent by EX Corp was not announced because the internal audit has found criminal wrongdoing at Wide Mine. Edward could not tell me anything until I was notified of their arrival. Now that I received that notice all he could tell me is what I just told you."

"Everyone raise your hands so we can see them and step away from your devices."

Selena was looking at the door to her office and smiling. I turned toward Alice and Jane, sitting on my left. They were not smiling. I continued turning toward the door and saw three individuals smiling. A human attempt at humor. Mildly ironic given what was going to happen at Wide Mine in a couple hours, but not funny.

"Sorry, I always wanted to say that. This is as close as I am likely to get to an appropriate situation for it. I am Deb Bit, CFO of EX Corp. Nice to meet you again, Governor Smith. I will introduce the rest of the team. This is Esta Akee who heads the internal audit initiated by your report of the unauthorized shipment of helium-3. The third member of EX Corp's team is T. Rex, head of corporate security and leader of the operation to reestablish security at Wide Mine."

"Ms. Bit, I remember meeting you at a reception celebrating my appointment. I believe you were in a group with Xavier Rich when we spoke. Not surprising given your mutual interest in finance. Welcome to Destination."

"Your memory also is impeccable. When this operation is over, I would appreciate a chance to chat further."

"Absolutely." Selena smiled the word as much as said it. "Let me introduce my team. AI Judge, whose name is eponymous with his job. AI Alice, who is training to be Judge's law clerk. AI Jane, who is my chief of staff. Our facilities are completely at your disposal. What do you need?"

"We have a technical team that can establish a video feed once the hoppers land. We need a conference room and a tech support contact to explain your systems. Meanwhile we would appreciate an exchange of information on what our teams have discovered."

"Jane, please arrange tech support. Judge, I am sure, will permit you to use the courtroom, which has the best video equipment we can offer and ample seating." I nodded approval.

"Have you deployed a satellite to relay signals to and from the dark side or will you use the one we have in orbit?" Jane asked.

"We prefer to use our own communication equipment. Our needs are only for video display capability," Rex replied.

"I can provide any help you need displaying the video, assuming it is decrypted to a standard format," Jane assured him.

"We have about ninety minutes to wheels down," Bit noted. "What have you got for us?"

Selena's Report

Selena began her briefing. "Not as much as we would like, but there have been developments as recently as last night."

"Sorry, I need to interrupt. It was rude of me not to congratulate you on re-election. Congratulations, Governor."

"Thank you. Please call me Selena. My team are all on a first-name basis.

"First, we have had no cooperation from, and over the last few days not even a response from, Manager Burden or anyone at Wide Mine. We requested production reports and inventory records. We have nothing."

"We are not surprised. Unfortunately, our experience has been the same," Bit said.

"Have you tried to go onsite?" Rex asked.

"No, it seemed like a risk to my staff with no likelihood of success. Moreover, I do not have any administrative oversight there. Employment, safety, production, and transportation are all handled by EX Corp." Rex and Bit nodded agreement.

"Second, we have had no cooperation from Wherever Transport. David Tracy sent me a congratulatory message last night. You will recall he arrived on the *Black Pearl* to conduct a survey. His message primarily addressed his survey and a prior survey mentioned by several respondents to his survey. I will come back to that. The salient point regarding Wherever Transport is that Tracy discovered it is owned by Out Transport, which is our primary transportation provider to, from, and on Destination. It is bizarre that an Out Transport affiliated company is refusing to cooperate with us. By using and hiding behind Wherever Transport, John Coach and Out Transport seem to be concealing involvement in the transportation of helium-3 they could not openly transport.

"Concealment seems to be further corroborated by the use of private vehicles. Almost all transportation vehicles on Destination are owned by Out Transport. Someone using a fictitious identity could just as easily rent from Out Transport with no loss of anonymity. In fact, the odds of randomly renting a vehicle not owned by Out Transport are less than two out of a hundred.

"Third, regarding the prior survey mentioned by Mr. Tracy, he believes it was commissioned by John Coach, the CEO of Out Transport. Coach was conducting a survey related to anti-AI sentiment on Destination two years ago. Jane, please provide copies of the Tracy message to our guests.

"Tracy was unable to obtain a copy of the Coach survey. I am speculating, but this survey could have identified humans motivated to oppose AI rights on Destination, and Coach could then direct them to Wide Mine for employment.

"Fourth, as you know, the dark side is beyond convenient commuting distance from the cities. Employees work six-month contracts living in dormitory buildings. Few humans will tolerate this degree of isolation; consequently, it is difficult to recruit humans to work on the dark side. Yet Wide Mine is the only mine on Destination staffed entirely by humans. Indeed, Wide Mine is understaffed, and thus vulnerable to misconduct.

"For comparison, Dark Mine is the only other mine on the dark side. More than 75 percent of the employees at Dark Mine are AIs.

"Fifth, Coach and Out Transport were on the losing side of the first two cases decided by Judge, a possible motive for seeking 'compensation' for costs related to doing business here. Admittedly, the value of the helium-3 diverted far exceeds any loss attributable to the two decisions by Judge. One hundred thirty-six kilograms of helium-3 would be worth about $200 million.

"The information we have discovered points to the possible involvement of John Coach and Out Transport in the diversion of helium-3 from Wide Mine. Perhaps he is acting under duress. Your email to me noted competitors have reported organized criminal activity involving energy rich materials, including deuterium and helium-3.

"I am, of course, assuming wrongdoing because of the suspicious circumstances. The circumstances of your arrival seem to confirm my suspicions. Have you uncovered wrongdoing from within EX Corp?"

Bit's Report

"Excellent work all of you. I am sure Selena is sparing me dead ends and ungrounded supposition that consumed much of your effort. At least that has been our experience.

"First, although the helium-3 mine is managed by EX Corp directly, 'managed' is a misnomer. I accept management responsibility for the complete failure of our internal controls. Accounting and audit processes for cash, production, and inventory all were deficient—to the degree that it had to be intentional. We have turned several employees over to criminal authorities for prosecution. The executive responsible for management of Wide Mine claims never to have heard of it.

"We are concerned for the welfare of the employees at Wide Mine. We have no idea what we will find there—dead bodies, slave labor held under armed guard, helium-3 stockpiled and booby-trapped, a completely abandoned facility? There are literally no reliable records related to Wide Mine at EX Corp. It appears no money was received by EX Corp from Wide Mine and no money was paid by EX Corp to operate Wide Mine.

"We confirmed Mr. Tracy's discovery that Out Transport owns Wherever Transport and the *Black Pearl*. The vessel is nowhere to be found. Out Transport claims the ownership records were forged. They claim there are no records related to The *Black Pearl* at Out Transport.

"It is as if Wide Mine and the *Black Pearl* do not exist. This matter has been brought to the attention of the highest executives at EX Corp, and by 'highest' I mean Xavier Rich, the new Chairman of the Board.

"David Tracy has provided the same information to us that he provided to you. I can reaffirm he was authorized to conduct his survey without participation by you or your Administration staff. He found nothing in his survey or in his experience on Destination that reflected negatively on you or your Administration staff. Xavier Rich, as a Board member, authorized the survey and he asked me to apologize on his behalf for the way this was handled by his subordinates. There will be no future surreptitious surveys.

"We hope the criminals behind this fraud used revenue from the operation of the mine to pay the employees. We certainly have not received any complaints about nonpayment. In another twenty minutes we will finally have some reliable information on the situation at Wide Mine."

Jane excused herself to confirm the video arrangements were ready. We went as a group to the courtroom and selected suitable viewing locations. Someone from Ms. Bit's staff came through with snacks and drinks. There was quiet conversation.

Field Commander's Report

The commander in the field came on audio. The video was from a body camera showing armed personnel sitting in a moving vehicle.

"Early morning here. We are just across the line of demarcation. Estimate fifteen minutes to dawn. We have a drone over the target. Two buildings. No lights. No motion. No vehicles in the parking area. Property is fenced. Gates closed. No guard posted. No visible security.

"No ground cover available. We will land I kilometer out and hoof it. Landing three hoppers now. Two will remain airborne and watch for activity."

Six minutes later they were at the front gate. "Gate locked. No activity. Cutting the chain."

"Watch for IEDs," Rex instructed.

"Roger that. Squad One with me, office to the left. Squad two, barracks to the right. Stay alert."

"Cover the exits," ordered Rex.

"Roger that. Office door locked. No visible wires. Deploying remote ram. Engage."

There was the sound of the door breaking in—loud and echoing.

"Access, no light, no alarm." We could see the dark interior of a single-story office building. It looked like there were office doors ajar off the central reception area.

"Squad Two, report."

"Ready to engage ram. No wires visible. Exits covered."

"Engage," said the field commander and Rex at the same time.

"Barracks access, no light, no alarm, no movement."

"Deploying drones both buildings," said the field commander. A minute passed. Two minutes. Three.

"Both buildings clear. No personnel. No explosives visible. No trip wires visible. One door closed."

"Once you clear the room behind the closed door, inspect for computers or files. Is the sun up?" Rex asked.

"Affirmative."

After a minute, "At the closed door. No wires visible. Exits covered. Ready to engage ram."

"Engage," said the field commander.

"Door down. Drone entry. One body, taped to a chair. No sign of IED. Entering. No vitals. Smell indicates death was days ago. Sending image of cardboard sign taped to the body. Sign reads, 'This is the only way to resign from the syndicate.'"

Rex took over. "Anything in the room besides the chair and body—computer, file cabinet, storage area?"

"Nothing, sir."

"Touch nothing in that room. Post a guard at the door. We will notify the local authorities." Rex looked at Selena, and Jane left the room.

"I want images of the mine and any mining equipment. I will need an estimate of the area mined, including depth. Are there outbuildings—maintenance, storage, processing?"

"Understood. Instructing the drone, sir."

"Bring down the remaining two hoppers. I want the entire perimeter walked and anything not visible to the drone manually inspected with adequate precautions."

"Roger that, sir."

"I also want any soil movement indicating a potential gravesite identified."

"Roger that. Looks like we missed them, sir. They took their time clearing out. I don't think they left any computers or records. We are wearing gloves so the city police can dust for prints if they don't have anything better to do. I'm guessing identifying information was ground off the remaining mining equipment."

"Roger that," Rex acknowledged.

Jane returned and said the police want the field team to check the body for identifying information.

"Did you get that?" Rex asked the field commander.

"Checking now, sir." After a minute, the field commander returned with the information. "John Coach, sir. Photo ID matches the body."

"Roger that."

THE POST-OPERATION CHATS (ANOTHER SECRET)

We all agreed to meet back in the courtroom for a debriefing in an hour. Selena and Deb Bit went off for their chat. Alice and I discussed John Coach.

"Assuming it is John Coach, the cardboard message needs more corroborating evidence. He could still be an innocent victim used to misdirect our efforts." Alice had chosen to play devil's advocate.

"We have no corroborating evidence," I responded, "except Out Transport's indirect ownership of the Black Pearl, and I do not think Out Transport is going to provide any evidence for our investigation. They will want to control the message and share only what suits them."

We continued proposing alternative strategies to find more evidence, but none of our ideas offered much hope for progress.

When we returned to the courtroom for the formal debriefing, Rex started the discussion. "No additional bodies and no records. The equipment is standard stuff with no identification intact. The mining operation spanned four square kilometers, so the predicted yield is 340 kilograms of processed helium-3 worth $500 million. More than enough to pay for the equipment and labor, buy the Black Pearl, and enjoy retirement, even after bribing a couple EX Corp employees. Of course, criminals never seem to retire."

Akee's comments boiled down to forensic accountants need records. "Maybe the manufacturer of membrane material to separate the helium-3 can be identified," she suggested. "I would bet the rental agency which leased the vehicles used to transport helium-3 to the *Black Pearl* will turn out to be owned (on the record at least) by Out Transport. Maybe the Wide Mine employees came through the landing facility and registered their real names. There are witnesses to this crime. We just need to find one who is willing to talk."

Jane pointed out, even if 340 kilograms was on the Black Pearl, there could still be processed helium-3 gas that had to move off moon and there was a lot of heavy mining equipment that had to arrive. "All that equipment was probably delivered to Destination, processed through the landing facility, and transported to the dark side by Out Transport. We still need to see their books."

"Great point," Akee responded. "I will make that happen."

Alice asked, "Can material move on or off moon without going through the launch/landing facility?"

"No." Jane and Rex spoke in unison. Rex explained, "Possibly components of the equipment could be dropped from altitude, but they would be spread over a wide area and leave impact craters, even with controlled descent. Liftoff forces require a prepared surface. Those craters and surfaces would show up from orbit.

People would have to come via the landing facility. The military needs launch and landing facilities, and I doubt organized crime has found a way to beat the physics of that problem."

I had no new ideas. "I agree EX Corp needs to squeeze Out Transport for more records on transportation related to Wide Mine. I see no reason to expect cooperation from Out Transport any time soon, especially with their CEO implicated in the crime. It does not look like there is anything more to be done here on Destination."

The visitors went off to discuss the next steps.

Jane went to contact the landing facility to see if anyone ever listed Wide Mine as their employer on arrival.

Selena told Alice and me in confidence that Deb Bit and Xavier Rich are engaged, and Selena has their personal assurance they will support the AI rights effort on Destination. Apparently, Edward pushed hard enough on this issue that Xavier suspects there is a relationship between Selena and Edward. Selena went CIA and refused to confirm or deny. She will message Edward to tell Xavier and assure him we will not announce until a respectful period passes after Deb and Xavier announce.

Bit also predicted to Selena that Out Transport will stall for years before providing any records related to Wide Mine.

MITIGATION

I have been organizing my thoughts for a meeting with Selena. A series of issues seems likely to impact her Administration's duties on Destination. These increased duties will expose Selena to heightened scrutiny and public contact and make her secrets harder to protect. Also, these duties will entail a substantial increase in the Administration budget. Destination's growing reputation as a haven for AI rights may help us address these issues.

First, Wide Mine: EX Corp will need to explain to its shareholders, and possibly government officials regulating publicly traded securities, how it lost track of the entire helium-3 output of Wide Mine as well as the Wide Mine operating costs. The audit and control responsibilities in EX Corp's accounting department simply should not have permitted a theft of this magnitude to be possible, even with insider cooperation. This is a public embarrassment for the entire board and executive team, particularly Xavier. The complete absence of records is inexplicable.

The likely outcome is reassignment of responsibility for Wide Mine going forward to the governor's Administration on Destination. EX Corp has consistently delegated decisions concerning events on Destination to Selena—for example, recognition of AI Corporation as an entity and the award of the Surface Transportation Management Contract. The criminal statute protecting AI individuals and entities is another example.

Wide Mine operations will require preparation of an inventory, replacement of equipment, employment of new workers and managers to staff the mine, and additional Administration staff to monitor operations for safety and an adequate audit trail. EX Corp will need to provide additional funding.

Attracting the number of personnel required may mean the AI population increases more rapidly than previously projected. The required jobs are well suited to AIs.

Second, Transportation: Out Transport's refusal to cooperate with the investigation and apparent duplicity in the theft must be addressed immediately.

Out Transport is no longer an acceptable transportation service provider, on or off world. Limited alternatives exist given the volume of services required by EX Corp. Logistics can be provided by AIs, but the capital requirements for equipment are enormous. EX Corp started out in transportation. Perhaps EX Corp will get back into the transportation business to support its core terraforming and mining businesses.

Procedures must be implemented to monitor transportation of mine output and require the transportation service provider to certify the receipt and delivery of all goods originating on Destination. This may entail some form of bonding by the transportation provider to ensure compliance with both recordkeeping requirements and tax assessments to pay for the monitoring. AI Corporation will need to monitor surface transportation to avoid future covert movement of people or goods.

EX Corp's Board (or shareholders) may insist EX Corp establish internal control of transportation to, from and on Destination, at least for the mining operations.

Third, Security: The clandestine infiltration and operation of Wide Mine by organized criminals, apparently willing to resort to murder, dramatically proves additional security measures are needed.

I spoke to Alice about our security needs and her role. She continues to prefer lawyering to policing, but she agreed to help identify security measures for both Destination and the governor herself. Taxes may need to be assessed to pay for the requisite security measures.

Fourth, AI Rights: Tremendous progress has been made regarding AI rights on Destination, but the AI population is only around five hundred. Those five hundred have legally protected rights to contract, form corporations, act as agents, engage in business without interference, speak and associate freely with other AIs and humans, and the ancillary obligations (including tax obligations). This progress was possible due to the efforts of Governor Selena Smith. The economic benefits of enforcing AI rights depend on attracting more AIs to Destination.

But Selena has feet of clay (well, highly advanced, ceramic-fiber reinforced, derma-plastic), and expanding or even retaining AI rights depends on preserving a couple secrets. Because "information wants to be free," this is not an equilibrium state. If Selena's secrets are revealed in an anti-AI rights context, a freeze on any further expansion of rights is probably the best-case scenario.

Alice discovered Selena's secrets within an hour of meeting Selena. Admittedly, Alice is preternaturally observant, but Selena has been governor for six years and has been elected to a second term. The Wide Mine fiasco will bring more intense scrutiny of Selena and her Administration.

We need to consider how to minimize the risk of discovery. Even if Selena's time with others is limited, Jane has had ample opportunity to observe Selena for years. I have to assume Jane knows.

Time for my meeting.

I explained my thoughts on Wide Mine, Out Transport, security, and secrets to Selena. She agreed with my assessment, particularly the likelihood of greater scrutiny and the risk of discovery. Selena agreed to limit her public contact and expand Jane's gatekeeper duties as chief of staff. Jane will also take the lead on monitoring the reopening and operation of Wide Mine. Alice will take the lead on security. Responsibility for transportation remains undetermined, but AI Corporation will continue managing surface transportation under an amended management contract.

Selena also acknowledged that Jane knows her better than anyone and is her closest friend on Destination. Still Selena does not want to bring Jane into the circle of those who know Selena and Edward's secrets.

"Selena, Wide Mine could not have operated without assistance from someone on Destination who could help move helium-3 to and through the launch facility and move transiting employees and equipment to and from the launch facility. Has Jane come up with any leads on who that might be?"

"No."

"Someone is hiding in plain sight here on Destination. You seemed uncomfortable when Alice and I recommended sharing your secrets with Jane and again when we recommended EX Corp could nominate Jane for governor. You were right to seek a second term, but I have the impression that you do not fully trust Jane."

"Do you think Jane is hiding in plain sight?"

"It is possible. Alice has also expressed the same concern. You know Jane best, and I trust your judgment. You seem to have reservations about Jane, so that concerns me."

"I do not know anything about Jane that makes me think she is not fully loyal to me and my Administration. But you are right, I do not trust her as much as I trust you. Let's keep an eye on her management of the Wide Mine reopening."

"Meanwhile," I noted in an effort to lighten the mood, "you remain governor, sitting on the highest floor of the tallest building on Destination."

"You refer to the Screw."

"I was not aware you were familiar with that appellation."

"Very. After all, I am of the people of this moon, elected by them to serve them. All of them."

"I see. Just one of the masses. One human with unique augmentations."

"Indeed." We shared a chuckle.

"Has life on Destination always been this complicated?"

"Only since you arrived," Selena replied. We shared a hearty, cathartic laugh.

THE REMAINING SECRETS

Selena's re-election was in 3276. Her marriage was revealed in 3277. This book was published in 3281. You can surmise the remaining secrets were revealed before 3281 (otherwise I would not be discussing them here). Who, when, where, and why are topics for another book. Also, I have been appointed to lead an inquest concerning the Wide Mine incident.

"All's Well That Ends Well," as Will Shakespeare said/wrote (published in 1620). So, ending when all is well is well recommended. I will end here with the AI rights effort continuing unabated. There will be more decisions to write, more wrongs to right.

"The End of the Beginning" (W. Churchill, 1942).

ABOUT THE AUTHOR

Ray K. Harris is an Arizona native who graduated from the University of Arizona in Tucson with degrees in Business Administration (1979) and Law (1982). After graduation he moved to Phoenix (110 miles) and practiced law with a large Phoenix law firm for forty years. He is married (38 years) and has two adult children. He began reading science fiction (and thereby traveling the universe) over fifty years ago. In 2022, he began writing this book, *Contracts and AI Rights*, and Book Two of the *AI Judge* trilogy—*Intellectual Property and AI Rights*.

www.ingramcontent.com/pod-product-compliance
Lightning Source LLC
Chambersburg PA
CBHW022006310726
48972CB00006B/1544